Anthony B. Norton

The Great Revolution of 1840

Anthony B. Norton

The Great Revolution of 1840

ISBN/EAN: 9783337234713

Printed in Europe, USA, Canada, Australia, Japan

Cover: Foto ©Andreas Hilbeck / pixelio.de

More available books at **www.hansebooks.com**

THE GREAT REVOLUTION OF 1840.

REMINISCENCES OF THE

Log Cabin   Hard Cider

CAMPAIGN

BY

A. B. NORTON.

"Truth is strange;
Stranger than fiction.

A. B. NORTON & CO.
MOUNT VERNON, O., AND DALLAS, TEXAS.

1888.

Werner Ptg. & Litho. Co.

AKRON, O.

DEDICATION.

To the Tippecanoe Veterans and Their Descendants,
These Reminiscences of the Great Revolution,
The Log Cabin and Hard Cider Campaign
of 1840, are Dedicated by the Author.

PREFACE.

The most remarkable political contest ever known was that of 1840, when Gen. William Henry Harrison was triumphantly elected to the Presidency of the United States over Martin Van Buren, the then incumbent. It was remarkable as the first campaign in which the women generally engaged, and, by their smiles and songs and encouragement, promoted the election. It was remarkable as the first campaign in which the lines were closely drawn between the people and the office-holders. It was remarkable as the first campaign in which the candidate was emphatically one of the people—a poor and honorable farmer. It was remarkable as the campaign in which the most slander, vituperation and abuse were used. It was remarkable from the fact that the great mass of the people rallied to the defense of the candidate they assailed. It was remarkable as being an uprising of the people to right themselves and redress the wrongs that had been done them, and to remove the imputations that had been placed upon them. Under the name of Democracy great outrages had been practiced by those claiming to be leaders. For about sixteen years power may be said to have been in the hands of one person. General Jackson, after having served two terms, designated his successor, whose boast was, that he "walked in the footsteps of his illustrious predecessor." General Jackson had been elected as a one-term candidate. In his message to Congress in 1829 he said, "It would seem advisable to limit the services of the Chief Magistrate to a *single term of either four or six years*." In his message to Congress in 1830 he reiterated and more strongly expressed this opinion in these words:

"It was a leading object with the framers of the Constitution to keep as separate as possible the

action of the legislative and executive branches
of the Government. To secure this object nothing
is more essential than to preserve the former from the
temptations of private interest, and, therefore, so to
direct the patronage of the latter as not to permit such
temptations to be offered. Experience abundantly
demonstrates that every precaution in this respect
is a valuable safeguard of liberty, and one which my
reflections upon the tendencies of our system incline
me to think should be still made stronger. It was
for this reason that, in connection with an amendment of the Constitution, removing all intermediate
agency in the choice of the President, I recommend
some restrictions upon the re-eligibility of that officer,
and upon the tenure of offices generally. The reason
still exists; and *I renew the recommendation,* with
an increased confidence that its adoption will strength-
en those checks by which the Constitution designed
to secure the independence of each department of the
Government, and promote the healthful and equitable
administration of all the trusts which it has created.

"*The agent most likely to contravene this design of
the Constitution is the* Chief Magistrate. In order
particularly that his appointment may as far as possible
be placed beyond the reach of improper influences ;
in order that he may approach the solemn responsibilities of the highest office in the gift of a free people,
uncommitted to any other course than the strict line of
constitutional duty, and that the securities for this independence may be rendered as strong as the nature of
power, and the weakness of its possessor, will admit,
*I cannot too earnestly invite your attention to the
propriety of promoting such an amendment of the
Constitution as will render him ineligible after one
term of service.*"

Right in the face of these declarations he acted, and
he trampled upon his own sentiments; and after
having set at naught his own teachings and violated
his own promises, he forced upon the country as his
successor "The Little Magician" De Witt Clinton,
speaking of the "political Grimalkin," Martin Van

Buren, said, " He was not of the race of the *lion* or the *tiger;* he belonged to the lower order, the *fox* and the *weasel*, and it would be in vain to expect that he could command the respect or acquire the confidence of those who had so little admiration of the qualities by which he was distinguished." He was known as the most cunning political trickster in our history. The brave Tennesseean, Davy Crockett, in his originality, correctly described him, when he said, " He could take a piece of meat on one side of his mouth, a piece of bread on the other, and cabbage in the middle, and chew and swallow each in its severalty, never mixing them together." He was skilled in sleight-of-hand as well as mouth tricks, and was regarded as full of deceit. His administration of the Government was oppressive and odious, and the recommendation of a standing army of 200,000 men, the employment of bloodhounds as allies, the sub-treasury scheme, low wages and free trade, and the profligacy and extravagance at the White House, together with the horde of defaulters, and the insolence of the office-holders, aroused popular indignation throughout the country. Even fair-minded and plain members of his own party could not but feel aware of his unworthiness. As an illustration it may be mentioned that the fourth-of-July celebration of 1840, at Vincennes, Indiana, brought together a large crowd. Abner T. Ellis, Esq., read the Declaration of Independence and Mr. Cannon delivered an oration. A Van Buren man was asked, " How do you like the proceedings?" "Why," said he, "I liked Cannon's speech *prime*, but I think Ellis's *bore rather too hard on Van Buren*, when you know it was agreed if we Democrats would join in the celebration nothing was to be said about parties." The Democrat regarded the Declaration of Independence, the great charter of our liberties, the most indignant rebuke that was ever penned of tyranny and oppression, as *a speech against Van Buren!*

> " Words are things ; and a small drop of ink,
> Falling like dew upon a thought, produces
> That which makes thousands, perhaps millions, think."

When Gen. William Henry Harrison was nominated
by the Whig national convention as a candidate for
the Presidency at the election of 1840, the administration writers and organs commenced ridiculing the
nominee and making light of his ability and qualifications.   The office-holding gentry and the codfish aristocracy turned up their noses and sneered contemptuously at his poverty.   In the columns of their leading
paper in the East these words of disparagement
appeared: "*Give him a barrel of hard cider and settle
a pension of two thousand a year upon him, and our
word for it, he will sit the remainder of his days
content in a log cabin.*"   This slur upon the brave old
soldier, who had served his country faithfully and long
on the battle-field, routing the British and Indian foes,
and endured the perils and toils of a pioneer life, and
had always shared his substance with the poor and
needy, filled the hearts of the hardy frontiersmen and
of the laboring men in the West and South, who lived
in humble log cabins, with indignation.   The dwellers
in log cabins in the valleys and on the mountain tops,
who lived in plainness and simplicity, took the epithets
of derision applied by his enemies as personal to
themselves, and gloried in their log-cabin candidate.
Honest men felt a just pride in the plain old farmer of
North Bend, and their families made the whole country
reverberate with the song:

> " They say that he lived in a cabin
>   And lived on old hard cider, too;
> Well, what if he did? I'm certain
>   He's the hero of Tippecanoe—
>   He's the hero of Tippecanoe!"

It became a log-cabin campaign, and demonstrated
the *power of the people* who lived in log cabins when
once aroused to action.   Wanting a just and honest
administration of the Government, and knowing Gen.
William Henry Harrison to be "honest, capable, and
faithful to the Constitution," they rallied around him
and elected him as their President.

The log cabin was everywhere to be seen, and log-
cabin songs were sung by old and young; log cabins

were built for places of meeting and crowds perambulated the country in log cabins on wheels.

Daniel Webster, in his great speech at Saratoga, New York, made the following patriotic allusion to his early life and to the manner in which log cabins had been assailed by the vile partisans of Martin Van Buren: " I agree that to live in a log cabin is no recommendation of a candidate for the Presidency, neither is it any disqualification. It is, however, to be assumed that a man who, by his capacity and industry, has raised himself from a log cabin to eminent station in the country, is of more than ordinary merit. I, sir, have a feeling for log cabins and their inhabitants. I was not myself born in one, but my elder brothers and sisters were— in the cabin in which, at the close of the Revolutionary war, in the perils and sufferings of which he bore his part, my father erected on the extreme frontiers of New Hampshire, where, beyond the smoke which curled from its chimney, not another stood between it and the walls of Quebec. In this humble cabin, amid the snow-drifts of New England, that father strove, by honest labor, to acquire the means of giving to his children a better education, and elevating them to a higher condition than his own. That cabin I honor, for the sake of the venerable man who dwelt in it. [Here Mr. Webster's voice became inarticulate from emotion.] That cabin I annually visit, and thither I carry my children, that they may learn to honor and to emulate the stern and simple virtues that there found their abode: and when I or they forget that cabin and what it teaches and recalls, may my name and their names perish from among men forever."

Harrison and Van Buren were the antipodes to each other in everything. Van Buren had been brought up in affluence and had lived in luxury, and had spent his days, as a lawyer and politician, in the fashionable circle, while Harrison had been from youth on the frontiers, a soldier enduring hardship and privation and baring his breast to the savage foe, a barrier to their inroads upon the settlements, and when the war ended he settled down as a plain farmer in what was then the "wild west." He had met the enemy often and never once had been vanquished. His heart was full of generosity and love for his comrades, and when taking leave of his soldiers he told them, "if they ever came that way they would always find a plate and a knife and fork at his table; "and I assure you," he added, "you will never find the string to the latch of my door pulled in." His name was "familiar as a household word" throughout the great Western country that he had rescued from the British and Indians; and the stories of his patriotism in war and generosity and kindness in peace had made the plain people everywhere love him. Hence it is not to be wondered that *there was magic in the name of Harrison throughout the Union, and the people, with a fervency and zeal unusual in politics, rally to the standard of a Harrison.* The name of the sturdy Republican, Gen. Thomas Harrison, who had signed the death warrant of the tyrant Charles I, the second of the Stuart kings of England, and that in an after revulsion he was himself subsequently hanged, drawn and quartered at Charing Cross, and his descendants emigrated to America and settled in Surry, Va., and one of them became the stanch Whig of the Revolution—Ben. Harrison—whose name stands among the fifty-six signers of the immortal Declaration of our Independence, and who was one of the most active in bringing about that great event. In fact, no man of the "times that tried men's souls" possessed more nerve and intrepidity, and he was an acknowledged leader of the greatest men. At the session of the Congress of the Colonies at Philadelphia, in May, 1775, when John Hancock had been elected President in place of Peyton Randolph, who had to return to Virginia to preside over the house of burgesses, and Mr. Hancock, modest and diffident, hesitating, Benjamin Harrison seized hold of and picked him up and carried him in his strong arms and placed him in the executive chair, then turned around to the members and boldly said, "We will show mother Britain how little we care for her by making a Massachusetts man our President, whom she has excluded from pardon by a public proclamation!"

He was a man of more than ordinary height, stout and muscular, and very heavy, and prided himself upon the position he held as chairman of the board of war having charge of the dispatches of General Washington and the regulation of trade and commercial affairs; and it was he who, on the 10th of June, 1776, brought up the resolution which declared the independence of the colonies, and on the 4th of July he reported that sacred instrument as having received the approbation of Congress, and with the other delegates of Virginia signed the same and, it is said, turned around to Mr. Gerry, a Massachusetts delegate, who was very spare and slender, and, as he raised his hand from the paper, exclaimed, "When the hanging scene comes to be exhibited I shall have all the advantage over you. It will be over with me in a minute; but you will be kicking in the air half an hour after I am gone."

Of this bold and resolute spirit we have found in our travels in Virginia many anecdotes, all characteristic of independence ; and the high estimate placed upon his services and usefulness and ability is second *only* to Washington. The many positions he filled evidences this fact.

The moderate party, at the head of which was Mr. Dickenson, succeeded in obtaining a vote for another petition to the King from the Congress of 1775. "On the success of this vote, Mr. D." says Mr. Jefferson, "was so much pleased that he expressed his satisfaction by saying: 'There is but one word, Mr. President, in the paper which I disapprove, and that word is *Congress.*'" Mr. Harrison immediately rose and said: "There is but one word in the paper, Mr. President, which I approve, and that word is *Congress.*"

This is the Harrison who, in the service of the country, *"sent forward as a private soldier"* into the western wilderness to fight the British and Indians, his son, with a letter dated October 10, 1793, addressed to Major-General Charles Scott. In this he states that, "Having received an appointment under General Wayne, I had intended accompanying him in his expedition against the Northwestern Indians, but I am unable to do so from having three of my ribs broken near the backbone; also loosened from my breast, and one broke near the middle. As there is not the smallest probability of my being serviceable on an active campaign, and moving would put me in great danger, it is prudent to stay at home." "Unwilling that an opportunity for the Harrison family to render some service to the country should pass, I determined to send my son. And now before I take my leave, permit me to tell you my son, a youth of nineteen years of age, I have sent forward in the character of a private soldier under Captain Rollins. His youth and inexperience, I make no doubt, will stand in need of your friendship; therefore, I pray you, *teach him the duties of his station,* and if any accident should happen him, pay some attention to him."

What a manly letter. How characteristic. There's no holding back and no begging for a position of light work for a youth of light weight as the paternal mind often suggests. But its very ruggedness impresses of nobility. "Teach him the duties of his station." The boy goes in with "his youth and inexperience," and by good work and square work wins promotion from a private soldier to a major-general.

The name immortalized in prose and verse—in tradition and history—the people could not but shout and sing for Harrison, who so fitly represented themselves. He accepted of their nomination and was willing to serve them to the best of his ability. At their call he sprang from retiracy and the log cabin into a full-fledged leader, only that he might bring back the Government to its pristine purity, when the people were recognized as the sovereigns. He was ready as their representative to act for one term and *one term only,* and if elected to let their chosen representatives make the laws and he would execute their wishes. He was opposed to the willful and flagitious use of the veto to thwart the will of the people. He did not believe that all the wisdom of the world was contained in the head of one small person that might fill the Executive chair. He was for building up American institutions and American interests, and while welcoming all honest immigrants, he desired to have them at once assimilate, become citizens, and own their own homes, and he would throw the broad ægis of the Constitution and the protection of the flag over all and make us an independent people.

The writer of these rough notes was,

> " One of the boys who, in 'forty, was true
> To the gallant old hero of Tippecanoe;"

and while an invalid, driven from his home in Texas by poison oak, to the banks of the Kokosing, has indulged in compiling these reminiscences, believing that they may be of interest to those who are at the verge or have passed their three-score and ten, and " perchance it will delight even them to have remembered it," as well as be of benefit to those still younger, who are now in the contest of young Tippecanoe, living over to some extent that of the old Tip of 1840. There can never again be a campaign of such enthusiasm and hurra as that of '40. The days of plain, honest simplicity, when the necessity existed for rigid economy, have passed and gone. The days of shinplasters and wild-cat paper money, when a silver dollar was as large as a wagon-wheel, and harder to get—the days of substantial " home-spun and hodden-gray"—of wool hats and linsey-woolsey—of innocence and integrity, of virtue and morality, of frugality and fidelity, and equality—when there were no millionaires and no Standard Oil or other combines or trusts, and when monopolies were unknown;

> " When none were for a party,
> And all were for the State;
> When the rich helped the poor,
> And the poor helped the great."

The times that created men like William Henry Harrison are gone and will not come again to this people.

We have grouped together many of the incidents as to meetings in various States, as to speakers and songs, and have aimed to put in form for presentation the speeches of some of the most prominent campaigners —the thrilling eloquence of Clay and Webster, and Prentiss and Rives, and Preston and Corwin, and other of the advocates of Harrison, Tyler and Reform, cannot be transferred to paper; but yet, the few addresses given will convey some idea of their character. As to their effect it cannot be portrayed to those who did not hear them and witness the enthusiasm of the masses.

The young men of the country can learn wisdom from the speeches given. We are sure that many will thank us for embodying in this work addresses that can be found in no publication in any of the libraries of the country. They are like "brands snatched from the burning." There were no stenographers or reporters a half century ago, as now, to catch down words as they fell from the inspired speaker.

General Harrison's speeches are worthy of preservation. His letters and expressions are finished productions—frank, outspoken, manly, as became an old soldier. His victory was complete. His term was short. A nation mourned the death of the honest old soldier and farmer and patriotic citizen, who sincerely loved the United States, and whose last words on earth were, "I wish you to understand the true principles of the Government. I wish them carried out."

A. B. NORTON.

Mt. Vernon, Ohio. October 10, 1888.

HARRISON NOMINATED.

PROCEEDINGS OF THE WHIG NATIONAL CONVENTION, AT HARRISBURG, PENNA.

FIRST DAY.

Wednesday, Dec. 4, 1839.

At 12 o'clock the convention assembled in the Lutheran Church, and was called to order by Mr. Williamson of Pennsylvania, who nominated Mr. Bates of Massachusetts, as chairman *pro tem.* for the purpose of organizing the convention.

On motion, Mr. Penrose and Mr. Swift of Pennsylvania, were appointed secretaries *pro tem.*

On motion of Mr. Lee, of Virginia, the list of delegates was called over by the secretary.

The following delegates then presented their credentials and took their seats.

Maine: Messrs. E. H. Allen, S. R. Lyman, S. Bradley, J. Neal, R. H. Vose, Z. Hyde, G. Pendleton.

New Hampshire: Messrs. Jas. Wilson, S. McNeil, J. Eastman, G. Stevens.

Massachusetts: Messrs. J. C. Bates, B. Burnell, P. Sprague, B. R. Hough, J. H. Duncan, S. Hoar, C. Hudson, A. Lee, H. Shaw, G. Ashman, W. Lovering, J. Howard, H. G. O. Colby, N. M. Davis.

Rhode Island: Messrs. J. F. Simons, W. Anthony, B. Diman, G. G. King.

Vermont: Messrs. W. Henry, S. H. Holley, A. B. W. Tenny, W. P. Briggs, C. Paine.

Connecticut: Messrs. C. Davies, W. H. Boardman, C. H. Phelps, C. Hawloy, Jos. S. Gladding, E. C. Bacon, E. Jackson, J. S. Peters.

New York: Messrs. Chandler Starr, Robt. C. Nichols, J. A. King, B. D. Silliman, Dudley Seldon, R. C. Wetmore, J. Hammond, Robert Smith, James A. Hamilton, P. R. Livingston, H. McFarland, E. Fay, E. Jenkins, H. Hamilton, A. Briggs, S. Van Rennssalaer, J. Knickerbocker, B. Blair, H. H. Ross, S. Gilbert, H. P. Voorhees, D. Petrie, C. P. Kirkland, A. L.

McCarty, J. Bradley, J. Russel, V. Whitney, D.
White, J. Dunn, D. D. Spencer, A. P. Granger, J. D.
Ledyard, G. II. Wood, G. V. Sacket, H. W. Taylor,
Jno. N. Dox, I. Lacy, P. L. Tracy, C. Tucker, L. F.
Allen, J. Chatterton.

New Jersey: Messrs. Asa Whitehead, D. S. Gregory,
E. Marsh, Jno. D. Hagar, T. A. Hartwell, C. Moffit,
R. E. Horner.

Delaware: Messrs. Thos. Stockton, T. M. Rodney,
R. Mansfield, P. F. Causey, J. Ferries, E. Spruance,
T. Wainwright, W. D. Wapples, D. Hazzard.

Pennsylvania: Messrs. J. A. Shulze, Alex. Quinton,
F. Fraley, Jno Swift, B. Badger, W. Darlington, E.
Darlington, J. Roberts, E. T. McDowell, J. A. Fisher,
W. R. Morris, C. B. Penrose, Jno. Williamson, A. O.
Cahoon, Jas. Merrill, S. M. Barclay, C. P. Markle, J.
Gray, C. C. Reed, T. H. Patterson, David Leech, Jno.
Dickey, J. Lawrence.

From the Fourth Congressional district, composed
of the counties of Delaware, Chester and Lancaster,
E. C. Reigart appeared and claimed his seat, T. G.
Henderson also appeared and claimed the same seat.

From the Twelfth Congressional district, composed
of the counties of Adams and Franklin, James Calhoun appeared and claimed to represent said district.
George Chambers also appeared and claimed the
said seat.

From the Seventeenth Congressional district, composed of the counties of Susquehanna, Bradford, Pot-
ter and McKean, Moses. J. Clark appeared and
claimed to represent said district. Edward Overton
also appeared and claimed to represent said district.

Whereupon, Mr. Roberts, of Pennsylvania, moved
that a committee of five delegates from other States
than Pennsylvania be appointed, to whom the cases of
the contested delegates from Pennsylvania be referred.
Mr. Williamson, of Pennsylvania, moved to amend
that motion bystriking out and inserting that the cases
of disputed seats in the delegation from Pennsylvania
be referred to said delegation.

Mr. Sprague, of Massachusetts, then moved that

the said motion, together with the amendment, be laid on the table, and that the secretary proceed with the call of the States.

Which motion prevailed, and the secretary proceeded with the call.

Maryland: Messrs. R. Johnson, J. L. Kerr, J. M. Goldsborough, R. W. Bowie, G. Howard, A. Alexander, Jas. Moore, R. J. Bowie.

Virginia: Messrs. B. W. Leigh, J. Barbour, J. W. Pegram, W. S. Archer, E. Chambers, Jno. Tyler, W. Newton, J. B. Harvey, I. A. Coles, J. Green, Jno. Janney, H. Berry, A. Waterman, B. G. Baldwin, J. Edginton.

North Carolina : Messrs. Jno. Owen, C. R. Kinney, W. W. Cherry, F. J. Hill, W. H. Battle, J. B. Kelly, H. W. Miller, N. M. Roan, I. Burns, T. A. Allison, B. S. Gaither, W. F. Davidson.

Kentucky: Messrs. Thos. Metcalf, L. Combs, M. Key, W. Preston, J. Shelby, J. Price, D. Banks, F. A. Andrews, C. M. Clay.

Ohio: Messrs. J. Burnett, N. G. Pendleton, J. Johnston, W. A. Rogers, W. S. Murphy, A. Toland, J. M. Creed, I. Belknap, E. Cutter, B. S. Cowen, C. T. Sherman, C. Prentiss, T. Bronson, H. Green, J. S. Lacy, B. Bentley.

Indiana: Messrs. D. McGuire, J. R. Mendenhall, A. Clarke, J. Perry, E. M. Huntington.

Louisiana: G. M. Graham.

Mississippi: Messrs. T. C. Tupper, A. S. Perkins.

Missouri: Messrs. W. H. Russel, Logan Hunton.

Illinois: Messrs. G. W. Ralph, W. S. Newberry, W. B. Warren.

Alabama: Messrs. H. W. Hilliard, W. H. Fleming, W. S. Smith.

Michigan: Messrs. G. C. Bates, T. J. Drake, D. S. Bacon.

Tennessee: South Carolina, Georgia, and Arkansas, not represented.

On motion of Mr. Sprague, of Massachusetts, a committee was appointed, consisting of one member from each State, to nominate officers for the permanent organization of the convention.

Mr. Johnson, of Ohio, moved that the convention be opened with prayer each morning, by the clergy-men of the different denominations, in the city of Har-risburg. Laid on the table, till the convention be per-manently organized.

On motion, adjourned till 10 o'clock to-morrow morn-ing.

SECOND DAY.

Thursday, Dec. 5.

Pursuant to adjournment, the convention met.

The Rev. Mr. Sprecher, officiating clergyman of the Lutheran Church, offered up to Almighty God a most fervent prayer for His blessing on the convention, our country and the world.

The following additional delegates appeared:

Ohio, Dr. Cyrus Faulconer; New York, Henry H. Ross; Virginia, William C. Mosley, Festus Dickin-son; Mississippi, Anderson Miller; North Carolina, J. C. Washington.

Col. Dickey, of Pennsylvania, announced that the Pennsylvania delegation had agreed that all the claim-ants of seats from this State ought to be admitted, and moved that the journal of yesterday be corrected ac-cordingly; which was agreed to.

Mr. Sprague, of Massachusetts, from the committee to nominate officers, made the following report, which was agreed to:

President: Gov. James Barbour, of Virginia.

Vice Presidents: Gov. Jno. S. Peters, of Connecti-cut; Gov. J. A. Shulze, of Pennsylvania; Gov. David Hazzard, of Delaware; Gov. George Howard, of Mary-land; Gov. Jno. Tyler, of Virginia; Gov. Jno. Owen, of North Carolina; Gov. Thomas Metcalf, of Kentucky; P. R. Livingston, of New York; Jacob Burnett, of Ohio; J. C. Bates, of Massachusetts; Jas. Wilson, of New Hampshire; E. M. Huntington, of Indiana; E. Marsh, of New Jersey.

Secretaries: Charles B. Penrose, of Pennsylvania: G. W. Ralph, of Illinois; S. R. Lyman, of Maine; C. Paine, of Vermont.

On taking the chair, Governor Barbour made one

of the most eloquent addresses ever listened to.

Mr. Graham, of Louisiana, said that a letter from t ie State of Arkansas, authorizing and requesting the delegates from Louisiana to cast the vote of Arkansas for candidates for President and Vice-President had been received, which he moved should be read. He said he was glad to find by the letter that the State of Arkansas was about moving forward in the cause of the country, and breaking from the shackles of Benton & Co., by whom it had been held in thraldrom.

The letter was from the chairman of the State Committee, and stated that the delegates elected by that State were in favor of Mr. Clay for President, and Governor Tyler, of Virginia, for Vice-President.

On motion of Mr. Roberts, of Ohio, the resolution offered by him yesterday instructing the president of the convention to procure the reverend clergy of Harrisburg to open the convention every morning with prayer, was taken up and adopted.

The following proposition of Mr. Sprague, as amended by Mr. Penrose, was unanimously agreed to:

Ordered, That the delegates from each State be requested to assemble as a delegation, and appoint a committee not exceeding three in number, to receive the views and opinions of such delegation, and communicate the same to the assembled committees of all the delegations, to be by them respectively reported to their principals; and that thereupon the delegates from each State be requested to assemble as a delegation, and ballot for candidates for the offices of President and Vice-President, and having done so, to commit the ballot designating the votes of each candidate, and by whom given, to its committee; and thereupon all the committees shall assemble and compare the several ballots, and report the result of the same to their several delegations, together with such facts as may bear upon the nomination; and such delegation shall forthwith reassemble and ballot again for candidates for the above offices, and again commit the result to the above committees, and if it shall appear that a majority of the ballots are for any one man for

candidate for President, said committee shall report
the result to the convention for its consideration; but
if there shall be no such majority, then the delegation
shall repeat the balloting until such a majority shall
be obtained, and then report the same to the convention for its consideration.

That the vote of a majority of each delegation shall
be reported as the vote of that State, and each State
represented here shall vote its full electoral vote by
such delegation in the committee.

THIRD DAY.

Friday, Dec. 6, 1839.

Convention met pursuant to adjournment.

A letter from the Whig State convention of Vermont, addressed to the president of the convention, was received and laid on the table.

Mr. A. P. McReynolds, of Michigan, and Mr. Preston, of Maryland, appeared as delegates, and took their
seats in convention.

Mr. Cassius Clay, of Kentucky, offered a resolution
that the ayes and noes be called, and the delegates
declare *viva voce* their choice as a candidate for President, and that where a delegation is not full, the
delegates present cast the votes of the absent members.

Mr. C. addressed the convention in favor of his
motion. He said he wished every portion of the people to be heard. He knew not that his own favorite
would be nominated—he did not know even the result
of the balloting, but he wished a full, fair, and candid
expression of opinion.

Mr. Davies, of Connecticut, opposed the motion of
Mr. Clay, and moved that it be laid upon the table.
Agreed to.

Mr. Hornor, of New Jersey, offered a resolution to
procure a correct list of the delegates and their post
offices, to be published with the proceedings of the
convention. Agreed to.

Mr. McFarland, of New York, laid before the convention the proceedings of a meeting in Orange county
in that State.

Mr. Williamson moved that a committee of finance be appointed: Mr. Lee, of Massachusetts, to be appointed chairman.

On motion the convention adjourned till 3 o'clock.

SAME DAY—AFTERNOON.

After prayer by the Rev. William Barnes, of the Methodist Episcopal Church.

Mr. Fisher, of Pennsylvania, from the committee, made report relative to the expenses of the convention.

Adjourned till 7 o'clock this evening.

SAME DAY—EVENING.

Mr. Williamson, of Pennsylvania, moved that Thos. E. Cochran, Esq., be admitted to a seat in the room of Mr. Morris, of Pennsylvania, who had left town. Agreed to.

Mr. Wetmore, of New York, offered several resolutions relative to the assembling of a national convention of young men to respond to the nomination of this convention.

Mr. Wetmore stated that the resolutions proceeded from a highly respectable body of Whigs in New York. He did not, however, press the resolutions at this time.

Some discussion now took place on a motion to take a recess till 9 o'clock. The motion prevailed.

NINE O'CLOCK P. M.

Mr. R. Johnson, of Maryland, said, that as no result had been arrived at in balloting by delegations, he would move that the committee on the subject be instructed to report progress, and that it then be discharged, and that the convention then proceed to vote for candidates for President and Vice President, *per capita.*

Mr. Richard Haughton was announced as a delegate from Massachusetts, in the room of Mr. Colby, who had gone home.

Mr. Harvie, of Virginia, moved to lay the resolution of Mr. R. Johnson on the table.

Mr. Harvie said the committee was now in session and could not report.

Mr. Williamson, of Pennsylvania, said the question was not debatable.

The question was then put on the motion to lay the resolution on the table; prevailed.

A motion was made that the convention do adjourn. Lost.

Mr. Harvie then said he understood the committee was in the house, and he therefore moved that the resolution be reconsidered.

Mr. McDowell, of Pennsylvania, said the committee would report in half an hour. [Applause.]

Mr. Harvie said he hoped that gentlemen would exercise a little patience.

Mr. Taylor, of New York, said he thought the resolution should not be acted on, as the convention would thereby be undoing what had been done for the last two days.

Mr. R. Johnson said he feared the committee would not report so soon.

Mr. McDowell said the committee would certainly report in half an hour.

Mr. R. W. Bowie, of Maryland, said the committee had adjourned, and no such order had been taken.

Mr. McDowell said he was assured by what might be considered the majority, that the committee would be able to report.

Mr. Hornor, of New Jersey, moved that the convention proceed to other business until the committee be able to report.

Mr. Harvie moved an adjournment. Lost.

Mr. Taylor, of New York, moved the convention take a recess for half an hour, which was afterwards altered to an hour, and agreed to.

HALF-PAST TEN P. M.

As soon as the convention was called to order, Governor Owen, of North Carolina, announced that the committee had had the subject-matter under consideration, and had instructed the chairman to report progress and ask leave to sit again; and that the following was the result of the ballotings for President:

Two hundred and fifty-four ballots were cast, of which Gen. Winfield Scott had 16, Hon. Henry Clay, 90; Gen. William Henry Harrison, 148.

One hundred and forty-eight ballots being a majority of the whole number, Gen. William Henry Harrison, of Ohio, was duly selected as the candidate for the Presidency.

The report was received and the committee had leave to sit again; whereupon the convention adjourned till 10 o'clock to-morrow.

FOURTH DAY.

Saturday, Dec. 7, 1839

Convention met persuant to adjournment.

A prayer was offered by the Rev. W. R. De Witt, of Harrisburg, when Mr. Banks, of Kentucky, rose and said, that as a delegate from Kentucky he had come here to acquiesce in the decision of the convention; he bowed before its determination, and he could assure the convention that the nomination made last evening would receive the hearty support of his constituents—at least it would not be his fault if it did not. The situation of the Kentucky delegation had, he said, been one of peculiar responsibility— they had their first choice, but they came here to sustain the nomination when made, and on their part he assured the convention they would do so. Among his constituents, Mr. Banks said, the nomination would be received as it deserved. They are uncompromising in their determined hostility to the administration of Martin Van Buren. By his own district he could assure the convention Gen. William Henry Harrison would receive as large a vote as Mr. Clay. My fellow-citizens, said Mr. Banks, prefer Mr. Clay, but they left me uninstructed, which I regarded as a liberal spirit; and the cultivation of such a spirit in all our relations cannot but have a salutary effect.

The Whigs of the State of Kentucky, said Mr. Banks, are sincere in their devotion to Henry Clay— not on his own account alone, for the measure of his fame is already full, but because they believe him to be the man of his country. But Kentucky will not prove unworthy of the man whose fame is but another name for her glory. She loves the country more than she loves Clay; and her delegates have met here as her people will meet at the ballot-boxes on the broad platform of determined hostility to Martin Van Buren. Side by side with their brethren from other States the Whigs of Kentucky will contend for the reformation of those abuses which now threaten the destruction of our beloved country, and strive to make her what present rulers will not—prosperous and happy.

Mr. Reverdy Johnson, of Maryland, said that Maryland's choice was well known—it was unnecessary now to mention the individual. The delegation had upheld that choice to the last. But satisfied, on consultation with the delegates from other sections of the Union, that the choice of Maryland would not be the choice of this convention, and that in opinion of a majority of the delegates there was another name that could carry dismay into the ranks of the enemy— he proposed, on the part of the delegation from Maryland, to offer a resolution that the result of the ballotings be unanimously confirmed, and that Gen. William Henry Harrison be presented to the American people with the sanction of this convention.

Under this banner. said Mr. J., we *can*. we *must* and we *will triumph ;* and in order to afford time for the report of the committee as to the candidate for the Vice-Presidency. he proposed that the convention take a recess for half an hour, and he felt satisfied that a name would be presented in connection with that office on which the friends of Harrison and Scott could unite with the same unanimity that prevails among the friends of Clay and Scott in regard to the nomination of Harrison. [Immense applause.]

Mr. Cherry, of North Carolina, said that the State he represented had remained comparatively quiet in the selection of the nominee. She had her first choice as well as other States. but she had too long fought

against the spoilers not to know her duty, and she
would stand by her sister States in the present contest, by giving Gen. William Henry Harrison a determined support, and when the election returns come
in, said Mr. Cherry, they will show that "*Old Rip is
wide awake again!*"

Mr. Preston, of Kentucky, said the convention had
already been correctly assured that the delegation from
his State came here for conciliation and compromise —
harmony and concession—and he was certain that the
resolution he was about to propose was one that would
meet the approbation of the convention. It might
naturally be thought, said Mr. Preston, that Kentucky
stands here in the attitude of one disappointed of her
favorite choice. Her people it was true had their preference: but they were Whigs and would sustain their
country; and to prove that their first choice will sustain
them in that course, said Mr. Preston. I will state that
there is now a letter in this convention from the Hon.
H. Clay, that if read will display the spirit that animates him in regard to General Harrison. He moved
that Mr. Combs, of Kentucky, in whose possession
the letter was, be requested to read it.

Mr. Combs said that his colleagues had truly represented their State. If, said he, the heart of Kentucky
is bruised, it is not broken; Kentucky was born a Whig
State, she has lived a Whig State, and I hope to God
she may die a Whig State! The life of her son,
Henry Clay, said Mr. C., is his eulogium, and the historian must do him justice.

Mr. Combs then read a letter from Mr. Clay, urging
upon the delegates from Kentucky the importance of
union among the elements of opposition to Van
Burenism, urging them to disregard his own position;
and paying a merited compliment to General Harrison,
whom he styled the "distinguished citizen of Ohio."

On motion, the letter was ordered to be entered on
the journals.

Governor Barbour, of Virginia, president of the convention, said he rejoiced the letter from Mr. Clay had
been read. For his own part, after the report of the

committee last evening, from rumors which he heard
he had been inclined to think that other action might
be taken. As regards the disinterested subject of the
proposed action, said Governor Barbour, distinguished
by the great crisis when the Union seemed to be threatened. I would say a word or two, with your permission. When danger portended it was his patrotism
and superior genius that weathered the storm. I
need not eulogize Mr. Clay. He will occupy through
all time one of the fairest pages of our country's history. When danger has threatened, Henry Clay has
always been the foremost to avert it, and his patriotism
and firmness on all occasions, will embalm his memory
in the hearts of the American people. But beyond
the consideration with which I, as a citizen of the Republic, regard Mr. Clay, said Governor Barbour, there
are other reasons for my ardent attachment to him.
I have known him from my infancy, and in the intercourse under the guard of honorable confidence and
private friendship, on no occasion have I ever heard
a sentiment from Henry Clay which was not that of an
ardent patriot and devoted friend of his country.
There is no selfishness about him—no petty scheming
for his own advancement. And had it been your
pleasure, gentlemen, to nominate him to the Presidency,
his election would have opened a new epoch in the
history of our country. He would not have been the
little, dirty, petty tool of a party; but would have
cleansed the Augean stable, and made us a happy
people.

But notwithstanding my feelings for Mr. Clay,
said Governor Barbour, and the hope I entertained
that he would receive your nomination, I have come
to the conclusion that so far as my vote and influence
go, they shall sustain the harmony of this convention,
and I shall therefore vote for the unanimous nomination of Gen. William Henry Harrison.

Mr. B. W. Leigh, of Virginia, said that he con-
curred in the sentiments of his colleague, [Governor
Barbour] and would join him in his vote for the unanimous entry of the nomination on the journal. The

letter of Mr. Clay was an evidence that in his heart disinterested patriotism was superior to all other feelings. He [Mr. L.] could not think that the ambition of such a man as Henry Clay could be gratified by being made President. He has already secured a fame that will live as long as pure government—a renown that will survive the marble monument that will cover his grave—and a renown more valuable in his [Mr. L.'s opinion] than any station, however high and exalted it may be.

Mr. Leigh said that one of the purposes for which the convention had met had been accomplished, and he for one would give his heart and hand to crown its labors with success.

Mr. Leigh also said that he too had had correspondence—correspondence with his intimate, old, personal friend, Gen. Winfield Scott, and he could assure the convention that he too would sanction their proceeding with his vote and influence.

Mr. J. A. King, of New York, said that as a representative of New York, he regretted that the choice of his State had not prevailed in the nomination; but, said Mr. King, we have surrendered him with manly firmness because we knew that the choice could not but fall upon an individual worthy of the support of American freemen. Our votes have been cast in the conviction that the candidate of this convention will ultimately carry. We have presented to the people a name unsullied by any spot of civil or military delinquency. We have given this distinguished individual our unhesitating support. We did not prefer General Scott because we believed him to be of sounder principles than him to whom we have thrown our votes, but for local reasons. The choice of the convention shall receive equal honor at our hands.

Mr. King said he would not detain the convention by a speech, but would merely remark that in the field General Harrison has displayed equal valor with General Scott—and he was certain the latter would respond to the convention, "God prosper your decision—God bless you all!"

Mr. Dudley Selden, of New York, said he was one of the minority who formed one-third of the delegation from that State, and went with the representatives of Kentucky and Virginia in the selection of a candidate. They had pursued that object till success became hopeless; but whatever may have been our preferences, said Mr. Selden, we concur heartily in carrying out the decision of the convention.

Mr. Jonathan Roberts, of Pennsylvania, addressed the convention in favor of the nomination. He said he had been in favor of the nomination of Mr. Clay: but being out-voted would not only acquiesce, but would unite heartily in the support of Gen. William Henry Harrison, and would do all in his power to further his election.

Mr. R. Johnson, of Maryland, then offered the following resolution:

Resolved, That this convention unanimously recommend to the people of the United States Gen. William Henry Harrison, of Ohio, as a candidate for President. and John Tyler, of Virginia, as a candidate for Vice-President.

Before the question was taken, Governor Owen, of North Carolina, said the balloting committee were ready to report on the subject of the Vice-Presidency; that 231 votes had been cast for Vice-President— the vote of Virginia not having been cast, and that the 231 votes had all been cast for John Tyler, of Virginia, who was accordingly reported by the committee as the candidate for the Vice-Presidency.

Mr. B. W. Leigh, of Virginia, then stated that the vote of Virginia had not been cast, because it was understood that Mr. Tyler, one of the delegation, would in all probability receive the nomination, and delicacy therefore forbade their participation.

Colonel Swift, of Pennsylvania, briefly expressed his original preference for the distinguished statesman of Kentucky, Henry Clay, and concluded by declaring his determination to yield his preference, and heartily and cordially to give his support to the nomination of the convention, and return to his constituents and recommend to them to do so likewise.

Mr. Sprague, of Massachusetts, next rose, and congratulated the convention on the happy result which was about to crown its labors. He referred to the fact that the delegates came much divided in opinion, and to the hopes entertained by our enemies that they would be divided in the selection of a candidate. Happily they have been disappointed. He alluded to the character and worth of Mr. Clay, his distinguished services to the country, and his high admiration of him. Massachusetts, he said, also had her favorite son; but she had yielded up her preferences—and yielded them early—for the sake of conciliation and success. She had made this sacrifice freely—cordially—and she would now rally under the banner of William Henry Harrison with the same zeal, and the same certainty of success as with her own favorite son.

Mr. Chambers, of Pennsylvania, was not only willing to support the resolution of the gentleman from Maryland, but to do so cordially and with all his heart. He was ready to rally under the banner of William Henry Harrison, and support that banner with all the influence that God and nature had given him.

Mr. Simmons, of Rhode Island, said in behalf of himself and his delegation, that though last to yield their preferences, they would be among the first to respond to the nomination.

Mr. Vose, of Maine, warmly responded to the nomination.

Judge Burnett, of Ohio, next addressed the convention at some length. After a brief eulogy of Mr. Clay, he referred to the early history of General Harrison, and his intimate acquaintance with him, and testified to the high estimation in which he was held by all who knew him. He concluded by recommending the unfurling the Union flag, with the motto of Mr. Wise of Virginia, *"Union for the sake of the Union!"*
Do this, said he, and all will be well.

Mr. Livingston, of New York, rose next. He commenced his remarks by asking the question, Where am

I? What has brought me here? and answered with the emphatic response, *Love of country!*—a wish to see the powers that be effectually prostrated and the country redeemed from the hands of the spoilers. He alluded to his old age and feebleness, stating that even then he was scarcely able to proceed; he said he had been a Democrat all his life, had never been out of the harness. He ever had and ever would adhere to the principle that the majority govern. When that principle was lost sight of there must be an end of the Republic.

Mr. Livingston briefly eulogized the character of Mr. Clay. The world, he said, would do him justice. His fame would be admired by after generations. Next he adverted to the character of General Harrison. He said he liked his character. He knew him well, and nothing had been said in his pra se that was not strictly true. Ohio, he said, would go for him by acclamation, and he was persuaded from what he had learned that the Keystone would yet be the arch of the Union. He then drew a vivid picture of Martin Van Buren, and referred to the downward tendency of the country under his administration, which, he said, had put the Republic radically wrong; but he had every confidence that we would soon get radically right. When he had realized this belief he would descend to the tomb happy and contented.

Governor Metcalf, of Kentucky, was particularly happy in his remarks. Kentucky's favorite son, he said, had lost the nomination, but had he himself been here he would have done precisely what the delegation from that State are prepared to do—enter heartily into the support of the nomination. Success is and ever has been his first object. The man who can best secure that success to the party is the man he would rally under—so will his friends. As regarded himself, he did not sacrifice so much as did many other of the friends of Mr. Clay; he moved only from the side of one noble friend to take his stand firmly by the side of another and no less noble friend. The country had not done General Harrison justice. He has done

more for his country and received less for his services
than any man living. He possessed both civil and
military capacities of the first order, which should entitle him to the admiration of the people. Governor
Metcalf said he came here in favor of Kentucky's favorite son, believing him to be the candidate most likely
to succeed. Since he had been here he had interchanged sentiments with the delegates from the various
States and had come to the conclusion that he was
mistaken. He was now prepared to go for the strongest man and overturn the powerful despotism under
which we were now suffering. Let not the song of
Democracy cheat the people. He had ever been a
Democrat—not one of the Democrats of the present
day—he was an old-fashioned Democrat. He verily
believed that the name of Democracy had cheated half
the people out of their senses. He here drew a vivid
picture of the corruption of the present powers that
be and the enormities committed under the name of
Democracy. He regarded it as his duty, he said, to
warn the people against such Democracy. He hoped,
he said, in conclusion, for triumph. The "Hunters
of Kentucky" will be found true to the great Whig
party of the Union.

Mr. Boardman, of Connecticut, earnestly supported
the nomination.

General Wilson, of New Hampshire, was very
happy in his remarks. He expressed the belief that
his State, though her prospects had been dark and
gloomy, would respond to the nomination of Harrison
and Tyler in a spirit of enthusiasm which would
enable her to triumph over the present corrupt party
in power. He related several anecdotes, and applied
them very happily.

Mr. Hilliard, of Alabama, said that he rejoiced to
hear the voice of congratulation sounding all around
him, and that he entertained the same patriotic feelings
as the gentleman who had preceded him. His own
preferences, he said, had been ardent for Clay, but he
would stand or fall with the nominee of this convention. He was resolved to sacrifice and risk everything

for the good of the cause; and he felt assured that the
delegates would all go home with an account of their
proceedings that will impart a corresponding enthusiasm in the bosoms of their constituents.

Mr. Merrill, of Pennsylvania, supported the resolution in a few excellent remarks.

Mr. Tupper, of Mississippi, said that the Mississippi
delegation had cast the vote of that State for Henry
Clay, and perhaps the Whigs of the State will be
disappointed in the result of our deliberations; but they
will go for the nominee of this convention, and the
land of Poindexter and Prentiss, as she has done
before, will do her duty still; and from the harmony
of this convention, and the enthusiasm manifested by
the members, he felt satisfied she can be rescued from
the spoilers under the banner of the hero of Tippecanoe.

Mr. Whitehead, of New Jersey, said he too had
had his first choice. He had been overruled by the
majority, but he did not complain, and would cheerfully abide by the decision of the convention. The
nominee had once before received the vote of New
Jersey, and was assured he would do so again.

Mr. Russel, of Missouri, commenced his remarks
by stating that he came from the State of the *great
expunger*. Dark clouds had long lowered over that
State, but light is now breaking through them. There
are still some green spots on which the eye loves to
rest. His first choice had not been selected, but we
leave him in the hands of his country, with the
wreath of fame covering his brow.

The Whigs of Missouri, said Mr. Russel, will support the nominee of this convention, General Harrison, and if their decision should fail in the latter, they
will hope to be rejoiced by the shout of victory from
their sister States.

There are considerations in Missouri that make the
name of General Harrison a tower of strength. He is
rich in the affections of his countrymen, and the
Whigs of Missouri will do their best—will die in the
last ditch.

Mr. Graham, of Louisiana, said that he and the Whigs of the State he represented had their first choice. But their prayer will be offered up for the success of the ticket.

A gentleman from Vermont, whose name the reporter could not learn, addressed the convention. He said the Whigs of that State will never surrender till the gates of the White House at Washington are demanded and secured in the name of the people of this great Republic.

Mr. Newton, of Virginia, said that the State which had the honor to be the birth-place of the first savior of his country, will prove to be the birth-place of the second savior of his country. He said the character of General Harrison is now much misunderstood, and when better understood will be better appreciated.

Mr. Bates, of Michigan, said he liked the eccentric Crockett's motto, "Be sure you're right, then go ahead!" With General Harrison, said Mr. Bates, we are right, and I assure the convention we will "go ahead."

Judge Huntingdon, of Indiana, said that that State has been Whig—and is Whig to the core. He was sure she would give General Harrison a large majority in 1840. He himself resided at Fort Harrison, and he knew there was no man there who supported the General in 1836, when the State gave him eight thousand majority, who would not do so again.

The Judge referred to the course of General Harrison in Congress in reference to the public lands and the early settlers, who, instead of an enemy, as they feared, found him their best friend. He also referred to the declaration of Col. R. M. Johnson that General Harrison had fought more battles than any man in the country and "never lost a battle."

The Judge said he was sure he never will lose a battle, and that his nomination will be received in the West with a burst of enthusiasm never before known in the country.

The question was then taken on the resolution of Mr. Johnson, when it was unanimously adopted.

A resolution was then offered and adopted congratulating the constituents of the convention on the result of its deliberations, and recommending the same harmony and enthusiasm among them that have characterized the proceedings of the delegates.

Mr. Preston, of Kentucky, offered a resolution relative to the adoption of an address to the people of the United States.

Mr. B. W. Leigh opposed the motion, believing no address necessary. He said he should be in favor of leaving the nomination to its own weight. He was not for acting on the defensive, but on the offensive. He was for carrying the war into Africa; for arraigning the spoilers before the bar of the American people for high crimes and misdemeanors, when they will receive the punishment due them, and the only punishment they can receive under our institutions—dismissal from office now and forever.

Mr. Pendleton, of Ohio, made some remarks which we could not hear.

Mr. Burnell, of Massachusetts, said there was no need of an address. If the voice of the West rolling down from the mountains and along the valleys of the Atlantic, be not better than all the addresses that ever were issued, then indeed a miracle has been wrought.

Mr. Preston's resolution was withdrawn.

Mr. Pendleton, of Ohio, stated that it was the wish of General Harrison only to serve but *one term*, if elected to the Presidency.

A resolution was then submitted by R. Johnson, of Maryland, and agreed to, recommending the friends of correct principles in the different States to hold conventions on the 22d of February next, or such day as may be agreed upon, for the purpose of nominating electoral tickets and general organization.

On motion of Governor Ewen, of North Carolina, a committee of one from each delegation was appointed to inform the nominees of the convention of their nomination.

Mr. Hornor, of New Jersey, said that in conformity

with the recommendation of the State convention of that State he offered the following:

Resolved, That this convention recommend to the Whig young men of the several States to assemble at Washington City on the first Monday of May next, for the purpose of advancing the cause of sound principles.

The resolution was agreed to after the substitution of Baltimore for Washington.

A resolution was passed tendering the thanks of the convention to the trustees of the Lutheran church, and to the reverend clergymen who attended the sessions.

Also a resolution tendering the thanks of the convention to the officers.

The president responded to the resolution in some very appropriate remarks, when the convention adjourned *sine die*.

ANECDOTE OF HARRISON.

The following circumstance was mentioned during the session of the Harrisburg convention by Judge Burnet, of Ohio, a warm personal friend of General Harrison.

Many years since, while the great tide of emigration was flowing through the Western States, the hero of the Thames having, for a while, exchanged the arduous duties of a statesman and general for the more peaceful pursuits of agriculture, was, on a hot summer evening, at the porch of his humble "log cabin," asked for shelter and a meal by a minister of the Gospel of the Methodist Episcopal persuasion. The jaded appearance of the steed and the soiled garments of the rider proclaimed the fatigue of the day, and with his usual courtesy the old General welcomed the stranger. After a plain and substantial supper the guest joined with his host in social conversation, and the latter, laying aside the character of the soldier and statesman, willingly listened to the pious instruction of the traveler. They retired to rest, the good old soldier thankful to a munificent Providence that he was enabled to administer to the wants of a fellow-creature and the worthy minister of Christ invoking the blessing of heaven upon the head of his kind benefactor. Morning came and the minister prepared to depart. He was in the act of taking leave when he was informed that his horse had died during the night. This loss, however severe, considering that he had yet two hundred miles to travel, did not discourage him in the exercise of his duty; but taking his saddle-bags on his arm he rose to depart with thanks for the kindness of his entertainer. The old General did not attempt to prevent him, though he offered his condolence upon his loss, but an observing eye could have detected a smile of inward satisfaction which the conciousness of doing good alone produces. The guest reached the door and to his astonishment found one of the General's horses accoutred with his own saddle and bridle in waiting for him. He returned and remonstrated, stating his inability to pay for it, and that in all probability he should never again visit that section of the country. But the General was inexorable and reminded the astonished divine that "He who giveth to the poor lendeth to the Lord," sent him on his way, his heart overflowing with gratitude and his prayers directed to heaven for blessings on the venerable hero.

HARRISON'S LETTER.

Reader, compare the two letters which we place before you, and if a Whig you will be proud of your candidate. Indeed, we thank General Harrison, from the bottom of our heart, for this, his best letter. It is indeed one most important step in the great reform which is to save our country—which brings us back to the fandamental principle in the Constitution, which would establish the independence and purity of Congress. It is indeed a reform.

Albany, Feb. 28, 1840.

SIR: On behalf of the Whig members of the legislature, being a majority of both the senate and the house of assembly, the undersigned have the honor to transmit to you the inclosed resolutions prepared by us and passed with perfect unanimity and the most enthusiastic feeling, by those members, at a meeting held on Saturday last, being the anniversary of Washington's birth-day.

We have also the honor to transmit to you a paper containing a report in full of the speeches and proceedings at that meeting.

We have the fullest confidence, that in the views there expressed as to the character and policy of the present administration, as well as in the tributes paid to your character and public services, and to those of the distinguished citizen associated with you in the Harrisburg nomination, we have given utterance not only to our own feelings and convictions, but to those of a large majority of the people of this State

We are, with high respect, your friends and fellow-citizens,

G. C. VERPLANCK, ⎫
MARTIN LEE, ⎬ Of the senate.
JOHN MAYNARD, ⎭

C. E. CLARK, ⎫
WM. DUER, ⎪
PETER B. PORTER, ⎬ Of the assembly.
D. B. ST. JOHN, ⎪
J. HUBBARD, ⎭

GEN. WILLIAM HENRY HARRISON.

North Bend, Ohio, May 23, 1840.

GENTLEMEN: I have the honor to acknowledge the receipt of your letter of the 28th February, conveying the proceedings of a meeting of the Whig members of the legislature convened in the Capitol of the State on the twenty-second of that month.

I beg you to believe, gentlemen, that I am deeply impressed with the honor which has been conferred upon me by the distinguished body whom on this occasion you represent. The great object of both my civil and military life has been to serve my country to the utmost of my abilities and to obtain its approbation. The hope of this has often cheered me in circumstances of great difficulty and embarrassment.

You will pardon me, I trust, if in this letter I go somewhat beyond the mere purpose of acknowledging the receipt of your communication and use the occasion for making a few remarks which circumstances seem to require from me in respect to a declaration of opinions or pledges, as to my future conduct, required of candidates for high offices.

My public life, not now a short one, is before the country. My opinions on important subjects have been expressed from time to time as those subjects have arisen; and since my name has been mentioned among those from whom a selection might be made for the office of President, I have in several letters to friends fully and frankly avowed my sentiments. Further than this I cannot suppose intelligent persons could desire me to go. The people of this country do not rely on professions, promises and pledges. They know that if a candidate is unprincipled he will not scruple to give any pledge that may be required of him, and as little will he hesitate to violate it.

I have already made public the principles by which I should be governed if elected President, so far as relates to the proper executive duties of that office. But almost innumerable applications have been made to me for my opinions relative to matters of legislation, or even to the proper mode of conducting business in the two houses of Congress.

My published letters to Mr. Williams and Mr. Denny will show that I do not consider the President a constituent branch of the legislature; yet it is impossible to read the letters that have been addressed to me without believing that many of the writers had adopted the opinion that the Presidential office was the proper source and origin of all the legislation of the country; an opinion, in my judgment, at war with every principle of the Constitution, and of deep and dangerous consequence. The prevalence of such sentiments, more than almost anything else, would tend to consolidate the whole substantial power of the Government in the hands of a single man, a tendency which, whether in or out of office, I feel it my most solemn duty to resist.

I have declined, therefore, to give any further pledge or opinions on the subjects which belong to the future legislation of Congress; because,

1. I conceive, for the reasons given in my letters to Mr. Williams and Mr. Denny, that Congress should be left as much as possible untrammeled by Executive influence in the discharge of its legislative functions; and that a better guarantee for the correct conduct of a Chief Magistrate may be found in his character the course of his former life, than in pledges and opinions given during the pendency of a doubtful contest; and that, although recognizing the right of the people to be informed of the leading political opinions of the candidates for offices of trust, yet as it regards the subjects upon which the legislature may be called to act, the pledges and opinions should be required, if required at all, of candidates for Congress.

2. Because the habit of considering a single individual as the source from which all the measures of government should emanate, is degrading to a republic, and of the most dangerous tendency.

3. Because upon all the questions in regard to which, under any circumstances, it would be at all proper for me to make answers, my sentiments have already been fully and clearly given to the public, in a manner to entitle them to credence, as I conceive that no honest man would suffer *his* friends to publish documents in his name which were not genuine, or containing opinions which he was not then willing to indorse. Accept, gentlemen, the assurance of my high regard.　　　WILLIAM HENRY HARRISON.

Messrs. Verplanck, Lee, Maynard, Duer, Clark, Porter, St. John and Hubbard.

In reply to a letter similar in substance to that of General Harrison, Governor Tyler thus writes :

Williamsburg, Va., March 20, 1840.

GENTLEMEN : I owe you my acknowledgments for your letter communicating to me the proceedings of the Whig members of the legislature of New York, and the paper containing the addresses made at their late meeting. I have read them with deep interest, not because of my present political relations to the country, relations which you are well aware are not in the slightest degree of my own seeking ; but because whatever proceeds from the accredited representatives of a majority of the people of the great State of New York, is entitled at all times, and more especially at the present, to excite the highest degree of attention. The influence and power which she exerts over the affairs of the Union devolve upon her a responsibility of the weightiest character, and when she announces herself on the side of the institutions of the country, the friends of civil liberty have cause to feel assured that all is safe. Such are the feelings which your late proceedings and addresses are calculated to inspire, and such, I am sure, will be the happy result.

For the complimentary notice which has been taken of myself by the Whig members of the legislature, I beg to be permitted to express my thanks, and to tender each of you, gentlemen, wishes for your health, happiness and prosperity.

I have the honor to be, yours, etc.,

JOHN TYLER.

Committee of the senate : Hon. G. C. Verplanck, Hon. Gen. Martin Lee, Hon. John Maynard.
Committee of the assembly : Messrs. C. E. Clark, Wm. Duer, Peter B. Porter, **D. B. St. John**, and J. Hubbard.

POLLOCK'S DEFENSE.

The Brave Soldier Defends His Old Chief.

Among the malicious inventions against General Harrison's character was that of cowardice. And, notwithstanding that in early youth he forsook the luxurious life of an Atlantic city to enlist in a war against the British and Indians among the primitive forests and prairies of the West, there were at times men so vile as to make such a charge. In the Ohio legislature, after two Van Buren members had indulged in this accusation, Mr. Pollock, thus replied to them:

Mr. Speaker: I have listened to the debate with much patience. I have heard abuse heaped upon General Harrison by men who are comparatively young, and although I am unaccustomed to speech-making, I hope the house will bear with me for a few moments, for I shall not trouble it long. I shall only reply to some particular matters. I shall not deal in generals; we have too many of them already. Sir, I have heard members of this house charge General Harrison with cowardice whom he defended and protected from the war knife and tomahawk of the Indian when they were sleeping in their mother's arms.

Mr. Speaker, I know something of General Harrison; and something of his history; and something of his deeds. I know individuals who were with him during the last war; who were with him in the battles of the Thames, Fort Meigs, and Fort Stephenson. I know, sir, that cannon balls, and chain shot, and bomb shells, flew thick around him in these battles. The gentleman from Clermont (Mr. Buchanan) said that General Harrison was not, during the battle of Fort Meigs, near enough to have the scales knocked off. He was near enough to have scales and dirt knocked on him by cannon balls. [Who saw it? asked some member.] I saw it, sir! I was in the battle. I saw a cannon ball strike within two feet of General Harrison during that fight. I was there. I saw bomb shells and chain shot flying all around him. I speak what I know, and what my eyes have seen. General Harrison is not a coward; and those who call him coward know nothing of him. He was a brave, prudent, and fearless general. He took the right course during the last war; he acted a noble part, and his country has honored him for it. Ask the soldiers who fought by his side; whose arms were nerved by his presence; whose hearts were cheered by his valor; and who were led to triumph and to victory by his courage, and bravery, and skill, if General Harrison was a coward: and they, sir, will tell you no!

Sir, I have done; I only wished to give my testimony in favor of General Harrison, and to state what I have seen, in opposition to the statements of those who are ignorant of his character, and who know nothing of his bravery and skill.

OHIO STATE CONVENTION.

THE MONSTER GATHERING OF THE CLANS OF OHIO. THE PEOPLE PARADE WITH LOG CABINS, HARD CIDER AND COONS.

> "The great twenty-second is coming,
>   And the Vanjacks begin to look blue,
> They know there's no chance for poor Matty,
>   If we'll stick to Old Tippecanoe,
>   If we'll stick to Old Tippecanoe."

On Friday, the 21st of February, 1840, the people of Ohio met in convention in the open air, at the corner of High and Broad streets, in Columbus, and James Wilson, the veteran editor, of Jefferson county, called the vast concourse to order. The convention was then and there fully organized by appointing the following persons officers:

President: *Gen. Reasin Beall,* of Wayne county.

Vice-presidents: first district, *Charles S. Clarkson,* of Hamilton county; second district, *William Carr.* of Butler county; third district, *Aurora Spofford,* of Wood county; fourth district, *Isaiah Morris,* of Clinton county; fifth district, *Thomas L. Shields,* of Clermont county; sixth district, *John C. Bestow,* of Meigs county; seventh district, *John Crouse, Sr.,* of Ross county; eighth district, *Forest Meeker,* of Delaware county; ninth district, *George Sanderson,* of Fairfield county; tenth district, *Charles Anthony,* of Clark county; eleventh district, *Solomon Bentley,* of Belmont county; twelfth district, *David Chambers,* of Muskingum county; thirteenth district, *Daniel S. Norton,* of Knox county; fourteenth district, *Eleutheros Cooke.* of Erie county; fifteenth district, *Frederick Wadsworth.* of Portage county; sixteenth district, *Storm Rosa,* of Geauga county; seventeenth district, *Joseph Mause.* of Columbiana county; eighteenth district, *Solomon Markham,* of Stark county; nineteenth district, *Hugh Downing,* of Jefferson county.

Secretaries: Chauncey Dewey, of Harrison; Robert Buchanan, of Hamilton; Thomas M. Kelley of Cuyahoga; James Watson Riley, of Mercer; Smithson E. Wright, of Franklin; William B. Thrall, of Pickaway; William M. Neeley, of Belmont; James M. Mason, of Monroe.

On taking the chair, General Beall delivered an animating address referring to the services of General Harrison and himself under Gen. Anthony Wayne, and to the later events in the active, varied and useful life of his old companion in arms. The assemblage was enthusiastic and uproarious in applause of the old soldier, whose seventy-one years had not impaired his vigor or patriotism. Hon. Richard Douglass, of Ross, offered resolutions as to appointment of various committees on business, which were adopted. Hon. Thomas Ewing, of Fairfield, Gen. Wm. S. Murphy, of Ross, and others, ably addressed the people, and the

body then adjourned until **Saturday** morning at 10
o'clock. The **great** 22d came, and the rain poured
down in torrents during the entire meeting and the
march of the procession. There was, in fact, no intermission. Gen. Charles Anthony, one of the vice-presidents, took the chair, and Nehemiah Allen, from a
committee of ten from each Congressional district,
presented a report recommending Hon. Thomas Corwin, of Warren county, for governor. General Anthony and others spoke in favor of the report, and
Thomas Corwin was unanimously nominated.

Gen. Allen Trimble presented from the committee
the names for an electoral **ticket, and the** following
were chosen by acclamation, **viz:**

Senatorial electors William R. **Putnam,** of Washington county; Reasin Beall, of Wayne county.

District electors: First district, Alexander Mahew,
of Hamilton county; second district, Henry Harter,
Preble county; third district, Aurora Spofford,
Wood county; fourth district, Joshua Collett, Warren
county; fifth district, Abram Wiley, Clermont county;
sixth district, Samuel F. **Vinton,** Gallia county; seventh
district, **John J. Van Meter, Pike** county; eighth
district, Aquilla Toland, Madison county; ninth district, Perley B. **Johnson,** Morgan county; tenth district, John **Dukes, Hancock county**; eleventh district, Otho Brashear, **Guernsey county**; twelfth district,
James Raguet, Muskingum county; **thirteenth district,**
Christopher S. Miller, **Coshocton county**; fourteenth
district, David King, Medina county; fifteenth district,
Storm Rosa, Geauga county; sixteenth district, John
Batty, Carroll county; seventeenth district, John
Carey, Crawford **county**; eighteenth district, John
Augustine, Stark **county**; nineteenth district, John
Jamison, Harrison county.

Resolutions in favor of **Harrison and** Tyler and
retrenchments **and reform were** presented from the
committee by Judge John C. Wright, of Hamilton,
Hon. Alfred Kelley, **of** Franklin, and Hon. Hiram
Griswold, of Stark. They contained a terrible arraign-
ment of the British party **in** power, the corruption

and profligacy of the office-holders, etc. Upon the
question of contributions they declared that, if it be
the interest of the office-holders to appropriate any
portion of their salaries to electioneering purposes,
with a view to sustaining those from whom they hold
appointments and themselves in office (as proved
to be the case with the custom-house officers in New
York), it is conclusive evidence that those salaries are
too high, and should be reduced. They declared in
favor of a change of the entire administration and of
governmental policy. They were opposed to the one-
man power and in favor of the people ruling. They
were for protecting the mechanical and manufacturing
and laboring interests of America, and the poor
people, wherever they might be, in the country.
Harrison, the log-cabin candidate, was the representative of the hardy yeomanry, and they would rally
around his standard. They declared for him as the
representative of the one-term principle, because no
one man should be elected President of the United
States for two terms in succession, and *Martin Van
Buren least of all!*

Resolutions of this character were carried with
a whoop.

General Murphy offered a resolution, recommending
to the Whig young men of Ohio, Kentucky, Indiana,
Illinois, Michigan, Western New York, Pennsylvania
and Virginia, to celebrate the next anniversary of the
raising of the siege of Fort Meigs, in June, 1813, on
the ground occupied by the fort. It was unanimously
adopted.

Charles Borland, of Fairfield, moved that it be recommended to the voters to organize Harrison and reform clubs in each and every county of the State.
Carried by acclamation.

The following central committee was appointed, to-
wit: Alfred Kelley, Joseph Ridgeway, Sr., John W.
Andrews, Robert Neil, John L. Miner, Francis Stewart, Lewis Heyl, Dr. Miller and Lyne Starling, Jr.

The condensation of the business of the convention
as relating to organization having been given, a brief

sketching of the incidents will enable the reader to judge
of the temper and spirit of the occasion.   When, simul-
taneously from all directions, on the 21st, immense
delegations came together on High street, at the corner
of Broad, and the **New**ark band played the Marseillaise
hymn, and more than twenty bands in the long lines
joined in, the crowd became fairly wild with yells and
shouts.   More than one thousand men came in procession from Ross, Pike and Jackson counties.   By
wagons and carriages, on canal boats, on horseback
and on foot, thousands upon thousands poured into the
streets, and thronged hotels and boarding-houses, and
filled the hundreds of dwellings whose "latch-strings
hung out," and over whose doors were the words,
"Welcome to all."

The grand procession on the 22d surpassed in enthusiasm anything ever before or since in the history
of Ohio.   The people had been gathering from Thursday morning, and from all the counties of the State
they had come together.

And to think that then the only easy conveyance
was by canal.   On the boats of the "raging canaul"
over seven hundred men came from Ross and
Pickaway.   By the next best way, the National road,
came the hosts from Madison, Clark, Greene, Champagne, Montgomery, Preble and the West, with their
log cabins and canoes on wheels; while from the East
came over that road the hardy men of Belmont, Jefferson, Guernsey, Muskingum and other counties with
cabins and canoes and banners flying with the names
of "Old Licking" and other counties emblazoned on
their folds.   From the North the Western Reserve
sent a horde of live Yankees, who were joined upon
the way by hundreds from the counties they crossed,
and the whole country through which the Cuyahoga
brig passed resounded with the songs for Old Tippecanoe.   And, O! what a joyful scene it was when
they met their brethren from the Darby plains and
Highland and Fayette and Brown and Clermont and
the southern counties!   What a sight, when the farmers
and pioneers, the mechanics and laborers mingle to-

gether in the streets of the State's Capitol. From the banks of the Scioto and the Miami and Mad rivers, and Muskingum and Licking and Killbuck and Jelloway and Hockhocking and Kokosing and Maumee and every river and creek between Lake Erie and the Ohio, every log cabin seemed to have contributed its stalwart Buckeye boys to make the great crowd to set "the ball a rolling on for Tippecanoe and Tyler too." They had come from the hill tops, and had come from the valleys to this grandest of all grand rallies, and the like of that enormous procession of the people never had been seen in the hundred years of Ohio's history or in all the nation's existence. It was an army with banners moving through streets, whose walls were hung with flags, streamers and decorations in honor of a brave old patriot and pioneer, who had given the best strength and years of his life to protecting the poor men, women and children on the frontiers, and who had settled down in a log cabin to spend his days as a humble farmer at North Bend; and when the people had called upon him in his retiracy to serve them, had been villified, slandered and traduced by the office-holders and a pensioned press.

Every banner and device and emblem spoke out in rebuke and expressed the honest indignation of the people. of Ohio. The log cabins spoke in language not to be misunderstood, and as the citizens marched in the mud over shoe tops, and with clothes drenching with rain, the people felt the loud beat of the pulse of victory. To the music of the drum and fife, brave Ohio soldiers, proud of the military services of General Harrison, kept time, as they lead in the procession with the stars and stripes unfurled. There were the Zanesville Guards, commanded by Captain Dulty, 50 rank and file; The Putnam Grays, Captain Hatch, 71 strong; The Warren Greens (Zanesville Rifles), Captain Hazlett, in one battalion under Colonel Curtis, accompanied by Brigadier General Watkins, of Zanesville, and his staff: The Jefferson Guards, Captain Hare; Columbus Guards, Captain Mills: Buckeye

Rangers, Captain Blaine; German Guards, Captain Frankenberg, all under Colonel Sanderson, accompanied by the field and staff officers of the Columbus brigade.

Then comes Lewis Bowyer, of Miami county, over eighty years of age, riding on a white horse with a banner inscribed, "The Last of the Life Guards of General Washington," and leading another white horse, on which was a standard to the saddle with the inscription, "The Saddle on which the Illustrious Father of his Country Rode when Leading his Countrymen to Battle;" and following them are a number of old soldiers of the Revolution. What an inspiration! What a thrill pervades the beholders! Then follows in the procession an ensign with a beautiful banner, on which is painted a life-like picture of the Farmer of North Bend, with his plow and team halted midway in the furrow, regaling himself with a cup of his favorite *hard cider*. Shouts upon shouts go up as it passes through the crowd.

Then comes the Cuyahoga delegation of eighty men with a full-sized brig on wheels, completely rigged and manned, with colors flying and Harrison's portrait at the masthead, with one hand holding a plow and his hat in the other ; resting underneath the legend, "The Farmer of North Bend." In the brig with the crew are William B. Lloyd, the bold and fearless representative of old Cuyahoga, John A. Briggs, the eloquent tariff advocate, and other as gallant tars as ever walked a deck. In the log cabin of the Mad river trappers behold Charley Anthony and others of "Old Tip's boys," eating corn bread and bacon, while coons run around the cabin roof and the fox, wolf, bear and deer skins, guns and axes, and barrels of hard cider are also visible. Shortly after there comes in sight Colonel Icil's large canoe drawn by eight beautiful gray horses, with a banner inscribed "Old Tippecanoe Forever," which calls forth loud cheers, while young Robert Neil beats the drum and the band plays and sings a campaign song. Another log cabin comes in for cheering, drawn by six bright bay horses and having a large picture of General Harrison drawing a gourd full of hard cider from a barrel and handing it to an old soldier.

Upon other banners in the procession are the inscriptions "The Log Cabin and Hard Cider Candidate"; "Hail Columbia and Harrison"; "He Never Yet Lost a Battle." The company with brooms on their shoulders and the motto, "We'll Cleanse the Augean Stable," attracts much notice. And there, too, is the old tin pan with the bottom knocked out, and in mourning because its glory has departed. And how the shouts go up at the long line of horsemen from "Old Knox" with the Owl creek canoe, and the big cavalcade from "Old Licking" and "Muskingum" and "Coshocton," with a steamboat under full head of steam and a "Harrison and Reform" banner flying.

Then comes the caricature exciting much laughter, of "The Sam Medary and the Quasi Quires" gouged out of the State's reams. The New York delegation, headed by Cols. E. A. Sevier and Babcock, with its beautiful flag and its tall pole, on the top of which is Jove's bird—a live American eagle. The ladies all along the line from windows and galleries and house tops greeted the men who marched in the mud and rain, with waving of handkerchiefs and cheers, and the soldiers of Tippecanoe felt their smiles and plaudits were a fitting recompense for what they endured. In platoons of eight they braved the storm and tempest regardless of health, and many of them without overcoats or other sufficient covering. As an illustration we may mention, that in the Knox delegation with G. B. Burr, G. A. Jones, Gen. William Bevans, R. C. Hurd, the Curtises, Daniel S. Norton and others, there was tramping in the mud and rain the venerable Judge Jesse B. Thomas, the distinguished ex-United States Senator from Illinois, who was the author of the Missouri Compromise, and he had raised his umbrella; when his attention was called to the fact that there was no other to be seen, he pitched it in the street and continued as a boy in the line, notwithstanding he had risen from his bed, where

he had been confined for weeks with rheumatism.
So deeply enthused were all that they lost sight
of their ailments and became oblivious to ague, rheumatism, gout, neuralgia and other ills in their zeal for
Harrison, while cheerily they rang out the song:

> "The times are bad and want curing,
> They are getting past all enduring;
> So let's turn out Martin Van Buren
> And put in Old Tippecanoe !"

Men sang who never had been known to sing before,
and many became noted as vocalists and orators who
were surprised to know their own abilities. Grand
as the pageant of the day parade the brilliancy of the
illumination and the grandeur of the scenes at night surpassed it when the discharge of oratory by Douglass
and Cooke and Andrews and Norton and Allen and
Goddard and Lloyd and Murphy and Mathiot and
others, fired the hearts and aroused the enthusiasm of
the masses. The Buckeye Blacksmith and the poor
Welch laborer on the canal, Sam White, like meteors
shot athwart the sky, and astonished by their brightness themselves as well as the vast multitude. It was
a general ground-swell, an upheaval that carried
consternation into the ranks of the administration
forces.

The great 22d convention electrified the nation. It
started a new epoch, and began a revolution that no
human power could check, no combination of parties
could control. The people were in it; they made it
apparent to unbelievers, infidels and heathen throughout the world that "the voice of the people is the voice
of God."

Feeling the inability of our descriptive power to
convey sufficiently an idea of the opening of the campaign by this convention, we avail ourselves of a
letter written at the time by a staid young gentleman
from New England, who came West to grow up with
Ohio, and has since become widely known as a lawyer
and statesman, the Hon. Aaron F. Perry, late member
of Congress from Cincinnati. He endeavors to give

to the Yankees through the columns of the *Boston Atlas,* a knowledge of the way things were moving in the land of old Tippecanoe:

Columbus, Ohio, Feb. 24, 1840.

The Ohio State convention of the friends of Harrison and Tyler came off here on the twenty-first and twenty-second. There was probably never before so great a turn out, such unanimity of thought, such universal enthusiasm at any political meeting in the United States. In giving a description there is no danger of exaggeration. You must bear in mind that Columbus is near the center of the State, from one hundred to one hundred and seventy-five miles from either boundary; that the weather was in transition from winter to spring; that the roads were all mud, deep mud, nothing but interminable unmitigated mud; that money was hard to be got for any purpose; that Harrison has been derided as the " log-cabin candidate," fond of "hard cider," and so forth. On the morning previous to the first day of the convention it began steadily to rain, and the people began to come in by delegations. The hotels were all filled by 10 o'clock in the forenoon. Soon crowds collected along the streets and about the public houses. You could hear occasional exclamations, " Old Tip," "Whoop," " Ho," " Harrison and Tyler," "For one term only!" As the delegates came in, soaked with rain and covered with mud one after another, the city becomes noisy and clamorous. They pass through High street in procession—each after its own band of music—recognizing continual shouts of welcome by the waving of hats, flags and handkerchiefs. Before night a concourse had collected larger than was ever before assembled in Ohio; and yet the day for the convention had not come, and many of the largest delegations had not arrived. Still it rained. Still on came the people with music, with banners and with shoutings.

A short time before sunset the clouds were suddenly broken up and rolled together in masses and driven by a brisk wind out of sight. An advance guard of the city rangers patrolled the streets with

martial music. Their rifle barrels glistened with
dazzling brightness as they were struck aslant by the
rays of the setting sun. The mind of the throng
seemed to revert all as one to the time when the bayonets of the Northwestern army under Harrison
were seen to glitter along the defiles of the Ohio
forests. And such was the general enthusiasm that
this little incident, simple as it was, called forth from
one end of Columbus to the other, a long, loud and
deafening "Whoo-oo-oo-o-ra-aa-ah for old Tippecanoe!" At night the doors of the citizens were thrown
open, straw beds, mattresses and even naked floors
were put in requisition. Some slept, some told anecdotes, some made speeches and some sung songs.

At break of day, on the morning of the twenty-first,
one of our best bands rode around the city, and filled
the air with animating music. During the night several
strips of canvas had been suspended from the house
tops across High street, on which were painted in
large letters "Harrison and Tyler" for one term only—
"Union for the sake of the Union." Soon shouts
were heard again. Delegations pour in afresh from
two to three and even up to eight hundred persons at a
time. Every neighborhood of farmers, every village
of mechanics seemed to have racked their ingenuity to
invent rare and expressive devices.

One delegation came armed with brooms, signifying
that the next election shall be made a sweeping
operation. Others bore full-length pictures of General
Harrison following his plow. One delegation bore
aloft upon a Buckeye pole a live eagle, that looked
around and received the plaudits of the multitude with
abundant camplacency. Several counties brought in
each a log canoe, fixed upon wheels, to answer the
purposes of a wagon, with various mottoes upon the
sides, and upon their horses' blinds were printed "Old
Tip." From one direction comes a steamboat, complete in all its parts, fixed upon wheels, loaded with
people and drawn by four horses tandem. The
paddles are made to revolve with a crank, the steam
rises in puffs from the pipe, each wheel-house bears

the name of "Harrison and Tyler." From another
direction comes a model of Fort Meigs, mounted
with small brass cannon, drawn by six horses and
large enough for twenty or thirty men to ride in. From
Cleveland, a distance of 145 miles, comes a brig,
mounted on wheels and drawn by six horses, manned
with delegates in sailor caps, with sails all set and
streamers flying, followed by half a mile of carriages
and curricles of all descriptions. The brig is called
"William Henry Harrison." Upon its sails is seen
in large characters, "Live Credit," "Flourish Commerce," "Don't Give Up the Ship." Yonder comes a
real, *bona fide* log cabin! See the raccoon-skins hanging
out upon its sides. Upon the door is written with
charcoal, in awkward characters, "Hard Cider." It is
filled with men in hunting shirts, eating corn-bread,
and as many of the same description as can sit on the
roof or hang upon it in any way, are singing rude
songs in praise of the "Log Cabin Candidate," "Old
Tippecanoe." It has been drawn on wheels through
the mud a distance of 40 or 50 miles, and now passes
through the throng in triumph, while shouts redouble
upon shouts and cheers upon cheers. There is still
another log cabin, brought from a different county,
and similar in appearance; also a board cabin purport-
ing to be occupied by "Mad River Trappers." These
are only a few of the most curious and prominent
devices. Countless numbers of others might be mentioned. Among the rest, an old "Tin Pan" stuck
upon a pole, with the bottom torn nearly out, the
seams ripped open and dressed in black crape, deserves
to be noticed. The Van Buren part of the Ohio legislature are in the habit of deliberating upon their
measures in secret ere they bring them before the public. This caucus operation has by some means come
to be known all over the State as the "Tin Pan."
The tin pan upon the pole is intended to foretell the
fate of the legislative "Tin Pan." But you can no
longer think of particulars. All is one dense, enthusiastic mass of human bodies. On either hand, so far
as the eye can extend, the streets are filled with

flags, pictures and all sorts of signs and symbols. Still they thicken, still on they come. Windows are all thrown up and filled with ladies, who join in the excitement and wave their white handkerchiefs to the crowd. The roofs of the public buildings are also filled with spectators, who swing their hats and shout.

On the night of the 21st it commenced raining, and continued incessantly till the evening of the 22d. Yet nobody seemed to heed it. A procession was formed on the morning of the 22d of all the delegations, and marched through the principal streets of the city, accompanied with the log cabins, brig, fort, steamboat, canoes, bands of music and all the badges, banners, insignia and paraphernalia that had been brought together from all over the State.

It might be supposed that men who had come through the mud from 100 to 150 miles, with forts, log cabins, and the like, on wheels, and who had been huzza'd from one end of their journey to the other, would, when they met so many others in the same spirit and condition as themselves, huzza also. But let me describe a different individual, and let him represent a class. He is a business man, or a scholar, a reader of ancient history, a gentleman—a philosopher in fact, he is a Whig—to be sure. But he says to himself, shouts convince nobody, shouts are not intellectual. He will do his business quietly, and go home as he came, in some decent and comfortable conveyance. You will not catch him in any sort of a flare-up—not he! But watch him as the delegates pass by, mass after mass. All are drenched with rain and covered with mud. Yet the white handkerchiefs of the ladies are seen waving from the windows. Yet shouts come down from the house-tops to meet the shouts that rise from below. Your philosopher gets excited, talks louder than usual, runs to and fro in the rain, and avers that mud is not a thing to be regarded at such a time. Yonder goes a beautiful white horse; on him are the empty military saddle and trappings of General Washington, which have been sent to the convention by a niece of Washington, who resides at Marietta. The horse is led by an old soldier of Washington's body guard, mounted upon another horse, and followed by a number of old men of the Revolution, who gaze upon the vacant saddle of their dead Chief, and then turn to the picture of Harrison, cast their eyes over the multitude and give a shout for " Old Tippecanoe." Will not our philosopher join them? Look at him! There he stands over shoes in mud. He is no longer silent. His arms are thrown back, his face upturned, his eyes shut, and he strains every muscle in shouts. as if it were a perfect business transaction. No one does it with such unction as your philosopher, and being a man of moral courage, he not only shouts when the rest do, but breaks forth occasionally alone, to show that he does it as a matter of principle.

In short, all classes and conditions in life, learned and unlearned, rich and poor, gentle and simple, seemed to remember for once that their interests were the same. All were covered with mud alike, all were zealous, all shouted. Cast your eye along the street, and you will see at one glance one hundred flags all bearing for a motto " The People are Coming!" Again you will see written upon wagon boxes, upon kegs, upon squares of cloth fixed upon staves, " Hard Cider." There is Harrison on his war-horse, Harrison at his plow. Harrison in the Cabinet. You will see floating over the multitude, in twenty different directions, "The People Must Do Their Own Voting." Several beautiful military companies are marching and parading every way. Twenty bands of music are emulating each other in the vivacity and stateliness of their music. Still it rains. Still you see nothing but smiles, you hear nothing but assurance of approaching victory.

If anything can be judged from the appearance of the convention and the universal opinion of delegates, Harrison and Tyler will carry the State almost by acclamation. The number assembled could not have been far from 20,000 persons. The nominations, which you will see in the newspapers, were made with the

utmost unanimity, and all went away amid cheers
and shouts, joyful and enthusiastic as when they
came.

Columbus, Ohio, April 17.

The most sanguine friends of Harrison did not know
what a tower of strength his name would be. No one
who has not seen the ebullitions of popular enthusiasm in this part of the country in his behalf, would
be likely to believe a tithe of what is really taking
place almost every day among us. I speak only of
what I see in and about this city, for I do not take an
active part in the strife myself; but I am told and believe that the same spirit prevails throughout the State
and country. The whole bosom of the mighty West
is literally heaving with emotions of gratitude and love
for the modest but gallant old farmer of North Bend.
It is not the temporary and evanescent glory of military achievements playing upon the passions of the
multitude and misleading the understanding of the
people. It is not merely the fellowship which the
laboring class feel for a man who has always been
more watchful of their interests than of his own, and
who from offices of honor and emolument has voluntarily retired to take them by the hand and become
one among them. It is because they revere him as a
man and a patriot, because they do not doubt his fitness for the Presidency, and because they know him
to be honest. Every slander upon his name has been
made to return and "plague the inventor," and every
new attack serves to bring out the proof of some noble
and generous achievement, which from his long retirement had been partially forgotten. Add to these
motives the general distress which some cause or other
has brought upon all classes and interests of the country,
and you can see why it is that here, at least, politics
have become the serious and absorbing business of all
classes of people. Last year the Whigs found difficulty to get men to serve upon committees and to assemble for meetings. Now meetings spring up spontaneously and continually, and almost every Whig con-
siders himself a committee of vigilance to do anything

and everything that men may honorably do to disseminate correct principles. Even the women and children have caught the spirit of revolution, and are lending their influence to animate and quicken those around them. Since the great convention I was conversing with a young lady, who inquired if I joined the procession and marched through the mud and rain with the multitude on that occasion. I told her I considered myself happy in being allowed to remain snugly in my office. "Then you are not a good Whig!" said a little girl of seven or eight years by her side with an air of astonishment and rebuke. She was so much abashed at her own boldness that she immediately hid her face in her hands, thinking she had done something wrong. I believe the children watch each other's politics as closely as the elders. To-day the friends of Harrison erected a log cabin in this city for political meetings, and the national flag will henceforth be seen flying over it in mid air during the campaign. The labor was mostly done by farming people from the country. For two weeks past they have been collecting and drawing logs for the cabin, appropriating particular days for the purpose, when they would form a procession with their teams, each bearing a flag and all uniting in some of the numerous Harrison songs with which the country is flooded. "It was Harrison that fought for the cabins long ago," is a favorite line with them, and they have sung it through the streets till no one in Columbus will be likely to forget it.

During the past week one of the Van Buren State central committee publicly announced his intention to vote for Harrison. The same man was the last candidate of the Van Buren party in this district for Congress. Indeed, there is every appearance of a radical and thoroughgoing revolution of popular opinion. I see many things to remind me of what I have been told by old people was the state of public feeling in Massachusetts at the opening of the Revolutionary war. The Whigs have adopted means in this county to circulate their papers and other matters independent of the post-office, and it is proposed to organize independent post routes through the State. Thus you may see that the ball of the revolution, though it trundled slowly at first, has now acquired a velocity that cannot be checked, and goes rolling, booming, thundering on.

Ohio expects a good deal from Massachusetts. We remember that "the bones of her sons, falling in the great struggle for independence, lie mouldering in every soil from Maine to Georgia." We look with reverence to the exalted patriotism of Davis, and we acknowledge with feelings of national pride the unrivaled genius of Webster. Massachusetts, with her numbers of great and good men, with her common schools and her churches and colleges, must give something more than a mere majority for correct principles. Massachusetts yielded her pretensions to the right of furnishing a commander-in-chief to the American armies in the war of Independence, and her complaisance was rewarded by the glorious career of Washington: she has now also yielded her preferred, her favorite and well worthy candidate for the Presidency. Should Harrison be elected, I firmly believe the wisdom of his administration will as *far* transcend the expectations of his friends at the Northern and Eastern States as the success and greatness of Washington transcended the expectations of *his* friends.

I have mentioned a few of the *signs* of the times; what the result may be you can judge as well as myself. I may mention further. Grain sells for a very low price; labor commands but little more than half the wages it did a year ago. And the mass of the people who make up the bulk of the Van Buren party begin seriously to think there is something wrong in the administration of the Government; they are reading, inquiring and coming over to Harrison in great numbers. I will not pretend to estimate the majority Ohio will give, but from what I see daily I shall be astonished at nothing. No Whig has any more doubt of *some* majority than he has of any future event whatever, and the feeling is that it *must* be a very large majority. The powers of the Government are busy in trying to check the progress of reform; but judging from what I see, I should suppose they might as well attempt to suppress an earthquake or stay the progress of a deluge, as to turn back or stay the tide of opinion which seems to have rent old party combinations asunder, and to be rushing on with accumulated force and sweeping everything away before it.

* * P.

JUDGE HANSON'S SPEECH.

WORDS OF WELCOME TO THE WHIG YOUNG MEN OF THE NATION AT THE CONVENTION IN BAL- TIMORE, APRIL 10, 1840.

It has become apparent to the great bulk of the American people that the present administration of their Government is not fitted to increase or preserve the blessings and privileges of a free and intelligent nation; to foster the pursuits of a laborious, inventive and spirited population; that it is not in accord- ance with the genius, past history, or future desti- nies of a vast republican empire; that its principles and measures are as ill-calculated to consolidate the credit, strength and resources of State sovereignties as they are to bind together and cement a confedera- tion; that it has failed to engender or keep alive a ven- eration for the Constitution, or to cherish an unalien- able love for the Union; that it has, on the contrary, by incessant and unrelenting assaults upon capital, good faith and enterprise, disunited the interest, and thereby torn asunder the good feelings which bind men to each other; that it has destroyed that salutary confidence which is essential to this commonwealth and all the communities that compose it; that it

has, in fine, chilled the hearts and the hopes of the
poor and shut the hands of the rich. It is, therefore, that we hail the approaching Whig national
convention, to be held in the city of Baltimore on
the 4th day of May next, as an unerring harbinger
to the coming of better things; that we greet the
numerical power (composed as it is of all classes)
and to which the intelligence from every quarter daily
adds rank to rank, and squadron to squadron as a perfect manifestation of the thorough and sweeping
change in the conduct of .public affairs resolved upon
by the people.   We rejoice that our fellow-citizens
(since what is passed cannot be recalled) are so far
benefited by present suffering as to be awakened to a
sense of impending evils more serious and calamitous,
and of which few can fail to perceive " the inevitable
ruin."   Surely, our administration presents us to the
whole world as a nation of contrarieties and contra-
dictions; we are held up to other nations in every
fantastic and antagonistic position that a people can
be regarded; our principles and our practice are perfect antipodes to each other; theories, abstractions,
solecisms and paradoxes, make up the sum of our
political economy; while political empirics have
driven from their moorings the once fast-anchored
axioms of the Constitution—a Constitution to which
Washington had affixed his seal and given verity by
experience.

Our perversions and absurdities, indeed, almost afford
plausibility to the assertion of the ancient philosopher,
that there once existed a race of men of a conformation
entirely different from those of our generation; and
who shall undertake to deny the possibility that, at
some distant era, when history shall again be handed
down by allegory and tradition, a people who are per-
petually moving one way and looking another shall
not be represented as a race of men who carried their
faces behind them and turned their backs upon themselves ?   So singular is the incongruity between our
words and our actions that no disinterested spectators,
even of the present age, can fail to be struck with

amazement by professions constantly at variance with conduct; with results diametrically opposite to those professed to be intended; and of causes stimulating effects, between the beginning and end of which no connecting consequences ever existed. Vain, however, would be the attempt to enumerate all the inconsistency of those who deal with the obliquity of partisan tacticians, instead of applying the established principles of statesmen.

The poor man is to be enriched by reducing the wages of labor; the rich are to be impoverished by the hoarding of their gold; the products of the earth, instead of being cultured by the sweat of the brow, are to wither and die amidst idleness, hunger and desolation; all surplus produce is to rot in the granary of the farmer for the want of markets furnished by the employments of artisans and laborers, fisheries, factories, work-shops, roads and canals; the condition of the country is to be improved by arresting all improvement; debts are to be paid by the annihilation of property. The interest on loans is to be discharged by borrowing from the lenders of the capital; gold and silver are to represent, instead of being represented, by paper and credit; and whilst the precious metals are promised in abundance they are again buried beneath the face of the earth in the vaults of banks—the strong-boxes of avaricious thrift, or melted down for the gold services of plate which adorns the Presidential dinner table of the very republican nabob in the palace at Washington.

Domestic productions are to be encouraged by bounties upon foreign fabrics; and whilst there is to be abundance of poverty, to furnish plenty of rags, readily converted into hieroglyphic shinplasters, and these are to be the only manufactories, which are sure to flourish, with or without a tariff; with or without foreign use or domestic consumption; unless indeed the treasury notes of the Government should enter the list as a competitor and thus clearly demonstrate the financial ability of the head of the treasury, and with the aid of Mr. Buchanan (be a capital Old Federalist),

home markets are to be shut up, and all labor to be rewarded *at a penny a day*, as in China and in Cuba.

Amidst these anomalies, *all* banks are to be put
down by the destruction of one, whilst in the place
of that one, thousands are to be erected and fostered,
by way of proving that *none* ought ever to have existed ; and whilst that *one*, consisting of three-fourths
of its capital of the hard earnings of husbands and
fathers, for the support of widows and children, is to
be crushed at all hazards, myriads are to start up *with
no capital at all*, for the benefit of speculators and adventurers, and thus the administration's sympathy for
the orphan and the aged soldier is to be illustrated, and
hard money only to be trusted in the hands of abscond-
ing sub-treasurers ; and if this war upon property,
upon the pursuits, business and enterprise of every
man and all classes of men, were not too much to be
endured, and too gross a fraud upon a sagacious and
thinking people, their morals, their religion, their ele-
mentary political creeds, coeval with their declaration
of independence, are all to be desecrated by absurdities, which have not even the "bad eminence" of
being compatible with themselves.

Truly the measures and the doctrines of this Northern man with Southern principles are sufficiently party
colored to denote that equivocation and paltering in a
double sense which none but a proficient in the black
arts of a magician in this age of reform could have the
temerity to practice. At one moment this Northern
man with southern principles, this harlequin, Proteus-
like diplomatist, holds out to the North General
Jackson's great proclamation, the force act, and the
second article of war, to-wit: that article, under which
the Prince of Nullifiers (now a repentant and par-
doned sinner) was to be hung up, drawn and quartered.
In the next, whilst in one breath he eulogizes in a
lovely song the Palmetto—he declares to the Unionist
of the South, that no colors are to be unfurled but the
colors of the Union: in another, he whispers to the
fanatic of amalgamation, with a word for Colonel
Dick, *that all colors are alike*, and that liberty knows

no distinction. But lo! and behold, in one month, nay
not one month, we see him (or rather hear him) ready
to shed the last drop of his Northern blood in the support of southern principles, and in defense of the rights
of the slaveholder; of rights to which the Abolitionist
contends Christianity affords not the least shadow or
pretense of existence. Christianity! yes, these administration tergiversators have Christianity in their mouth;
that sort of Christianity which would expel from the
national councils the ministers of God; that Christianity
which would extend to the poor Indian its blessings
of civilization, by extermination and indiscriminate
murder; yes, the Christianity of those, who would, as
if there were not already more than enough of yelpers
at the Capital, augment the pack by the importation
of bloodhounds from Cuba: of bloodhounds to act the
part of a Christian army: of bloodhounds in the place
of holy missionaries; of bloodhounds, curs and mon-
grels, pampered upon the bread and substance of the
land, whilst the poor Revolutionary pensioner, without whose heroic achievements (with Lafayette, not
bloodhounds, for an ally) this land would never have
been a land of liberty, are naked and starving for the
want of the miserable pittance, which is, at this moment, withheld from them; not in order that a "better
currency" than rags should cover their nakedness and
stay their hunger, but that a "better currency" should
line the pockets of minions and favorites, who would
never have earned it by honest industry. It seems,
however, that this importation of bloodhounds: this
stain upon the escutcheon of the nation is to be forever
obliterated; and how do you think, Mr. President and
gentlemen? Why, forsooth, I am told that it is asserted
(I know not upon what authority it is avouched) that
when an Indian shook his blanket at one of these
bloodhounds, he put his tail between his legs and ran
like a sub-treasurer. But we forbear; let there be no
acrimonious feelings, bitterness or wrath in the midst
of the cheers and hopes that surround us. We are all
one people, and we trust that there is more of error
than of vice among us. We are ready to open our

arms, and take to our bosoms every deluded son of our
country, and go hand in hand to the rescue. We see
the day not far distant, when those who infest the
palace, block up the avenues of the Senate, forestall
public opinion, waste their time and compromit their
honor and independence, in pursuit of office and emolument, may be reformed into better citizens and more
useful men.

The day of deliverance is approaching. The day
of our travail is come; the day when we may all rejoice
that the old petticoat granny, William Henry Harrison,
is at hand. We do, therefore, hail him as our *deliverer;*
we are not ashamed in our agony and dismay, to cry
out for his help; yes, the old petticoat General, William Henry Harrison, comes to our rescue. He comes,
the coward ! who in every battle was victorious; the
coward! who never turned his back upon the enemy
of his country; the coward ! who in every conflict,
from Tippecanoe to the Thames, was seen " 'with
his beaver up,' to course along the lists scattering his
lightnings around;" and whilst, in the hottest of the fight,
and in every post of danger, the fire of his eye gleamed
like a sword, and his own peculiar voice was heard
ringing in the ears of every soldier, those memorable
words, "Stand to your guns, my boys; never surrender," till not a foe was left upon the field. 'Tis he we
claim as our deliverer; the defaulter. We look to him;
yes, to him, William Henry Harrison, to restore the
perished credit and fill the exhausted and pillaged cof-
fers of the country. We look to him, William Henry
Harrison, the public robber, who retired from the office
poor and in debt, whilst he replenished and filled the
national treasury with millions of dollars, not one of
which ever stuck in his palm in passing through his
hands. It is to him, William Henry Harrison, the
oppressor of the poor, we turn, who was the ad-
viser, the friend, the father to every poor emigrant
who settled beyond the mountains; who was always
ready to take by the hand the poorest settler of the
meanest log cabin in the wilderness; it is to him that
we look once more for peace and plenty, for private

and national prosperity, for a restoration of all the privileges and blessings of freemen ; in a word, we look to him under the blessings of Providence for the *great consummation of public and private faith.* 'Tis to such a deliverer we look; to "our old, well-tried, weather-beaten, hard-cider, log-cabin, Tippecanoe." Not to such a deliverer as the Emperor Alexander, of Russia; he the deliverer, who delivered kings, emperors, and the whole continent of nations, into the hands of the Holy Alliance; but we seek to be delivered from an alliance, than which none was ever more *unholy*, and from under the pressure of which no people ever groaned more than we, the people of the United States; 'tis to such a deliverer we look. And if, in as mongrel a pack as was ever littered in a kennel, there be not included in the deliverance a pair of as notable twins as was ever engendered in the cabinet of the kitchen, then, in the language of the facetious old knight, "there is no skill in surgery."

But let us no longer linger with the past, for the time has come to give thanks and rejoice .Those upon the lookout are proclaiming joyful tidings from all around us. Land is once more in sight, and our perils at an end. Too long have we been at sea, without chart or compass. "tossed about by every wind of doctrine ;" but the great swell of public opinion is resetting ; the undertow of intrigue and corruption is running out, sweeping along with it the turbid feculence that polluted the land we trust to be forever "in the dark ocean of oblivion buried"; the rainbow of promise is again to be seen ; distempered elements are everywhere dispersing, and the prow of our bark once more points to the haven of safety.

With the memorable words of Harrison for our motto, if we unfurl upon our banners, "Stand to your guns, my boys, and never surrender," and inscribe upon our ballots "The people must do their own voting and their own fighting," then we hazard nothing in the prediction that they will fill three-fourths of the ballot-boxes in thecountry. Animated, then, by these hopes, and toiling in one cause, there is every incentive to greet our coming friends, to Maryland, at the approaching national convention. We therefore hope that our Whig fellow-citizens need only to be reminded of the duty to extend the hand of good fellowship, and open wide the door of hospitality throughout the State, to the friends of him, the string of whose latch was never pulled in when the stranger needed shelter; and as it is expected that at the approaching celebration, the public houses of accommodation may not be sufficient for the reception of all our numerous visitors, we undertake to assure all those who may honor us with their company of the shelter and comfort of at least our own roof-trees, and with as good entertainment as ever log cabin and hard cider afforded.

CHARLES OGLE'S SPEECH.

REMARKS OF MR. OGLE, OF PENNSYLVANIA, BEFORE THE HOUSE OF REPRESENTATIVES, APRIL 16, 1840, ON THE CIVIL AND DIPLOMATIC APPROPRIATION BILL.

I am glad to see the committee becoming a little patient; we were somewhat otherwise a few days ago. This bill appropriates nine millions of the people's money, and I have regretted to witness such exhibitions of hot haste in many of the representatives of the people, day in and day out, to force us to vote away millions without due examination. To my knowledge, there never has been a bill before Congress which involved so large an amount of money, except the ten millions "*Maine War*" bill of the last session; and we all knew that *that* money would never be spent. But here is a bill appropriating nine millions of the hard cash of my constituents and yours, and yet in such

violent haste are some gentlemen to pass it, that we
must stay here all night for the purpose. For my part,
I tell gentlemen that I will stand out, night and day,
until I see the bottom of every dollar, before I will
permit the question to be taken. And if Representatives go before their constituents with a different principle, they will find they have got the wrong side of
the argument. The people will tell them, We love the
Representative who looks to our money, and sees that
it is expended on proper objects.

Have gentlemen ever tried the rule of division to ascertain what the President has spent *yearly*, *monthly*,
weekly, *daily*, *hourly*; ay, sir, for each and every
minute since Martin Van Buren's inauguration on the
4th day of March, 1837. The actual expenditures, during the first three years of his administration, have
reached the enormous sum of one hundred and eleven
million four hundred and six thousand nine hundred
and sixty-three dollars.

Average per year	$37,135,654 33
Average per month	3,094,637 86
Average per week	714,147 17
Average per day	102,021 07
Average per hour	4,250 87
Average per minute	70 84

Let us compare and contrast these prodigious expenditures with the disbursements made by all the
former Presidents since the adoption of the Constitution in 1789.

You will observe, sir, by the statement which I
here present, and which has been prepared with
great care, that the annual expenses of Martin Van
Buren's administration are greater by $6,538,325.66 than
the entire yearly disbursements of Presidents Washington, Adams, Jefferson and Madison, altogether. You
will also see that the yearly expenses of Martin Van
Buren's government have been more than one hundred
per cent. larger than Mr. Madison's, notwithstanding
the latter had been engaged in a most expensive war
of three years with the most powerful nation of the
world.

A Table of Comparison of the Expenditures Under the Administration of the Several Presidents of the United States.

Presidents.	Years.	Total Amount.	Average Per Year.	Average Per Month.	Average Per Week.	Average Daily.
Washington,	8	$15,892,188 55	$1,986,524 82	$165,543 73	$38,202 40	$5,457 48
John Adams,	4	21,450,351 19	5,362,587 79	446,882 31	103,126 68	14,732 38
Jefferson,	8	41,300,788 68	5,162,598 58	430,216 55	91,588 43	13,084 06
Madison,	8	144,684,939 86	18,085,617 48	1,507,034 79	347,800 33	49,685 61
Monroe,	8	104,463,400 59	13,057,925 07	1,088,160 42	251,113 94	35,873 42
J. Q. Adams,	4	50,501,914 31	12,625,478 58	1,052,122 12	242,411 12	34,630 16
Jackson,	8	145,792,735 00	18,224,091 88	1,518,674 32	350,463 39	50,066 18

Yes, sir, Martin Van Buren has spent more than seventy dollars for each and every minute since he was sworn into the Presidential office. How often has the clock ticked since that fatal hour? During the four months of last year that he passed on his electioneering tour in the State of New York, how many times did the clock tick then? The people's hard dollars were going at the rate of $70 a minute, while he was dancing with the Countess of Westmoreland at Saratoga. That was dancing to a pretty dear tune, but the people paid the piper.

Now the very best remedy which I can suggest to prevent this profligate waste of the public money will be to displace that lavish spendthrift, Martin Van Buren, and to substitute in his stead, at the head of the Government, that plain, frugal, economical, and well-tried citizen, William Henry Harrison. I shall, therefore, proceed to make such further remarks in relation to the conduct, principles. and public services of the latter, and in regard to the conduct and principles of the former, as may, in some degree, assist the people in arriving at proper conclusions in the premises. I will first turn to some of the evidences which exist as to the favor in which Harrison has been held by the country, both for his military and civil services. And I will say in the outset, that there has no man lived, since the days of Washington, who has drawn out from his political enemies so strong a certificate of character, as he has done. Could Jefferson, if he were now alive, and a candidate for the Presidency, produce such testimony? You could call the Hon. James Buchanan, who might tell you, what he had many years ago declared, that during the administration of that President, "our ships were laid up to rot, as melancholy monuments of the weak and wicked policy of our Government"—and who could not find time in a 4th of July oration even "to enumerate all the other wild and wicked projects of the Democratic administrations!" Could James Madison, if he were a candidate, produce such testimony? You might call up that plain, economical, hard-handed Democrat, Martin

Van Buren, who would, without hesitation, testify that, "according to the best of his knowledge and belief, James Madison was either too imbecile in mind, or too dishonest in principle, to be re-elected President of the United States in 1812;" and that with the design and settled purpose to prevent and defeat that re-election, he (Martin Van Buren) had patriotically conspired and associated with the Essex Junto federalists, and the men who subsequently devised and organized the Hartford convention.

But what testimony has General Harrison in his favor? The first is the commission of George Washington. Brought up in revolutionary times "in the days that tried men's souls"—his sire, one of the noble signers of the Declaration of Independence—his guardian, the able financier of the Continental Congress—his friend and patron, the glorious chief who led the armies of liberty to battle and to victory—George Washington, Robert Morris, Benjamin Harrison—what a brilliant association! It was among such men that William Henry Harrison learnt his principles, and it was under the command of the gallant and impetuous General Anthony Wayne that he first put those principles into practice. Let me read you, sir, a short extract from the official account of the battle on the banks of the Miami, on the 20th of August, 1794:

"The bravery and conduct of every officer belonging to the army, from the General down to the Ensigns, merit my highest approbation. There were, however, some whose rank and situation placed their conduct in a very conspicuous point of view, and which I observed with pleasure and the most lively gratitude; among whom I beg leave to mention Brigadier General Wilkinson and Colonel Hamtranck, the commandants of the right and left wings of the legion, whose brave example inspired the troops; and to these I would add the names of my faithful and gallant aides-de-camp, Captain DeButts, and T. Lewis, and Lieutenant Harrison, who with the Adjutant General, Major Mill, rendered the most essential services by communicating my orders in every direction, and by their conduct and bravery exciting the troops to press for victory."

This battle of the Miami Rapids was fought with the utmost desperation by the combined Indian and British forces, which amounted to 2,000 combatants, while the troops actually engaged against them " were short of nine hundred." You have seen, sir, that the commanding General, in an official dispatch, expressed his gratitude to Lieutenant Harrison for "rendering the most essential services" during the engagement. "Mad Anthony," as he was familiarly called by Whigs of that day, was too bold and too brave a soldier to award the meed of praise to a coward, and possessed a soul too generous to withhold the tribute of justice for deeds of valor done by his young hero and aid-de-camp. By the way, as to General Wayne, let me remark that he, like Harrison, was called "Granny" by the British red-coats and their tory allies, during the Revolution. At the battle of Stony Point, on the night of the 15th of July, 1779, the bayonet was the only weapon relied upon. The assailants, by the order of Wayne, silently advanced with unloaded muskets. Mad Anthony was the first to mount the ramparts of the enemy. The captain of the British guard inquired what that meant? It means " Granny Wayne," said he, as he severed his head from his shoulders. When did Martin Van Buren, who has the audacity and meanness to call Harrison, through his official organ a granny, receive the thanks of his commanding general for "rendering essential services" on the battle-field? Under what chieftain did Martin Van Buren win his military trophies? I well remember that, in the letter of this redoutable champion of the toilet, dated at London, February 24, 1832, he assumed the air of a knight-errant, mounted his gold epaulets, and blue and buff, and strutted the hero, while he recounted his valiant services in the army of "Old Hickory." "To have served," said he, "under such a chief, at such a time, and to have won his confidence and esteem, is a sufficient glory; and of that, thank God, my enemies cannot deprive me." I would inquire, sir, whether it was on the plains of New Orleans, that Martin Van Buren performed those self-glorifying, self-satisfying services? Was he an aid-de-camp of "Old Hickory" at Talladega, or the Horse Shoe? Why does he, as arrant a coward as was ever cast in "Nature's mold," thus gasconade like another Bobadil? Does this braggart plume himself for procuring the dissolution of Old Hickory's first Cabinet, through the influence of a female court favorite? Or does he take credit to himself for the instructions he gave as Secretary of State to Mr. McLane, our Minister at the Court of St. James, and on account of which his own nomination to that court was subsequently rejected by the casting vote of the then Vice-President, John C. Calhoun? I cannot forbear, on this subject, to read three or four lines from the Richmond *Enquirer* in relation to that rejection:

" Mr. Clay was aware of the keen and canine appetite with which Mr. Calhoun was prepared to devour his victim, and therefore insidiously continued to place the banquet before him. With what eager delight he seized upon it we have already seen."

Old Father Time, Mr. Chairman, makes sad havoc of the consistency of poor mortals. Where is the "keen and canine appetite" of Mr. Calhoun now? Surfeited, satiated. Who is the "victim" now? I have known men who, if they could not get the lion, would be well content to take the skin. But let us return to the examination of the testimony to establish the distinguished services which General Harrison has rendered the nation. The legislature of Kentucky, on the 7th of January, 1812,

Resolved, That in the late campaign against the Indians upon the Wabash, Gen. William Henry Harrison has behaved like a hero, a patriot and a general; and that for his cool, deliberate, skillful and gallant conduct in the battle of Tippecanoe, he well deserves the warmest thanks of his country and the nation."

Pray, sir, on what occasion did Martin Van Buren, whose "official organ" calls General Harrison a

"coward" and a "granny," ever behave like a "hero"
and a "patriot?" On what field of honor and carnage did
he exhibit "cool," "deliberate," "skillful" and "gallant"
conduct? Why, sir, I have been told that on the very
same night on which Harrison and his brave companions were engaged in deadly strife with the merciless savages at Tippecanoe, Martin Van Buren, per-
fumed like a milliner, and spruce as a popinjay, was
manifesting his gallantry and heroism by tripping "on
the light fantastic toe" through mazy French cotillions
in a ball-room. For the truth of this fact, however, I
do not vouch, but I have heard it from a most respectable quarter, and place full reliance upon it myself.

In the legislature of Indiana, on the 19th of November, 1811, Gen. William Johnson, the speaker of the
house of representatives, thus addressed General Harrison:

"SIR: The house of representatives of the Indiana
Territory, in their own name, and in behalf of their
constituents, most cordially reciprocate the congratulations of your excellency on the glorious result of the
late sanguinary conflict with the Shawnee Prophet
and the tribes of Indians confederated with him.
When we see displayed in behalf of our country, not
only the consummate abilities of the general, but the
heroism of the man, and when we take into view the
benefits which must result to that country from those
exertions, we cannot, for a moment, withhold our meed
of applause."

And yet Martin Van Buren's "official organ" has
the unblushing impudence to call the old veteran, who
has displayed the "consummate abilities of the general" and "the heroism of the man," a "coward," a
"granny," and a "petticoat hero."

On the 4th of April, 1818, James Monroe, President
of the United States, approved a resolution, passed by
Congress, directing two gold medals to be struck and
presented to Maj. Gen. William Henry Harrison and
Gov. Isaac Shelby, "for their gallantry and good conduct in defeating the combined British and Indian
forces under Major-General Proctor, on the Thames

in Upper Canada, on the 5th of October, 1813, capturing the British army, with their baggage and artillery."

Still Martin Van Buren's "official organ" continues to reiterate "coward" and "granny" and **"petticoat hero."**

On the 18th of December, 1811, President Madison, in a special **message** to Congress, said:

" While it is deeply **lamented** that so many valuable **lives have been lost** in the action which took place on the 7th ultimo, Congress will see with satisfaction the dauntless spirit of fortitude victoriously displayed by every description of troops engaged, as well as the collected firmness which distinguished their commander on an **occasion** requiring the utmost exertions of valor and discipline."

And again, in his message to Congress in December, 1813, Mr. Madison said:

" **The success** on Lake Erie having opened a passage to the territory of the enemy, the officer commanding the Northwestern army transferred the war thither, **and,** rapidly pursuing the hostile troops, fleeing with their savage associates, forced a general action, which quickly terminated in **the** capture of the British **and** dispersion of the savage force.

" This result is signally honorable to Major-General Harrison, by whose military talents it was prepared."

And still Mr. **Van** Buren's "official organ" cries "coward," "granny," "petticoat hero."

Simon Snyder, **the** pure, honest, Democratic governor of Pennsylvania, during the war, in his message to the legislature of that State, on December 10, 1813, said:

" The blessings of thousands of women and children, rescued from the scalping knife of the ruthless savage of the wilderness, and from the still more ruthless Proctor, **rest on Harrison and** his gallant army."

" The old **hero has,** by his valor secured, **"the blessings of thousands of w**omen and children," but he has **also secured the curses** of British Tories and Martin Van Buren's official organ. By the latter he is still denounced as a "coward," "granny," and "petticoat hero."

Governor **Shelby** to Mr. Madison, May 18, 1814, says:

" I feel no hesitation to declare to you that I believe General Harrison to be one of the first military characters I ever knew."

But Martin Van Buren's "official organ" says that General Harrison is a "coward," a "granny," and a "petticoat hero."

Col. Richard M. Johnson, to General Harrison, July 4, 1813, says:

" We did not want to serve under cowards or traitors but under Harrison who had proved himself to be wise, prudent and brave."

But Martin Van Buren's official organ calls Harrison a "coward," a "granny," and a "petticoat hero."

The honorable Langdon Cheves, speaking on the battle of the Thames, said:

" The victory of Harrison, was such as would have secured to a Roman general, in the best days of the Republic, the honors of a triumph! He put an end to the war in the Upper Canada."

And yet Martin Van Buren's "official organ" calls Harrison a "coward," a "granny," and a "petticoat hero."

Commodore Perry to General Harrison, August 18, 1817, says:

" The prompt change made by you in the order of battle on discovering the position of the enemy, has always appeared to me to have evinced a high degree of military talent. I concur with the venerable Shelby in his general approbation of your conduct in that campaign."

Still Martin Van Buren's "official organ" insists that Harrison is a "coward," a "granny," and a "petticoat hero."

Eleven of the officers who fought under General Harrison, at the battle of Tippecanoe, paid him the following tribute of justice and praise soon after the engagement:

" Should our country again require our services to

oppose a civilized or a savage foe, we should march
under General Harrison with the most perfect confidence of victory and fame."

" JOEL COOK,	JOSIAH SNELLING,
" R. B. BURTON,	O. G. BURTON,
" N. ADAMS,	C. FULLER,
" A. HAWKINS,	G. GOODING,
" H. BURCHSTEAD,	J. D. FOSTER,
" HOSEA BLOOD."	

But still Martin Van Buren's "official organ" contends that General Harrison is a "coward," a "granny,"
and a "petticoat hero."

The following is an extract of a letter from Colonel
Davies, who was killed at the battle of Tippecanoe,
August 24, 1811:

"I make free to declare that I have imagined there
were two military men in the West, and General Harrison is the first of the two."

But Martin Van Buren's "official organ" calls General Harrison a "coward," a "granny," and a "petticoat hero."

The Richmond *Enquirer* of January 9, 1813, speaks
of General Harrison in the following manner:

"General Harrison, in spite of the difficulties which
surround him, seems determined to press on to Detroit.
Neither the cold nor the badness of the roads can deter
him from his enterprise. If he fails, the world will excuse him on account of the difficulties which encom-
pass his path. If he succeeds, these very difficulties
will enhance the luster of his success.

"If he has been reported rightly, Harrison is a man
of no ordinary promise. War has been his favorite
study. At a very early age he was with Wayne in his
famous campaign against the Indians. A gentleman
of very high standing, who had an important post
under him during last fall, compares him to Washington. He is as circumspect as he is enterprising; as
prudent in collecting the means of an attack as he is
vigorous in striking the blow."

Again the Richmond *Enquirer* of the 19th of October, 1813, referring to the battle of the Thames, says:

"We have not words to express the joy we feel for the victory of Harrison. Never have we seen the public pulse beat so high. And well may we rejoice. We rejoice not so much for the splendor of this achievement as for the solid benefits which it will produce. Yet, in point of splendor, we have no reason to believe that when we shall receive the official accounts we shall sustain any disappointment," etc.

"But its solid benefits require no official accounts to emblazon them; almost every eye sees them, and almost every tongue can tell them. It gives security to the frontier. Ohio may now sleep in security. The trembling mother that nightly used to clasp her infant to her breast may rock its cradle in peace. The chain which bound the red man to the English white man is broken," etc.

"These benefits we owe to the intrepidity of Perry, who paved the way, and to Harrison, whose skill, prudence and zeal have at length reaped their just reward. This general has now put all his enemies to shame. After struggling with difficulties under which an ordinary man would have sunk ; after passing through a wilderness of morass and mud, so difficult of access that the wagon-horses could not carry provender enough to support them during the journey, he reached the consummation of all his labors; repairs the vices of Hull; wipes off the stain which he had cast upon our arms; stands on the ruins of Malden; muzzles the Indian war dog, and proves to the world that Americans want only an opportunity to display the same gallantry on the shore which they have done upon the wave."

But again: In the spring of 1814 a proposition was made in Congress to create the office of lieutenant-general. The Richmond *Enquirer* named General Harrison for the elevated station in the following eloquent and patriotic language:

"If any one should ask where such a man is to be met with, we answer to the best of our abilities, in the man who has washed away the disasters of Detroit; who had everything to collect for a new campaign,

and who got everything together; who waded through
morasses and snows, and surmounted the most frightful climate in the Union; the man who was neither to
be daunted by disaster nor difficulties under any shape
by the skill of the civilized or the barbarity of a savage
foe; the man who won the hearts of the people by
his spirit, the respect of his officers by his zeal, the
love of his army by a participation of their hardships;
the man who has finally triumphed over his enemy.
Such a man is William Henry Harrison."

And after all this testimony given by the editor of
the Richmond *Enquirer* in regard to the courage,
skill, capacity, patriotism and services of General Har-
son, Martin Van Buren's official organ presumes to call
him "coward," "granny" and a "petticoat hero."

John M. Niles, in his life of Perry, published in 1821,
after giving a general biography of General Harrison,
said: .

"The defense of Fort Meigs and the subsequent
capture of the British army may be fairly considered
the most brilliant and extraordinary events of the late
war."

In alluding to the battle of the Thames he said:

"It must be conceded that this victory reflected
great honor upon the national arms, and upon the
troops by whom it was achieved."

"The action and the movements which preceded it
afford ample testimony of the judgment and cool
intrepidity of General Harrison ; and, indeed, all the
events of the campaign support these characteristics;
the disasters attending it having in no instance been
imputable to him."

And yet Martin Van Buren's "official organ" still
dares to call General Harrison a "coward," "granny,"
and a "petticoat hero."

Ex-Governor Isaac Hill, Nov. 23, 1813, in the New
Hampshire *Patriot*, said:

"What man lives whose whole heart and soul is not
British that cannot sincerely rejoice in the late victories of Perry and Harrison; that does not feel a
pride in the valor and patriotism of the heroes of the

West, who have freed a country large as the Empire of Alexander the Great from the Indian tomahawk and scalping-knife. If there be such a one he is a traitor to his country; he possesses the spirit of a murderer."

Still Martin Van Buren's "official organ" continues to call Harrison a "coward," a "granny," and a "petticoat hero."

I will in the next place, Mr. Chairman, claim the attention of the committee to the testimony given by a portion of the surviving members of the Petersburg, Virginia, volunteers, who had served under General Harrison. Before, however, I introduce this testimony, I will furnish some evidence of its high worth and character by reading the discharge given to that "patriotic and gallant corps" of citizen soldiers by Brigadier General Cass. He says:

"In granting a discharge to this patriotic and gallant corps, the general feels at a loss for words adequately to convey his sense of their exalted merits. Almost exclusively composed of individuals who had been nursed in the lap of ease, they have, for twelve months, borne the hardships and privations of a military life, in the midst of an inhospitable wilderness, with a cheerfulness and alacrity which has never been surpassed; their conduct in the field has been excelled by no other corps."

Let us now see what the brave and gallant men say:

"We, the undersigned, a portion of the surviving members of the Petersburg, Virginia, Volunteers, now residing in Petersburg, have seen in some public prints, with much surprise, the imputation of cowardice attempted to be cast upon our old commander, Gen. William Henry Harrison. We, as an act of sheer justice to that individual, deem it a duty to state that during the siege of Fort Meigs in the spring of 1813, we frequently saw General Harrison placed in dangerous and perilous situations; and one day of the several sorties, 5th of May, 1813, we as frequently saw him coolly and deliberately encouraging his officers and men to do their duty. No coward, we think could act with coolness and deliberation on such occasions.

6

"In September following, we crossed the lake and landed on the Canada shore a few miles below Malden, in which neighborhood we expected to meet the enemy. At and after the landing, on our march towards Malden, Harrison and Shelby were seen at the heads of their respective commands, in the active discharge of their duties. And at the Thames, in October, it was conceded by all that General Harrison's conduct was brave and meritorious.

"In February or March of the same year, the time of service of the militia was about to expire, and, had they left the army, we should have been left with but a few volunteers and regulars exposed to the combined enemy. At that time Meigs was not fortified. In this situation, the general rallied the troops together and addressed them in a feeling and patriotic manner, impressing upon them the necessity of remaining only a few days longer, at the same time pledging himself to see them paid from his own private resources, should the Government refuse to do it, for the time they might serve after their legal time of service had expired.

"We cannot forbear acknowledging a debt of gratitude of long standing, and yet due to General Harrison, for his kind and personal attention to those of our company who were wounded in the engagement on the 5th of May, at Fort Meigs, and for his general deportment towards our corps during our term of service.

"Joseph Scott,
"John H. Smith,
"Joseph Mason,
"Wm. R. Chieves,
"James Page,
"Wm. P. Burton,
"R. Clements."

Notwithstanding the foregoing conclusive testimony to the contrary, Martin Van Buren's "official organ" alleges that General Harrison is a "coward," a "granny" and a "petticoat hero."

In addition to all the testimonials I have here enumerated—testimonials from friends and from foes, some of whom have since gone to their rest—I will now present the committee a few others, some of whom have never been extensively before the public. In September, 1836, there was a convention of the citizens of Western Pennsylvania held at Pittsburgh. A committee, consisting of officers who had served nearest the person of General Harrison in the Northwestern army, during the late war, was appointed to "report to the convention their personal knowledge of his courage and ability as a commander." At the head of that committee stood Col. John B. Alexander, a brave and gallant officer, who was equally distinguished for his legal and scientific attainments as for his accurate and intimate acquaintance with military science and the art of war. With him were associated Gen. Joseph Markle, Major Reeves, Colonel Daily and Dr. McGheehan, all gentlemen of admitted gallantry, intelligence and high character. And now, sir, let me read you a short extract from the report of that committee :

"That they served as officers in the Northwestern army, under the command of General Harrison, in the campaign of 1812-13. They have had many opportunities to observe the character and tendency of his orders and arrangements, and were witnesses of the obstacles presented by an extensive wilderness and dreary swamps to the transportation of the material of the army and the accomplishment of his views. Yet his industry and perseverance overcame these difficulties.

"The members of the committee have also seen him in battle and noticed his conduct. In command, he was composed, yet vigorous. Under the fire of the enemy, he was tranquil, calm and deliberate. During the protracted siege of Fort Meigs, and amid the shower of shot and shells which poured into the works without intermission, no one saw the eye of the General to falter or a nerve to quiver. In his purposes he was steady; in his manners kind and urbane, yet dignified and commanding."

And now, sir, if there were no other testimonials to establish the courage, ability, and services of General

Harrison than the one to which I have last referred, that
alone would be entirely satisfactory to my mind, emi-
nating, as I know it did, from gentlemen who have
manifested their patriotism, not by merely calling
themselves Democrats, and talking about Democracy,
but by deeds of heroism at Massassinewa and other
bloody fields in the Northwest.

Still Martin Van Buren's "official organ" calls General
Harrison a "coward," a "granny," and a "petticoat
hero."

But, sir, here is another testimonial from some of the
brave men of Western Pennsylvania, who served an
arduous campaign under the command of General Harrison in the Northwestern army:

"To his Excellency Major General William Henry Harrison, Commander-in-Chief of the Northwestern
army.

"Fort Meigs, April 16, 1813.

"SIR: We feel it a particular duty and pleasure to
acknowledge to you and our countrymen the confidence we have entertained of your excellency as our
general and commander-in-chief of the Northwestern
army. Fifteen days since we were prepared to return
home, our six months' tour of duty expired; but, by
your solicitations in a letter addressed to General
Crooks, and that of the State government of which we
are citizens together with the impending dangers that
threatened all around by our hostile foes, we again
engaged ourselves in the service of the United States
for the fifteen days past, and to-morrow we expect
again to be discharged from the service, the danger
threatened appearing principally to have abated.
Reinforcements having arrived, and the preparations
much increased, we shall retire from the field
with peculiar satisfaction, asking of Heaven its protection for you, your army, and our country; trusting that
our Western enemies will be taught a lesson of submission not to be forgotten, and that the inhabitants of our
Western frontier will again enjoy the peaceful pleasures of their homes.

" Most respectfully, your excellency's humble servants, " DAVID NELSON, Major.

" THOMAS LINGHAM, Major.

" ROBERT ORR, Major.

" E. CASSETTS, Surgeon.

" JOHN JUNKINS,

" J. BARACMAN,

" WM. HARPER,

" JAMES BONNER,

" WM. JOHNSON,

" THOMAS JACK.

" JOSHUA LOGAN, Adjutant."

These gentlemen were alike distinguished for bravery, heroism, and all the sterling virtues. One of them,
Major Orr, some years after the termination of the
war, had the honor of a seat on this floor.

But Martin Van Buren's official organ still vouches
that General Harrison is a "coward," a "granny," and
a " petticoat hero."

Major Willock, of Pittsburgh, has borne witness to
the bravery and courage of General Harrison. "He
had been present on the field of battle when British
balls were flying thick around the head of Harrison,
and the old hero never blanched or quailed in that hour
of peril."

John D. Davis, Esq., of Pittsburgh, testifies that he
was an "eyewitness to the services of General Harrison on the field of battle; to his courage, humanity,
and devotion to the interests of the troops during some
of the most trying scenes of the last war, and that his
conduct towards his suffering soldiers was that of a
father in his family."

Mr. John W. Lynch, of Pittsburgh, testifies "that
on the field of battle and in the army, no man ever
questioned the courage and benevolence of General
Harrison."

Major Willock, John D. Davis, Esq., and Mr. Lynch
are brave and patriotic citizens, and had served in the
Northwestern army under General Harrison.

Yet Martin Van Buren's "official organ" denounces

General Harrison as a "coward," a "granny," and a "petticoat hero."

Mr. Pollock, of Muskingum county, Ohio, in a recent debate in the house of representatives of that State, speaking relative to the battle of Fort Meigs, said:

" I was in the battle. I saw a cannon ball strike within two feet of General Harrison during that fight. I was there. I saw bomb shells and chain shot flying thick around him. Horses were shot down under him. I saw General Harrison there, and he was in the hottest of the fight; and where balls flew the thickest, and where steel met steel the fiercest, there you would find General Harrison. I speak what I know my eyes have seen. General Harrison is not a coward; and those who call him a coward know nothing of him. He was a brave, prudent and fearless general. He took the right course during the last war; he acted a noble part, and his country has honored him for it. Ask the soldiers who fought by his side, whose hearts were cheered by his valor, and who were led to triumph and to victory by his courage, and bravery and skill, if General Harrison was a coward; and they, sir, will tell you no!"

But Martin Van Buren's "official organ" still hesitates not to proclaim General Harrison a "coward," a a "granny," and a "petticoat hero."

General Tipton, late of the United States Senate from the State of Indiana, who had served as an ensign in the battle of Tippecanoe, testifies in regard to General Harrison's courage and behavior in that engagement in the following manner:

" I think him as brave a man as ever lived; no man could have behaved with more true courage than he did. While the engagement was hottest and when bullets flew thickest he was to be seen speaking in his ordinary tone and giving commands with the greatest precision. "The company to which I belonged," said General Tipton, "went into action eighty strong and only twenty survived. The firing upon us was most tremendous. After the general had made his arrange-

ments for repelling the attack of the Indians at either
point, he rode up to where I was, and made the following inquiries: 'Where's your captain?' 'He is
dead, sir.' 'Where is the first or second lieutenant?'
'They are both dead,' was the reply. 'Well, where is
the ensign?' 'He stands before you, general.' 'Well,
my brave fellow,' said Harrison, 'hold your ground
for five minutes longer and all will be safe.'" In fifteen minutes the enemy was repulsed on all sides;
Tipton gallantly led on his few remaining comrades to
the charge, and victory perched upon the American
banner.

"As an evidence of Harrison's coolness in the midst
of danger, General Tipton stated that, at the moment
the conversation ended between himself and General
Harrison, and as the horse on which was mounted his
aide, the late General Taylor, of Indiana, was in the
act of turning, a rifle ball pierced him through the
body and brought him to the ground, catching his
rider's leg under him. It was a favorite black horse
of the general's, and he exclaimed, 'Ah! is my gallant
old black gone?' ' Well, rise and mount again, for we
have no time to mourn the loss of a horse when so
many brave ones are exposed to a similar fate,' and,
having remounted his aide, he dashed into the midst of
the danger. In a few minutes the battle was over."

Notwithstanding the statement of General Tipton,
Martin Van Buren's "official organ" continues to con-
nect the name of General Harrison with "coward,"
"granny" and "petticoat hero."

Mr. Will, of Ross county, Ohio, in relation to the
battle of the Miami rapids, states as follows:

"That he had been a soldier under Wayne; that he
had risen from the post of a private to that of a captain in the regular service. It was at the battle of
the Miami rapids that he first saw General Harrison.
He was then the aide of General Wayne. He saw the
youthful Harrison in the hardest, the hottest and the
thickest of the fight. I was shot through the body. I
fell and was for some time unable to get up. I succeeded, however, after great difficulty, in struggling to

my feet. Just at this moment Harrison came up to me
and exclaimed, 'Soldier, why are you not fighting with
your company?' The blood was then gushing out of
my shoes. I informed him of my situation, and he
rushed on into the worst dangers of the fight. Some
denounce him as a coward. It is a base slander upon
a good and a brave man. I know and feel what I am
saying. He was a brave man, and a better officer I
never saw."

Still Martin Van Buren's "official organ" cries aloud
"coward," "granny" "petticoat hero."

Joseph Loranger, a respectable citizen of Monroe,
Michigan, gives his testimony in favor as follows:

"I was with General Harrison at Fort Meigs, and
when I hear those who were in their cradles at the
time or fleeing from danger stigmatize him as a 'coward,' I feel bound no longer to remain silent, but to tell
my fellow-citizens what I know. I was near him
when General Proctor demanded the surrender of the
fort, and I heard General Harrison say that he would
never surrender; he would die in its defense rather
than give up the fort; and he called upon all his
subordinate officers to join in his resolution; and that,
if he did fall, to never give up the conflict. Stimulated
by the firmness of their general, whom every officer
and soldier in the fort loved for his amiable qualities
and unflinching bravery, all resolved to die rather than
to dishonor their country by a surrender. You know,
fellow-citizens, the result. By his untiring perserver-
ance, by his late and early attention to duty, by his
constant encouragement of the private soldier by his
own example, and by his extraordinary skill, prudence
and bravery as a commander, the enemy were repulsed,
and the flag of their beloved country waved in triumph
over the fort which General Harrison and his brave
companions so gallantly defended."

But Martin Van Buren's "official organ" proclaims
General Harrison a "coward," a "granny," and a
"petticoat hero."

The following extracts of a letter from the hero of
Brownstown, Gen. James Miller, afford additional

evidence of the "bravery, skill and judgment" of General Harrison. At the time of the battle of Tippecanoe General Miller was at Fort Harrison, about seventy miles up the Wabash. He says :

"Although I was not in the battle still I took great interest in it, had much conversation with all the officers on their return and made every inquiry I could think of respecting their movement and encampments, the attack and defense, and the operations of the battle throughout; and I made up my mind unhesitatingly that the campaign had been conducted with great bravery, skill and judgment, and that nothing was left undone that could be done consistently with the general's express orders from the War Department, which I saw and read. Nor have I ever known or heard of any act of his which has in the least degree altered the opinion I then formed of him. I will add that if I ever had any military skill I am more indebted for it to General Harrison than to any other man.

" In those days I never heard that General Harrison was a coward or wore petticoats.

" To conclude, I freely express my opinion, after following him through all his civil and military career, after living with him in his family more than six months, that Gen. William Henry Harrison is as free from stain or blemish as it falls to the lot of man to be."

This is the testimony of as brave an officer as ever wielded a sword; of the officer who, at the battle of Lundy's Lane, gave the memorable reply, " I'll try," to General Brown, when the latter inquired, if Miller could dislodge the British artillery from their commanding position, and forthwith accomplished his purpose by the aid of his favorite weapon, the bayonet.

And yet Martin Van Buren's "official organ" calls Harrison a "coward," a "granny" and a "petticoat hero."

The following general, field and staff officers of the Northwestern army gave to the world their testimonial in writing, in which they express their surprise and regret "that charges as improper in form as in substance" have been made against General Harrison. And they conclude by stating, that, " With a ready acquiescence, beyond the mere claim of military duty, we are prepared to obey a general whose measures meet our most deliberate approbation and merit that of his country:"

Lewis Cass, brigadier general United States Army.

Samuel Wells, colonel Seventeenth regiment United States Infantry.

Thomas D. Owings, colonel Twenty-eighth regiment United States Infantry.

George Paull, colonel Seventeenth regiment United States Infantry.

J. C. Bartlett, colonel quartermaster-general.

James V. Ball, lieutenant-colonel.

Robert Morrison, lieutenant-colonel.

George Todd, major Nineteenth regiment United States Infantry.

William Trigg, major Twenty-eighth regiment United States Infantry.

James Smiley, major Twenty-eighth regiment United States Infantry.

Rd. Graham, major Seventeenth regiment United States Infantry.

Geo. Croghan, major Seventeenth regiment United States Infantry.

L. Hukill, major and assistant inspector-general.

Ed. Wood, major engineers.

But still Martin Van Buren's "official organ" reiterates "coward," "granny" and "petticoat hero."

After their term of service in the Northwestern army had expired, the following officers addressed General Harrison in this manner:

"On retiring from service, sir, we are happy in assuring you of our fullest confidence and that of our respective commands in the measures you have taken; they have been cautious and guarded, such as would at this time have carried our arms to the walls of Malden had not the unhappy occurrences at the river Raisin checked your progress, and for a short time thwarted your plans of operation. That you may soon teach the enemy the distinction between an honorable and savage warfare by planting our standard in the heart of their country and regain the honor and territory we have lost, and, as a just tribute to valor, toils and suffering, receive the grateful thanks of a generous and free people, is among the first, the warmest wishes of our hearts.

    " Edward W. Tupper, Brigadier-General.
    " Simon Perkins, Brigadier-General.
    " Charles Miller, Colonel.
    " John Andrews, Lieutenant-Colonel.
    " William Rayan, Colonel.
    " R. Spafford, Lt. Col. 2d Regt. Ohio quota.
    " N. Beasley, Major.
    " James Galloway, Major.
    " Solomon Bentley, Major.
    " George Darrow, Major
    " W. W. Cotgreave, Major.
    " Jacob Frederick, Major.

" His Excellency, William Henry Harrison, commander-in-chief of the Northwestern Army."

Still, Martin Van Buren's "official organ" persists in calling General Harrison a "coward," a "granny," and a "petticoat hero."

I have it in my power, sir, to adduce many other valuable testimonials in relation to the courage, skill, ability and conduct of Gen. William Henry Harrison, and particularly the statements of Gen. John O'Fallon, of St. Louis, Colonel Chambers, of Kentucky, and Majors Todd and Smith; but I will no longer test the patience of the committee by heaping certificate upon certificate, and testimony upon testimony. I might also call upon at least four honorable gentlemen on this floor, who gallantly fought at the side of the hero of North Bend, to bear their testimony in favor of that brave veteran and the cause of truth. But, sir, I forbear; for if men will not be convinced with the ample evidence which has been produced, neither would they be convinced "though one rose from the dead." General Harrison had in his army several thousand men from

Western Pennsylvania. Many of them are now residing in my district; men as bold and brave as ever
breathed the "breath of life," and if the gentleman dared
to tell them that William Henry Harrison was a "petticoat hero," he would very quickly have his mouth
stopped. Indeed, I never in my life saw a man who
had fought under Harrison that was not his warm
friend. But stay, I almost take that back; I did hear
once of six men in the county of Fayette, in Pennsylvania, who had been in his army, and yet were violently opposed to his election; but, on inquiry, it turned
out that the whole six had been deserters and notorious scamps, insomuch that the General had printed a
hand-bill offering a reward for the apprehension of
every one of them. These men who deserted the
stars and stripes of their country are the only political
deserters I ever heard of from the Harrison standard.

But now let us look a little at the civil qualifications
and services of General Harrison, for he is still more
distinguished for his capacity and conduct in the civil
offices he has filled than for his qualifications as a military chieftain. As the governor of the Northwestern
Territory, which then embraced a region of the country that has since formed five States of this Union, and
afterwards as governor of the State of Indiana, he won
for himself the illustrious title of the "Father of the
Western Country." As a member, both of this House
and the Senate, and not less when Minister to the Republic of Colombia, he conducted himself in a manner
to secure his own reputation, and to reflect honor upon
his country.

In every situation the polar star that governed all
his actions was the love of justice. When he was a
member of Congress, and a bill was up to increase the
pay of its members, *he refused his vote to take up this
bill until justice had been done to the men who had
been his companions in arms, by passing that pension
bill of which he was the earnest, ardent, inflexible, per-
severing advocate. He refused to do justice to himself
till he had seen justice done to the old heroes who had
fought for the national liberty.* Whoever wishes to

form a correct opinion in regard to this portion of the life of General Harrison, and to peruse a compendium of the speeches he delivered, and the principles he advocated in this and in the other house, has only to consult a series of editorial articles, which were prepared by Mr. Gales, the editor of the *Intelligencer*, where they will see, as in a picture, the honest, manly, patriotic, feeling character of the venerated hero whom the people of the West so enthusiastically admire. Let any man consider what was the weight of responsibility imposed on General Harrison when he was appointed commander-in-chief over the whole Northwestern Territory by President Madison, whose election Mr. Van Buren so zealously opposed. Hear what the Secretary of War, by direction of the President, wrote to him on that occasion: " You will command such means as may be practicable, exercise your own discretion, and act in all cases according to your own judgment."

Here is *carte blanche* unlimited—discretionary power over the whole West; the country and its interests were placed at his disposal. Such was the confidence reposed in him by James Madison. Subsequently Mr. Monroe, acting Secretary of War, wrote General Harrison in relation to the invasion of Upper Canada as follows:

" No person can be so competent to that decision as yourself, and the President has great confidence in the solidity of the opinion you may form. He wishes you to weigh maturely this important subject, and take that part which your judgment may dictate."

Such an amount of power was never intrusted to any other officer of this Government. And did Harrison betray the trust? Did he basely violate this confidence of the Chief Magistrate? No. Never; never in a single instance.

Do you know how it was that this same man acquired, in so eminent a degree, the affections and love of the officers and soldiers in the army? He, himself, has disclosed the secret in four lines:

" By treating them with affection and kindness, by

always recollecting that they were fellow-citizens, whose feelings I was bound to respect, and by sharing, on every occasion, the hardships which they were obliged to undergo."

General Harrison possessed the confidence and approbation of every President of the United States, from George Washington down to the election of General Jackson.

In 1791, when nineteen years of age, he was appointed by Washington an ensign in our army.

In 1792 was promoted to the rank of lieutenant.

In 1795 he was made a captain and placed in command of Fort Washington.

In 1797 he was appointed by President Adams secretary of the Northwestern Territory, and ex-officio lieutenant-governor.

In 1798 he was chosen a Delegate to Congress.

In 1801 he was appointed governor of Indiana, and in the same year President Jefferson appointed him sole commissioner for treating with the Indians.

In 1803 and 1806 he was reappointed governor by President Jefferson.

In 1809 he was appointed by President Madison governor of Indiana.

In 1814 he was appointed by Madison one of the commissioners to treat with the Indians, and in the same year, with his colleagues, Governor Shelby and General Cass, concluded the celebrated treaty of Greenville.

In 1815 he was again appointed such commissioner, with General McArthur and Mr. Graham, and negotiated a treaty at Detroit.

In 1816 he was elected a member of Congress.

In January, 1818, he introduced a resolution in honor of Kosciusko and supported it in one of the most feeling and classical and eloquent speeches ever delivered in the House of Representatives.

In 1819 he was elected a member of the Ohio senate.

In 1824 he was elected Senator in Congress, and was apointed in 1825 chairman of the military committee in place of General Jackson, who had resigned.

In 1827 he was appointed minister to Colombia, and in 1829 wrote his immortal letter to Bolivar, the deliverer of South America.

These, sir, are some of the public stations which General Harrison has filled with so much honor to his own character and with so great advantage to his country.

RATIFICATION CONVENTION.

THE YOUNG MEN'S WHIG NATIONAL CONVENTION AT BALTIMORE MAY 4—ORDER OF THE PROCESSION, BANNERS, ETC.

Sunday evening it rained, and the appearance of the clouds foretokened an unpleasant Monday; but He, who "tempers the wind" dispersed the lowering clouds. The day was auspicious, sufficiently cool to prevent exhaustion, and sufficiently warm for comfort. The streets were filled at an early hour in the morning with notes of preparation—delegations assembling in private meetings, delegates hurrying to and fro in search of friends or badges, and the arrival of delegations from the country, inspired an expectation of an uncommonly interesting day. Before 8 o'clock the marshals began to ride through the streets to their various appointments; and then commenced the rush of thousands; the sidewalks of Baltimore street for two miles presented an almost unbroken mass of eager expectants waiting for the march of the procession. As the hour advanced the roofs of the houses were scaled, and hundreds from their lofty perches looked for the Whig array. The ladies, the bright-eyed beautiful ladies of Baltimore, filled the windows.

At half past nine the firing of the national salute, the signal for the march of the procession, began. Before it was concluded the delegation from Philadelphia

City and county arrived, and, with their baggage in their hands, hastened to their position in Cove street.

The front of the procession, led by the chief marshal, accompanied by two aids, commenced its march.

THE PROCESSION.

The procession was led by Capt. James O. Law, chief marshal of the day, and an aid on each side on horseback. He had appointed five assistants; they were Messrs. James H. Milliken, Washington Booth, Charles H. Wilder, Levi Fahnestock and J. W. Osborne. A fine band of music immediately followed the marshal, playing "Harrison's March," as composed by Professor Deilman. Then came the president and officers of the Baltimore city delegation, bearing a large white banner on a frame, with the following appropriate inscription from a new and popular song:

> "The people are coming from plain and from mountain,
>   To join the brave band of the honest and free,
> Which grows as the stream from the leaf-sheltered fountain,
>   Spreads broad and more broad till it reaches the sea;
> No strength can restrain it, no force can retain it,
> Whate'er may resist, it breaks gallantly through,
> And borne by its motion as a ship on the ocean
>   Speeds on in his glory—
>   Old Tippecanoe!
> The iron-arm'd soldier, the true hearted soldier,
> The gallant old soldier
>   Of Tippecanoe!"

An eagle was represented at the head of the inscription, and beneath it was a barrel of "hard cider."

INVITED GUESTS.

A number of barouches followed, containing the invited guests of the convention, in the first of which we observed the Hon. Daniel Webster, of the United States Senate, and his honor, Sheppard C. Leakin, mayor of the city of Baltimore.

Next to the carriages, and on foot, came the subcommittee of arrangements, the Harrison convention, and the central committee, distinguished by sashes and appropriate badges, expressive of their official position in the duties of the convention.

The above composed that portion of the line resting on Baltimore street, which, as it passed down, was joined by the delegation from

NEW HAMPSHIRE.

It was preceded by the State banner, with the motto, "Crescit Sub Pondere Virtus." The delegation was larger than was anticipated, and admirably did the fine body of men which represented the "Granite State" sustain their distinctive appellation.

MASSACHUSETTS.

The delegation from the Old Bay State was alike imposing for the strength of its numbers and the high respectability of those arrayed under its numerous and significant banners. It comprised about a thousand delegates. It was preceded by an elegant banner borne by the Boston members, having a view of the city of Boston with the motto, "We are Where We Have Been, and Ever Mean to Be." On the reverse of the banner, "Sicut Patribus sit Deus Nobis. Bostonia Condita, Civitatis Regime Donata, A. D. 1822."

The various sections of this delegation were distinguished by banners with appropriate devices and inscriptions. On the first of these was the figure of "Fame," and inscribed on the reverse, "Harrison and Tyler." This was followed by one representing "The Book of Laws," and on the reverse, "Honor to the Majesty of Law." Two richly finished silk scrolls, one representing the "Constitution of the United States," and having therefrom a sentence in letters of gold: the other the "Constitution of Massachusetts," with a sentence therefrom in the same letters. A silk banner encircled with pictorial illustrations of General Harrison's career, closing with the Presidency, and bearing the words, "The Rising of Harrison."

The members from Bunker Hill with a banner bearing those two words only, were very numerous, and were cheered with the deepest enthusiasm. Succeed-

ing them was a banner with a device of a golden goblet
overflowing with gold pieces; on the reverse the
words, "The Golden Humbug." On the next was
represented a quantity of mechanics' implements of
labor, and on the other side the pithy expression.
"Buchanan; Beware of Edge Tools." It will be remembered that Mr. Buchanan, in the course of a speech
some time since, exclaimed: "I would that the whole
of New England might hear my voice." They appear
to have heard it, and Mr. Buchanan is thus honored with
their reply. New England, like all other sections of
the Union, is not well pleased with that political
theory which would begin its practice by a reduction
of the price of labor. A banner followed with the device of the sword and balance, bearing the motto,
"Equal Rights and Equal Justice." Amongst others
we noticed banners with the following inscriptions:
"Glad Tidings for the People;" "Union for the Sake of
Union;" "Success to our Cause." The device of an
arm and hammer with the motto, "Strong Arms and
Stout Hearts."

The Cape Cod delegation were distinguished by
banners with the following inscriptions: "The Fisheries—By These We Thrive." "Bounty and Prosperity
to the Fishermen."

The banner of the arms of the State was borne in the
rear of this long line of the young Whigs of Massachusetts, and it was encircled by the motto, "There is
Lexington, and Concord and Bunker Hill, and There
They will be Forever."

The Massachusetts delegation was accompanied
with a remarkably fine band of music which came on
with them, and whose performances excited much admiration.

RHODE ISLAND.

This gallant little State, which came with "victory
yet green upon her brow," was well represented. Her
sons moved on with an elastic step under the folds of
her State banner, representing an anchor hove, with
the appropriate motto, "Fast Anchored to Her An-

cient Principles." Her representation was very large
for her population.

CONNECTICUT.

Connecticut, too, has but recently added a new leaf
to her laurels, and on the present occasion was represented by a goodly number of her sons, who had just
reason to be proud of the station which she has per-
manently assumed among her Whig sisters of the national confederacy. She followed her State banner,
inscribed with the motto, "Connecticut Has Said, and
Connecticut Has Done It."

A fine band of music occupied the interval in the
line, and was followed by the delegation from

NEW YORK.

The proud "Excelsior" of the Empire State met the
eye in the van of the long line of intelligent, enterprising and patriotic citizens who composed her numerous delegation. Almost every one of her many counties
was represented, and at the head of the delegation we
recognized its chairman, J. N. Reynolds, Esq. The
eyes of the spectators appeared to sparkle with new
interest and pleasure as the long line passed before
them, "the observed of all observers." The cry of
"Rescue" is in the shouts of her sons ; we know "she
can;" we hope "she will;" may we live to write "she
has!" The motto on the armorial banner consisted of
the words, "New York, the Ebbs and Flows of Whose
Single Soul are Tides to the Rest of Mankind."

NEW JERSEY.

The wronged New Jersey next appeared, and with
the free air and fearless port of men who know their
rights and dare maintain them, followed that banner
which they have preserved in the hands of the undismayed defender of their rights, their worthy governor. The State banner bore the significant inscription, "The Next Impression of Her Broad Seal Will
Be Respected." A very elegant banner represented a
fac-simile of the seal of the State over which were
the words, "Our State Sovereignty Shall Not Be

Violated." Around it, "The Great Seal of the State of New Jersey." We cannot doubt but that it will make a due impression in the fall.

The Nottingham delegation displayed a rich silk banner inscribed, "Our Cause is Our Country, Our Candidate Its Gallant Defender; Presented by the Young Ladies at Mill Hill, April 8, 1840." Each corner was beautifully embroidered with roses.

A banner in the West Jersey delegation contained the motto, "Jerseymen Choose Their Own Representatives."

The members from Princeton, whose ranks were well filled, were distinguished by a rich silk banner representing the American eagle, with the words, "Princeton Whig Association," and on the reverse, "Harrison and Tyler."

PENNSYLVANIA.

The delegation from the Keystone State was immense, and presented a scene that in itself would dignify the name of a procession. Its approach was indicated by a large white banner. on which was inscribed, "Keystone State. It is Coming." Then followed the "Philadelphia City and County Delegation," with a banner signifying the same, and another rich one bearing the arms of the State.

Another banner had on it a ship with the sentence above, "Labor is Wealth," and below, "Don't Give Up the Ship." In the rear of the Philadelphia members was carried a transparency, being a full-length portrait of General Harrison, encircled by the words, "Honor Be to Him Who Defends Our Homes and Friends." On the reverse it stated that, "This transparency was displayed in Philadelphia in 1813, by the people, after the defeat of Proctor by the gallant Harrison." A relic of the time when people en masse offered honor to the victorious soldier.

York county was represented by about 150 "good men and true" with their six marshals. In front of the delegation from Democratic York was borne a beautiful banner, on which was tastefully displayed a white rose with the motto, "The White Rose of Pennsylvania Defends the Fair Fame of Harrison." On the reverse was inscribed the "York County Delegation."

Cumberland county was also strongly represented. Among her highly respectable delegation we noticed the Hon. Charles B. Penrose, late Speaker of the Senate, who afterwards addressed the convention with great effect, at Monument Square. On the banner in front of the delegation was inscribed these expressive words: "Old Mother Cumberland—She'll bag the Fox."

From Schuylkill county a large number were present; their banner, "W. H. H.—In peace the Farmer and His Plowshare: in War the Soldier and his Sword." On the reverse, "Harrison and Tyler."

The Dauphin county delegation exhibited an elegant banner, on one side of which she announced her principles as "First for Jackson; First for Harrison. Always Honest—She Gave Up Cæsar for Rome, and Now to the Aid of Rome She Calls the Cincinnatus of the West." On the other side was, "Pro Patria—Harrison and Tyler."

In the same delegation there was also a beautiful banner, which attracted particular notice. This banner was got up by two members of the Harrisburg Tippecanoe Club, Messrs. A. Jones, and T. Fenn. On one side of the banner, the body of which was black satin, was a log cabin, in gilt, surrounded with thirteen stars, indicative of the thirteen original States; and attached to the cabin was a barrel of hard cider, also in gilt. The string of the door of the cabin was not drawn in. On the same side was "Harrison, Tyler and True Democracy," and "The Ball is Rolling," all also in gilt. On the other side was the Pennsylvania coat of arms, and the inscription, "To Preserve Their Liberties the People Must Do Their Own Fighting and Voting," all also in gilt. The banner was splendidly decorated and trimmed.

The delegation from Fayette county conveyed a portion of its members in a complete log cabin, built

upon wheels and drawn by six horses. Upon the roof
a banner was displayed, inscribed "Laurel Mountain
Boys, from Fayette County, Pennsylvania, Head of the
Mississippi Valley." Deer and fox skins, buck-horns,
with sundry implements of husbandry, adorned the
sides and roof of the cabin, and boughs of green trees
decorated the top. The appearance of such a thing in
our streets was not a little interesting to many as a
curiosity in the way of architecture, and of novelty to
all. A barrel of hard cider was placed in the rear
of the cabin, and a gourd was suspended by it. A flag
in front announced whence it came, "From Fort
Necessity, Washington's First Battle Ground."

The Bucks county delegation followed it with the
banner, brief but expressive, "Huzza for Old Tippecanoe."

Lancaster county was preceded by a banner that
announced herself as "The Gibraltar of the Keystone
State, Good for 4,000 Majority for Old Tip." A club
from Lancaster city had a beautiful flag bearing the
words of General Harrison to his soldiers at parting
with them.

Mifflin county with an appropriate flag followed,
and

Adams county was largely represented, her banners
having a variety of devices. On the first banner was
"Adams County, Pennsylvania, Opposed to Reducing
the Wages of the Laborer and Mechanics." On
another, "Harrison the Conqueror of Proctor Shall
Lead Us to Victory."

The Delaware county delegation carried a banner
bearing the motto, "Tippecanoe; No Reduction of
Wages."

From Pittsburgh the delegation, was large and consisted of substantial looking men, the iron of Pennsylvania. They carried a banner consisting of a painting
representing Harrison and his staff, and on the reverse
a log cabin with Harrison at the plow in the foreground.

Mercer county was well represented. The banner
of the delegation presented a likeness of Harrison and

around it, "Our Candidate, Fort Meigs, The Thames, Tippecanoe, William Henry Harrison, the Poor Man's Friend." On the reverse, "Our Candidates, Harrison and Tyler."

DELAWARE.

The delegation of this gallant little State reached the city at an early hour yesterday morning. It comprised representatives from all the counties. The banner borne in front had on it the arms of the State, and on the reverse the motto, "The First to Adopt—the Last to Abandon the Constitution." On another banner was the motto, "Our Country—Our Rights." The New Castle Tippecanoe Club had its appropriate banner, as had also the Sussex and Kent members.

The banners of the Kent county delegation had on them the "Blue Hen's Chickens;" a name given to the Delaware line in the glorious war of the Revolution. As the worthy sons of worthy sires have arrayed themselves under this banner, its appropriateness will be seen from the following explanation, furnished by one who took part in the struggle for our National Independence:

"In the Revolutionary war Delaware was among the most densely populated portions of our country, and is said to have furnished five thousand fighting men to the Revolutionary army. The regiment of 'Delaware Blues' was so called from their blue uniforms. When they marched from Wilmington, in 1776, they were indeed a gallant sight. Eight hundred men, with such perfect discipline in their march that when advancing in line, it was said a bullet might have passed from one end of the regiment to the other between the ankles of every soldier without touching a man, exhibited a spectacle such as has not been exceeded since that day.

"They were exposed in every action from Long Island to Charleston, and as fast as they fell in battle their ranks were recruited from Delaware alone. Jaquett, who was one of their officers, used to say that he could march all day with them, from sunrise to sunset, and when, on Green's retreat, everybody else was tired and asleep, his Sussex soldiers alone would get a fiddle and dance around their watch fires. They were engaged in thirty-two pitched battles, and were always the last to retreat.   It was natural that they should have been then the pride and boast of the State in which scarcely a man was left who had not a relation or friend in the regiment.

"Captain Caldwell had a company recruited from Kent and Sussex called 'Caldwell's Game Cocks,' and the regiment after a time in Carolina was nicknamed from this 'The Blue Hen's Chickens,' and 'The Blue Chickens,' as the fun and fancy of their comrades preferred the phrase.   But after they had been distinguished in the South the name of the Blue Hen was applied to the State whenever after a battle the recruiting officers were sent home to get more chickens of her raising, and those who came from Kent were chiefly taken from her forests of white oak. The poor fellows for the most part died in the battles of the Revolution, and but a very few of those who returned ever received any reward for their services, being paid off in Continental money. But the Whigs of the Revolution never ceased to boast of the Blue Hen and her chickens, and to this day their descendants will often boast in Kent that they are the cocks of that brood, and were taken from the stooping white oak."

At this point of the procession was another log cabin, with its appendages of dried skins and emblems of the agricultural life, and, as an indispensable accompaniment, a barrel of hard cider with its pendent gourd.

An elegant full-length portrait of General Harrison, by Otis, was borne in front of the cabin.

Maryland occupied, of course, a large portion of the line, and was rich in devices and decorations. The Baltimore city delegation, under the banner of the State, with the motto, "Religious Toleration and Public Liberty," was in the van; they also carried an elegant banner representing the "Battle Monument."

The delegation from St. Mary's, which followed, was distinguished by a large banner inscribed, "Old

St. Mary's, the Adopted Land of Lord Baltimore, and
Now the Advocate of Old Tippecanoe." They were
accompanied by a very neatly finished log cabin,
drawn by eight gray horses, and having a variety of
tasteful decorations in character. It was the favorite
establishment of the kind with the ladies, and was
particularly honored with their attention. A banner
in the rear of the delegation exhibited the words, "Tip,
Tyler and the Tariff."

Worcester county followed with a banner representing a log cabin and having the inscription, "Harrison
and Tyler; Worcester County is Pledged to Support
Maryland."

A portion of the Frederick City delegation occupied
a well-built log cabin drawn by six horses; on the side
a placard was suspended with the words, "The Cabin
in Which This Morus Multicaulis Administration May
Winter," on another, "Sweep the Augean Stable," for
which purpose a most ominous broom discovered itself
at the chimney top. On the branch of a tree on the
roof of the cabin was perched a mountain eagle, which
produced an excellent effect.

The new made Howard district, victorious in their
first election, carried a banner inscribed "The Young
Whigs of Young Howard District, the True Blood of
the Old Maryland Line." On the other side was "No
Reduction of Wages."

A large log cabin from Sharpsburg here diversi-
fied the line; it was a most substantial one, built on a
frame fixed on six wheels and drawn by eight beautiful horses, each wearing a set of bells. In this cabin a
delegation of forty came down from Washington
county, and from a peep into the interior their quarters
were quite comfortable.

A man was seated on a barrel of hard cider behind; on the sides were a number of skins of various
animals; in one of the windows a hat without a crown
was thrust; cooking utensils and farming implements,
with tools peculiar to the labor of the log-cabin occu-
pants abounded about it, and upon the roof an opossum
was seen clinging to a branch of a gum tree. This

was the favorite of the men, and a capital specimen it was.

Carroll county also came in with a log cabin similar to those we have described.

Talbot county delegation was distinguished by an appropriate flag.

The delegates from Queen Anne's carried a handsome flag, bearing the motto, " When Our Country Calls, Obey—Cincinnatus."

A large delegation from the Laurel Factory followed with a magnificent and very costly banner. This splendid ornament of the procession contains forty yards of silk; its principal picture represents the Factory village, including the river and all the prominent buildings connected with it. Its motto above was, " Protect American Industry," below the words " Laurel Factory, Prince George's County, Maryland, May 4th, 1840." On the reverse, a screw-and-lever press, under which is a figure intended to represent the President, and a laboring man at the lever; above is the quotation, "A pressure which no honest man need regret." The banner, trimmed in superb style by Sisco, is suspended from a gilt spear across the top, the feather projecting at one end and the point at the other; this supported by gold cord attached to gilt-banner poles. It was borne in the procession by six persons. Mr. A. C Smith, was the painter. A large gilt eagle is at the cap of the banner.

A delegation followed bearing the motto, " Old Kent Co.; Union for the Sake of the Union."

The next made the candid acknowledgment, " The Whigs of Cecil—Often Beaten, Never Conquered." Another banner was inscribed, "Hard Cider—Harrison and Reform;" and on the other side, " Retrenchment and Reform—No Standing Army of 200,000 Men."

A curious affair followed here, which was immediately preceded by a flag announcing that "Alleghany is Coming." It was a huge ball, about ten feet in diameter, which was rolled along by a number of the members of this delegation: the ball was apparently a wooden frame covered with linen painted divers colors, and bearing a multitude of inscriptions, apt quotations, original stanzas and pithy sentences, which it was impossible to collect in consequence of the motion of the ball. We think there was other evidence yesterday that "the ball is in motion."

The Cumberland delegation was preceded by an elegant satin flag, worked by the ladies of that town. On another flag of the same delegation was the motto: " Buff and Blue—Good and True—For Tippecanoe."

Hartford, Cecil, Kent and other counties were designated by their appropriate banners.

The Govanstown district displayed a banner representing a log cabin, with the inscription " General Harrison Elected to the Presidency by the Hard-Handed Yeomanry."

DISTRICT OF COLUMBIA.

The delegation from the " Ten-Mile Square" was numerous. The members from Washington headed the delegation with a banner representing the Capitol, and a motto, " Insensible Alike to Blandishments or Threats." A very beautiful banner, having a painting of the genius of Columbia, and the inscription, " Columbia the Sentinel of the Republic," was second in order. This was followed by a flag with the significant motto, " The Liberty of Speech, if Not the Right of Suffrage."

Georgetown came next, and exhibited a banner, having thereon the appropriate sentences, "As Sentinels on the Tower of Liberty We Sound the Alarm. Young Whigs to the Rescue." and on the reverse, " Under the Shadow of the Throne, the Throb of Liberty Still Beats On."

From Alexandria the delegation was large. Their banner, which was very beautiful, represented a figure on a pedestal, and bore the motto, " Public Good Our Only Aim."

VIRGINIA.

Virginia—just fresh from the encounter in which she has added to her renown and given a new zest to the hopes of the American people, and to their confi-

dence in her strength and ability—brought her own
good welcome with her welcome news. The delegation was very large. In every respect the flag of the
" Old Dominion " and its followers did justice to the
place of the nativity of the gallant Harrison.

The Norfolk borough delegation bore a large banner with the picture of the balance, over which were
the words of warning first given to Belshazzar, " Mene,
mene, Tekel Upharsin—Thou Art Weighed in the
Balance and Found Wanting." On the opposite side
the significant expression, " Treasury Pap Inopera-
tive."

From Hampshire county there was a considerable
delegation with an appropriate banner, and lively
green badges.

There was a delegation quite numerous bearing a
banner whose familiar motto especially belonged to
them. On the front an eagle was painted among the
clouds and lettered above, " Wise's District;" on the
reverse the hand-in-hand, with the well-known expression which originated with Mr. Wise, and was so
interestingly exemplified yesterday, " The Union of
the Whigs for the Sake of the Union."

NORTH CAROLINA.

This delegation was comprised in one body under
the banner of the arms of the State, the motto upon
which was, " On, Stanly! On!"

SOUTH CAROLINA.

A similar deputation from this State took its place
in the line, and hoisted the State banner in the cause.
It bore the motto, " The Palmetto Resists Oppression."

GEORGIA.

The enthusiasm which has circulated like electricity
throughout so large a portion of the Union, has not
been more thoroughly felt than among the warm tem-
peraments of the sons of the South. Georgia, but a
short time since avowing her apathy in the Presidential campaign, has felt the kindly influences of a renewed hope, and sends forth her representatives to

the convention; while at home the name of Harrison is cherished as the talisman that is to protect the Union. Her banner bore the motto, " She Has Aroused From Her Lethargy."

VERMONT

Came next, preceded by her armorial standard, and presented a goodly array both in numbers and appearance. The Green Mountain boys who have ever proved the inflexible supporters of the doctrine of equal rights, received a hearty welcome. We know Vermont and can rely on her, and in the language they have adopted on their flag, we feel assured that "The Green Mountain Boys Will Do Their Own Voting and Their Own Fighting."

TENNESSEE

Came with the sable weeds of solemn mourning on her flag for one of her great and good men who had just passed away. This token of respect to the memory of the talented and virtuous Hugh L. White, produced a deep sympathy of feeling on the beholder. The motto of the standard was, " Not that She Loved Cæsar Less, but Rome More."

KENTUCKY.

There was a full delegation from this State, and larger than was expected. The standard bore the name of " Henry Clay " and the Latin passage " Tanto Nomine Nullem per Eulogium." It was no doubt a great gratification to the gentlemen from Kentucky to have the pleasure of meeting their distinguished representative in the Senate, Mr. Clay, at the convention, as it was to many others.

A band of music, as in the order of the procession, followed Kentucky, and preceded a large delegation from

OHIO.

The banner of the State with the well-selected motto. " She Offers Her Cincinnatus to Redeem the Republic," led the procession from Ohio.

A large body of men from Hamilton county, in

which General Harrison resides, followed, bearing a beautiful banner representing Harrison at the plow: on the reverse a view of Cincinnati, the Ohio river and the landing. They also brought on with them a miniature log cabin, built of the buckeye, grown on the farm at North Bend.

Next, a miniature log cabin, built of buckeye timber, taken from North Bend, and brought here by the Cincinnati boys.

Next, flag, an eagle; above, "Franklin County, Ohio," under, "Harrison, Tyler and Reform—One Term;" on the reverse, above the eagle, "Our Country's Good is all Our Aim," and under, "The Buckeyes of Columbus, Ohio."

Next, a small flag, representing a barrel of hard cider with the name of the Franklin County Reform Club, "Straight Outs."

And last, a large painting from Muskingum county representing the demand made by the British general Proctor, upon General Harrison for the surrender of Fort Meigs. Above, "General Proctor Demands the Surrender of This Post," underneath, "Tell Your General Its Capture Will Do Him More Honor Than a Thousand Surrenders." On the reverse, "William Henry Harrison Has Done More for His Country, and Received Less, Than any Man Now Living."—Metcalf, of Kentucky. "The People of the United States—May They Ever Remember, that to Preserve Their Liberties, They Must Do Their Own Voting and Their Own Fighting."—Harrison.

LOUISIANA.

The convention received some addition to its members from this State under their coat of arms, and the motto "Sans Peur et Sans Reproche," upon a banner with a pelican feeding her young.

INDIANA.

A very fine delegation was in attendance from the "Buffalo" State, whose sons have cause to be known and to appreciate the gallantry of the man they have thus publicly honored. The flag was inscribed, " She

Will Cherish in Her Manhood the Defender of Her Infancy."

MISSISSIPPI.

The banner of Mississippi, which preceded a liberal delegation, bore the motto, "Once More To the Rescue —We Honor Him Who Gave up Office for Our Sake."

A band of music here varied the procession; and it was followed by the delegation from

ILLINOIS.

The banner was inscribed, "She will Teach Palace Slaves to Respect the Log Cabin;" at the base, "The Prairies Are on Fire!"

ALABAMA.

This delegation followed under the banner of their State with the pithy motto, "She will Soon Renounce Allegiance to a King."

MAINE.

The delegation from Maine was very full. A fine body of men supported the banner which bore the apt sentences, "Her Honor is Our Honor—Her Quarrel Shall be Our Quarrel."

MISSOURI.

From this State the delegates followed their banner, which was inscribed, "Missouri Remembers her Early Friend."

MICHIGAN.

The delegation was limited in number, but not the less welcome on that account. The banner had the motto, "Oh May'st Thou Ever Be what Thou Now Art." a sentence to which we all respond, amen.

ARKANSAS.

From this State there was a small delegation to unite with their brethren in the distinguished honors of a day that will ever be brilliant in the civil annals of American history. Under a banner with the words, "We Remember Him Who Gave Up Office for Our Sake."

BALTIMORE CITY TIPPECANOE CLUBS,

Came next, from the First to the Twelfth ward, inclusive.

The club of each ward had an appropriate banner.

As the procession moved on through the city and stretched out a lengthened line, the array was most imposing. Such an immense concourse moving like an "army with banners," never before on such an occasion thronged the avenues; while from one end of the mighty column to the other loud acclamations ran, renewed from rank to rank, and bespeaking the strong enthusiasm which prevailed in every heart. Baltimore street was one long gallery of beauty. Innumerable white handkerchiefs waved by fair hands greeted each advancing pennon, and to the waving of handkerchiefs and to smiles, and bright glances from the windows, the young Whigs returned loud cheers with uplifted hats. It may be safely calculated that for every three rounds given for the Whig cause generally, one was especially devoted to the ladies of Baltimore. From Baltimore street bridge the view of the coming procession was in the highest degree striking, and gave a very comprehensive sight of the multitude, inasmuch as from Cove street to this point the avenue is perfectly straight, while a slight elevation at the bridge afforded a commanding view of the whole distance westward. The wide thoroughfare of Baltimore street, viewed from that point, seemed wedged by a solid mass of men, and no end could be seen to the lengthened column. The extent of the procession could not have been less than two miles, marching in platoons six to ten abreast.

Throughout the whole course of the procession as far as the extremity of the city, the most cheering demonstrations were given from windows, doors, and crowded balconies. In several of the streets flags and mottoes were suspended across, and on one house in Market street F. P. a splendid oil painting of General Harrison was suspended amidst patriotic decorations. The procession loudly cheered it as it passed.

In entering the inclosed ground appropriated for

the meeting of the convention, the procession passed
through a triumphal arch decorated with flags. This
spot, known as the Canton race-course, is even and
smooth and covered with a rich grassy sward. On
the right of the entrance stood a log cabin, constructed
in the backwoods style, the crevices between the logs
being well plastered with clay, a stick chimney at each
extremity, and a door well provided with a latch, and
the string outside. Across the lawn at some distance
a representation of Fort Meigs appeared in the shape
of a fortress, with port-holes and guns and surmounted
by the national flag waving gallantly in the breeze, a
sight which required no great stretch of fancy to bring
to mind the thought of the memorable day when the
stars and stripes floated over no emblematical structure amid the smoke and roar of artillery, and the shouts
of brave men fighting valiantly. Towards the western
end of the ground a pavilion rose, inclosing the trunk
of a large tree, above the top of which ascended a flag-
staff bearing the broad banner of the Union.

The invited guests, distinguished strangers, clergy-
men, members of Congress, several Revolutionary soldiers, and others, were conducted to one of the plat-
forms, over which floated the "stars and stripes of
liberty." The other was reserved for the president
and officers of the convention. The various delegations, with banners flying and bands playing, ranged
themselves around, amidst a salute of twenty-six guns
from Fort Meigs. While the extreme of the procession was drawing near the distinguished strangers on
the platform were severally introduced to the assembled
multitude, and greeted with long and deafening
cheers.

Among those who were thus particularly distinguished, were Mr. Henry Clay, Mr. Webster, Mr.
Preston and Mr. Crittenden, of the United States Senate; Mr. Montgomery, of Pennsylvania; Mr. Graves,
of Kentucky; Mr. Cushing, of Massachusetts; Mr.
Grinnell, of New York; Mr. Bond, of Ohio; Mr. Penrose, of Pennsylvania; Mr. Crary, of Michigan; Mr.
Monroe, Mr. Ogden Hoffman, Mr. Carter, Mr. Granger

8

and Mr. Fillmore, of New York; Mr. Corwin, Ohio; Mr. Jenifer, of Maryland; Ex-Governer Howard, Col. G. C. Washington, and some others.

Not the least interesting part of this ceremony was the introduction to the convention from the rostrum of Mr. Ely, of Philadelphia, a soldier of the Revolution, now in the eighty-fourth year of age. As this venerable man, with an energy arising out of the enthusiasm of the occasion, bared his whitened head to the multitude in approval of the cause which they had assembled to promote, a triumphant shout of applause showed how much they valued the presence and approbation of their hoary-headed fellow-citizen.

The Reverend Henry B. Bascom, of Kentucky, then fervently and eloquently addressed the Throne of Divine Grace, after which the Hon. Henry A. Wise, of Virginia, introduced John B. Thompson, Esq., of Kentucky, the chairman of the committee of chairmen of the several delegations represented, by whom the convention was called to order. Mr. Thompson, on behalf of the same committee, then announced the following nominations for president, vice-presidents and secretaries, which nominations were agreed to by acclamation.

President: John V. L. McMahon, of Maryland.

Vice-Presidents: W. Willis, of Maine; J. W. Emory, of New Hampshire; R. Babcock, Jr., of Rhode Island; J. B. Eldridge, of Connecticut; Charles Hopkins, of Vermont; Thomas E. Sawyer, of New Hampshire; D. P. King, of Massachusetts; J. N. Reynolds, of New York; J. M. Keim, of Pennsylvania; Charles H. Black, of Delaware; William Irick, of New Jersey; A. Wilson, of Virginia; T. O. Edwards, of Ohio; J. H. Crozier, of Tennessee; G. R. Clark, of Missouri; J. Dillet, of Alabama; G. Mason Graham, of Louisana; J. H. Wright, of Indiana, J. Constable, of Illinois; J. R. Gilliam, of North Carolina; Thomas Allen, of District of Columbia; F. M. Robertson, of Georgia; R. Wickliffe, Jr., of Kentucky; M. Gooding, of Michigan; Henry Page, of Maryland; Edward Gamage, of South Carolina.

SECRETARIES.

M. S. Appleton, of Maine; S. E. Garfield, Jr., of New Hampshire; B. C. Hill, of Rhode Island; Austin Baldwin, of Connecticut: E. P. Walton, Jr., of Vermont; E. G. Austin, of Massachusetts; Alexander Kelsey, of New York; J. Wash. Tyson, of Pennsylvania; J. Burton, of Delaware; Jos. H. Nicholson, of Maryland; N. J. Winder of Virginia; J. A. Corwin, of Ohio; C. C. Norvell, of Tennessee; J. White, of Missouri; W. S. Oliver, of Alabama; J. Warfield, of Louisiana; John Hutton, of Indiana; C. J. Randall, of Illinois; W. M'Phitees, of North Carolina; A. C. M. Pennington, of New Jersey; George Dawson, of Michigan; R. L. Brent, of District of Columbia; F. Cooper, of Kentucky; J. E. Harvey, of South Carolina; R. Clarke, of Georgia.

' The following resolutions, recommended to the adoption of the convention by the committee of chairmen, were then read by Mr. Thompson of the committee, and unanimously adopted:

Resolved, By the Convention of the Whig Young Men assembled at Baltimore, the fourth day of May, 1840, that the nomination of William Henry Harrison, of Ohio, for the office of President of the United States, and of John Tyler, of Virginia, for the office of Vice-President of the United States, by the late Whig convention at Harrisburg, is hereby cordially approved and ratified, and earnestly recommended to the support of the people of the United States.

Resolved, That to sustain the said nomination, the young men of the Union should unite their zeal, enthusiasm, and vigor, to the wisdom, experience and judgment of their seniors; and to insure its triumph and success, they should immediately adopt, thorough and efficient organization.

Resolved, That for that purpose it be recommended to Democratic Whigs everywhere to form Democratic Tippecanoe clubs, or Harrison associations, in the respective towns, counties and cities of the States which shall establish and maintain an active political correspondence, and procure and circulate political information.

Resolved, That these clubs and associations, when formed, shall select and appoint the ablest and most efficient orators to address the people on all proper occasions, as may be deemed advisable, to proclaim the truths of Republican liberty, and to expose the abuses and corruptions of a spoils party which would enslave the people by an odious and insufferable Federal despotism in the form of an unchecked and unbalanced executive, arrogantly assuming the purse, dictating laws of revenue and finance, recommending standing armies in time of peace, demolishing the co-ordinate departments of the Federal Government, proscribing individual citizens, and daringly attacking the rights and sovereignty of the States.

Resolved, That we will not yield or relax until the great work of reform and of redress of grievances be finished; and to insure perseverance to the end of this noble but arduous struggle for civil and political liberty, we will meet in our clubs at stated times, regularly; we will print and publish useful matter; we will address ourselves in every reasonable and respectful form to our fellow-countrymen; and, finally, we will immediately preceding the Presidential election in the fall, at such times as the central clubs of the respective States may appoint, assemble in State conventions throughout the Union to consider of preparations for the coming contest.

Resolved, That to carry out these resolutions the " Republican Committee of Seventy-six," appointed by opponents of the present administration, at public meetings in the city of Washington, February 15th and 18th, 1840, and the " Young Men's Committee of Forty-one" be, and the same are hereby, constituted the central Democratic Tippecanoe club of the Union; and the central Whig committee of the States, respectively, be, and they are hereby, constituted the Democratic Tippecanoe clubs or Harrison associations, whose duty it shall be to correspond immediately for the formation of city, town and county clubs, and to superintend all the other interests of the great and glorious cause, to which we here pledge our dearest devotion and most patriotic exertions.

Resolved, That it be recommended to each delegation to raise a free contribution of one dollar from each of its members to support the opposition press at the city of Washington, and generally to oppose the tyrannical tax upon the office-holders of the Presidential party.

Resolved, That the fund thus raised shall be placed in the hands of the executive committee of Seventy-six at Washington.

These resolutions were unanimously adopted by the convention, and the following was then offered and adopted also:

Resolved, That the president of this convention be requested to call on the several States, through their vice-presidents, for brief statements of their present political condition and prospects.

In pursuance of this resolution, the president of the convention severally called on the following gentlemen, who addressed the convention in regard to the current of popular opinion in their several States, the ruin of business and destruction of trade growing out of the measures of the administration, the necessity that was felt for a change, and the conviction experienced that nothing but the election of General Harrison could arrest the disasters that threatened to overwhelm them. The names of the speakers were:

Mr. Babcock, of Rhode Island.

Mr. Eldridge, of Connecticut.

Mr. Clarke, of Missouri.

Governor Duncan, of Illinois.

Mr. Emory, of New Hampshire.

The Hon. Henry A. Wise was called for, and appearing at the front of the stand, thanked the convention for the honor they had done him, and assured them that it would afford him great pleasure to address them on an occasion so deeply interesting to his feelings. He was sorry to say that the state of his health would not permit such an effort. On Saturday last he had almost worn himself down in addressing twenty-five hundred of his fellow-citizens of Delaware, and he now found himself totally inadequate to the task of addressing twenty-five thousand. He hoped, however, that his health would improve, and that he should yet be able successfully to war against that system of government which had entailed on us so many evils.

The following gentlemen were, by the committee appointed for the purpose, introduced to the thousands who were present. They appeared on the stand in the order in which their names follow:

Henry Clay, Daniel Webster, Messrs. Wise, Hoffman, Preston, Graves, Curtis, Wm. Cost Johnson, Williams, North Carolinia. Fillmore, Saltonstall, Jenifer and Kennedy. Another shout for Clay and Webster brought both of these gentlemen, arm-in-arm, to meet the salutations of the people. Nine cheers greeted them. Then followed Crittenden, of Kentucky; Hall, of Vermont; Colonel Ely, of Philadelphia (who was at the battles of Bunker Hill and Lexington); ex-Governor Thomas and Colonel Washington, of Maryland, and numerous other distinguished gentlemen, all of whom were recognized and welcomed by the thousands of men determined to be free, assembled from the sea-shore and the mountain-top.

"OLD MASSACHUSETTS."

Daniel B. King spoke for the "Old Bay State." Twelve hundred men had come 500 miles to represent her. He told the people that her present governor had been elected by only *one* majority, but that he should go out by a vote of ten thousand majority against him.

NEW YORK,

The Empire State. Mr. Reynolds, of her delegation, said that all who knew her history for three years past required no pledge of her devotion to the cause of "Harrison and reform." "Wake her up at two o'clock in the morning, and she can, whilst rubbing her eyes, vote down Martin Van Buren."

VERMONT.

Mr. Hopkins said the "Green Mountain boys" had a thousand majority for Harrison, and that they could "do their own voting and fighting."

PENNSYLVANIA,

The Keystone State. Mr. Brady proclaimed that next fall Pennsylvania should be found "right side up," that "she never was a Van Buren State." That "when Van Buren was a candidate for the Vice-Presidency, she threw away her vote rather than to vote for him." He pledged that she would give 20,000 majority for old Tippecanoe at the next Presidential election.

Mr. Southard, for the "Jersey Blues," said they were not yet subdued. "She was not depressed in the Revolution, she was not depressed now. When she speaks again it will be in no small voice, and she will teach a lesson to the wretched men who have dared to insult her they will never forget.

"Corruption," said Mr. Southard, "has made the party in power deaf, but the noise from Fort Meigs will open their ears."

VIRGINIA.

Mr. Wilson of the "Old Dominion," appeared for her. He said she had just spoken for herself. A shout for Wise brought him out again. Though he was evidently in ill-health, the people were almost crazy to see and hear him. "I have," said Mr. Wise, "been speaking so long against this wicked and corrupt administration, that I have worn out the best pair of lungs ever given to man."

Mr. Edwards from Ohio, the Buckeye State, remarked that as speeches were all the go, he would give a song. And he did so, and a good speech also. He said they had a barrel of hard cider to bet that Ohio would give the largest majority for Harrison of any State in the Union. Who'll take that bet?

Mr. Humes, of Tennessee, was in mourning for Hugh Lawson White. He commenced by remarking that "On the mountains of Tennessee, the Whig fires were blazing." When he spoke in memory of Judge White, who, he stated had "died a martyr to freedom," the convention felt the justness and propriety of the remark.

Ex-Governor Duncan, from Illinois, appeared for that noble State. When he said the "Prairies were on fire" and that the alarm was sounded, the shout of the multitude responded to the declaration that Van Burenism was extinguished in that "Jackson State." Said Governor Duncan, she was formerly Jackson and Van Buren, the latter of whom is now entirely repudiated, so ruinous are the measures of his administration.

While the gentlemen mentioned above were addressing the convention, a portion of the delegations withdrew to the side of the second rostrum, and called upon several of the gentlemen upon it, who successively addressed them.

The first speaker was Mr. Clay, a sketch of whose address we subjoin.

MR. CLAY'S ADDRESS.

Mr. Clay commenced by reference to the northwest wind, which blew almost a gale, and compared it happily to the popular voice of the immense multitude who were present. Difficult as it was to be heard by such a throng, he said he could not refrain from obeying the general summons and responding to the call. He was truly grateful for the honor conferred upon him. "This," said he, "is no time to argue; the time for discussion has passed; the nation has already pronounced its sentence. I behold here the advance guard. A revolution by the grace of God and the will of the people will be achieved. William Henry Harrison will be elected President of the United States.

"We behold," continued Mr. Clay, in his emphatic and eloquent manner, "the ravages brought upon our country under the revolutionary administrations of the present and the past. We see them in a disturbed country, in broken hopes, in deranged exchanges, in the mutilation of the highest Constitutional records of the country. All these are the fruits of the party in power, and a part of that revolution which has been in progress for the last ten years. But this party," Mr. Clay thought he could say, "had been or was demolished. As it had demolished the institutions of the country, so it had fallen itself. As institution after institution had fallen by it; and with them interest after interest, until a general and wide-spread ruin had come upon the country, so now the revolution was to end in the destruction of the party and the principles which had been instrumental in our national sufferings.

"This," said Mr. Clay, "is a proud day for the patriot. It animated his own bosom with hope, and I," he added, "am here to mingle my hopes with yours, my heart with yours, and my exertions with your exertions. Our enemies hope to conquer us, but they are deluded and doomed to disappointment."

Mr. Clay then alluded most happily, and amid the cheers of all around him, to the union of the Whigs. "We are," said he, "all Whigs: we are all Harrison men. We are united. We must triumph.

"One word of myself," he said, referring to the national convention which met at Harrisburg in December last. "That convention was composed of as enlightened and as respectable a body of men as were ever assembled in the country. They met, deliberated, and after a full and impartial deliberation, decided that William Henry Harrison was the man best calculated to unite the Whigs of the Union against the present executive. General Harrison was nominated, and cheerfully and without a moment's hesitation I gave my hearty concurrence in that nomination. From that moment to the present, I have had but one wish, one object, one desire, and that to secure the election of the distinguished citizen who received the suffrages of the convention.

"Allow me here to say," continued Mr. Clay, "that his election is certain. This I say, not in any boasting or over-confident sense; far from it. But I feel sure

that there are **twenty States who** will give their votes
for Harrison. Do not the glories of this day authorize
the anticipation of **such a victory?** I behold before
me more than **twenty thousand freemen, and is it an-
ticipating too much to say that such an assembly as this
is a sign ominous of triumph?**"

Mr. Clay then warned his friends of two great errors
in political warfare—too much confidence and too
much despondency. Both were to be feared. There
should be no relaxation. The enemy were yet powerful in numbers and strong in organization. It became
the Whigs, **therefore, to abstain from no** laudable exertion **necessary to success.** Should we fail, he added,
should Mr. Van. Buren be re-elected, **which** calamity
God avert, **though he would be the last man** to despair
of the Republic, **he believed the struggle of** restoring
the country to its former glory **would be almost** a hopeless one. **That calamity, however, or the** alternative,
**was left with the twenty thousand Whigs here assem-
bled.**

"**We received our liberty.**" said Mr. Clay in conclusion, "**from our Revolutionary** ancestors, and we are
bound in all honor to transfer it unimpaired to our
posterity. The breeze which this day blows from the
right **quarter is the promise of that** popular breeze
which will **defeat our** adversaries and make **William
Henry Harrison the President of the United** States."

Mr. Webster was now loudly called for, and addressed the multitude from another quarter of the
stage to the following effect:

Mr. Webster said that he "feared the attempt to make
himself heard would be a vain one. Never before
had the land in which we lived seen a spectacle like
the present. We count **men by the** thousands, and
**they are here from the borders of Canada and the
rivers of Georgia. They are here from** the sea-coast
and the heart of the country. **The States are here—**
every **one of them** through their representatives. The
'Old **Thirteen' of the** Republic are here from every

city and every county, between the hills of Vermont
and the rivers of the South. The new thirteen, too,
are here, without a blot or stain upon them. The
twenty-six States are here. No local or limited feeling
has brought them here—no feeling but an American
one—a hearty attachment to the country. We are
here with the common sentiment and the common
feeling that we are one people. We may assure
ourselves that we belong to a country where one part
has a common feeling and a common interest with the
other.

" The time has come," continued Mr. Webster, "when
the cry is change. Every breeze says change. Every
interest of the country demands it. The watchword
and the hope of the people is that William Henry
Harrison should be placed at the head of affairs. We
may assure ourselves," said Mr. Webster, "that this
change will come—come to give joy to the many, and
sorrow only to the few. Mr. Van Buren's administration is to be of one term and of one project, and that
project, new to us, not yet consummated. It is new to
our country, and so novel that those with whom it
originated, after hammering it for years, have not been
able to give form or shape to the substance.

"All agree," continued Mr. Webster, "that we have hard
times, and many," he amusingly remarked, "supposed
the remedy to be hard cider." Changing his subject and
his manner, he exhorted in a strong and stentorian
voice the members of the convention to go hence fully
impressed with a solemn sense of the obligations they
owed to the country. "We were called upon to accomplish not a momentary victory, but one which should
last at least half a century. It was not to be expected
that every year, or every four years, would bring
together such an assemblage as we have now before us.
The revolution should be one which should last for
years, and the benefits of which should be felt forever.
Let us, then, act with firmness. Let us give up ourselves entirely to this new revolution. When we see
the morning light grow bright, it is the sign of the
noon-day sun. This sign around me is no less lumin-

ous of the brightness which is to succeed the present rays of light.

"Go to your work, then," said Mr. Webster, in conclusion;" "I will return to mine. When next we meet, and wherever we meet, I hope to say that this Convention has been the means of good to you and to me and to all. I go to my appropriate sphere and you to yours—each to act, I trust, for the good of the country in the advancement of the cause we all have so much at heart."

Mr. Webster retired, as Mr. Clay did, amidst the plaudits of the thousands in hearing.

Mr. John Sergeant, of Pennsylvania, succeeded Mr. Webster upon the rostrum. "What have you come here for?" said Mr. Sergeant. "I will answer. To bring back to the people, and through the log cabins of the country the neglected and lost Constitution. In the man you have selected for your suffrages, you have one possessing those qualifications in which the head of this administration is most deficient—political integrity. He is the disciple of Washington—of his school and of his instruction. In his hands the country will be safe, that which has been lost, in him will be found again. The unjust and unskillful men in power have run our national engine from the track made by George Washington. He, the father of the Republic, left good advice to his successors, but some of them, alas! have disregarded it, and driven this engine from the track.

"It is for the disciple of Washington to place it on again. As Harrison received from Washington lessons of wisdom which he regarded when young, so he will maintain them when called, like Washington, to maintain the honor of the country. No change," said Mr. Sergeant, "can be for the worse. Through Harrison we shall be brought to safety. In the history of the world there is hardly a calamity recorded greater than our own in the mal-administration of public officers. In war there has been no greater calamity.

"Let us, then, go back as near as we can to the times of that illustrious man, George Washington, whom General Harrison, both in his private and public life, so much resembles. Washington when a young man was a surveyor. Harrison when quite a youth was a pioneer in the wilderness and a companion of the brave General Wayne. It was the name of Harrison which had brought more than twenty thousand people here; of Harrison who had fought and gained the battle of the country. The people will elect him, for he is the candidate of the people."

The Hon. William C. Preston, the eloquent and distinguished senator from South Carolina, next responded to the call of the convention. " This," said he, "is the happiest day of my life. I see here the consummation of almost all that I had hoped for from the earliest day I entered public life. I hate tyranny, and from my infancy was taught to despise a Tory. I was born a Whig, and am yet a Whig. The Whigs have met here," continued Mr. Preston, "to bring peace and prosperity to the land, and I take pleasure in expressing the belief that the man of their choice will maintain and strengthen and consolidate the great national institutions and enterprises of the country."

Continuing his remarks, Mr. Preston alluded to the self-denying, magnanimous and patriotic conduct of Henry Clay. The eulogium was the most eloquent we have heard, and the audience heard it with interest and delight. Returning to General Harrison, he said, " I will devote to him my labor, my thoughts, my person and my purse. I regard the Ohio farmer as a true and devoted patriot, and I would the news of this day's meeting could be borne to him upon the wings of the wind."

Mr. Preston, in concluding his remaks, said he was a Southern man, and happily, in connection with this subject, did he allude to the recent demonstration of opinion from the " Old Dominion." "Harrison, too," he was proud to say, "was a Virginian born and a son of a signer of the Declaration of Independence. He sprung, too, from the best of the Anglo Saxon blood. He was a descendant of that Harrison who, in the reign of the tyrant Charles, said that 'as he was a tyrant I slew him." Who," said Mr. Preston, "can boast of better

blood in his veins than this descendant of the king-de-
stroying, despot-killing, tyrant-hating Harrison?"

Mr. Preston, in a manner peculiar to himself, after
exhorting the Whigs to use their anticipated triumph
as not abusing it, left the grave for a moment for the
gay. "Alas, poor Democrats! farewell, dear Loco
Focos! you have had your day. Every dog has his
day! It is necessary, Mr. Van Buren, that you should
go for diminished wages, and the country says you shall
go for diminished wages!" Again, Mr. Preston drew a
happy picture of the 4th of March, 1841. He supposed
that Prince of Democrats, Martin Van Buren, to be
here in his coach and four horses. Following him
comes Amos Kendall, and succeeding him Levi Woodbury with his empty bags, and still behind these worthies, the head of the War Department, Mr. Poinsett, the
author of the system for two hundred thousand militia
and thirty-four bloodhounds. "I see them now," said
Mr. Preston, "in my mind's eye. They come from
Washington, are seen at Fell's Point, now at Canton,
and some one says to the party, there is the race-course
where met the national convention in May last."

Again Mr. Preston changed his manner and in a
burst of eloquence which electrified his hearers, exhorted them to go into the possession of the administration of public affairs with clean hands and honest
hearts; and first of all to proscribe that system of proscription which had dishonored the country. "Let us
wash the ermine and purify the seats of government."
Mr. Preston also made a happy allusion to Cincinnatus
the plowman, citizen and general. In many respects
Harrison was like him, but the spectacle of selecting
the humble American citizen to rule over the nation
was of the moral sublime, and far eclipsed anything in
Grecian or Roman history.

"In General Harrison," said Mr. Preston, in conclusion, "I believe in after time we may be able to say
that the country has a second Washington in the second Harrison. When this day comes, and God speed
the time, for one, I will be content, rest satisfied, leave
the field of labor and say, like one of old, 'Now, Lord,

lettest Thy servant depart in peace, for mine eyes have seen Thy glory.'"

Mr. Preston was followed by Hon. S. Southard, of New Jersey, who made a brief and eloquent address. His allusions to New Jersey were very happy, and we regret that we are without room to publish them.

Mr. Graves, of Kentucky, followed with a forcible and stirring appeal. Others would have spoken, but the hour admonished an adjournment.

The president then announced that the lateness of the hour and the fatigue which they had undergone rendered it necessary to suspend further proceedings for the day, and he submitted a motion that the convention adjourn to meet on Tuesday morning, 5th inst., in Monument Square, at nine o'clock.

The convention adjourned accordingly, at 4 o'clock.

MEETING IN MONUMENT SQUARE TUESDAY, MAY 5, 1840.

Monument square was thronged through the morning and the day. The president of the convention, John V. L. McMahon, Esq., presided with great dignity, and perfect order prevailed among the mass.

Pursuant to the adjournment of yesterday, thousands assembled to hear the further deliberations of the convention.

The crowd was so great that it was impossible for those on the outskirts to hear the speakers from the rostrum elevated in front of the court-house, and a separate rostrum being erected, several distinguished Whigs came forward at the call of the people and addressed them from it.

Mr. McMahon, the president of the convention, announced that in furtherance of the resolution adopted yesterday, the several vice-presidents or other persons representing them from the several States, would inform them of the prospects of the Whig party in the State from whence they came, and be accordingly introduced:

Mr. Dillett, Alabama ; Mr. Thompson, Delaware ; Mr. Stanley, North Carolina; Mr. Willis, Maine, Mr. Graham, Louisiana ; Mr. Wickliffe, Kentucky; Mr.

Allen, District of Columbia; Mr. Robertson, Georgia;
Mr. Emory, New Hampshire; Mr. Proffit, Indiana;
Mr. Dawson, Micnigan; Mr. Bryan, South Carolina;
Mr. Tyler (a grand-son of General Putnam), Connecticut; ———, Rhode Island; Mr. Wise, Virginia;
Mr. Stannard, Virginia, who addressed the convention
with great power and effect. Their speeches were responded to by repeated cheers from the assembled
multitude, who presented a living mass covering a
large space of ground as far as the voice could reach,
and who remained upon the ground from early in the
morning until the convention adjourned for dinner.

INDIANA.

Mr. Proffit spoke eloquently and effectively for this
State. He called upon the Whigs of the Union to
reason mildly and kindly with their political opponents. He said the patriotism of the American people
was sound to the core, and he earnestly hoped every
delegate to this convention would go to his home and
endeavor to reason with and conciliate his neighbor.
Such a course, and such a course only, was the proper
one. Whilst he lived he was for the Whigs.

NEW YORK.

Mr. King spoke eloquently this morning for those
he represented. "All the local differences of that State
were settled," said Mr. King, "and she would, on the
day of election, be foremost in the ranks."

OHIO.

Mr. Frazier said he was from North Bend, Harrison's own log cabin, where the string of the latch was
never pulled in, and if he were Loco Foco to the core,
he would be compelled to hurrah for Harrison's military achievements, as he used, when a boy, to hurrah
for General Jackson. In his county, at the recent election, there were sixty-four Van Buren candidates, only
one of whom was elected, and he avowed afterwards
that he was elected by Whig votes.

KENTUCKY.

Governor Pope, of Kentucky, being called for, addressed the assemblage for a considerable length of

time, in a peculiarly happy manner. He said he was once a Jackson man, but that he "had now come to atone for past mistakes."

The speaking went on during the day from several stands. We can but briefly refer to the speakers.

Among the members of Congress were Henry Clay and Wm. C. Preston, of the Senate

Both of these distinguished gentlemen spoke with that feeling of popular enthusiasm to be expected from the cheering signs and congratulations around them.

Mr. Clay was received with enthusiastic demonstrations of applause, and his stirring appeals and forcible pictures of the sad experiments brought upon the country, prompted a response in every bosom.

Mr. Preston, of South Carolina, was hardly less eloquent than on Monday, and none the less interesting to those who heard him, for many now heard him for the first time.

Mr. Legare, of South Carolina, also made an eloquent and spirited address. Few men in the country have more power to interest, and no one has a more brilliant imagination with which to illustrate the good or bad principles of a government.

Mr. Stanley, of North Carolina, spoke eloquently from the court-house rostrum, and after a stirring address of an hour, the cry was, " On, Stanley, on!"

Henry A. Wise, of Virginia, was also called for, and introduced to the convention by the president. The appearance of the bold and talented Virginian was responded to by the thousands present in loud and repeated cheers. Mr. Wise, though much indisposed, spoke with great energy and power, and especially in reference to the many national peculiarities of his own district, one of the most national of the Old Dominion. "There Harrison and Tyler both were born. There, too, old Ben. Harrison, the signer of the Declaration of Independence, and Patrick Henry, the renowned champion of our national independence, had their homes. There also was fought the last naval battle of the Revolution, and there sprung up Bacon's rebellion. The history of the district was eventful, and it was a Whig

9

district. The Old Dominion, God bless her! had now
joined his district, and Virginia was a Whig State,
ready to give her electoral vote to William Henry Harrison and John Tyler." Mr. Wise spoke eloquently and
with great effect. Retiring, he was greeted with the
hearty and unanimous applause of the convention.

Mr. Willis, of Maine, was introduced to the assembled thousands by the president, and as one of the
vice-presidents, gave a good account of the Northeast
State. In the name of the Whigs of Maine he
promised ten electoral votes for Harrison and Tyler
upon the "ides of November."

No less interesting were the speech and pledge
given by Mr. Graham, another vice-president, from
the State of Louisiana. He, too, promised the electoral
vote of the Southwestern border State for Harrison
and Tyler.

Mr. Allen, of the District of Columbia, made a
report of the popular movements in the District, and
gave his reasons for the demonstration of public feeling among a people who are unjustly deprived of the
right of suffrage.

Mr. J. N. Emory spoke for New Hampshire. The
work in the Granite State, he said, was an up-hill
business, but the delegates here present would promise
at least a spirited contest.

Mr. E. S. Thomas from North Bend, Ohio, and
formerly of Baltimore, made a spirited address, and
many happy illustrations drawn from the history of
the Government and the times.

Mr. Reynolds, of New York city, delighted his
hearers with a sensible and practical address upon the
character and importance of the contest.

Mr. Robertson, of Georgia, a true Southron, spoke
eloquently of Georgia. His address was brief, and
one of the best made in the convention. "Georgia,"
he said, "was awake to the importance of the coming
contest, and the fires kindled within her were of her
own irresistible and spontaneous lighting."

Mr. Wickliffe, of Kentucky; Mr. Bryan, of South
Carolina; Mr. Dawson, of Michigan; Mr. Tyler, of

Connecticut: Mr. Proffit, of Indiana, Mr. Thompson, of Delaware; Mr. Stannard, of Virginia, and others also spoke, but in the crowd it was impossible to hear the names of half who spoke or of the thousandth of what was said.

Mr. Penrose, of Pennsylvania, offered the following resolutions, which were seconded by Mr. Myers, of the same State, and unanimously adopted:

Resolved, That the delegates from each State represented in this convention be, and they are hereby, requested to raise by contribution of not exceeding one dollar for each person, a sum of money for the use of the bereaved family of Thomas H. Laughlin, carpenter, of the Eighth ward of the city of Baltimore, and a member of the convention, who was killed in the procession of yesterday, while in the exercise of the undoubted right of freemen peaceably to assemble and deliberate upon the conduct of the officers of government, "a right inestimable to them and formidable to tyrants only."

Resolved, That the sum so raised be paid to the president of the convention, to be by him applied for the relief of the widow and children of our deceased fellow member, to whom we hereby tender our condolence for his death in the glorious cause of his country.

At the close of the addresses the convention unanimously resolved to attend the funeral of the lamented Laughlin, at four o'clock in the afternoon.

The convention then adjourned until 5 o'clock P. M.

FUNERAL OF THOMAS H. LAUGHLIN.

The solemn duty of committing the remains of Mr. Laughlin to the grave was performed by the delegates to the convention in a body. The procession, accompanied by a band of music playing a dead march, moved from the late residence of the deceased, at the corner of Light street and Guilford alley, between 4 and 5 o'clock, P. M., to the burial ground of the Methodist Episcopal congregation. The chief marshal of the convention, Capt. James O. Law, supported the weeping and bereaved widow of the deceased from the carriage to the grave, where her condition was most pitiable, as she stood convulsed with an agony of grief at her sudden and irreparable loss. The ceremonies, by the officiating clergyman, Dr. Baker, of New York, were brief and impressive, at the close of which the immense concourse returned to the city.

AFTERNOON.

At five o'clock the convention reassembled. The president having taken the chair, the committee of chairmen of the State delegations reported the following resolution, which was seconded and advocated by Mr. C. L. Talfourd, of Ohio, and unanimously agreed to. The speech of Mr. Talfourd was one of great beauty, exhibiting eloquence of the highest order, and drew from the crowd loud, repeated and enthusiastic cheers:

Resolved, That the president be directed to transmit to Gen. William Henry Harrison and John Tyler, the compliments of this convention, together with a copy of its proceedings, signed by the president and secretaries.

The people called for more speakers, and thereupon the vast assemblage was severally addressed by distinguished gentlemen from the different States.

Mr. Bradford, of Baltimore city, said it required stronger nerves and cooler blood than his to withstand the enthusiasm of the present occasion. As one of the delegation from Baltimore, he had intended to remain silent and listen to his brethren from abroad; but his bosom was full of the inspiration which he had caught from the scenes before him, and he could no longer hold his peace. His speech throughout was full of thrilling and patriotic sentiments, expressed with force and listened to with attention.

Mr. S. T. Hurd, of Ohio, followed in an eloquent and effective speech, some portions of which were particularly sarcastic and amusing.

"After listening," said Mr. Hurd, "to the eloquent speeches of the most talented men in the nation, he had lost all confidence in his ability to entertain, for a single moment, the vast assemblage before him. They had been hearing big guns; he could not hope to entertain them with a mere pistol shot. But when called to raise his voice on an occasion like this, he would not shrink from a duty which he owed to those who had sent him here, because he might not be able to perform his duty so acceptably as others."

He "felt proud to stand there as the representative of a portion of that State which would claim the distinguished honor of 'offering her Cincinnatus to redeem the Republic,' and in and near which were laid the scenes of many of his brilliant achievements.

His brother delegates from the Buckeye State had given "eloquent and stirring accounts of her southern and central counties, and it devolved upon him to say a word for old Cuyahoga, who never slumbered at home; and he would be sorry to find her napping here. She and her sister counties, constituting the ' Western Reserve,' of which he could speak more definitely than of other portions of the State, were 'under bonds' to give 'Old Tip' a heavy majority in the coming contest. No one could calculate on the number that might slip the collar between this and November."

He knew of "many in his vicinity whose necks had become so sore from wearing the iron collar of the administration that they found it extremely difficult to swallow their accustomed doses of Loco Focoism. They began to acknowledge that they felt also an extreme pressure about the chest. The doctors had recommended Harrison plasters (not shin plasters) applied to the parts affected, and think they will find perfect relief by the fourth of March next.

Mr. Hurd retired from the stand amid the deafening cheers of the immense multitude, and was succeeded by Mr. Grund, of Philadelphia, who stated that "he was a native German; that like others of his countrymen, he had come here from his native land, with a bosom swelling with the love of liberty. There was a charm in the name of Democracy—that name had long deceived his countrymen who had emigrated hither, but thank God, the scales were falling from their eyes, and they were beginning to distinguish between the substance and the shadow. The Germans in his vicinity were coming over by hundreds to the Harrison standard. He had been the political friend and the biographer in German and English of Martin Van Buren. He was now the friend and biographer of General Harrison".

Mr. English, of Philadelphia, next took the stand. "He had," he said, "heretofore been a supporter of the administration of General Jackson and Martin Van Buren;" he had "listened to their promises of retrenchment and reform;" he had "pondered upon the seductive arguments which the party had put forth to gull and deceive the people;" he had "witnessed the manner in which those promises had been fulfilled, or rather in which they had failed; and, as a true American and friend of his country, he could no longer wink at the corruptions of the present administration."

The committee of chairmen of the State delegations also submitted the following resolutions, which were seconded by Mr. McQuern, of North Carolina, and unanimously adopted by the convention:

Resolved, That the members of this convention entertain a most grateful sense of the generous hospitality of the citizens of Baltimore, who have, by receiving us as guests, evinced their devotion to the cause in which we are engaged, and given to the country another evidence of their enlightened and zealous patriotism; and that we shall return to our homes cheered by their confidence and resolved individually to imitate their patriotic example.

Resolved, That the generous liberality, the untiring devotion, and the judicious plans of the Baltimore committee of arrangements demand their most hearty acknowledgments.

The president having temporarily retired from the chair, Mr. Gill, of Ohio, on behalf of the committee of chairmen, offered the following resolution; which was adopted by acclamation:

Resolved, That the unanimous thanks of this convention be and they are hereby tendered to John V. L.

McMahon, Esq., president of the convention, for the prompt, dignified and successful manner in which he has presided over its deliberations.

After the adoption of this resolution, Mr. McMahon again appeared before the people, and expressed his acknowledgments for the distinguished honor which had been conferred upon him in elevating him to the dignity of presiding over this convention of the *elite* of the young men of our country, and for the additional mark of kindness which had been shown in the adoption of the last resolution. He then proceeded to address the large assemblage before him with a fervor and energy of eloquence, which, we believe, he never surpassed; and which called forth, at every sentence, the most rapturous and hearty applause. He closed by saying that as the organ of the convention, he had hitherto not felt at liberty to present any resolution or proposition of his own, but now as they were about to separate, after two days spent in such a manner that would long make every member recall the recollections of this time with a glow of pleasure and pride; and as he sincerely wished that all those now before him should meet together once more in this world, he would submit for their adoption a resolution that when this convention adjourns, it should adjourn to meet in Washington on the 4th day of March, 1841, to attend the inauguration of President William Henry Harrison. This resolution, we need scarcely say, was adopted unanimously, and amidst the most enthusiastic cheering. The convention then adjourned.

OTHER MEETINGS AND INCIDENTS.

After the adjournment of the great meeting on Monday at the Canton ground, a large number, consisting of portions of various delegations, guests at the Eutaw House, spent the remainder of the afternoon in the social enjoyments of the table, rendered doubly refreshing by the active exercise and excitement of the previous part of the day. After the cloth was removed, General McDonald, of Virginia, was called to the chair, and at his right was placed Mr.

Horner, of New Jersey, who was introduced to the company as the gentleman who, at the Harrisburg convention, last December, offered the resolution which gave birth to the Young Men's Whig Convention of the 4th of May in Baltimore.

Upon this announcement, the company all rose and received Mr. Horner with cheers. The toasts, speeches, and songs were all good, and were worthy of being specially particularized, if the means were at hand of preserving them. The Hon. C. B. Penrose, of Pennsylvania, being present, a toast was offered alluding to him as a Pennsylvania senator, expelled by lawless violence from the senate chamber. In reply to this toast, Mr. Penrose spoke with great eloquence. He referred to the incident alluded to in the toast, and spoke of it as an act perpetrated by the same hand which had recently obliterated New Jersey from the galaxy of States, and which before had expunged the sacred record of the Senate of the United States. He dwelt upon the fearful prevalence of the spirit thus rife throughout the land, and threatening destruction to all principles of Constitutional liberty, dear to every true American heart. Mr. Penrose spoke twice during the festival, being called up by special allusions, and in both addresses he gave an able exposition of the Democratic-Whig principles which are the real basis of the present organized opposition to the administration. In reference to his own course during the Harrisburg riots, he showed how his conduct had been in strict accordance with the law of the Commonwealth. He spoke of the state of feeling now prevailing in Pennsylvania; of the great reaction which was going on among the sensible yeomanry of that State. "Virginia and Pennsylvania," said Mr. Penrose, "have always gone together; and now that the Old Dominion has thrown off the yoke, the hour of Pennsylvania's deliverance is at hand.

Speeches were made by gentlemen from Alabama, Tennessee, New Jersey and other States, according as delegates from abroad happened to be present, the whole affair being without previous arrangement and

most of the company being strangers personally to one
another. Yet, as each knew his neighbors to be good
Whigs, it was not long before a cordial fellowship
united all in excellent concord and good humor, so that
everything passed off in a very spirited manner. There
were no doubt similar festivals in other parts of the
city, the particulars of which, if known, would tend
still further to give some adequate idea of the general
state of things existing in the city during the last few
days.

AND STILL THE PEOPLE CALL FOR MORE SPEECHES.

Tuesday evening about 7 o'clock Monument Square
was again filled with an assemblage of five or six
thousand, consisting of large detachments from the
different delegations and citizens, all animated by the
same desire to hear the distinguished speakers whom the
occasion has brought here, which they had displayed
the foregoing day.

They were successively addressed by a number of
gentlemen. Among the speakers were Mr. Wickliffe,
Jr., of Kentucky; Mr. Patterson, of New York: Mr.
Crittenden, of Kentucky; Mr. Bell, of Tennessee; Mr.
A. W. Bradford, Mr. Charles H. Pitts, Mr. Wallis, Mr.
Jenifer and Mr. Pope, of Kentucky. Mr. Reverdy
Johnson closed the series of speeches with a most vig-
orous and eloquent address, and the assemblage dis-
persed to their several quarters about 11 o'clock.

THE MURDER OF LAUGHLIN.

The circumstances connected with the killing of
Laughlin show the malicious and vicious opposition
to General Harrison, and hence we copy the following
from the Baltimore *American* of May 6, 1840:

"The shocking outrage which was perpetrated last
Monday on a respectable citizen of Baltimore, employed in the lawful exercise of his rights as a freeman, will awaken a feeling of just and strong indignation, if we mistake not, throughout the whole country.
The *Sun* of yesterday, whose account corresponds
with the facts of the case so far as we have been able
to ascertain them, says:

"'The particulars of this melancholy and disgraceful affair, are these: As the procession was proceeding down Baltimore street, a gang of half-grown boys was marching up, carrying on the top of a pole a stuffed figure, representing General Harrison as a petticoat hero, and when they arrived near Howard street they attempted to form in with the procession; Mr. Laughlin stepped out of the ranks with the view to stop them, when he received the blow over the head from a stick, which deprived him of life. An inquest was held over the body by A. H. Greenfield, Esq., coroner, and the jury returned as a verdict that "he came to his death by a blow from a stick, in the hands of some persons unknown to the jurors." If these fellows came out for the purpose of insulting and disturbing the procession, they ought to have been arrested and severely punished for their insolence and blackguardism.'"

Mr. Laughlin has left a wife and four children, one an infant. He was a respectable mechanic, a carpenter, residing on Federal Hill. The excitement in the city is very great at this wanton and brutal murder. We feel at present unprepared to comment upon it. The act itself speaks in a language than which we can add none stronger, nor is it easy to find any terms fit to convey the feelings of indignation and horror which such an outrage naturally inspires.

PETTICOAT SLANDER REBUKED..

The following letter from Gen. William S. Murphy, in reply to a letter of inquiry, to the citizens of Erie, Pennsylvania, sets at rest the vile slander put in circulation by Major Allen:

Chillicothe, May 2, 1840.

GENTLEMEN: The only candid and true statement of the matter that can be made, is this: that the charge which was thus first made by Major Allen, of the Senate of the United States, whilst he was a subordinate officer of my brigade, is, and was, utterly and absolutely false. It has no sort of foundation whatever. Such a thing never was done, never was intended to be done, and never entered into the heads or the hearts of the fair, virtuous and patriotic ladies of Chillicothe to do. It was a falsehood in the beginning. It was concocted and conceived as a falsehood, told and uttered as a falsehood, published as a falsehood, and republished as a falsehood, known to be false, received as false, and talked about as false, all over the Union, for years since it was uttered.

In the convention of this State, held in Columbus, not long after the publication of that falsehood, about one hundred and fifty delegates (if my memory serves me as to this number) from this county, branded the charge as false, and their solemn attestation was received and made part of the proceedings of the convention; and the oldest and most respectable of our citizens have done the same in their often-published certificates.

With my best wishes for your welfare, I am, gentlemen, yours, very respectfully,

W. S. MURPHY.

THE PETTICOAT HERO.

It is too true General Harrison, as will be seen by the following letter, has had something to do with the "petticoats:"

A CARD.

Headquarters St. Mary's, Sept. 29, 1812.

General Harrison presents his compliments to the ladies of Dayton and its vicinity, and solicits their assistance in making shirts for their brave defenders who compose his army, many of whom are almost destitute of that article, so necessary to their health and comfort. The materials will be furnished by the quartermaster; and the general confidently expects that the opportunity for the display of female patriotism and industry will be eagerly embraced by his fair countrywomen.

WILLIAM HENRY HARRISON.

In consequence of this call, the ladies of Dayton and
its neighborhood, within ten days after it was received,
made up about eighteen hundred shirts for the use of
the army. They were made of calico furnished by the
Indian department, and from the annuities which had
been withheld from the tribes that had taken up arms
against the Americans.

A CURIOUS DOCUMENT.

A gentleman of the highest respectability, says the
editor of the Louisville Journal, has sent us the annexed document, which he vouches for as genuine.
It was handed to him by one of the signers of it, a
half-breed Indian and a relative of Tecumseh.

Council Bluffs, March 23, 1840.

To GENERAL HARRISON'S FRIENDS: The other day,
several newspapers were brought to us, and peeping
over them, to our astonishment we find the hero of
the late war called coward. This would have surprised the tall braves, Tecumseh of the Shawnees and
Round Head and Walk-in-the-Water of the Wyan-
dots. If the departed could rise again they would say
to the white man that General Harrison was the terror
of the late tomahawkers. The first time we got acquainted with General Harrison, it was at the council
fire of the late old Tempest (General Wayne), at
Greenville, on the headwaters of the Wabash, 1796.
From that period until 1811, we had many friendly
smokes with him, but from 1812 we changed our to-
bacco smoke into powder smoke; then we found General Harrison was a brave warrior and humane to his
prisoners, as reported to us by two of Tecumseh's
young men who were taken in the fleet with Captain
Barclay on the 10th of September 1813; and on the
Thames, where he routed both the British and red men,

and where he showed his **courage and his humanity** to
his prisoners both white and red—report of Adam
Brown and family taken the morning of the battle,
October 5, 1813. We are the only two surviving of
that day in this **country.** We hope the good white
men will protect the name of General Harrison.

We remain your friends forever,
CHAMBLEE, Aid to Tecumseh,
B. CALDWELL, Captain.

IN MISSOURI.

THE LOG CABIN RAISIN'—GLORIOUS DAY FOR ST.
LOUIS AND THE STATE—THE PEOPLE HAVE
COME!

We recognize among those who bore a prominent
part the names of some who were the supporters of
Colonel Benton and original Jackson men. There
were signs of a breaking up of the old party lines,
and of a reorganization of the people to assert their
own power, and to enforce their authority that could
not be understood. The following report is from the
St. Louis *New Era:*

We cannot believe that any friend of Harrison
could, in his most sanguine moments, have anticipated
so glorious a day, such a turn-out of the people, as was
witnessed on Tuesday last in this city. Everything
was auspicious. The heavens, the air, the earth, all
seemed to have combined to assist in doing honor to
the services, the patriotism and the virtues of William
Henry Harrison. Never have we seen so much enthusiasm, so much honest, impassioned and eloquent
feeling displayed in the countenances and bursting
from the lips of freemen. It was a day of jubilee.
The people felt that the time had come when they
could breathe freely—when they were about to cast

from them the incubus of a polluted and abandoned
party, and when they could look forward to better
and happier days in store for them and for the country.
The city itself bore, in some respects, the remarkable
character of a Sabbath day. By the Whigs, and even
among the Democrats, there was little work done.
The doors of all places of business were closed, and
nothing was thought of on this carnival day but joy
and gratitude. We noticed upon the ground people
from all parts of the State and of the Union, and they
can give to their neighbors and friends a true description of what they saw and heard. We shall, ourselves,
give such an account of the proceedings as our time
and opportunities permitted us to gather, leaving it
to the imagination to fill up the *tout ensemble* of the
picture. Any sketch of this kind must be necessarily
imperfect, for it is impossible for any one person to
see, hear, and describe everything that occurred.

Preparations had been made for the reception and
entertainment of the company, by the proper committees, at Mrs. Ashley's residence. The extensive
park was so arranged as to accommodate the throng
of persons who were expected. Seats were erected
for the officers of the day, for the speakers and for the
ladies. At the hour appointed by the marshal of the
day, the people commenced to assemble at the court
house, and several associations and crafts were formed
in the procession as they advanced on the ground.
While this was going on, the steamboats bringing delegations from St. Charles, Hannibal, Adams county,
Ill., and Alton, arrived at the wharf, with banners
unfurled to the breeze, and presenting a most cheering
sight. The order of procession, so far as we have been
able to obtain it, was as follows:

Music : Brass band.

1. Banner, borne by farmers from the northern part
of St. Louis township. This banner represented the
" Raising of the Siege of Fort Meigs " and bore as its
motto, "It Has Pleased Providence, We Are Victorious." (Harrison's dispatch.)

2. Officers and members of the Tippecanoe club,

preceded by the president, Col. John O'Fallon, with a splendid banner, representing a hemisphere surmounted by an American eagle, strangling with his beak a serpent, its folds grasped within its talons, and its head having the face of a fox in the throes of death. Above was a rainbow, emblematic of hope, in which was the name of the club. Below the hemisphere was the motto, "The Victor in '11, Will be the Victor in '40." On the reverse side, the letters "T. C." The members six abreast.

3. Log cabin committee, six abreast.

4. The president and vice-presidents of the day.

5. Soldiers who served under Harrison in the late war—in a car, adorned with banners on each side—one, a view of a steamboat named Tippecanoe, with a sign board, "For Washington City." On the other, a view of the cabin at North Bend, the farmer at his plow, with the inscription, "Harrison, the Old Soldier, Honest Man, and Pure Patriot."

6. Invited guests in carriages.

7. Citizens on foot, six abreast, bearing banners inscribed, "Harrison, the Friend of Pre-emption Rights," "One Term for the Presidency;" "Harrison, the People's Candidate;" "Harrison, the People's Sober Second Thought;" "Harrison, He Never Lost a Battle;" "Harrison, the Protector of the Pioneers of the West;" "Harrison, Tyler and Reform;" "Harrison, the Poor Man's Friend;" "Harrison, the Friend of Equal Laws and Equal Rights."

8. Citizens on horseback, six abreast.

9. Delegation from Columbia Bottom.

10. Canoe, "North Bend."

11. Boys with banners, upon one of which was inscribed, "Our Country's Hope," and on another, "Just as the Twig is Bent, the Tree's Inclined."

These boys belonged to the several schools of the city; were regularly marshaled, and presented, by the regularity of their conduct, a most interesting spectacle.

12. Laborers, with their horses and carts, shovels, picks, etc., with a banner bearing the inscription,

" Harrison, the Poor Man's Friend—We Want Work."

13. A printing press on a platform with banners, and the pressman striking off Tippecanoe songs, and distributing them to the throng of people as they passed along, followed in order by the members of the craft.

14. Drays, with barrels of hard cider.

15. A log cabin mounted on wheels, and drawn by six beautiful horses, followed by the craft of carpenters in great numbers. Over the door of the cabin, the words, "The String of the Latch Never Pulled In."

16. The blacksmiths, with forge, bellows, etc., mounted on cars, the men at work. Banner, "We Strike for Our Country's Good."

17. The joiners and cabinet-makers: a miniature shop mounted on wheels; men at work; the craft following it.

17. A large canoe, drawn by six horses, and filled with men.

19. Two canoes, mounted, and filled by sailors.

20. Fort Meigs, in miniature, 40 by 15 feet, drawn by nine yoke of oxen. The interior filled with soldiers, in the usual dress of that day, hunting shirts, leggins, leather breeches, etc.; and one of the men a participant in the defense of Fort Meigs. At every bastion of the fort the muzzle of a piece of ordnance protruded itself, and from another point a piece of artillery was fired, at short intervals, during the day. The whole was most admirably got up, and reflects much credit upon the friends of "Old Tip," to be found at the "Floating Dock."

21. Delegation of brickmakers, with apparatus, clay, etc., and men at work.

22. Delegation of bricklayers, with a beautiful banner, representing a log cabin, brick house going up, etc., and followed by the craft, six abreast.

Band of music.

23. Delegation from Carondelet.

24. Delegation from Belleville, Ill., with banners.

25. Delegation from Alton, with canoe, drawn by four horses, and banners representing the state of the country, the peculiar notions of the Loco Foco party about the reduction of the prices of labor to the stand-

ard of the hard-money countries of Europe and of Cuba; a sub-treasury box, with illustrations, etc. One of the banners bore the inscription, "Connecticut Election, 4,600 Majority; Rhode Island, 1,500 Majority;" and a cunning looking fellow, with his thumb on his nose, and twisting his fingers in regular Samuel Weller style, saying, "You Can't Come It, Matty." This delegation numbered about two hundred men.

26. Delegations from Hannibal and Pike counties with banners, etc.

27. Delegation from Rockport with a log cabin, canoe, banners, etc.

28. Delegation from St. Charles, with banners bearing the names of the twenty-six States, borne by as many individuals, and having with them a handsome canoe drawn by four horses.

Arrived at the southern extremity of the park, the procession halted and formed in open order, the rear passing to the front. The president of the day, John F. Darby, Esq., Mayor of St. Louis, soon afterwards took his seat, assisted by J. Russel, J. P. Gratiot, J. Perry, William Tyler, Robert Walsh, Dr. James W. Moss, Thomas Sappington, H. Von Paul, Edward Tracy, L. J. Chauvin, James Clemens, Jr., John Porcelle, John K. Walker, James McDonald, Samuel Mount, John D. Daggett, James J. Wilkinson, William Carr Lane, Frederick Hyatt, Thomas D. Yeats, John W. Johnson, Stewart Matthews, John Bobb, William H. Boyce, George Bushy, and Peter Lindell, as vice-presidents. Charles D. Drake, Esq., then arose and addressed the assembled multitude.

The people were then successively addressed by Mr. John Hogan, of Illinois, who, as was also Mr. Baker, was called out several times during the day; by L. V. Bogy, Logan Hunton, Lewis F. Thomas, Wilson Primm, Benj. Lawhead, Jas. Denny, J. J. Hardin, of Jacksonville, and J. L. Dorsey.

Colonel John O'Fallon was then called for, and mounted on Fort Meigs, he thus addressed the people:

"My Fellow Citizens: I feel deeply sensible of the honor you confer upon me by calling me to address this vast concourse of intelligent freemen. My pursuits in life have led me into retirement; I am wholly unused to speaking in public. This fact, although well known to many of you, I had reason to believe, would not excuse me on the present occasion. Aware that my known acquaintance with the eventful scenes which we have this day assembled to commemorate, is the only reason for this call, I shall, consequently, in responding to it, state something of what I know in relation to them.

"It was on the first day of February, 1813, that the army of General Harrison pitched their tents upon, and adjacent to, the ground where Fort Meigs was erected, and commenced the construction of a stockade, which was afterwards surrounded by a ditch and embankments, embracing several acres of ground. The snow was deep upon the ground, and the weather extremely cold; and although the troops were raw and greatly unaccustomed to such severe exposure, their ardor never abated. Under many deprivations, they performed their several duties with zeal and alacrity; that zeal and alacrity which spring from the soldier's deep confidence in the tried skill and courage of his commander, and his warm attachment to his person. Early in April, 1813, the garrison of Fort Meigs numbered about 1,000 effective men; two brigades of militia having been discharged in consequence of the termination of their period of service. This fact being early ascertained by the British general commanding at Malden, an expedition against Fort Meigs was immediately projected. His army of British and Indians was near 4,000 strong, and he gave his Indian allies the most confident assurances that he could carry the fort by storm, should his invitation to General Harrison to surrender with the honors of war be refused. He had a heavy park of artillery, and this, with imagined weakness of our defenses, he fancied would give him a ready and easy conquest of the fort. And it was even stipulated between the British general and the celebrated Tecumseh, that, should the garrison be taken and General Harrison remain alive, the Ameri-

can commander was to be delivered to the Indian, who
designed to wreak upon him his savage vengeance for
the death of his many braves and warriors who fell at
the battle of Tippecanoe. Vain calculation! Vain,
this premediated purpose of base and barbarous
malice! The god of battles was with the brave
American general, and he was reserved by a wise and
far-seeing Providence, to be, in after times, the proud
hope, the high blessings, the bright prospects, the
noble deliverer of his country.

" Fort Meigs was invested and cannonaded with
bombs shells and red-hot balls for seven days, during
all which time General Harrison was ever at the point
of danger, planning and directing the defense, and by
his manner, his voice, his sagacious conduct, and his
undaunted courage, inspiring his officers and men with
an abiding confidence of ultimate victory. General
Proctor was at length driven to confess that he was
contending with a commander whose courage and
military talents were equal to any emergency; and
despairing of redeeming the pledge he had given to
his army, to make an easy conquest of the garrison,
and being informed by intercepted communication
that General Harrison was in daily expectation of
re-enforcements, he determined to effect that by strata-
gem which he now despaired of accomplishing by
open warfare. He calculated by a timely and well
concerted deception to decoy into an ambuscade a
large detachment of our garrison—then scarcely sufficient effectually to man the defenses. Should he
succeed in this the ready sacrifice of the fort would
inevitably follow. Suddenly a brisk and sharp firing
was heard in a thick wood near the fort, through
which passed the road to the interior. The alarm
strongly represented, as it was designed to do, an
Indian engagement. Shortly afterwards loud wailing
and groans were heard, as would naturally proceed
from wounded and dying men. The whole garrison,
at once concluded that an attack was made on our
brothers in arms on their way to our relief, and who
had the strongest claim to our assistance. Not so,

however, with General Harrison. He alone was incredulous. Many of his officers waited upon him, and almost demanded permission to fly to the rescue. For a time the greatest excitement prevailed in the garrison at the idea of the sacrifice of their gallant comrades without an attempt to save them. General Harrison's sagacity caught the design of the enemy in a moment, and it required the exercise of all his powerful influence and authority to subdue the impetuosity of his officers and men, and to convince them of this cunning device of the enemy planned for their desruction.

"About 2 o'clock on the morning of the 5th of May, 1813, two officers came, expresses from Gen. Green Clay, who had passed the Indian lines, under cover of the night, at the most imminent hazard of their lives. They brought information that General Clay, with his brigade of Kentucky militia, was encamped on the river, a few miles above the fort, to which he would proceed early that morning. This was most cheering intelligence to General Harrison; and with this addition to his force he determined at once to commence offensive operations by attacking the enemy at every assailable point, dislodge them from their position, destroy their batteries, and thus terminate the siege of Fort Meigs. With this view, two officers were immediately dispatched to General Clay with orders to land about a mile above the fort, on the opposite side of the river, a detachment of 800 men under one of his most trustworthy officers—to move upon the British batteries, to carry them, spike the cannon, destroy the ammunition with their carriages, and immediately upon the accomplishment of this, to cross the river to the fort under cover of our artillery.

"The brave Colonel Dudley did, in a most gallant manner, take the British batteries and spiked some pieces of their cannon; but, too confident of his own strength, and ignorant of that of the enemy, to be soon made available, he was induced, in violation of his instructions, to occupy the ground taken until the enemy had time to collect their forces in an adjacent wood, into

which he was cunningly enticed by a partial firing of
a few Indians, where, after a bloody conflict, the largest of his command was taken.

"General Harrison displayed, in the judgment of all
his officers, the highest order of military talent during
the siege, for his efficient plans of defense, by traveses
through and across the encampment, as a cover for his,
the manner of protecting his magazine, the object of
constant attack, as well as for the plan, direction and
most opportune execution of the grand objects of the
two sorties, made by detachments from the garrison of
Fort Meigs on the 5th of May, 1813.

"The first sortie was directed against that portion of
the Indians and Canadian militia investing the south and
west end of the fort, for the purpose of drawing them
from the river, whilst General Clay's detachment was
effecting their entrance into the fort.

"The second sortie commenced its movement just at
the moment of their appearance, on the opposite side of
Dudley's detachment, advancing upon the British batteries, having the double effect of engaging the Indians
and preventing them from crossing the river to co-op-
erate against Dudley, and accomplishing the destruction of the enemy's batteries on the southeast side of
the river.

"On no occasion during the last war were greater
honors acquired than by General Harrison, who conceived and directed, and the gallent men who executed
his orders in these two brilliant sorties.

"In both engagements our troops, whilst utterly exposed, advanced upon and repulsed the enemy, sheltered as he was by his position, and outnumbering our
men four to one.

"In the last sortie our men marched as firmly as veterans to the very mouths of the British cannon, receiving, unmoved, their constant fire of grape shot, accompanied by a most galling and destructive fire from
thousands of Indians and militia on our front and flanks.
Although a large number of our men fell and perished
upon the field of honor, their surviving comrades never
paused in their forward march until the batteries, with

a large portion of the British regulars in charge of them, were captured, and the whole Indian and militia force was dispersed and routed. Thus ended the memorable siege of Fort Meigs.

"In conclusion, fellow-citizens, allow me to say that I had the honor of serving under General Harrison at the battle of Tippecanoe, during the siege of Fort Meigs, and at the battle of the Thames. I can say that, from the commencement to the termination of his military services in the last war, I was almost constantly by his side. I was familiar with his conduct as governor and superintendent of Indian affairs of the Territory of Indiana, and after the return of peace, as commissioner to treat with all the hostile Indians of the last war in the Northwest, for the establishment of a permanent reconciliation and peace. I saw also much of General Harrison whilst he was in the Congress of the United States.

"Opportunities have thus been afforded me of knowing him in all the relations of life, as an officer and as a man, and of being enabled to form a pretty correct estimate of his military and civil services, as well as his qualifications and fitness for office. I know him to be open and brave in his disposition, of active and industrious habits, uncompromising in his principles, above all guile and intrigue, and a pure, honest, noble-minded man, with a heart ever overflowing with warm and generous sympathies for his fellow-man. As a military man, his daring, chivalrous courage inspired his men with confidence and spread dismay and terror to his enemies. In all his plans he was successful. In all his engagements he was victorious. He has filled all the various civil and military offices committed to him by his country, with sound judgment and spotless fidelity. In every situation he was cautious and prudent, firm and energetic, and his decisions always judicious. His acquirements as a scholar are varied and extensive, his principles as a statesman sound, pure and republican.

" If chosen President he will be the President of the people rather than of a party. The Government will then be administered for the general good and welfare.

His election will be the dawn of a new era! The reform of the abuses of a most corrupt, prolifigate and oppressive Government. Then will end the ten years' war upon the currency and institutions of the country. The hard-money cry and hard times will disappear together. Then will cease further attempts to increase the wages of the office-holders and reduce the wages of the people to the standard of European labor.

"Then shall we see restored the general prosperity of the people, by giving them a sound local currency, mixed with a currency of a uniform value throughout the land. The revival of commerce, of trade, enterprise and general confidence. Then the return of happier, more peaceful and more prosperous days, when cheerfulness and plenty will, once more, smile around the poor man's table."

About sunset Fort Meigs was brought into the city and stationed opposite the court-house, and an adjournment took place until after supper. At that time a considerable portion of the toughest of the multitude reassembled, and were addressed until eleven o'clock by Messrs. Geyer, Tunstall, Logan, John Bobb, Drake and Captain Mallet in animated speeches, which were responded to with undiminished enthusiasm. About the close of the meeting the following resolutions were offered by Mr. Drake, and adopted with three cheers:

Resolved, That the Whig young men of St. Louis county will respond to the call for a young men's convention at Rocheport on the 20th of June, and that the cause of old Tippecanoe shall not suffer because they are not on the ground.

Resolved, That five hundred of the real "log cabin and hard cider boys" of St. Louis county will stand at a corner of the Rocheport cabin on the 18th, and join in the convention of the 20th, when they hope to meet ten thousand of their brethren and join with them in doing honor to the farmer-statesman of the West.

Resolved, That a committee of twenty be appointed to select the five hundred who shall go.

After the adoption of these resolutions, a song was sung, and the company dispersed.

Thus ended this day's proceedings. Such a day of political excitement never has been known in Missouri. Such an assemblage of people has never taken place within her borders. We do not wish to mislead by exaggerating the number who were in the park, but we are certain that we fall short of, rather than over-estimate it, when we put it at from eight to ten thousand. This glorious day cannot soon be forgotten by those who were present. The young and the old will speak of it with mingled delight and wonder; and we hope and believe that it is but the precursor of many such meetings in Missouri, by which she may yet be saved from the reproach of being the last State to desert the fortunes of Mr. Van Buren.

TOM. CORWIN AT PORTSMOUTH.

The Hon. Thomas Corwin came down the river last Wednesday in the steamer General Scott. So retired and unassuming is he in his deportment, that the captain and passengers were not aware who he was. But scarce had the boat landed at our wharf before he was recognized by some of our citizens. The word was soon spread, and a crowd of our people gathered together at the American House, anxious to shake the hand of this distinguished and talented son of Ohio. The number soon became too large to enter any room of the hotel, and they took their position on the pavement in front of the hotel and called for "Tom Corwin." This call brought Mr. Corwin to the platform in front of the house, from which, for an hour and a half, he addressed the assemblage in that eloquent and forcible style so peculiarly his own, upon the leading political topics of the day. He most justly sustained his high reputation as a stump speaker, and left the Whigs of Portsmouth proud of their candidate for governor.

It is due to Captain Dustam, of the General Scott, that it should be known, that as soon as he was informed who his passenger was he kindly lay at the wharf long enough to enable Mr. Corwin to receive the visits of our people and to address them.

On leaving the wharf the boat passed up the river near the opposite shore until above the upper part of our town, when she turned round and passed down close to the wharf. When opposite the hotel, her engine was stopped for a few moments, and while floating in the stream, the citizens along the street gave three cheers for "Tom Corwin."

Mr. Corwin is on his way home to visit his family, having obtained leave of absence for three weeks. He has not yet resigned; and whether he resigns at all depends upon the action of his constituents.—*Portsmouth Tribune.*

WILLIAM C. RIVES,

A Patriotic Son of the Old Dominion, Comes Straight Out.

Hon. William C. Rives, of Virginia, on the 22d of February, ably addressed his fellow-citizens upon the leading political topics of the day, having specially in view the exhibition of Mr. Van Buren's unworthiness for the executive office, and the propriety of sustaining General Harrison in opposition to him. He sums up his reasons for supporting Harrison in this manner:

"Regarding General Harrison, for reasons I have mentioned, as the true Republican candidate for the Presidency of the two now presented to the choice of the country, I shall unhesitatingly give him my support. I shall do so with the more cheerfulness because, while best consulting thereby, as I honestly believe, those great Republican principles which I have ever considered to be inseparably united with the happiness of my country, I shall assist to confer its highest meed on an

eminent citizen who has rendered it the most signal
and important services at a time, when, to serve meant
something far other than merely to receive the emoluments of office; on one who, having successively enjoyed the confidence of Washington, Jefferson and
Madison, would be naturally prompted to emulate their
high example, who, in all the various and delicate trusts
he has held, has ever shown that he preferred his
country to himself, and has retired from all, amid the
numerous and alluring temptations they presented to
private gain, with clean hands and unsuspected honor,
neither guilty of infidelity himself nor winking at it
in others; and who now in the honorable retirement
of private life, combining the ennobling pursuits of the
agriculturist, the scholar and the patriotic citizen, is
emphatically one of the people, knowing how to appreciate their interests, as well as to maintain and
defend their rights.

MEETINGS IN MAY.

GREAT WHIG MEETINGS IN MASSACHUSETTS AND VERMONT.

Thousands of people from Springfield, Amherst,
Northampton and the adjacent country met at Greenfield on May 10. More than six thousand farmers
were there with their sunburnt faces and horny hands,
marching in procession that they might testify their
devotion to the cause of old Tippecanoe. The Deer-
field farmers wheeled into the procession with a team
of thirteen yoke of prime cattle, banners streaming from
the head of each. Bunches of ears of corn hung from
the sides of the huge car. But the most interesting
sight in the line was a company of five Revolutionary soldiers from Coleraine—their ages averaging 86—
with these impressive words on their banner, "The
Last Blood of '76." There was an immense assemblage

of ladies and others on the brow of the hill, which cheered each delegation as it passed. One of the banners had a Florida blood-hound dressed in military. A large company of Vermont mountaineers were present with a log cabin.

The convention was organized in a beautiful field in the rear of the First Congregational church, Hon. George Grinnell presiding. Patriotic speeches were made by General Maltoon, a Revolutionary sage of 86 years, I. C. Bates, Myron Laurence, and General Wilson, of New Hampshire. At the close of the services the assembly partook of "the soldier's fare" for the old soldier's friend, at the log cabin. The highest enthusiasm prevails through the hills and valleys of New England.

At old Feneuil Hall, Boston, there was a grand meeting on the 12th of May to hear the report of the delegates to the young men's national convention at Baltimore. Speeches were made by Crozier and Hosmer, of Tennessee, Wickliffe, of Kentucky, Governor Everett, and others. Hon. Edward Everett presided.

At a Whig meeting at Bennington, Vermont, on the 11th, there was a procession several miles long. In it a wagon drawn by twenty-five yoke of oxen, and a wagon containing one hundred ladies and drawn by twenty-five horses, with the banner flying, "Vermont, the Star that Never Sets."

VARIOUS MEETINGS.

THE TIPPECANOE CLANS ARE RALLYING FOR BATTLE EVERYWHERE.

On the 2d, 3d, and 4th of June, there was a big camp meeting of the friends of Harrison and reform at Springfield, Illinois. It was largely attended by the people of Sangamon, and all the surrounding counties, and also from Missouri, Indiana, and Illinois, and was addressed by Edwards, Lincoln, Stewart, Linder, and others. Upwards of 20,000 people were present, and the zeal and enthusiasm kindled a flame that fairly set the prairies on fire.

On the 15th there was a grand rally in Philadelphia. The Pennsylvania *Inquirer* says:

"The meeting was one of the largest and most enthusiastic ever held on any occasion in Philadelphia. The hardy Democracy turned out in thousands, determined to omit no opportunity for the expression of their sentiments against the existing dynasty, with its sub-treasury and standing army, and in favor of the long tried and deeply cherished hero and civilian, whom the people are about to elevate to the Chief Magistracy of the nation. Citizens of every class and rank in society mingled in the multitude, all devoted to the same cause, all animated by the same feeling, all looking forward to the results of the coming struggle, as to the bright future which is to renerve the prostrate arm of enterprise, and once more rouse the mechanic and the manufacturer into activity and business. The feeling throughout was of the right kind indeed—earnest and harmonious."

Among the banners were the following inscriptions: "Third District—We Set the Ball in Motion;" on another, "Kensington is Coming;" on a third, "This Banner Was Displayed in 1813, by the People, After the Defeat of Proctor, by General Harrison."

Spring Garden, Germantown, and Southwark, turned out in great force; the Cohocksink boys were also present with a neat banner; so also a deputation from Delaware county, and from various parts of the county of Philadelphia. When arrived at the square, the scene was exciting, gratifying, and imposing in an extraordinary degree. Even the most sanguine of our friends, who expected a great meeting, "did not venture to hope that a popular display, called at a brief notice, would have surpassed anything of the kind that had taken place in Pennsylvania since the commencement of the present Presidential campaign."

The venerable John Ely, a soldier of the Revolution, presided, assisted by a number of vice-presidents.

A series of resolutions were offered by W. B. Reed, Esq., and unanimously adopted. They went to express the sentiments of those present, in reference to the abuses of the administration; the prostration of credit and confidence produced by the policy of the executive; the necessity for a change of rulers before the country can be again made prosperous and happy; the confidence of the people in the wisdom, the sagacity, and patriotism of William Henry Harrison and John Tyler, and the fixed resolve to use every honorable effort to promote the elevation of those distinguished citizens to the highest offices in the gift of a free people.

After the adoption of the resolutions, the celebrated "Ohio Blacksmith," Mr. Bear, made his appearance, and was received with shouts of applause. He threw off his coat, rolled up his sleeves, and, for the space of nearly two hours held the attention of the meeting in a speech of great argumentative power and effect, enlivened and illustrated by choice and appropriate anecdotes.

The meeting was further addressed by Major Conover, of North Bend; the Hon. Waddy Thompson, of South Carolina; Mr. Pope, of Tennessee; Mr. Jenifer, of Maryland; Mr. Grinnell, of New York, and several other gentlemen.

There was a grand rally at St. Louis, July 16, at which Hon. S. S. Prentiss delivered one of the most eloquent speeches that ever fell from the lips of man.

The Whigs of Vermont met in a monster convention on the 4th, and chose Hon. Solomon Foot president, and fourteen vice-presidents. Hon. Samuel C. Craft and Hon. Ezra Meek were chosen electors for the State-at-large. The old State officers were nominated with entire unanimity. The Whitehall *Chronicle* says:

The assemblage was, by far, the largest ever known

in Vermont, and variously estimated at from 10,000 to 15,000.

This vast assemblage, from every county in the State, was early erganized under the direction of Col. H. Thomas, marshal of the day, in procession and marched through the principal streets of the village, then to College hill, thence north to Pearl street, down which to the square, at which time the last of the procession were just falling into line. It was more than three miles long.

In the afternoon the people were addressed from a platform in front of the court house by Messrs. Adams and Upham, of Vermont; E. D. Culver, of New York, and General Wilson of New Hampshire, with their usual eloquence and ability, for more than six hours. Acres of men were listening to them with an intensity of interest commensurate with the great objects for which they were assembled.

At Worcester, Massachusetts, there was a mighty gathering of Whigs. The following electors were chosen: Isaac M. Bates, Peleg Sprague, Robert G. Shaw, Stephen C. Phillips, Rufus Longley, Sydney Willard, Ira M. Benton, George Grennell, Thaddeus Pomeroy, Samuel Mixter, Thomas, French, Wilks, Wood, Joseph Tripp and John B. Thomas.

There was a large meeting at Westminster, Maryland. Jacob Matthias was president; Thomas Hook vice-president, and Elias Youghing, which was addressed by William Pitts and others.

At Tuscaloosa, Alabama, June 1st, over one thousand Whigs met in convention, and were presided over by Judge Hunter, who had headed the Van Buren electorial ticket in 1836, and had voted the party ticket since. They nominated for Presidential electors Arthur F. Hopkins, James Abercrombie, John Gayle, Henry W. Hilliard, Thomas Williams, Harry J. Thornton and Nicholas Davis. The gathering was eloquently addressed by Hon. H. W. Hilliard and others.

The Whigs of Maryland met in State convention and nominated for Harrison electors, David Hoffman, John

L. Kerr, Thomas A. Spencer, Theodore E. Lockerman, George Howard, John T. Kennedy, Richard J. Bowie, Jacob A. Preston, James M. Coole and Wm. T. Cotton. Hon. Reverdy Johnson, Charles H. Pitts, J. L. Ridgley, William Pitts, and others addressed them,

The Whig convention of Maine, at Augusta, on the 17th, had over two thousand present. Edward Kent was nominated for Governor, and the State went "hell bent" for him. Isaac Ilsley and Gen. Isaac Hodedon were nominated for electors at large. There was great enthusiasm.

The Whig State convention of New Hampshire met at Concord and put a strong ticket in the field. The electors chosen were as follows: Joseph Healey, George W. Nesmith, Joseph Cilley, Andrew Pierce, William Bixley, Thomas D. Edwards, and Amos A. Brewster. Over five thousand were present.

Over twenty thousand people were at the great Fort Meigs convention. The steamboat General Wayne carried twelve hundred to the grand rally for the old hero, Harrison.

On the 19th of June the largest meeting ever in Delaware was held at Delaware city, to do honor to the hero of Fort Meigs.

The Whigs of New Orleans had a tremendous meeting on the 24th, which was addressed by the gallant Prentiss, of Mississippi, who exhorted them to meet the expectations of the country and to send up their voice to the National Capital in a tone of thunder. A correspondent says, " We did so, though we expect to hear of the death of some of the young Kendalls. Prentiss gave us the most brilliant speech we ever heard. Wit, sarcasm, logic, declamation, humor—all were blended together in a style of magnificence never surpassed. He says Van Buren is a little yawl attached to the great steamboat, General Jackson. That it comes with ill-grace from him to denounce General Harrison as an imbecile and no general, when he himself is nothing more than a commander-in-chief of Cuban blood-hounds."

IN MARYLAND.

THE SHARPSBURG MEETING—ITS PROCESSION, MOTTOES AND ORATORS.

June 8, 1840.

DEAR GENERAL: More than six thousand persons are assembled here to respond to the nomination of Harrison and Tyler. This is a spontaneous burst of enthusiasm. From mountain and valley, over rivers and streamlets, they came to evince their hearty and enthusiastic admiration of the pure hero of Tippecanoe, and their disapprobation of the bloodhound, standing army, sub-treasury administration of Martin Van Buren. Berkley and Jefferson counties, of Virginia, sent fifteen hundred Whigs over the Potomac; Washington and Frederick counties made up, with a little help from Allegany, the balance. It is a miniature of the great convention of the 4th of May.

After the people had assembled they were called to order by a song, sung by an Ohioan. Mr. Weisel, of Hagerstown, then addressed them from a stand erected in the square, in a happy and animated speech. His allusions to Virginia, her eminent statesmen, and her late glorious conduct were peculiarly appropriate.

He was responded to by Dr. Quigley, of Virginia, who addressed the assemblage in a short but spirited speech. Dr. Quigley was followed by Capt. John Snyder, of Harper's Ferry; he has been on the stump before, or I am much mistaken; his speech was an excellent one. Mr. Perry Orndorff, a soldeir under Harrison at the siege of Fort Meigs, followed Captain Snyder, and spoke nearly as follows: "I have heard my general slandered and defamed; I have even heard him represented as a coward. My fellow-citizens, it makes my blood boil in my veins to hear the man who was foremost when the battle was hardest, slandered by men whose lives have been a reproach to those masculine exercises and virtues which have distinguished his, and for which all men are formed. Yes, my fellow-citizens, these men, whose infancy was cradled in down, and whose riper years have been fed on treasury pap from a golden spoon, without the slightest knowledge of hardship or a soldier's sufferings, stigmatize my old commander as a coward. Fellow-citizens, it is false. I know General Harrison is a brave and wise man. I fought under him at Fort Meigs against the British and Indians: and I cheerfully fight under him now, against a standing army of 200,000 men, against an army of defaulting office holders, and against the human bloodhounds who remorselessly hunt down and murder private reputation and martial fame. He led me to victory in the first war, and he will lead me and all of us to victory over his and our bloodhound persecutors." As soon as the old soldier concluded, the procession was formed by John Brinn, of Antietam iron works, chief marshal, assisted by the district marshals, whose names will be given with their districts in the following order:

The chief marshal and three aids led the procession; then followed a band of music, next came the Clear Spring delegation, bearing in advance a banner, having for a motto the candid confession and game defiance: "Clear Spring District, No. 4; Often Beaten But Never Conquered." Their second banner was a portrait of Harrison, with the inscription, "Hero of Tippecanoe;" their third banner was the national flag with an eagle holding a scroll, on it was the national motto, "E Pluribus Unum." The Sharpsburg district came next, attended by its marshals, David Smith, Samuel Mumma, David Hill, Thomas G. Harris, Joseph Porter, David R. Miller and Jonathan Hill; their first banner in front represented a blacksmith at work; above this picture was, "Antietam Iron Works," below, the motto, "Strike While the Iron Is Hot;" on the reverse the motto, "By Industry We Thrive;" their second banner bore the motto, "Harrison and Tyler, Our Country's Hope,"

"Martin Van Buren you won't do,
The people's choice is Tippecanoe."

11

Their third banner had, "The Voters of Antietam Iron
Works Know How to Appreciate the Worth of Gen.
William Henry Harrison." The people from Middletown Valley, in Frederick county, followed next, their
marshals were the same as Boonsboro's; below their
banner was a starred blue satin flag, with blue streamers, on which were Harrison and Tyler; the motto on
the flag was, "From Mountain and Valley, We Rally.
We Rally." The gallant array of Tippecanoe boys
from Harper's Ferry, preceded by martial music, came
next; their first banner was a likeness of General Harrison, with the descriptive inscription, "Farmer of
North Bend and Hero of Tippecanoe;" their next ornamental display was the river Thames, with a canoe
named Tippecanoe in it, and in the canoe was a miniature Fort Meigs, and in the fort was John Orndorff,
the old soldier who assisted in the defense of the real
Fort Meigs, the stars and stripes raised over every bastion; their third was a ship and plow with the motto,
"Commerce and Agriculture." The officers of this
delegation were, Captain J. Stryder, chief marshal,
John T. Hinkle, Lewis W. Washington, Thomas Boet-
ter, Collin Peter and Samuel Stryder, assistant marshals. The Shepherdstown district followed the Harper's Ferry boys; they were led by Major Hamtranck,
their chief marshal, and his aide, Wm. Fouke, Esq.,
assisted by Alexander R. Boteler, Dr. Thomas Hammond, Henry Boteler, B. T. Towner, James Chap-
lino, Wm. Lemmon, John Ernst and A. Cameron,
assistant marshals; their first banner was the Virginia
coat of arms (the goddess of liberty with one foot on
the neck of a satyr), on the reverse were the mottoes,
"Domestic Manufactures," and "No Reduction of
Wages," "No Standing Army in Time of Peace;"
their second banner bore the inscription, "Tip and
Tyler," and the motto, "Harrison, the Hero of Tippecanoe."

Next came the Boonsboro' Harrison men; their mar-
shals were, Jos. Weast, chief marshal; Elias Davis,
Robert Fowler, Elias Snavely, Josiah Snavely and
—— Allen, assistant marshals. The Boonsboro' and

Middletown delegations were consolidated. Their first banner bore in front the motto, "Our Country's Good, Our Only Aim;" on the reverse, "We Honor Virtue," "We Reward the Brave." Their second banner bore a pair of scales, with a sub-treasury and standing army on one side, and a barrel of hard cider on the other; the cider weighed them down.

Hagerstown, Beaver Creek, Cavetown and Lectersbury consolidated into one, and numbering more than one thousand, came next; their marshals, Dr. J. C. Dorsey, chief marshal: Henry J. Bentz, Jno. Martenny, William Miller, Jno. Thruston, Samuel McCarty, Jno. Gantz, Samuel Bloom, Jacob Windens, assistant marshals of Hagerstown. Peter Coblentz, chief marshal; Samuel Keedy, chief marshal; Jos. Snavely, Samuel Baker, John Kerr, assistant marshals, etc. The banners of this party were sixteen in number.

1. American flag and gilt eagle.
2. "The Tip of All Tips is Tippecanoe."
3. Motto, "We Go for a Strong Team, and Old Tip for the Driver."

The others, to the twelfth, were not different from some we have given.

12. A large box of provisions behind a wagon, with the label, "Farmers' Fare and Some to Spare."
13. A wagon, with eight black horses, each horse bearing a flag with the motto, "Tip's Coming."
14. Motto, "General Harrison's Beaver Creek Friends."

The noble farmers, from Pleasant Valley, came next, with the expressive motto on their banner, "Pleasant Valley, a Terror to Loco Focoism."

Berkley county, Virginia, wound up the procession with a splendid array of banners borne in wagons, log cabins, etc. Their log cabin had a full-length portrait of Harrison in front.

1. Banner, motto, "The Yeoman."
2. "Liberty and Union, Now and Forever, One and Inseparable." "For President, William Henry Harrison; for Vice-President, John Tyler."
3. Motto, "One Presidential Term."

4. " Safety of the Public Money."
5. "General Good of the People."
6. "Integrity of the Public Servants."
7. " We Have Flung the Broad Banner of Our
Country to the Breeze." "Union of the Whigs for
the Sake of the Union."

On a wagon were the following mottoes:

{"50 Cents."   "1 Cent." }
{(Wild Cat.)   (Red Dog.)}
           "The Hard Currency."

A painting of Van Buren running from Capitol Hill
and a big ball rolling down after him.

A painting of Benton rolling a ball, solitary and
alone.

A motto, " Down with Van Buren Principles, Sub-
Treasury and Standing Army."

A painting of Van Buren, sword in hand, re-
viewing his regiment of bloodhounds. This was
one of the most laughable caricatures I have ever
seen.

After the procession had marched through the village and countermarched to the square, William
Price. Esq., was elected president. So enthusiastic
was the multitude that, without any further organization, Mr. Price was called out by acclamation. He
spoke about fifteen minutes, and was followed by Col.
James M. Coale, elector for this district. Colonel Coale
spoke about an hour. It is not sufficient to say Messrs.
Price and Coale spoke well; they both spoke with
eloquence: the latter, from the length of time he
occupied, had a better opportunity than the former of
indulging in that quaint humor which is suited to the
stump. Mr. J. P. Kennedy spoke in his best style; his
speech was an able one. Mr. David Hoffman spoke
but a short time, and concluded by introducing one of
nature's noblemen, Mr. Baer, the Ohio Blacksmith.
He made the best speech I have ever heard; not in
manner; but in matter.

The meeting dispersed before sundown to enable
the sturdy Whigs of Virginia and Maryland to return
home.

I had forgotten to mention a beautiful evergreen arch thrown across the principal street of Sharpsburg, and surmounted by the star-spangled banner: and also the Sharpsburg log cabin, the same you saw in Baltimore on the 4th of last month. It was placed in the square with a living bear chained on the roof, and several living opossums, racoons, etc., perched among the branches of a tree, which seemed to shoot from its center.   Yours,   F. II.

DISTRICT OF COLUMBIA.

GREAT HARRISON FESTIVAL AT ALEXANDRIA, DISTRICT OF COLUMBIA.

The *Madisonian* of June 19, contains a full account of the proceedings of the meeting of the friends of Harrison and reform, at Alexandria, from which we are only enabled to give extracts. Washington and Georgetown were fully and ably represented.

"Among the distinguished visitors from Washington, we noticed Mr. Webster, Mr. Crittenden, Mr. Preston, and Mr. Phelps, of the Senate; Messrs. King, of Georgia, Jenifer, Graves, Waddy Thompson, Biddle, Hill, Hoffman, Wise, Graham, James Garland, the mayor of Washington, Colonel Washington, and several others. Upon landing from the boats, they were received by the committee and welcomed in a very beautiful and appropriate address by the mayor."

The honor of replying to this address, was, by the spontaneous concurrence of all, conceded to Mr. Webster. His remarks were brief, but admirably appropriate and imbued throughout with deep and genuine emotion.

The ladies are represented as having taken, as they always do, the most noticeable share in the proceedings of the day.

On arriving at the spot selected for the festival, excellent arrangements were found to have been made for the accommodation of those who wished to participate. A number of patriotic toasts were drank, and Mr. Webster again, in response to calls, made one of his most eloquent responses, concluding thus: "Can we lose anything by a *change?* Let us, then, go forward together. We have made William Henry Harrison the bearer of our standard, and while he holds it, it shall not fall, unless we fall along with it." Mr. Crittenden pronounced a glowing eulogium upon the character and services of General Harrison, and related many anecdotes illustrative of his courage, his disinterestedness, his moderation and his humanity. Messrs. Wm. Preston, Ogden Hoffman, Biddle, of Pennsylvania, Wise, King, Waddy Thompson, Phelps, of Vermont; James Garland, Graves, Hill, of Virginia; Graham, of North Carolina, and Mr. Janney, the Whig elector for Loudon county, Virginia, severally addressed the meeting. The proceedings closed by a speech of uncommon force and spirit from Mr. Wise.

HARRISON AMONG THE PEOPLE.

HIS SPEECH AT COLUMBUS, OHIO, JUNE 11, 1840.

General Harrison left his home to visit the site of old Fort Meigs. He arrived at Columbus on the afternoon of Friday week, and left at 10 o'clock next morning. The short period he was present in that city was remarkably interesting. At the moment he was about to depart he was constrained to answer the calls of the sovereign people, and he accordingly addressed them nearly an hour in the frank and manly spirit of a soldier. We have read his remarks with unalloyed delight. No man of any party who has a heart can peruse them without an honest emotion of satisfaction.

What a relief is such a speech from the bitter tirades of party slang-whangers? The following we find in the Ohio *Confederate* of the 11th of June:

"General Harrison left Cincinnati on Thursday; he arrived here, a distance of one hundred and twenty miles, at 5 o'clock P. M. on Friday.· He was on his feet receiving the calls and congratulations of our citizens for hours after his arrival. In the evening he repaired, by invitation, to the log cabin, where additional hundreds had congregated to meet this beloved and venerated patriot. Here, with the frankness and unreservedness which have marked his character through life, did he mingle for two hours with the "log cabin boys" of the capital. Long before the sun and before our youth were astir, the general was, on the morning of the morrow, up and about. Having breakfasted with a friend at a remote part of the city, he was soon again surrounded by the multitude of our people, who refused to be satisfied without seeing and communing with him. The period of his departure was at hand— the crowd increased; it was impossible that in the brief interval every one could be presented individually to the general, and all were anxious to see and hear him. At the instance of a friend, who noticed the popular solicitude, the general, from the platform of the door of the National Hotel, addressed the people for half an hour or more. We wish that every man in America had heard that speech. How would the defamers of this great and good man have dwindled in their estimation into merited insignificance. How would the slanderers who impute to him motives which never actuated him, and opinions which he never held, and designs which he never entertained, and principles which he never cherished, and who infamously ascribe to him imbecility and decrepitude and cowardice—how would these slanderers have been indignantly rebuked by the righteous judgment of an honest and insulted people? But as they did not and could not hear it, we will endeavor to possess them of its substance. We took no notes. Neither General Harrison nor any other person thought of his making a public address two minutes before he commenced it. It arose out of the circumstances which surrounded him at the moment, and signally illustrated a quality of his character to which we have before alluded, the ability always to say and to do exactly what is proper to be said and done. The reader will bear in mind, therefore, that we profess only to give him the subject-matter, not the style and expression of

GENERAL HARRISON'S REMARKS.

General Harrison said he was greatly indebted to his fellow-citizens of Columbus and Franklin county; the most cordial hospitality had at all times been accorded to him by them. So long ago as the time when he was honored with the command of the Northwestern army, and held his headquarters at Franklinton, on the other side of the river, it was his fortune to find in the people of Franklin county not only good citizens, but patriots and soldiers. Their unvarying kindness to him had laid him under many previous obligations, and their generous attentions on the present occasion he cheerfully and gratefully acknowledged.

He said he had no intention to detain his friends by making a speech, and he did so in obedience to what he understood to be the desire of those whom he addressed. He was not surprised that public curiosity was awakened in reference to some things which had been lately published concerning him, nor was he unwilling to satisfy the feelings of his fellow-citizens by such proper explanations as became him in his present position before the country. He confessed that he had suffered deep mortification since he had been placed before the people as a candidate for the highest office in their gift—nay, the most exalted station in the world—that any portion of his countrymen should think it necessary or expedient to abuse, slander or villify him. His sorrow arose not so much from personal—dear as was to him the humble reputation he had earned—as from public considerations. He might draw consolation, under this species of injury, from the revelations of history, which showed

that the best of men, who had devoted their lives
to the public service, had been the victims of tra-
duction. But virtue and truth are the foundations
of our republican system. When these are disregarded,
our free institutions must fall; he looked, therefore, at
symptoms of demoralization with sincere regret as
betokening danger to public liberty. A part of the
political press, supporting the existing administration,
and certain partizans of Mr. Van Buren, also a candidate for that high office, to which some of those whom
he addressed desired to elevate him, had invented and
propagated many calumnies against him, but he proposed on the present occasion to speak of one only of
the numerous perversions and slanders which filled
the columns of the newspapers, and misrepresented
his character and conduct. He alluded to the story of
his famous "confidential committee," as they called it.
"The story goes," said General Harrison, "that I have
not only a committee of conscience-keepers, but that
they put me in a cage, fastened with iron bars, and
kept me in that." To one who looked at his bright
and sparkling eye, the light which beamed in its rich
expression, the smile which played upon his countenance, blending the lineaments of benevolence and
firmness; who remembered also that he was listening
to the voice of a son of old Governor Harrison, one of
"the signers," the pupil of old "Mad Anthony," the
hero of Tippecanoe, the defender of Fort Meigs, the
conqueror of Proctor—the idea of William Henry
Harrison in a cage was irresistibly ludicrous!

When the laughter had subsided, the General proceeded; "I have no committee, fellow-citizens, confidential or other. It is true that I employed my friend, Major Gwynn, to aid me in returning replies to some of the
numerous questions propounded to me by letters; but
to such only as any man could answer as well as another.
There is scarcely a question of a political nature now
agitating the public mind on which I have not long
since promulgated my opinions, by speeches, published
letters or official acts. A large majority of letters
addressed to me purported to seek my views of aboli-

tion, United States bank, and other matter, concerning
which my views are already in possession of the public.
The most suitable answers to these and to well-inten-
tioned persons the most satisfactory, was a reference
to the documents in which my opinions already expressed were to be found.   Such answers I intrusted to
my well-tried and faithful friend, Major Gwynn.   Letters requiring more particular attention I answered myself. Everybody who knows Major Gwynn, knows that
he is not one whom I would employ to write a political
letter.   He is a self-made man, a soldier and a gentleman, but neither a politician nor a scholar.   I asked the
service of him, because he was my friend, and I
confided in him, and it was plain and simple.   My
habit is to receive, open and read my letters myself.
Such as require special attention I reply to myself.
Such as may be easily answered by another, I hand to
my friend, with an indorsation indicating where the
information sought may be found—as thus—'Refer
the writer to speech at Vincennes'—or 'the answer is
seen in my letter to Mr. Denny,' etc.   But it seems that
Major Gwynn was chairman of a committee of the citizens of Cincinnati, or of Hamilton county.   When the
famous Oswego letter was received, it was read, and,
as usual with such letters, I indorsed it and handed it
to Major Gwynn.   But, it seems, when the answer was
prepared, it was signed also by his colleagues of the
county or city committee.   Of all this I knew nothing,
nor in their capacity of committee had they anything
to do with my letters.   Yet, by a little mistake and
much perversion, these gentlemen have been erected
into a committee of my conscience-keepers, and made
to shut me up in a cage to prevent me from answering
interrogatories."   General Harrison remarked that, had
he, indeed, called to his assistance the services of a
friend in conducting his correspondence, he would
have had high authority to justify him in the measure.
It had been said of General Washington, that many of
the papers which bear his signature were written by
others, and he believed it had never been contra-
dicted; and General Breckenridge, aide to General Jack-

son, in the late war, had represented himself to be the author of much of General Jackson's correspondence. But he had not done so, to any extent, or in any sense, than as he had now explained it—in requesting Major Gwynn to refer those addressing inquiries to him to the public sources of information. And he would here say, that in all his public life, civil and military, there was no letter, report, speech or order, bearing his name, which was not written wholly by his own hand. He said, to open, read, and answer all the letters received by him was physically impossible, though he should do nothing else whatever.

To give his hearers an idea of the labor it would require, he said, a gentleman then present was with him the morning he left Cincinnati when he took from the post-office sixteen letters—there was usually half the number at the post-office near his residence—twenty-four letters per day. "Could any man," he asked, "give the requisite attention to such a daily correspondence, even to the neglect of every other engagement?" True it was, that many communications were sent which were not entitled to his notice, sent by persons who had no other object but to draw from him something which might be used to his injury, and the injury of the cause with which he was identified; yet, there were enough of those which claimed his respectful consideration for the sources from which they came and the subjects to which they referred, to occupy more time and labor than any one man could bestow upon them.

General Harrison said he had alluded particularly to this action of the committee because it had so recently been the occasion of so much animadversion by his political adversaries. But it was one only of many misrepresentations of him, his conduct, his principles and his opinions, with which the party press was teeming. He said it would occupy him many hours to discuss them, if it were necessary or proper for him to do so. He referred, however, to the Richmond *Enquirer*, and expressed his surprise at the manner in which his name and character had been treated by that paper. He did

so, as it afforded an example of the prostitution of the
press to party purposes. That paper—which formerly
did him more than justice and paid him the highest
compliments as a soldier and civilian, whose editor at
one time could designate no other man whom he considered so well qualified for the responsible place of
Secretary of War—was now lending itself to the circulation of the most discreditable calumnies against him
and endeavoring to persuade his countrymen that he
was a coward and a Federalist. He alluded to the
evidence upon which the *Enquirer* sought to fasten
the accusation that he was a black cockade Federalist
—i. e., the remarks of Mr. Randolph in the Senate of
the United States. He said that the attack of Mr.
Randolph was met at the moment it was made, and
effectually disproved. He passed high encomiums upon
the genius of that remarkable man, and said, that
those who knew Mr. Randolph knew that he never
gave up a point in debate, or receded from his ground
anywhere, until convicted of error. The fact that he
made no reply to his answer to the charge is proof to
any familiar with his character that he himself was satisfied that he had erred. General Harrison explained
the foundation of Mr. Randolph's charge, made at a
moment of temporary irritation. He said that old Mr.
Adams refused to adopt against France the measures
which his party desired, and showed himself in that
respect, at least, more an American than a partisan.
It was that course of policy of Mr. Adams which commanded his approbation and induced him so to express
himself at the time. Mr. Randolph remembered the
expression, but probably forgot the particular subject
of it, and thus the very fact which proved him to belong to the Republican party of 1800, long years after-
ward, is separated from its attendant circumstances
and used to prove him a Federalist. General Harrison
expressed himself with much earnestness on the injustice which was thus attempted to be inflicted on his
character in his native State, in which, when truth and
virtue, and honor, had suffered violence everywhere
else, he had hoped they would survive.

General Harrison alluded to several other instances of gross misrepresentation or absolute falsehoods, industriously and shamefully propagated by a party press.

"It seems almost incredible, fellow-citizens," said he, "but it is true, that from a long speech, filling several columns of a paper, two short sentences have been taken from different parts of it, these two sentences, separated from their context, are put together. my name attached to them, and published throughout the land as an authentic document."

He deplored that state of public sentiment which could tolerate such a system of party action, and trusted for the honor of his country and the hopes of liberty, that the reformation of such abuses would soon be wrought out by the force of a pure and healthy public opinion.

"Why, fellow-citizens," said General Harrison, "I have recently, in that house (pointing to the State house) been charged with high offenses against my country, which, if true, ought to cost me my life. Yes," continued he, "accusations were there laid to my charge which, being established, would subject me, even now, to the severest penalties which military law inflicts; for I have always held that an officer may not escape the responsibilities of misconduct by resigning his commission.

"These charges are not made by my companions in arms—by the eye-witnesses of my actions—by the great and good and brave men who fought by my side or under my command. They tell a different story. But their evidence, clear, unequivocal and distinct: the testimony of Governor Shelby, the venerable hero of King's mountain. of the gallant Perry, and of many brave and generous spirits who saw and knew and participated in all the operations connected with the battle of the Thames; the evidence of impartial and honorable men, the concurrent records of history and the authority of universal public opinion, are all cast aside in deference to the reckless assertions of those who were either not in being or dandled in the arms of their nurses!"

General Harrison said he acknowledged that these calumnies were disagreeable to him. His good name, such as it was, was his most precious treasure and he did not like to have it mangled by such calumnies. Were it his land which they were seeking to destroy, were it the title-deeds to his farm that they were endeavoring to mutilate, he could bear their efforts with patience, and smile even at their success. But he confessed, notwithstanding his perfect confidence in the justice of his country, and the decision of an impartial posterity, that these ruthless attacks upon his military character affected him unpleasantly. This policy of his adversaries constrained him to consider himself as now on trial before his country. He was not reluctant to be tried fairly—the American people being his court and jury. His adversaries held to those rules of evidence established by common sense and common right. He feared not the results of the strictest scrutiny, and would cheerfully submit to the decision of a virtuous and enlightened community. He asked but fair dealing and final justice; no more.

General Harrison alluded to several other instances of gratuitous and unfounded calumny, having no shadow of apology in any fact for their invention and publication. He spoke of the battle of Tippecanoe, of the death of the brave and lamented Davies, whose fall had been ascribed to him. He said the whole story about the white horse was entirely false, and that the fate of the gallant Kentuckian had no connection whatever with his own white mare which, by accident, was not rode on that occasion by any one. In remarking upon the slanders connected with the battle of Tippecanoe he said their refutation, one and all, was found in the proceedings of the legislature of Kentucky, and especially in the extraordinary confidence reposed in him by the governor and people of that State, when they subsequently honored him with the command of their army, composed of the choice spirits of the land, the best blood of Kentucky. General Harrison spoke with deep emotion of the trust reposed in him by Kentucky on the occasion alluded to, and said

that the commission which made him the commander
of that brave and patriotic army of Kentuckians he
had always held as the most honorable commission
which it had been the fortune of his life to have conferred upon him.

He referred to a very recent story got up in his own
neighborhood and sent forth to the world, corrobor-
ated by the sanctity of an affidavit, which represented
him as confessing to a young man on a steamboat that
he was an Abolitionist, and that, although he voted
against restrictions on Missouri, he did so in opposition
to the suggestions of his conscience, etc. He said the
narrative bore on its face the proofs of its absolute
falsity, and when he pronounced it a fabrication without the semblance of a fact or a word for its basis, it
was not because he thought it required a contradiction, but to evince the recklesⸯness and desperation of
his political enemies, who seemed to have given up
every ground of hope, save that which they found in
villifying his name. " It is a melancholy fact, fellow-
citizens," said General Harrison, "that the advocates of
Mr. Van Buren should so far forget what belongs to
the character of an American citizen, and do so much
violence to the nature of our free institutions as to
place the great political contest in which we are now
striving upon an issue such as this. I would not
accept the lofty station to which some of you are
proposing to elevate me, if it came to me by such
means. I would not, if I had the power to prevent it,
allow the fair fame of my competitor to be unjustly
assailed and wounded even for the attainment of that
lofty aim of a noble ambition. Nay, I have often
defended Mr. Van Buren against what I believed to
be the misrepresentations of my own mistaken friends
and others. Fellow-citizens, if Mr. Van Buren be the
better statesman, let us say so. I shall be the last man
to raise an objection against, or to desire to impose
restraints upon, the utmost independence of thought
and action, and the freest expression of feeling and
opinion. I love a frank and generous adversary; such
a man I delight to embrace, and will serve him ac-

cording to my ability as cheerfully as my professed friend. But that political warfare which seeks success by foul detraction, and strives for ascendency by the ruin of personal character, merits the indignation of honest men, is hateful to every generous mind, and tends too surely to the destruction of public virtue, and, as a consequence, to the downfall of public liberty."

General Harrison apologized for occupying his fellow-citizens so long. He said he would but mention one more of the latest slanders which had come to his knowledge. A German paper, published in Cincinnati, almost under his own eye, puts it forth with apparent sincerity, that " General Harrison, now a candidate for the Presidency of the United States, was, many years ago, when a young man, an aide to General Wayne during his Indian wars, and that, whenever young Harrison found that a battle was coming on, he always ran off into the woods." [Again there was loud and irrepressible laughter.] " The editor forgot," said the General, "when he served up this little dish, that the only possible security to young Harrison's scalp, on the approach of a battle with the Indians, was in keeping out of the woods. Such a story as this can only excite a smile here, it is true," said General Harrison; "but this paper circulates not alone in the United States, copies of it are probably read in Europe, where our history is less known, and where the contradiction of such silly falsehoods may possibly never come.

" It has long been proverbial of old soldiers, fellow-citizens," continued General Harrison, "that they delight to go back to other days and fight their battles over again. When I began this address to you, I intended only to speak of my far-famed 'committee of conscience keepers,' and the 'iron cage' in which they confined me; but I have unwittingly taken advantage of your kind disposition to listen to me and extended my remarks to other though kindred topics. I will only add that, although they have made a wide mistake who make me dwell in an 'iron cage,' the unlucky wight who put me in a log cabin was a little nearer the truth than he probably supposed himself to be. It is true that a part of my dwelling-house is a log cabin, but as to the hard cider——" [The laughter which followed the allusion to the "hard-cider" branch of the story, drowned the voice of the speaker.]

"But," said General Harrison, "admonished by the proverb, that you may ascribe my long speech to the common infirmity of an old soldier, and bring me under the suspicion of the loquacity of age, I will conclude these hasty and unpremeditated remarks, by thanking my fellow-citizens of Columbus for their politeness on the present occasion, as well as for the friendly feeling of which they have uniformly and often heretofore given me so many gratifying proofs."

The general retired, leaving the crowd which had accumulated while he spoke delighted with the prompt and satisfactory manner in which he had met the wishes of the citizens. The uppermost idea in the mind of every one with whom the writer interchanged a thought, was the wish that every man in the Union had heard this unpremeditated and extemporaneous address. Upon every candid mind it impressed the conviction that the opposition candidate for the Presidency was the last man in the world to be made the instrument of a committee of "conscience-keepers," or to conceal his opinions of public measures from sinister motives, when the disclosure of them was called for by the propriety and fitness of things.

The general left the city about 10 o'clock, escorted by a numerous cavalcade on horseback, and attended by the mayor and the chairman of the State central committee. The escort parted with their guest a mile or so from the city on his journey northward.

The general was addressed, on parting, by the mayor in a brief valedictory on behalf of the citizens of the capital, to which he replied in his uniformly happy manner.

HARRISON'S FORT MEIGS SPEECH.

" Fellow-citizens, I am not, upon this occasion, before you in accordance with my own individual views or wishes. It has ever appeared to me that the office of President of the United States should not be sought after by any individual; but that the people should spontaneously, and with their own free will, accord the distinguished honor to the man whom they believed would best perform its important duties. Entertaining these views I should, fellow-citizens, have remained at home but for the pressing and friendly invitation which I have received from the citizens of Perrysburg, and the earnestness with which its acceptation was urged upon me by friends in whom I trusted, and whom I am now proud to see around me. If, however, fellow-citizens, I had not complied with that invitation—If I had remained at home—believe me, my friends, that my spirit would have been with you; for where, in this beautiful land, is there a place calculated as this is to recall long past reminiscences, and revive long-slumbering, but not wholly extinguished, emotions in my bosom?

" In casting my eyes around, fellow-citizens, they rest upon the spot where the gallant Wayne triumphed so gloriously over his enemies, and carried out those principles which it seemed his pleasure to impress upon my mind, and in which it has ever been my happiness humbly to attempt to imitate him. It was there, fellow-citizens, I saw the banner of the United States float in triumph over the flag of the enemy. There it was where was first laid the foundation of the prosperity of the now wide-spread and beautiful West. It was there I beheld the indignant Eagle frown upon the British Lion. It was there I saw the youth of our land carry out the lesson they imbibed from the gallant Wayne, the noblest and best an American can acquire, to die for his country when called to do so in its defense.

[At this moment the speaker's eye fell upon General

Hedges, when he said: "General Hedges, will you come up here? You have stood by my side in the hour of battle, and I cannot bear to see you at so great a distance now." Immense cheering followed this considerate recognition, and the cries of "Raise him up," "Place him by the side of his old general," had scarcely been uttered, when General Hedges was carried forward to the stand.] .

The General continued: " It was there I saw interred my beloved companions—the companions of my youth. It was not in accordance with the stern etiquet of military life then to mourn their departure; but I may now drop a tear over their graves at the recollections of their virtues and worth.

"In 1793, fellow-citizens, I received my commission to serve under General Wayne. In 1794 I was his aid at the battle of Miami. Nineteen years afterwards I had the honor of again being associated with many of those who were my companions in arms then. Nineteen years afterwards I found myself commander-in-chief of the Northwestern army, but I found no diminution in the bravery of the American soldier. I found the same spirit of valor in all—not in the regular soldier only, but in the enrolled militia and volunteer also.

"What glorious reminiscences does the view of all these scenes around me draw to my mind! When I consented to visit this memorable spot, I expected that a thousand pleasant associations (would to God there were no painful associations mingled with them) would be recalled—that I should meet thousands of my fellow-citizens here, and among them many of my old companions, met here to rear a new altar to liberty in the place of the one which bad men have prostrated.

[Here the general looked around as if for some water, when the cry was raised, " Give the general some hard cider." This was done, much to the satisfaction of the multitude.]

"And fellow-citizens," continued the general, " I will not attempt to conceal from you that, in coming here, I expected that I should receive from you those evidences of regard which a generous people are ever

willing to bestow upon those whom they believe to be
honest in their endeavors to serve their country. I receive these evidences of regard and esteem as the only
reward at all adequate to compensate for the anxieties
and anguish which in the past I experienced upon this
spot. Is there any man of sensibility, or possessing a
feeling of self-respect, who asks what those feelings
were? Do you suppose that the commander-in-chief
finds his reward in the glitter and splendor of the
camp? or in the forced obedience of the camp around
him? These are not pleasures under all circumstances,
these are not the rewards which a soldier seeks. I
ask any man to place himself in my situation, and then
say whether the extreme pain and anguish which endured, and which every person similarly situated must
have endured, can meet with any adequate compensa-
tion, except by such expressions of the confidence and
gratitude of the people, as that with which you, fellow-
citizens, have this day honored me? These feelings
are common to all commanders of sense and sensibility.
The commanders of Europe possess them, although
placed at the head of armies reared to war. How
much more naturally would those feelings attach to a
commander situated as I was? For of what materials
was the army composed which was placed under my
command? The soldiers who fought, and bled, and
triumphed here, were lawyers, who had thrown up
their briefs, physicians, who had laid aside their instruments; mechanics, who had put by their tools, and, in
far the largest proportions, agriculturists who had
their plows in the furrow, although their families depended for their bread upon their exertions, and who
hastened to the battle-field to give their life to their
country, if it were necessary to maintain her rights. I
could point from where I now stand to places where
I felt this anxiety pressing heavily upon me, as I
thought of the fearful consequences of a mistake on
my part, or the want of judgment on the part of others.
I knew there were wives who had given their husbands to the field, mothers who had clothed their sons
for battle; and I knew that these expecting wives and

mothers were looking for the safe return of their husbands and sons. When to this was added the recollection that the peace of the entire West would be
broken up, and the glory of my country tarnished if I
failed, you may possibly conceive the anguish which
my situation was calculated to produce. Feeling my
responsibility, I personally supervised and directed the
arrangement of the army under my command. I
trusted to no Colonel or other officer. No person had
any hand in any disposition of the army. Every step
of warfare, whether for good or ill, was taken under
my own direction, and of no other, as many who now
hear me know. Whether every movement would or
would not pass the criticism of Bonaparte or Welling-
ton, I know not; but whether they would induce applause or censure, upon myself it must fall."

"But, fellow-citizens, still another motive induced me
to accept the invitation which had been so kindly extended to me. I knew that here I should meet with
many who had fought and bled under my command—
that I should have the pleasure of taking them by the
hand, and recurring, with them, to the scenes of the
past. I expected, too, to meet with a few of the great
and good men yet surviving, by whose efforts our freedom was achieved. This pleasure alone would have
been sufficient to induce my visit to this interesting
spot upon this equally interesting occasion. I see my
old companions here, and I see not a few of the Revolutionary veterans around me. Would to God that it
had ever been in my power to have made them comfortable and happy, that their sun might go down in
peace! But, fellow-citizens, they remain unprovided
for—monuments of the ingratitude of my country. It
was with the greatest difficulty that the existing pension act was passed through Congress. But why was
it restricted? Why were the brave soldiers who fought
under Wayne excluded? soldiers who suffered far more
than they who fought in the Revolution proper. The
Revolution, in fact, did not terminate until 1794—until
the battle was fought upon the battle ground upon
which my eye now rests. [Miami.] War continued

with them from the commencement of the Revolution until the victory of Wayne, to which I have just alluded.

"The great highway to the West was the scene of unceasing slaughter. Then why this unjust discrimination? Why are the soldiers who terminated the war of the Revolution, in fact, excluded, while those by whom it was begun, or a portion of them, are rewarded? I will tell you why. The poor remnant of Wayne's army had but few advocates, while those who had served in the Revolution proper had plenty of friends. Scattered, as they were, over all parts of the Union, and in large numbers, they could exert an influence at the ballot-box. They could whisper thus in the ears of those who sought their influence at the polls. 'Take care, for I have waited long enough for what has been promised. The former plea of poverty can no longer be made. The Treasury is now full. Take care, your seat is in danger.' 'Oh! yes, everything that has been promised shall be attended to if you will give me your votes.' In this way, fellow-citizens, tardy, but partial, justice was done to the soldiers of the Revolution. They made friends by their influence at the ballot-box. But it was different with General Wayne's soldiers. They were but few in number, and they had but one or two humble advocates to speak for them in Congress. The result has been, justice has been withheld.

"I have said that the soldiers under Wayne experienced greater hardships even than the soldiers of the Revolution. This is so. Every one can appreciate the difference between an Indian and a regular war. When wounded in battle the soldier must have warmth and shelter before he can recover. This could always be secured by the soldier of the Revolution. In those days the latch-string of no door was pulled in. When wounded he was sure to find shelter and very many of those comforts which are so essential to the sick, but which the soldiers in an Indian war cannot procure. Instead of shelter and warmth, he is exposed to the thousand ills incident to Indian warfare. Yet no relief was extended to those who had thus suffered !

" After the war closed under Wayne, I retired; and when I saw a man poorer than all others, wandering about the land decrepid and decayed by intemperance, it was unnecessary to inquire whether he had ever belonged to Wayne's army. His condition was a guarantee of that—was a sufficient assurance that he had wasted his energies among the unwholesome swamps of the West, in the defense of the rights of his fellow-citizens, and for the maintenance of the honor and glory of his country.

" Well, fellow-citizens, I can only say, that if it should ever be in my power to pay the debt which is due these brave but neglected men, that debt shall first of all be paid. And I am very well satisfied that the Government can afford it, provided the latch-string of the Treasury shall ever be more carefully pulled in. Perhaps you will ask me for some proof of my friendship for old soldiers. If so, I can give it you from the records of Congress. When the fifteen-hundred-dollar law was repealed, I opposed it, as I opposed changing the pay of members of Congress from six to eight dollars, until we had done justice to and provided for these soldiers. You will find my votes upon this question upon the records of Congress, and my speech upon it in the public debates of the same.

" I will now, my fellow-citizens, give you my reasons for having refused to give pledges and opinions more freely than I have done since my nomination to the Presidency. Many of the statements published upon the subject are by no means correct; but it is that it is true my opinion that no pledge should be made by an individual when in nomination for any office in the gift of the people. And why? Once adopt it, and the battle will no longer be to the strong, to the virtuous, or to the sincere lover of his country; but to him who is prepared to tell the greatest number of lies, and to proffer the largest number of pledges which he never intends to carry out. I suppose that the best guarantee which an American citizen could have of the correctness of the conduct of an individual in the future would be his conduct in the past when he had no temptation before him to practice deceit.

"Now, fellow-citizens, I have not altogether grown gray under the helmet of my country, although I have worn it for some time. A large portion of my life has been passed in the civil departments of government. Examine my conduct there, and the most tenacious Democrat—I use the word in its proper sense; I mean not to confine it to parties, for there are good in both—may doubtless discover faults, but he will find no single act calculated to derogate from the rights of the people.

"However, to prove the reverse of this, I have been called a Federalist. [Here was a loud cry of "The charge is a lie—a base lie. You are no Federalist."] Well, what is a Federalist? I recollect what the word formerly signified, and there are many others present who recollect its former signification also. They know that the Federal party were accused of a design to strengthen the hands of the General Government at the expense of the separate States. That accusation could not nor cannot apply to me. I was brought up after the strictest manner of Virginian anti-Federalism. St. Paul himself was not a greater devotee to the doctrines of the Pharisees than was I, by inclination and a father's precepts and example, to anti-Federalism. I was taught to believe that sooner or later that fatal catastrophe to human liberty would take place—that the General Government would swallow up all the State governments, and that one department of the Government would swallow up all the other departments. I do not know whether my friend, Mr. Van Buren (and he is, and I hope will ever be, my personal friend), has a gullet that can swallow everything; but I do know but that if his measures are all carried out, he will lay a foundation for others to do so if he does not.

"What reflecting man, fellow-citizens, cannot see this? The representatives of the people were once the source of power. Is it so now? Nay. It is to the Executive

Mansion now that every eye is turned—that every wish is directed. The men of office and party, who are governed by the principles of John Randolph, to wit: the five loaves and two fishes, seem to have their ears constantly directed to the bell at headquarters, to indicate how the little ones shall ring.

" But to return: I have but to remark that my anti-Federalism has been tempered by my long service in the employ of my country, and my frequent oaths to support her General Government; but I am as ready to resist the encroachments on State rights as I am to support the legitimate authority of the executive or the General Government.

" Now, fellow-citizens, I have very little more to say, except to exhort you to go on, peacefully if you can—and you can—to effect that reform, upon which your hearts are fixed. What calamitous consequences will ensue to the world if you fail! If you should fail, how the tryants of Europe will rejoice. If you fail, how will the friends of freedom, scattered like the few planets of heaven over the world, mourn, when they see the beacon-light of liberty extinguished—the light whose rays they had hoped would yet penetrate the whole benighted world.

" If you triumph, it will only be done with vigilance and attention. Our personal friends, but political enemies, remind each other, that ' Eternal vigilance is the price of liberty.' While journeying thitherward I observed this motto waving at the head of a procession, composed of the friends of the present administration. From this I inferred that discrimination was necessary in order to know who to watch. Under Jefferson, Madison, and Monroe, the eye of the people was turned to the right source—to the administration. The administration, however, now say to the people, ' You must not watch us, but you must watch the Whigs! Only do that, and all is safe!' But that, my friends, is not the way. The old-fashioned Republican rule is to watch the Government. See that the Government does not acquire too much power. Keep a check upon your rulers. Do this, and liberty is safe. And if your efforts

should result successfully, and I should be placed in the
Presidential chair, I shall invite a recurrence to the old
Republican rule, to watch the administration, and to
condemn all its acts which are not in accordance with
the strictest mode of republicanism.   Our rulers, fellow-
citizens, must be watched.   Power is insinuating.   Few
men are satisfied with less power than they are able to
procure.   If the ladies, whom I see around me, were
near enough to hear me, and of sufficient age to give
an experimental answer, they would tell you that no
lover is ever satisfied with the first smile of his mistress.

" It is necessary, therefore, to watch, not the political
opponents of the administration, but the administration itself, and to see that it keeps within the bounds
of the Constitution and the laws of the land.   The
executive of the Union has immense power to do
mischief if he sees fit to exercise that power.   He may
prostrate the country.   Indeed this country has been
already prostrated.   It has already fallen from pure
republicanism to a monarchy in spirit if not in name.
A celebrated author defines monarchy to be that form
of government in which the executive has at once the
command of the army, the execution of the laws and
the control of the purse.   Now how is it with our
present executive?   The Constitution gives to him the
control of the army and the execution of the laws.
He now only awaits the possession of the purse to
make him a monarch.   Not a monarch simply, with
the power of England, but a monarch with powers
of the autocrat of Russia.   For Gibbon says that an
individual possessed of these powers 'will, unless
closely watched, make himself a despot.'

" The passage of the sub-treasury bill will give to the
President an accumulation of power—the single additional power that the Constitution withholds from him,
and the possession of which will make him a monarch.
This catastrophe to freedom should be and can be prevented by vigilance, union and perseverance.

["We will do it," resounded from twenty thousand
voices, "we will do it."]

"In conclusion, then, fellow-citizens, I would impress it upon all, Democrats and Whigs, *give up the idea of watching each other, and direct your eye to the Government.* Do that, and your children, and your children's children, to the latest posterity, will be as happy and as free as you and your fathers have been."

[At the close of this speech the vast multitude gave "three times three," with an unanimity and heartiness which spoke eloquently the unanimity of their sentiments as to the force, truth and beauty of the speech, and the worth, merit and virtue of the speaker.]— *Detroit Advertiser.*

SPEECH OF HENRY CLAY

At Taylorsville, Hanover County, Virginia, June 27, 1840.*

After a longer delay than we expected, we have to-day the pleasure of presenting to our readers the speech delivered by Mr. Clay at Taylorsville, Hanover county, on the 27th ult. It will be read with interest by his friends and opponents. It is worthy of his high fame as an orator and a statesman, and contains matter for the serious reflection of every lover of his country.

The sentiment in compliment to Mr. Clay was received with long-continued applause. That gentleman rose and addressed the company substantially as follows:

"I think, friends and fellow-citizens, that, availing myself of the privilege of my long service in the public councils just adverted to, the resolution which I have adopted is not unreasonable, of leaving to younger men, generally, the performance of the duty, and the enjoyment of the pleasure of addressing the people in their primary assemblies. After the event which

___

*From the Fredericksburg *Arens*, July 10, 1840.

occurred last winter at the capitol of Pennsylvania, I believe it due to myself, to the Whig cause and to the country, to announce to the public, with perfect truth and sincerity, and without any reserve, my fixed determination heartily to support the nomination of William Henry Harrison there made. To put down all misrepresentations, I have, on suitable occasions, repeated this annunciation; and now declare my solemn conviction that the purity and security of the prosperity of the country imperatively demand the election of that citizen to the office of Chief Magistrate of the United States.

" But this occasion forms an exception from the rule which I have prescribed to myself. I have come here to the county of my nativity, in the spirit of a pilgrim, to meet, perhaps for the last time, the companions and the descendants of the companions of my youth. Wherever we roam, in whatever climate or land we are cast by the accidents of human life, beyond the mountains or beyond the ocean, in the legislative halls of the Capitol, or in the retreats and shades of private life, our hearts turn with an irresistible instinct to the cherished spot which ushered us into existence. And we dwell with delightful associations on the recollection of the streams in which, during our boyish days we bathed, the fountains at which we drunk, the piney fields, the hills and the valleys where we sported, and the friends who shared these enjoyments with us. Alas! too many of these friends of mine have gone whither we must all shortly go, and the presence here of the small remnant left behind attests both our loss and our early attachment. I would greatly prefer, my friends, to employ the time which this visit affords, in friendly and familiar conversation on the virtues of our departed companions, and on the scenes and adventures of our younger days; but the expectation which prevails, the awful state of our beloved country, and the opportunities which I have enjoyed in its public councils, impose on me the obligation of touching on topics less congenial with the feelings of my heart, but possessing higher public interest. I assure you, fellow-citizens, however, that I present myself before you for no purpose of exciting prejudices or inflaming passions, but to speak to you in all soberness and truth, and to testify to the things which I know or the convictions which I entertain, as an ancient friend, who has lived long, and whose career is rapidly drawing to a close. Throughout an arduous life I have endeavored to make truth and the good of our common country the guides of my public conduct; but in Hanover county, for which I cherish sentiments of respect, gratitude and veneration above all other places, would I avoid saying anything that I did not sincerely and truly believe.

"Why is the plow deserted, the tools of the mechanic laid aside, and all are seen rushing to gatherings of the people? What occasions those vast and unusual assemblages which we behold in every State, and in almost every neighborhood? Why those conventions of the people, at a common center, from all extremities of this vast Union, to consult together upon the sufferings of the community, and to deliberate on the means of deliverance? Why this rabid appetite for public discussions? What is the solution of the phenomenon, which we observe, of a great nation agitated upon its whole surface, and at its lowest depths, like the ocean when convulsed by some terrible storm? There must be a cause, and no ordinary cause.

"It has been truly said, in the most memorable document that ever issued from the pen of man, that 'all experience hath shown that mankind are more disposed to suffer, while evils are sufferable, than to right themselves by abolishing the forms to which they are accustomed.' The recent history of our people furnishes confirmation of that truth. They are active, enterprising and intelligent, but are not prone to make groundless complaints against public servants. If we now everywhere behold them in motion, it is because they feel that the grievances under which they are writhing can be no longer tolerated. They feel the absolute necessity of a change, that no change can render their condition worse, and that any change must better it. This is the judgment to which they have come; this, the brief and compendious logic which we daily hear. They know that, in all the dispensations of Providence, they have reason to be thankful and grateful; and if they had not, they would be borne with fortitude and resignation. But there is a pervading conviction and persuasion that, in the administration of government, there has been something wrong, radically wrong, and that the vessel of State has been in the hands of selfish, faithless, and unskillful pilots, who have conducted it amidst the breakers.

" In my deliberate opinion, the present distressed and distracted state of the country may be traced to the single cause of the action, the encroachments, and the usurpations of the executive branch of the Government. I have not time here to exhibit and to dwell upon all the instances of these, as they have occurred in succession, during the last twelve years. They have been again and again exposed on other more fit occasions. But I have thought this a proper opportunity to point out the enormity of the pretensions, principles and practices of that department, as they have been, from time to time, disclosed in these late years, and to show the rapid progress which has been made in the fulfillment of the remarkable language of our illustrious countryman, that the Federal executive had an awful squinting towards monarchy. Here in the county of his birth, surrounded by sons, some of whose sires with him were the first to raise their arms in defense of American liberty against a foreign monarch, is an appropriate place to expose the impending danger of creating a domestic monarch. And may I not, without presumption, indulge the hope that the warning voice of another, although far humbler son of Hanover, may not pass unheeded?

" The President of the United States advanced certain new and alarming pretensions for the executive department of the Government, the effect of which, if established and recognized by the people, must inevitably convert it into a monarchy. The first of these, and it was a favorite principle with him, was, that the executive department should be regarded as a unit. By this principle of unity he meant and intended that all the executive officers of Government should be bound to obey the commands and execute the orders of the President of the United States, and that they should be amenable to him, and be responsible for them. Prior to his administration, it had been considered that they were bound to observe and obey the Constitution and laws, subject to the general superintedence of the President, and responsible by impeachment, and to the tribunals of justice, for injuries inflicted on private citizens.

"But the annunciation of this new and extraordinary principle was not of itself sufficient for the purposes of President Jackson; it was essential that the subjection to his will, which was its object, should be secured by some adequate sanction. That he sought to effect, by an extension of another principle, that of dismission from office, beyond all precedent, and in cases and under circumstances which would have furnished just grounds of his impeachment, according to the solemn opinion of Mr. Madison and other members of the first Congress under the present Constitution.

"Now, if the whole official corps, subordinate to the President of the United States, are made to know and to feel that they hold their respective offices by the tenure of conformity and obedience to his will, it is manifest that they must look to that will, and not to the Constitution and laws, as a guide of their official conduct. The weakness of human nature, the love and emoluments of office, perhaps the bread necessary to the support of their families, would make this result absolutely certain.

"The development of this new character to the power of dismission would have fallen short of the aims in view, without the exercise of it were held to be a prerogative, for which the President was to be wholly irresponsible. If he were compelled to expose the grounds and reasons upon which he acted, in dismissals from office, the apprehension of public censure would temper the arbitrary nature of the power and throw some protection around the subordinate officer. Hence the new and monstrous pretension has been advanced, that although the concurrence of the Senate is necessary by the Constitution to the confirmation of an appointment, the President may, subsequently, dismiss the person appointed, not only without communicating the grounds on which he has acted to the Senate, but without any such communication to the people themselves, for whose benefit all offices are created. And so bold and daring has the executive branch of the Government become, that one of its Cabinet ministers, himself a subordinate officer, has contemptuously refused to members of the House of Representatives to disclose the grounds on which he has undertaken to dismiss from office persons acting as deputy postmasters in his department.

" As to the gratuitous assumption by President Jackson, of responsibility for all the subordinate execut.ve officers, it is the merest mockery that was ever put forth. They will escape punishment by pleading his orders, and he by alleging the hardship of being punished, not for his own acts, but for theirs. We have a practical exposition of this principle in the case of the 200,000 militia. The Secretary of War comes out to screen the President, by testifying that he never saw what he strongly recommended; and the President reciprocated that favor by retaining the Secretary in place, notwithstanding he has proposed a plan for organizing the militia, which is acknowledged to be unconstitutional. If the President is not to be held responsible for a Cabinet minister, in daily intercourse with him, how is he to be rendered so for a receiver in Wisconsin or Iowa? To concentrate all reponsibility in the President is to annihilate all responsibility. For who ever expects to see the day arrive when a President of the United States will be impeached; or, if impeached, when he cannot command more than one-third of the Senate to defeat the impeachment?

" But to construct the scheme of practical despotism, whilst all the forms of free government remained, it was necessary to take one farther step. By the Constitution the President is enjoined to take care that the laws be executed. This injunction was merely intended to impose on him the duty of a general superintendence; to see that offices were filled, officers at their respective posts in the discharge of their official functions, and all obstructions to the enforcement of the laws were removed, and, when necessary for that purpose, to carry out the militia. No one ever imagined, prior to the administration of President Jackson, that a President of the United States was to occupy himself with supervising and attending to the execution of all the minute details of every one of the host of offices in the United States.

"Under the constitutional injunction just mentioned, the late President put forward that most extraordinary pretension that the Constitution and laws of the United States were to be executed *as he understood them;* and this pretension was attempted to be sustained by an argument equally extraordinary, that the President, being a sworn officer, must carry them into effect according to his sense of their meaning. The Constitution and laws were to be executed, not according to their import as handed down to us by our ancestors, as interpreted by contemporaneous expositions, as expounded by concurrent judicial decisions, as fixed by an uninterrupted course of Congressional legislation, but in that sense which a President of the United States happened to understand them!

"To complete this executive usurpation one further object remained. By the Constitution, the command of the Army and the Navy is conferred on the President. If he could unite the purse to the sword nothing would be left to gratify the insatiable thirst for power. In 1833 the President seized the Treasury of the United States, and from that day to this it has continued substantially under his control. This seizure was effected by the removal of one Secretary of the Treasury understood to be opposed to the measure, and by the dismissal of another, who refused to violate the law of the land upon the orders of the President.

"It is, indeed, said that not a dollar in the Treasury

13

can be touched without a previous appropriation by law, nor drawn out of the Treasury without the concurrence and signatures of the Secretary, the Treasurer, the Register and the Comptroller. But are not all these pretended securities idle and unavailing forms? We have seen that, by the operation of the irresponsible power of dismission, all those officers are reduced to automata, absolutely subjected to the will of the President. What resistance would any of them make, with the penalty of dismission suspended over their heads, to any order of the President to pour out the treasure of the United States whether an act of appropriation existed or not? Do not mock us with the vain assurance of the honor and probity of a President, nor remind us of the confidence which we ought to repose in his imagined virtues. The pervading principle of our system of Government—of all free governments—is not merely the possibility, but the absolute certainty of infidelity and treachery with even the highest functionary of the State; and hence all the restrictions, securities, and guarantees which the wisdom of our ancestors or the sad experience of history had inculcated have been devised and thrown around the Chief Magistrate.

"Here, friends and fellow-citizens, let us pause and contemplate this stupendous structure of executive machinery and despotism which has been reared in our young Republic. The executive branch of this government is a unit; throughout all its arteries and veins there is but one heart, one head, one will. The number of the subordinate executive officers and dependents in the United States has been estimated, in an official report, founded on public documents, made by a Senator from South Carolina (Mr. Calhoun), at one hundred thousand. Whatever it may be, all of them, wherever they are situated, are bound implicitly to obey the orders of the President. And absolute obedience to his will is secured and enforced by the power of dismissing them, at his pleasure, from their respective places. To make this terrible power of dismission more certain and efficacious, its exercise is covered up in mysterious secrecy, without exposure, without the smallest responsibility. The Constitution and laws of the United States are to be executed in the sense in which the President understands them, although that sense may be at variance with the understanding of every other man in the United States. It follows, as a necessary consequence from the principle deduced by the President from the constitutional injunction as to the execution of the laws, that, if an act of Congress be passed, in his opinion, contrary to the Constitution, or if a decision be pronounced by the courts in his opinion contrary to the Constitution or the laws, that act or that decision the President is not obliged to enforce, and he could not cause it to be enforced without a violation, as is pretended, of his official oath. Candor requires the admission that the principle has not yet been pushed in practice to these cases; but it manifestly comprehends them, and who doubts that, if the spirit of usurpation is not arrested and rebuked, they will be finally reached? *The march of power is ever onward.* As times and seasons admonish, it openly and boldly, in broad day, makes its progress; or, if alarm be excited by the enormity of its pretensions, it silently and secretly, in the dark of the night, steals its devious way. It now storms and mounts the ramparts of the fortress of liberty; it now saps and undermines its foundations. Finally, the command of the Army and Navy being already in the President, and having acquired a perfect control over the Treasury of the United States, *he has consummated that frightful union of purse and sword*, so long, so much so earnestly deprecated by all true lovers of civil liberty. And our present Chief Magistrate stands solemnly and voluntarily pledged, in the face of the whole world, to follow in the footsteps and carry out the measures and the principles of his illustrious predecessor!

"The sum of the whole is, that there is but one power, one control, one will in the State. All is concentrated in the President. He directs, orders, commands the whole machinery of the State. Through the official agencies, scattered throughout the land, and absolutely subjected to his will, he executes according to his pleasure or caprice, the whole power of the commonwealth, which has been absorbed and engrossed by him. And one sole will predominates in, and animates the whole of this community. If this be not practical despotism I am incapable of conceiving or defining it. Names are nothing. The existence or non-existence of arbitrary government does not depend upon the title or denomination bestowed on the chief of the State, but upon the quantum of power which he possesses and wields. Autocrat, sultan, emperor, dictator, king, doge, president, are all mere names, in which the power respectively possessed by them is not to be found, but is to be looked for in the Constitution, or the established usages and practices of the several States which they govern and control. If the Autocrat of Russia were called president of all the Russias, the actual power remaining unchanged, his authority under his new denomination would continue undiminished; and if the President of the United States were to receive the title of Autocrat of the United States, the amount of his authority would not be increased without an alteration of the Constitution.

"General Jackson was a bold and fearless reaper, carrying a wide row, but he did not gather the whole harvest; he left some gleanings to his faithful successor, and he seems resolved to sweep clean the field of power. The duty of inculcating on the official corps the active exertion of their personal and official influence was left by him to be enforced by Mr. Van Buren, in all popular elections. It was not sufficient that the official corps was bound implicitly to obey the will of the President. It was not sufficient that this obedience was coerced by the tremendous power of dismission. It soon became apparent that this corps might be beneficially employed to promote in other matters than the business of their offices, the views and interests of the President and his party. They are far more efficient than any standing army of equal numbers. A standing army would be separated, and stand

out from the people; would be an object of jealousy and
suspicion; and being always in corps, or in detachments,
could exert no influence on popular elections. But the
official corps is dispersed throughout the country, in
every town, village and city, mixing with the people,
attending their meetings and conventions, becoming
chairmen and members of committees and urging and
stimulating partisans to active and vigorous exertion.
Acting in concert, and throughout the whole Union
obeying orders issued from the center, their influence,
aided by executive patronage, by the Post-Office Department, and all the vast other means of the executive,
is almost irresistible.

"To correct this procedure, and to restrain the sub-
ordinates of the executive from all interference with
popular elections, my colleague (Mr. Crittenden) now
present, introduced a bill in the Senate. He had the
weight of Mr. Jefferson's opinion, who issued a circular to restrain Federal officers from intermeddling in
popular elections. He had before him the British example, according to which, placemen and pensioners
were not only forbidden to interfere, but were not,
some of them, even allowed to vote at popular elections.
But this bill left them free to excercise the elective
franchise, prohibiting only the use of their official
influence. And how was this bill received in the Senate? Passed by those who profess to admire the character and to pursue the principles of Mr. Jefferson?
No such thing. It was denounced as a sedition bill.
And the just odium of that sedition bill, which was
intended to protect office-holders against the people
was successfully used to defeat a measure of protection
of the people against the office-holders! Not only
were they left unrestrained, but they were urged and
stimulated by an official report to employ their influence in behalf of the administration, at the elections of
the people.

Hitherto the Army and Navy have remained unaf-
fected by the power of dismission, and they have not
been called into the political service of the executive.
But no attentive observer of the principles and pro-

ceedings of the men in power could fail to see that the
day was not distant when they, too, would be required
to perform the partisan offices of the President.   Accordingly, the process of converting them into executive instruments has commenced in a court-martial
assembled at Baltimore.   Two officers of the Army of
the United States have been put upon their solemn
trial, on the charge of prejudicing the Democratic
party by making purchases for the supply of the Army
from members of the Whig party.   It is not pretended
that the United States were prejudiced by those purchases; on the contrary, it was, I believe, established
that they were cheaper than could have been made
from the supporters of the administration.   But the
charge was that to purchase at all from the opponents,
instead of friends of the administration, was an injury
to the Democratic party which required that the offend-
ers should be put upon their trial before a court-martial.   And this trial was commenced at the instance of
a committee of a Democratic convention, and conducted and prosecuted by them.   The scandalous spectacle is presented to an enlightened world of the Chief
Magistrate of a great people executing the orders of a
self-created power, organized within the bosom of the
State, and upon such an accusation, arraigning, before
a military tribunal, gallant men, who are charged with
the defense of the honor and interest of their country,
and with bearing its eagles in the presence of an
enemy.

"But the Army and Navy are too small, and in com-
position are too patriotic to subserve all the purposes
of this administration.   Hence the recent proposition
of the Secretary of War, strongly recommended by the
President, under color of a new organization of the
militia, *to create a standing force of two hundred thousand men*, an amount which no conceivable foreign
exigency can ever make necessary.   It is not my purpose now to enter upon an examination of that alarming and dangerous plan of the Executive Department
of the Federal Government.   It has justly excited a
burst of general indignation; and nowhere has the dis-

approbation of it been more emphatically expressed than in this ancient and venerable commonwealth.

" The monstrous project may be described in a few words. It proposes to create the force by breaking down Mason and Dixson's line, expunging the boundaries of States, melting them up into a confluent mass, to be subsequently cut up into ten military parts, alienates the militia from its natural association, withdraws it from the authority and command and sympathy of its constitutional officers, appointed by the States, puts it under the command of the President, authorizes him to cause it to be trained, in palpable violation of the Constitution, and subjects it to be called out from remote and distant places, at his pleasure, and on occasions not warranted by the Constitution!

" Indefensible as this project is, fellow-citizens, do not be deceived by supposing that it has been or will be abandoned. It is a principle of those who are now in power that an election or re-election of the President implies the sanction of the people to all the measures which he had proposed, and all the opinions which he had expressed, on public affairs, prior to that event. We have seen this principle applied on various occasions. Let Mr. Van Buren be re-elected in November next, and it will be claimed that the people have thereby approved of this plan of the Secretary of War. All entertain the opinion that it is important to train the milita and render it effective; and it will be insisted, in the contingency mentioned, that the people have demonstrated that they approve of that specific plan. There is more reason to apprehend such consequence from the fact that a committee of the Senate, to which this subject was referred, instead of denouncing the scheme as unconstitutional and dangerous to liberty, presented a labored apologetic report, and the administration majority in that body ordered twenty thousand copies of the apology to be printed for circulation among the people. I take pleasure in testifying that one administration Senator had the manly independence to denounce, in his place, the project as unconsittutional. The Senator was from your own State.

" I have thus, fellow-citizens, exhibited to you a true and faithful picture of Executive power, as it has been enlarged and expanded within the last few years, and as it has been proposed further to extend it. It overshadows every other branch of the Government. The source of legislative power is no longer to be found in the Capital but in the palace of the President. In assuming to be a part of the legislative power, as the President recently did contrary to the Constitution, he would have been nearer the actual fact if he had alleged that he was the sole legislative power of the Union. How is it possible for public liberty to be preserved, and the constitutional distributions of power, among the departments of Government, to be maintained, unless the executive career be checked and restrained?

" It may be urged that two securities exist: first, that the Presidential term is of short duration; and secondly, the elective franchise. But it has been already shown that whether a depository power be arbitrary or compatible with liberty, does not depend upon the duration of the official term, but upon the amount of power invested. The Dictatorship in Rome was an office of brief existence, generally shorter than the Presidential term. Whether the elective franchise be an adequate security or not, is a problem to be solved next November. I hope and believe it yet is. But if Mr. Van Buren shall be re-elected, the power already acquired by the executive be retained, and that which is in progress be added to that department, it is my deliberate judgment that there will be no hope remaining for the continuance of the liberties of the country.

" And yet the partisans of this tremendous executive power arrogate to themselves the name of Democrats, and bestow upon us who are opposed to it the denomination of Federalists! In the Senate of the United States there are five gentlemen who were members of the Federal party, and four of them have been suddenly transformed into Democrats; and are now warm supporters of this administration, whilst I, who had exerted the humblest of my humble abilities to arouse the nation to a vindication of its insulted honor and its violated rights, and to the vigorous prosecution of the war against Great Britain, to which they were violently opposed, find myself, by a sort of magical influence, converted into a Federalist! The only American citizen that I ever met with, who was an avowed monarchist, was a supporter of the administration of General Jackson; and he acknowledged to me that his motive was to bring about the system of monarchy which his judgment preferred.

"There were other points of difference between the Federalist and the Democratic or rather Republican party of 1798; but the great, leading, prominent discrimination between them related to the constitution of the executive department of the Government. The Federalists believed that, in its structure, it was too weak and was in danger of being crushed by the preponderating weight of the legislative branch Hence, they rallied around the executive, and sought to give to it strength and energy. A strong Government, an energetic executive was among them the common language and the great object of that day. The Republicans, on the contrary, believed that the real danger lay on the side of the executive; that, having a continuous and uninterrupted existence, it was always on the alert, ready to defend the power it had, and prompt in acquiring more; and that the experience of history demonstrated that it was the encroaching and usurping department. They therefore rallied around the people and the legislature.

"What are the positions of the two great parties of the present day? Modern Democracy has reduced the Federal theory of a strong and energetic executive to practical operation. It has turned from the people, the natural ally of genuine Democracy, to the executive, and, instead of vigilance, jealousy, and distrust, has given to that department all its confidence, and made to it a virtual surrender of all the powers of Government. The recognized maxim of royal infallibility is transplanted from the British monarchy into modern American Democracy, and the President can do no wrong. This new school adopts, modifies, changes, renounces, renews opinions at the pleasure of the executive. Is the bank of the United States a useful and valuable institution? Yes, unanimously pronounces the Democratic legislature of Pennsylvania. The President vetoes it as a pernicious and dangerous establishment. The Democratic majority in the same legislature pronounce it to be pernicious and dangerous. The Democratic majority of the House of Representatives of the United States declare the deposits of the public money in the bank of the United States to be safe. The President says they are unsafe, and removes them. The Democracy say they are unsafe, and approve the removal. The President says that a scheme of a sub-treasury is revolutionary and disorganizing. The Democracy say it is revolutionary and disorganizing. The President says it is wise and salutary. The Democracy say it is wise and salutary.

"*The Whigs of 1840 stand where the Republicans of 1798 stood, and where the Whigs of the Revolution were, battling for liberty, for the people, for free institutions, against power, against corruption, against executive encroachments, against monarchy.*

" We are reproached with struggling for offices and their emoluments. If we acted on the avowed and acknowledged principle of our opponents, 'that the spoils belong to the victors,' we should indeed be unworthy of the support of the people. No, fellow-citizens, higher, nobler, more patriotic motives actuate the Whig party. Their object is the restoration of the Constitution, the preservation of liberty, the rescue of the country. If they were governed by the sordid and selfish motives acted upon by their opponents, and unjustly imputed to them, to acquire office and emolument, they have only to change their names, and enter the Presidential palace. The gate is always wide open, and the path is no narrow one which leads through it. The last comer, too, often fares best.

"On a resurvey of the past few years we behold enough to sicken and sadden the hearts of true patriots. Executive encroachment has quickly followed upon executive encroachment; persons honored by public confidence, and from whom nothing but grateful and parental measures should have flowed, have inflicted stunning blow after blow in such rapid succession that before the people could recover from the reeling effects of one, another has fallen heavily upon them. Had either of various instances of executive misrule stood out separate and alone, so that its enormity might have been seen and dwelt upon with composure, the condemnation of the executive would have long since been pronounced; but it has hitherto found safety and impunity in the bewildering effects of the multitude of its misdeeds. The nation has been in the condition of a man who, having gone to bed after his barn has been consumed by fire, is aroused in the morning to witness his dwelling-house wrapt in flames. So bold and presumptuous had the executive become that penetrating in its influence the hall of a co-ordinate branch of the Government by means of a submissive or instructed majority of the Senate *it has caused a record of the country to be effaced and expunged, the inviolability of which was guaranteed by a solemn injunction of the Constitution.* And that memorable and scandalous scene was enacted only because the offensive record contained an expression of disapprobation of an executive proceeding.

" If this state of things were to remain; if the progress of executive usurpation were to continue unchecked, hopeless despair would seize the public mind, or the people would be goaded to acts of open and violent resistance. But, thank God, the power of the President, fearful and rapid as its strides have been, is not yet too great for the power of the elective franchise; and a bright and glorious prospect in the election of William Henry Harrison has opened upon the country. The necessity of a change of rulers has deeply penetrated the heart of the people, and we everywhere behold cheering manifestations of that happy event. The fact of his election alone, without reference to the measures of his administration, will powerfully contribute to the security and happiness of the people. It will bring assurance of the cessation of

that long series of disastrous experiments which have
so greatly afflicted the people. Confidence will immediately revive, credit be restored, active business
will return, prices of products will rise, and the people will feel and know that, instead of their servants
being occupied in devising measures for their ruin and
destruction, they will be assiduously employed in promoting their welfare and prosperity.

" Whatever is the work of man, necessarily partakes
of his imperfections; and it was not to be expected
that, with all the acknowledged wish and virtues of
the framers of our Constitution they could have sent
forth a plan of Government so free from all defect, and
so full of guarantees, that it should not, in the conflict
of embittered parties and excited passions be perverted
and misinterpreted. Misconceptions or erroneous con-
structions of the powers granted in the Constitution
would probably have occurred, after the lapse of many
years, in seasons of entire calm and with a regular and
temperate administration of the Government; but during the last twelve years the machine, driven by a
reckless charioteer with a frightful impetuosity, has been
greatly jarred and jolted, and it needs careful examination and a thorough repair.

" With a view, therefore, to the fundamental character of the Government itself, and especially of the executive branch, it seems to me that, either by amend-
ments of the Constitution, when they are necessary, or
by remedial legislation, when the object falls within
the scope of the powers of Congress, there should be,

1. *A provision to render a person ineligible to the
office of President of the United States after a service of one term.*

" Much observation and deliberate reflection have
satisfied me that too much of the time, the thoughts, and
the exertions of the incumbent are occupied during his
first term, in securing his re-election. The public business, consequently, suffers; and measures are proposed
or executed with less regard to the general prosperity
than to their influence upon the approaching election.
If the limitation to one term existed, the President

would be exclusively devoted to the discharge of his public duties; and he would endeavor to signalize his administration by the beneficence and wisdom of its measures.

"*2. That the veto power should be more precisely defined, and be subjected to further limitations and qualifications.* Although a large, perhaps the largest, proportion of all the acts of Congress, since the commencement of the Government, were passed within the three last days of the session, and when of course the President for the time being had not the ten days for consideration allowed by the Constitution, President Jackson, availing himself of that allowance, has failed to return important bills. When not returned by the President within the ten days, it is questionable whether they are laws or not. It is very certain that the next Congress cannot act upon them by deciding whether or not they shall become laws, the President's objections notwithstanding. All this ought to be provided for.

"At present, a bill returned by the President can only become a law by the concurrence of two-thirds of the members of each House. I think if Congress passes a bill after discussion and consideration, and, after weighing the objections of the President, still believes it ought to pass, it should become a law, provided a majority of all the members of each House concur in its passage. If the weight of his argument and the weight of his influence conjointly cannot prevail on a majority, against their previous convictions, in my opinion, the bill ought not to be arrested. Such is the provision of the constitutions of several of the States, and that of Kentucky among them.

"*3. The power of dismission from office should be restricted, and the exercise of it be rendered responsible.*

"The constitutional concurrence of the Senate is necessary to the confirmation of all important appointments; but, without consulting the Senate, without any other motive than resentment or caprice, the President may dismiss, at his sole pleasure, an officer created by the joint action of himself and the Senate.

The practical effect is to nullify the agency of the Senate. There may be, occasionally, cases in which the public interest requires an immediate dismission without waiting for the assembling of the Senate; but, in all such cases the President should be bound to communicate fully the grounds and motives of the dismission. The power would be thus rendered responsible. Without it, the exercise of the power is utterly repugnant to free institutions, the basis of which is perfect responsibility and dangerous to the public liberty, as has been allready shown.

"*4. That the control over the Treasury of the United States should be confided and confined exclusively to Congress; and all authority of the President over it by means of dismissing the Secretary of the Treasury, or other persons having the immediate charge of it, be rigorously precluded.*

" You have heard much, fellow-citizens, of the divorce of banks and government. After crippling them and impairing their utility, the executive and its partisans have systematically denounced them. The executive and the country were warned again and again of the fatal course that has been pursued; but the execctive nevertheless persevered, commencing by praising and ending by decrying the State banks. Under cover of the smoke which has been raised, the real object all along has been, and yet is to obtain the possession of the money-power of the Union. That accomplished and sanctioned by the people—the union of the sword and the purse in the hands of the President effectually secured—and farewell to American liberty. The subtreasury is the scheme for effecting that union; and, I am told, that of all the days in the year, that which gave birth to our national existence and freedom is the selected day to be disgraced by ushering into existence a measure imminently perilous to the liberty which, on that anniversary, we commemorate in joyous festivals. Thus, in the spirit of destruction which animates our rulers, would they convert a day of gladness and of glory into a day of sadness and mourning. Fellow-citizens, there is one divorce urgently demanded by the safety and highest interests of the country, a divorce of the President from the treasury of the United States.

"*And 5. That the appointment of members of Congress to any office, or any but a few specified offices, during their continuance in office, and for one year thereafter be prohibited.*

"This is a hackneyed theme, but it is not less deserving serious consideration. The Constitution now interdicts the appointment of a member of Congress to any office created, or the emoluments of which had been increased whilst he was in office. In the purer days of the Republic that restriction might have been sufficient, but in these more degenerate times. it is necessary, by an amendment of the Constitution to give the principles greater extent.

"These are the subjects, in relation to the permanent character of the Government itself, which, it seems to me, are worthy of the serious attention of the people, and of a new administration. There are others, of an administrative nature, which require prompt and careful consideration.

"1. The currency of the country, its stability and uniform value, and, as intimately and indissolubly connected with it, the insurance of the faithful performance of the fiscal services necessary to the Government should be maintained and secured by exercising all the powers requisite to those objects with which Congress is constitutionally invested. These are the great ends to be aimed at, the means are of subordinate importance. Whether these ends, indispensable to the well-being of both the people and the Government, are to be attained by sound and safe State banks, carefully selected and properly distributed, or by a new bank of the United States, with such limitations, conditions, and restrictions as have been indicated by experience, should be left to the arbitrament of enlightened public opinion.

"Candor and truth require me to say that, in my judgment, whilst banks continue to exist in the country, the services of a bank of the United States cannot be safely dispensed with. I think that the power to

establish such a bank is a settled question; settled by
Washington and by Madison, by forty years' acquiescence, by the judiciary, and by both of the great parties which so long held sway in this country. I know
and I respect the contrary opinion, which is entertained in this State. But, in my deliberate view of the
matter, the power to establish such a bank being settled, and being a necessary and proper power, the
only question is as to the expediency of its exercise.
And on questions of mere expediency, public opinion ought to have a controlling influence. Without banks, I believe we cannot have a sufficient currency; without a bank of the United States I fear we
cannot have a sound currency. But it is the end, that
of a sound and sufficient currency, and a faithful execution of the fiscal duties of Government, that should
engage the dispassionate and candid consideration of
the whole community. There is nothing in the name
of a bank of the United States which has any magical charm, or to which any one need be wedded. It is
to secure certain great objects, without which society
cannot prosper; and if, contrary to my apprehension,
these objects can be accomplished by dispensing with
the agency of a bank of the United States, and em-
ploying that of State banks, all ought to rejoice and
heartily acquiesce, and none would more than I should.

" 2. That the public lands, in conformity with the
trusts created expressly, or by just implication, on
their acquisition, be administered in a spirit of liberality towards the new States and Territories, and in
a spirit of justice towards all the States.

" The land bill, which was rejected by President Jackson, and acts of occasional legislation, will accomplish
both these objects. I regret that the time does not admit of my exposing here the nefarious plans and purposes of the administration as to this vast national re-
source. That, like every other great interest of the
country, is administered with the sole view of the effect upon the interests of the party in power. A bill has
passed the Senate, and is now pending before the
House, according to which forty millions of dollars are

stricken from the real value of a certain portion of the
public lands by a short process; and a citizen of Virginia
residing on the southwest side of the Ohio is not allowed to purchase lands as cheap by half a dollar per
acre as a citizen living on the northwest side of that
river. I have no hesitation in expressing my conviction that the whole public domain is gone if Mr. Van
Buren be re-elected.

"3. THAT THE POLICY OF PROTECTING AND ENCOUR-
AGING THE PRODUCTIONS OF AMERICAN INDUSTRY, EN-
TERING INTO COMPETITION WITH THE RIVAL PRODUC-
TIONS OF FOREIGN INDUSTRY, HE ADHERED TO AND
MAINTAINED ON THE BASIS OF THE PRINCIPLES AND
IN THE SPIRIT OF THE COMPROMISE OF MARCH, 1833.

"PROTECTION AND NATIONAL INDEPENDENCE ARE,
IN MY OPINON, IDENTICAL AND SYNONYMOUS. THE
PRINCIPLE OF ABANDONMENT OF THE ONE CANNOT BE
SURRENDERED WITHOUT A FORFEITURE OF THE OTHER.
Who, with just pride and national sensibility, can think
of subjecting the products of our industry to all the
taxation and restraints of foreign powers, without effort on our part to counteract their prohibitions and
burdens by suitable countervailing legislation? These
questions cannot be, ought not to be, one of principle,
but of measure and degree. I adopt that of the compromise act, not because that act is irrepealable, but because it met with the sanction of the nation. Stability
with moderate and certain protection, is far more important than instability, the necessary consequence of
high protection. But the protection of the compromise
act will be adequate, in most, if not as to all interests.
The twenty per cent. which it stipulates, cash duties,
home valuations, and the list of free articles inserted in
the act for the particular advantage of the manufacturer,
will insure, I trust, sufficient protection. All together,
they will amount probably to not less than thirty per
cent.—a greater extent of protection than was secured
prior to the act of 1828, which no one stands up to
defend. Now, the valuation of foreign goods is not
made by the American authority, except in suspected
cases, but by foreigners and abroad. They assess the

14

value and we the duty; but, as the duty depends, in most cases on the value, it is manifest that those who assess the value fix the duty. The home valuation will give our Government what it rightfully possesses, both the power to ascertain the true valuation of the thing which it taxes, as well as the amount of that tax.

"*4. That a strict and wise economy in the disburse-ment of the public money be steadily enforced; and that, to that end, all useless establishments, all unnecessary offices and places, foreign and domestic, and all extrav-agance, either in the collection or expenditure of the public revenue be abolished and repressed.*

" I have not time to dwell on details in the applica-tion of this principle. I will say that a pruning knife, long, broad, and sharp, should be applied to every de-partment or the Government. There is abundant scope for honest and skillful surgery. The annual ex-penditure may, in reasonable time, be brought down from its present amount of about forty millions to near one-third of that sum.

"*5.* That several States have made such great and *gratifying progress in their respective systems of in-ternal improvement,* and have been so aided by the distribution under the deposit act, that, in future, the erection of new roads and canals should be left to them with such further aid only from the General Govern-ment as they would derive from the payment of the last installment under that act, from an absolute re-linquishment of the right of Congress to call upon them to refund the previous instalments, and from that equal and just quotas, to be received by the future dis-tribution of the net proceeds from the sales of public lands. And

"6. That the right to slave property being guaranteed by the Constitution and recognized as one of the com-promises incorporated in that instrument by our an-cestors, should be left where the Constitution has placed it, undisturbed and unagitated by Congress.

" These, fellow-citizens, are views both of the struc-ture of the Government and its administration which appear to me worthy of commanding the grave attention of the public and its new servants. Although, I repeat, I have neither authority nor purpose to commit anybody else, I believe most, if not all of them are entertained by the political friends with whom I have acted. Whether the salutary reforms which they include will be effected or considered, depends upon the issue of that great struggle which is now going on throughout all this country. *This contest has had no parallel since the period of the Revolution. In both instances there is a similarity of object. That was to achieve, this is to preserve the liberties of the country.* Let us catch the spirit which animated and imitate the virtues which adorned our noble ancestors. Their devotion, their constancy, their untiring activity, their perseverence, their indomitable resolution, their sacrifices, their valor! If they fought for liberty or death, in the memorable language of one of the most illustrious of them, let us never forget that the prize now at hazard is liberty or slavery. We should be encouraged by the fact that the contest, to the success of which they solemnly pledged their fortunes, their lives, and their sacred honor, was far more unequal than that in which we are engaged. But, on the other hand, let us cautiously guard against too much confidence. History and experience prove that more has been lost by self-confidence and contempt of enemies than won by skill and courage. Our opponents are powerful in numbers and in organization; active, insidious, possessed of ample means, and wholly unscrupulous in the use of them. They count upon success by the use of two words, Democracy and Federalism Democracy, which, in violation of all truth, they appropriate to themselves, and Federalism, which, in violation of all justice, they apply to us. And allow me to conjure you not to suffer yourselves to be diverted, deceived, or discouraged by the false rumors which will be industriously circulated between the present time and the period of the election, by our opponents. They will put them forth in every variety, and without number, in the most imposing forms, certified and sworn to by conspicuous names. They will brag, they will boast, they will threaten.

Regardless of all their arts, let us keep steadily and faithfully and fearlessly at work.

"But if the opposition perform its whole duty; if every member of it act as in the celebrated battle of Lord Nelson, as if the eyes of the whole nation were fixed on him, and as if on his sole exertions depended the issue of the day, I sincerely believe that at least twenty of the States of the Union will unite in the glorious work of the salvation of the Constitution and the redemption of the country.

"Friends and fellow-citizens, I have detained you too long. Accept my cordial thanks and my profound acknowledgments for the honors of this day, and for all your feelings of attachment towards me; and allow me, in conclusion, to propose a sentiment:

"Hanover county: It was the first, in the commencement of the Revolution, to raise its arms, under the lead of Patrick Henry, in defense of American liberty; it will be the last to prove false or recreant to the holy cause."

LOG CABIN RAISING AT ALBANY.

The People are Coming, Ha, Ha! Ha, Ha!

The great log cabin raising at Albany, New York, on July 10, brought in the old Dutch farmers from the ancient settlements of the county, and the timbers went up in quick time. Over 5,000 Whigs were present. The ladies thronged Stanwise Hall and buildings around, and the feasting on corn bread, cheese and hard cider, together with speeches from Mr. Edmonds and others went on to a late hour.

The Whigs of New York had a great celebration of the 4th at the Tabernacle. The Declaration was read by Samuel G. Raymond, Esq., and there was an eloquent oration by John A. Sargeant, Esq.

At Poughkeepsie and Hudson there were also large Whig gatherings.

At Newcastle, Georgia, on the 4th, there was an immense Harrison meeting.

The Whigs of Philadelphia had a glorious celebration on the island opposite that city on the 4th of July, and were addressed by John M. Botts, of Virginia; Alford, of Georgia; White, of Kentucky; R. Biddle and John Sergeant, of Pennsylvania, and others.

A large log cabin was raised at New Orleans on the 13th of June for a place of meeting.

There was a great Whig meeting and log-cabin raising at "North Bend," in Talbot county, Maryland, on the 16th of June; "open house was kept" in the peculiar way of the Eastern Shore, and the invitation was general, "Won't you take pot luck with me?"

At Easton, there was a mammoth meeting July 15, whereat the Eastern Shore, with its 130 miles and aggregate population greater than Delaware or Rhode Island, turned out over 25,000 people to shout and work for Harrison and Tyler. All the classes were represented, and log cabins and canoes were numerous, and hard cider as liberally dispensed in gourds, and joy reigned supreme.

At Vienna, on Barren Creek, Maryland, Whig celebration, a splendid batteau labeled, "Tippecanoe" decorated with banners and flags, placed on wheels and drawn by four horses, commanded by F. Chelton. Mr. Allison Parsons, of Salsbury, was there with his fine canoe, "Tip," also on wheels and decorated with flags. Mr. Isaac Leonard had another beautiful canoe, and other devices were there. Speeches were made by C. H. Pitts, Yates Walsh, John L. Kerr. Much enthusiasm, and hospitality was unbounded.

Over one thousand sturdy Whigs of Arkansas met at Little Rock, on the 13th and 14th, and were addressed by Albert Pike, William Byers and others.

At Steubenville, Ohio, over ten thousand freemen met in convention and were addressed by Gen. Sam. Stokely, Colonel James Collier and others.

New Jersey met in convention at Trenton, and chose as electors, Dr. Lewis Condict, Cornelius Lupton, James Iliff, J. M. Ryerson, John Rank, Sam.

C. Wright, Thomas Newbold and Joshua Townsend.

At Cadiz, Ohio, on July 4, there was a strange and exciting scene. There were two meetings held, and, as the processions were passing, a "Harrison" banner was unfurled in the Democratic line by one who spoke to them and then marched out with sixty others into the Republican crowd. On the banner were lettered the noble words of Levi Mallonee, "Strike My Name From the Nottingham List! I Can Do That Work No More."

On the 30th of July there was an immense Republican meeting at Charlestown, Virginia.

The Whig State central committee, of New York, from Albany, on the 20th, put out a rousing address to the Whigs of the Union.

At Henderson, Kentucky, over three thousand people met July 20 and were addressed by Judge Underwood and others.

The patriotic Whigs of Pittsylvania, Virginia, gave a public dinner on the 25th to Hon. Waddy Thompson, of South Carolina, who delivered to them an eloquent address.

At Columbus, Georgia, more than three thousand persons attended a Tippecanoe celebration.

At Tallahassee, Florida, a grand Harrison and reform meeting was addressed by General Clinch and General Floyd.

HILLSBOROUGH, OHIO, MEETING.

A Sample of Ohio Gatherings for Harrison and Reform.

Notice had been given a few weeks previously, and arrangements made for a convention of the three counties of Adams, Fayette, and Highland, to select and nominate their candidates for the legislature and prepare for the coming contest in October.

Our friends everywhere were invited to attend on the 30th of July, and as it was designed to make this a proud day for Harrison and reform, we specially addressed Messrs. Corwin, Bond, and Governor Morrow, of Ohio; and Hon. H. Clay, Southgate, and General Collins, of Kentucky. Mr. Corwin (whom we delight to honor as the late representative in Congress from this district) was obliged to be at Steubenville to meet Governor Shannon; and Mr. Clay, from pressing private engagements, was prevented from being present. The other gentlemen named above were, with Richard Douglass, Esq., of Chillicothe, and other champions, on the ground; Professor Galloway, of Indiana, and young Buckeye Carson, of Ross county, also addressed the meeting. But the people were here! The hardy and industrious yeomany of the Buckeye soil— the laborer and the mechanic, the merchant and professional man, with their families, their wives, their sons and daughters, all, all were with us, with appropriate badges and banners, with log cabins, Fort Meigs, and balls rolling, with bands of music pealing their martial notes, reverberating wildly through our highland hills and valleys for many a mile. The delegates arriving from every point of the compass, in heavy columns of thousands, and processions from three different roads, extending upwards of a mile, presented a scene the most thrilling and imposing. Here was an army of peaceful and patriotic citizens, whose march was that of firmness and devotion to the cause of their country. The wide and ample streets of our handsome village could not contain even the advance guard of the swelling columns of freemen, and our marshals were obliged to conduct the different divisions as they arrived to the extensive and beautiful grove adjacent, which was prepared for the convention. There they were all concentrated by 11 a. m., and during the day from fifteen to twenty thousand people listened attentively to the eloquent and forcible appeals of Bond, Southgate, and that well-tried and veteran statesman, Governor Morrow. Tables, upwards of twelve thousand feet in length, and provisions to cover them, were at hand, where ladies and gentlemen (during a recess of thirty minutes) partook of substantial log cabin fare.

The speaker's stand was again occupied; Bond was at home, with facts for the people, while Southgate's fervid and impassioned eloquence sent them home to the conviction of every honest and unprejudiced mind. Governor Morrow's plain and practical speech, characterized by good sense and enforced by that sterling integrity and political honesty, unimpeached and unimpeachable, was well adapted to the occasion, and produced a strong and deep impression. In the absence of General Collins at the moment, Mr. Galloway followed Governor Morrow in an able speech, and closed the discussion of the day. Hundreds, perhaps thousands, remained during the night, crowding the private dwellings of our citizens. The public square was splendidly illuminated, and our speakers were again called to the stand. R. Douglass, Esq., of Chillicothe, a well-tried soldier and patriot of 1812, was first called for, and he responded in an able and effective speech. Next was presented a native "Buckeye Boy," Mr. Carson, of Ross county, a tanner and currier, who, amid the loud and repeated cheers of the audience, occupied the stump for about three hours, in which time he tanned and curried Kendall & Co. with neatness and dispatch. Southgate gave the valedictory the next morning, and left for a convention next day in Warren. Revolutionary soldiers, soldiers of Wayne and of Harrison's campaign of 1813, were here, all joyously responding to the tribute paid to the worth of Harrison, and repelling indignantly the insults offered to their gallant chief by Kendall and his tribe of pensioned slanderers.

Hope and joy seemed to animate every breast, while the smiles of the virtuous fair chastened and subdued the strong and indignant feeling of freemen, aroused to a sense of the wrongs and outrages which they have suffered and borne with patience too long.

We are prepared to engage in the approaching contest against a hitherto superior force, and we hope not only to maintain our outposts, but to plant the standard of Harrison and reform firmly upon the ramparts of the enemy, and force him from his strongholds in Adams, Highland and Fayette.

GEN. VAN RENSSELAER'S SPEECH.

REMARKS OF GEN. STEPHEN VAN RENSSELAER, AT THE DINNER GIVEN TO HIM IN CINCINNATI, IN JULY, 1840.

After the sixth toast was read, General Van Rensselaer returned his thanks for the compliment by the following remarks, which were read by his friend, Colonel Pendleton, in consequence of General Van Rensselaer's voice having been impaired by the wound in the lungs received at the battle of Maumee :

"GENTLEMEN: I am altogether unaccustomed to public speaking; my life has been one of action rather than words; my hand has been more conversant with the sword than the pen. I cannot, however, suffer the sentiment which you have just given to pass without the expression of my most grateful acknowledgments. While that sentiment, gentlemen, received with so much cordiality, is justly flattering to the pride of an old soldier, it recalls events and scenes productive of other and better emotions. Your allusion to the Maumee carries me back to the year 1792, when a youth of eighteen years of age, with the commission of General Washington in my pocket, and I trust, some share of his principles in my bosom. I first landed in Cincinnati. And what a mighty change has been wrought in that short period ! What higher eulogy can be passed upon the enlightened enterprise of your people than the simple fact that the humble individual who now addresses you saw the site of your noble city when there were no houses but a few rudely constructed log cabins along the bank of your river, and

the challenge of the sentinels on the parapet of old
Fort Washington alone interrupted the universal
silence. The line of the canal was then our Northern
frontier, beyond which the lurking Indian made it unsafe
to penetrate; and the pursuit of a stray horse among this
magnificent amphitheatre of hills surrounding your
city was conducted with little of the pomp, to be sure,
but much of the precaution of a military incursion.
With the exception of a few old settlements on the
Wabash and Mississippi, whose inhabitants had become incorporated with the surrounding Indian tribes,
there were no white men in the whole Northwest
Territory, comprising now your great State and the
States of Indiana, Illinois, Michigan and Wisconsin
Territory. The roaming Indian alone possessed it.
Where are they now? They are gone like the falling
leaves of their own boundless forests; but unlike those
leaves, no reviving Spring shall witness their return.
Such was Cincinnati. What is it now after the lapse
of forty-eight years? I was indebted to the politeness
of the Mechanics' Institute for an invitation to their
fair last evening, and had I a catalogue of the articles
there exhibited, I would produce it as the most eloquent and comprehensive answer to the interesting
question, "What is Cincinnati now?" The exquisite symmetry and beauty of the various articles bore
ample testimony to the skill of your workers in wood,
and in brass and in iron, while nothing can exceed the
good taste exhibited in the many ornamental specimens
of the Institute.

"I cannot, however, omit to remark, and, if it will
not be considered invidious, commend the vast proportion in which the useful exceeds the merely ornamental. The combined effect of the whole exhibition
forces upon the mind the reflection that he who would
discover the secret of the unparalleled growth of Cincinnati, and its comparative exemption from the general
embarrassment of the times, must seek it in her work-
shops and in her factories.

"From this balcony, fellow-citizens, my eye rests
upon the ground where it was my daily duty to ma-

neuver my troops; and when I recall the scene as it
then existed and compare it with what I now see, it
fills me with emotions which no language is adequate
to express. The thoughtless inconsideration of youth
is proverbially short-sighted; but what imagination
could then have boded forth the grand realities which
now surround it? The inclosures of some dozen miserable huts, Fort Washington and the low ground on
what is now Columbia street, then called Hudson's
Choice, were the only points which had been cleared
of the Forest. Your handsome private buildings, your
noble public school-houses, your magnificent churches
have succeeded, and a log cabin is not to be found
within the bounds of your fair city, except as an appropriate emblem of the youthful ardor, the indomitable spirit, the pure and disinterested public virtue,
which, through years of toil and danger, such as they
only can conceive who have felt them, have watched
over the infant settlement of the great West, and protected the log cabins and their hardy and adventurous
inmates from the tomahawk and scalping knife of the
relentless savage.

"At this period I first became acquainted with Harrison, he nineteen years old, and I one year younger.
We were, for a long time, the youngest officers in the
army, and I am happy to say, at this distant period,
that the friendship*thus formed upon youthful sympathies and congenial dispositions proved too strong for
time and absence, and we met in New York in 1827,
after a separation of thirty years, the same warm friends
as we had parted on this spot in '97. This period recalls to my mind the inauguration of the elder Adams,
and with it the charge against General Harrison of
"ancient Federalism." I am a living witness that, at
the period to which I refer, the charge was without
the slightest foundation. The republican principles of
Harrison were then as well known as his chivalric
spirit, and he had no superior in either. It has been
reserved for the politicians of the present day, even
while surrounded by the monuments of his civil and
military virtues, to question both. General Wayne was

a severe disciplinarian as well as an able general and a gallant soldier. He exacted the most punctilious conformity to all the rules of militaty life; particularly did he exhibit himself and require his staff to exhibit a constant example of the conduct he required of others. Brave, temperate and laborious himself, he selected his staff for qualities similar to his own. Of such a military family thus organized Harrison became a member in the confidential relation of aide-de-camp. The delicate duties of that responsible station he performed, not only with the entire approbation of Wayne, but the satisfaction of every officer in the army with whom his duties brought him into a most daily intercourse; and such was his uniform urbanity and kindness to the soldiers that their respect for him as an officer was only equaled by their love for him as a man.

"The first Northwest army, while in winter quarters in the wilderness, had few amusements to vary the dull routine of camp duty. The consequence was that habits of dissipation were acquired by many of the officers, whose rank and age made the habit contagious. Harrison, though of an age peculiarly weak against such temptations, was strengthened to successful resistance by an unquenchable thirst for knowledge, both general and professional. Temperate, active and studious—then, as now, he lost no time. Then, as now, the sun never found him in bed; and the intervals of military duty were devoted to a course of extensive historical reading.

"The battle of the Maumee, on 20th August, 1794, was fought by the Indians with the most desperate courage. There was no point of the line at which the danger was not imminent. As aide-de-camp it was Harrison's duty to carry the orders of the general to any part of the army. Thes eorders, of course, were most frequent where the fight was thickest, and in those parts of the fight I generally saw him on that eventful day.

"I can attest the truth of the remark said to be made by General Wilkinson and Colonel Shambaugh, that Harrison was in the front of the hottest battle; his person was exposed from the commencement to the close of the action; wherever duty called he hastened, regardless of danger, and by his efforts and example contributed as much to secure the fortunes of the day as any other subordinate to the commander-in-chief.

"General Wayne, in his official account of the battle, after naming several officers who distinguished themselves, says: 'I must add the names of my faithful and gallant aides-de-camp. Captains De Butts and T. Lewis, and Lieutenant Harrison, who, with the Adjutant-General Major Mills, rendered the most essential service by communicating my orders in every direction, and by their conduct and bravery exciting the troops to press for victory.'

"I was stationed with my troop on the extreme left, and the order to me to charge was delivered by Harrison. In that charge I was severely, it was thought, mortally, wounded. Perhaps I owe my life to the prompt attention of my young friend, who carried me to the general's tent, and nursed and watched me with the tenderness and affection of a brother.

"Of the officers of that army, so far as my knowledge extends, there were but four who survive, Generals Harrison and Brady, and Major John Posey, of Kentucky, who was a cornet in my troop, and myself. General Wayne, whose best eulogy is the grateful and affectionate remembrance of the people of the West, was wholly unnoticed by Congress, and died at a miserable hovel in Pennsylvania; and there, without a stone to mark the place, his body was deposited. And now, when the people are calling their friend and neighbor from his farm by acclamation, to redeem the country from degradation to which it has been reduced by a selfish and designing politician, the others have gone forth to charge upon him, whom the people assemble in unheard-of numbers to honor, the most detestable crimes, civil and military, which the wildest imagination, unrestrained by a single moral sense, can conceive; military crimes which, if true, would long since have consigned his body to a felon's tomb and his memory to general execration; civil offenses and delinquencies, which, if true, think you he would now stand first, as he does stand first, in the hearts of his countrymen?

"People of Ohio and Indiana! You who have been the objects of his civil administration, upon you, especially, devolves the grateful task of asserting the civil virtues of your old and best-tried friend—to raise his fair fame far out of the range of the puny shafts of low ambition; and I hesitate not to believe it will be efficiently performed. You are now called upon in his old age to repay that immense and accumulating debt of gratitude which I, an eye witness, not from hearsay, now testify your fathers incurred in his early youth.

"The inheritance has descended upon you, and I will not do you the injustice to doubt, that in November next, you will entitle yourselves to a receipt in full, from my gallant old friend. Is this the language of General Harrison? No! disinterested and generous as brave, he advances no claim upon his country for services he has rendered. It is the language of his friend, and your friend—of one removed by age far from the temptation to flatter either friend or foe.

"What shall I say of charges against his military character? Nothing. One old soldier cannot be brought to vindicate the reputation of another old soldier from a charge of cowardice; indignation would choke my utterance. I appeal from the living to the dead; I appeal from Van Buren and Kendall to Shelby and Perry.

"I thank you again, gentlemen, for the kind manner in which you have been pleased to refer to my early and humble services.

"Permit me to propose the following sentiment: 'The City of Cincinnati—The wonderful creation of virtue, intelligence, and enterprise. Her name associates in our remembrance the patriotic farmers of old Rome and young Ohio.'"

During the entertainment, a large concourse of persons had collected in the street opposite to the hotel, and a solicitation being expressed to hear addresses from the balcony, the company adjourned to that place, when a call was made for the reading of General Van Rensselaer's speech. When it was concluded, Governor Poindexter, an invited guest, was called for by the crowd, and addressed them extensively upon the subject of general politics. Animated addresses were then made, by request, by Messrs. White, of Indiana, Major Chambers and W. W. Southgate, Esq., of Kentucky, William Johnson, Esq., of Cincinnati, and Mr. Turner, of Baltimore. This entertainment continued until the approach of night, when the crowd dispersed in great harmony.

INSULT TO MECHANICS.

The present party in power pretend to be the friends of the poor man, and insist that they are for reducing prices by way of aiding the laboring man and the mechanic. It was but the other day that an esteemed correspondent quoted the language of a distinguished partisan of Mr. Van Buren, who boldly avowed that they were for putting down the banks, because the use of credit enabled the poor man to rise above his condition in life, and to obtrude his sons into the learned professions. His language. that if the banks were put down they would not have the use of credit, and the tinker's son must be a tinker like his father, and the cobler's son must be a cobler too, but we did not expect to see the *Republican* insulting the mechanics of this city, by denouncing such men as the honest and patriotic blacksmith of Ohio, and by proclaiming as the creed of the party, that the blacksmith should stick to his anvil and the shoemaker to his last. Yet here is the language of the *Republican* itself. Mechanics, read:

COLD IRON FOR THE BUCKEYE BLACKSMITH, OR AN IMPOSTOR LAID BARE.

When this old hat was new, then I heard my mother say
Mechanics stuck close to their work, and seldom went astray,
No growling bears prowl'd through the land—loafers then
    were few;
And everything went on so snug, when this old hat was new.

When this old hat was new, by hammer and by hand
Each blacksmith and mechanic lad, throughout our happy land,
Stuck to his anvil or his last, never hard times knew;
For banks were scarce as white black birds, when this old hat
    was new!

It would seem that the infatuation of party spirit would sacrifice every principle that is dear to us as a people, that all the sources of prosperity are to be dried up, and that all the avenues to honor and preferment are to be closed, except it be to the servile instruments of faction and misrule. Miles Hotchkiss can be rewarded by an office for playing the hypocrite and writing an insolent letter to General Harrison. Negroes can be admitted as witnesses against high-minded officers of your Navy, but if a blacksmith or a shoemaker dares to interfere in politics, he and all mechanics are insulted by being told he should stick to his anvil or his last!!! And this is done in this city of Baltimore. and in the face of a population consisting so largely of the mechanic classes!

It is in such things that the arrogance of the purse-proud office-holder shows itself, and the hypocrisy of those who would use the mechanics is manifested.— *The Pilot.*

WEBSTER AT SARATOGA.

SPEECH OF DNNIEL WEBSTER, AT THE GREAT
MASS MEETING AT SARATOGA, ON THE 19TH OF
AUGUST, 1840.

We are here, my friends, in the midst of a great
movement of the people. That a revolution in public
sentiment on some important questions of public policy
has begun, and is in progress, it is vain to attempt to
conceal, and folly to deny. What will be the extent of
this revolution, what its immediate effects upon political men and political measures—what ultimate
influence it may have on the integrity of the Constitution, and the permanent prosperity of the country, remains to be seen. Meantime, no one can deny that an
extraordinary excitement exists in the country, such as
has not been witnessed for more than half a century
—not local, not confined to any two, or three, or ten
States, but pervading the whole, from North to South,
and from East to West, with equal force and intensity.
For an effect so general, a cause of equal extent must
exist. No cause, local or partial, can produce consequences so general and universal. In some parts of
the country, indeed, local causes may in some degree
add to the flame; but no local cause, nor any number
of local causes, can account for the general excited
state of the public mind.

In portions of the country devoted to agriculture
and manufactures, we hear complaints of want of
market and of low prices. Yet there are other portions of the country which are consumers, and not
producers of food and manufactures, and as purchasers,
they should, it would seem, be satisfied with the low
prices of which the sellers complain; but in these portions too of the country, there is dissatisfaction and
discontent. Everywhere there is complaining and a
desire for change.

There are those who think this excitement among the
people transitory and evanescent. I am not of that

15

opinion. So far as I can judge, attention to public affairs among the people of the United States has increased, is increasing, and is not likely to be diminished,
and this not in one part of the country, but all over.
This certainly is a fact, if we may judge from recent
information. The breeze of popular excitement is
blowing everywhere. It fans the air in Alabama, and
the Carolinas, and I am of the opinion that when it
shall cross the Potomac, and range along the northern
Alleghanies, it will grow stronger and stronger, until
mingling with the gales of the Empire State and the
mountain blasts of New England, it will blow a perfect hurricane.

There are those, again, who think these vast public
meetings are got up by effort, but I say that no effort
can get them up and no effort can keep them down.
There must, then, be some general cause that animates
the whole country. What is that cause? It is upon
this point I propose to give my opinion to-day. I have
no design to offend any feeling, but in perfect plainness to express my views to the vast multitude assembled here. I know there are among them many
who from first to last supported General Jackson. I
know there are many who, if conscience and patriotism had permitted, would support his successor, and I
should ill repay the attention with which they may
honor me by any reviling or denunciation. Again, I
come to play no part of oratory before you. If there
have been times and occasions in my life when I might
be supposed anxious to exhibit myself in such a light,
that period has passed, and this is not one of the occasions. I come to dictate or prescribe to no man. If
my experience, not now short in the affairs of government, entitle my opinions to any respect, those opinions are at the service of my fellow citizens. What I
shall state as facts I shall hold myself and my character
responsible for; what I shall state as opinions, all are
alike at liberty to reject or receive; asking only such
fair interpretation of them as the fairness and sincerity
with which they are uttered may claim.

What, then, has excited the whole land from Maine

to Georgia, and that gives us assurance that while we here are meeting in New York in such vast numbers, other like meetings are holding throughout all the States? That this cause must be general in its effect is certain, for it agitates the whole country and not parts only.

When that fluid in the human system indispensable to life becomes disordered, corrupted, or obstructed in its circulation, not the head or the heart alone suffers, but the whole body, head, heart and hand. all the members and all the extremities are affected with debility, paralysis, numbness, and death. The analogy between the human system and the social and political system is complete, and what the life-blood is to the former circulation, money, currency, is to the latter; and if that be disordered or corrupted, paralysis must fall on the system.

Mr. Webster went into the discussion of the sub-treasury at great length, which for want of space is omitted.

PROTECTION TO AMERICAN LABOR.

This leads me naturally to the great subject of American labor, which has hardly been considered or discussed as carefully as it deserves. What is American labor? It is best described by saying, it is not European labor. Nine-tenths of the whole labor of this country is performed by those who cultivate the land they or their fathers own, or who in their work-shops employ some little capital of their own, and mix it up with their labor. Where does this exist else-where? Look at the different departments of in-dustry, whether agricultural, manufacturing or mechanical, and you will find that in all, the laborers mix up some little capital with the work of their hands. The laborer of the United States is the United States; strike out the laborers of the United States, including therein all who in some way belong to the industrious or working classes, and you reduce the population of the United States from sixteen millions to one million. The American laborer is expected to have a comforta-

ble home, decent, though frugal living; to clothe and
educate his children, to qualify them to take part, as
we are called to do, in the political affairs and Government of their country.   Can this be said of any European laborer ?   Does he take any share in the government of his country, or feel it an obligation to educate
his children?   There, nine-tenths of the laborers have
no interest in the soil they cultivate, nor in the fabrics
they produce; no hope under any circumstances of raising themselves, or raising their children above the condition of a day laborer at wages, and only know the
government under which they live by the sense of its
oppressions, which they have no voice in mitigating.

To compare such a state of labor with the labor of
this country, or to reason from that to ours, is prepost-
erous.   And yet, the doctrine now is, not of individuals only, but of the administration, that the wages of
American labor must be brought down to the level of
those of Europe.

I have said this is not the doctrine of a few individuals, and on that head I think injustice has been
done to a Senator from Pennsylvania, who has been
made to bear a large share of the responsibility of sug-
gesting such a policy.   If I mistake not, the same idea
is thrown out in the President's message of ——, and
in the Treasury report.   Hear what Mr. Woodbury
says:

" Should the States not speedily suspend more of their
undertaking which are unproductive, but by new loans
or otherwise find means to employ armies of laborers,
in consuming, rather than raising crops, and should
prices thus continue in many cases to be unnaturally
inflated, as they have been of late years, in the face of
a contracting currency, the effect of it on our finances
would be still more to lessen exports, and consequently,
the prosperity and revenue of our foreign trade."

He is for turning off from the public works these
"armies of laborers" who consume without producing
crops, and thus bring down prices, both of crops and
labor.   Diminish the mouths that consume, and multiply the arms that produce, and you have the Treasury

prescription for mitigating distress and raising prices ! How would that operate in this great State. You have, perhaps, some fifteen thousand men employed on your public works—works of the kind that the Secretary calls "unproductive"—and even with such a demand as they must produce for provisions, prices are very low. The Secretary's remedy is to set them to raise provisions themselves, and thus augmet the supply while they diminish the demand. In this way the wages of labor are to be reduced, as well as the prices of agricultural productions. But this is not all. I have in my hand an extract from a speech in the House of Representatives, of a gentleman from New Hampshire, Mr. Burke, a zealous supporter of the administration, who maintains that, other things being reduced in proportion, you may reduce the wages of labor without evil consequences. And where does he seek his example? In the Mediterranean. He fixed himself upon Corsica and Sardinia. But what is the Corsican laborer that he should be the model upon which American labor is to be formed ? Does he know anything himself ? Has he any education, or does he give any to his children ? Has he a home, a freehold, and the comforts of life around him ? No. With a crust of bread and a handful of olives, his daily wants are satisfied. And yet from such a state of society the laborer of New England, the laborer of the United States, is to be taught submission to low wages. The extract before me states that the wages of Corsica are, for the male laborer, 24 cents a day, and the female laborer, 11 cents a day. And the honorable gentleman argues, that owing to the greater cheapness of other articles, this is relatively as much as the American laborer gets, and he illustrates the fact by this bill of clothing for a Corsican laborer: Jacket, lasting 24 months, 8 francs; cap, lasting 24 months, 2 francs; waistcoat lasting 36 months, 4 francs; pantaloons, lasting 18 months, 5 francs; shirt, lasting 12 months, 3 francs; pair of shoes, lasting 6 monts, 6 francs; total, 28 francs.

Now what say you, my friends—what will the farmer of New York, of Pennsylvania, and New England say,

to the idea of walking on Sunday to church at the
head of his family, in his jacket two years old? What
will the young man say, when, his work ended, he desires to visit the families of his neighbors, to the one
pair of pantaloons, not quite two years old indeed, but,
as the farmers say of a colt, coming two next grass,
and which for 18 months have done yeoman's service?
Away with it all—away with this plan for humbling
and degrading the free, intelligent, well educated, and
well-paid labor of the United States to the level of the
almost brute labor of Europe.

There is not much danger that schemes and doctrines
such as these shall find favor with the people. They
understand their own interest too well for that. Gentlemen, I am a farmer, on the sea-shore, and have, of
course, occasion to employ some degree of agricultural
labor. I am sometimes also rowed out to sea, being,
like other New England men fond of occasionally catching a fish, and finding health and recreation in warm
weather from the air of the ocean. For the few months
during which I am able to enjoy this retreat from labor,
public or professional, I do not often trouble my neighbors, or they me, with conversation on politics. It
happened, however, about three weeks ago, that on
such an excursion as I have mentioned, with one man
only with me, I mentioned this doctrine of the reduction of prices, and asked him his opinion of it.

He said he did not like it. I replied, the wages of
labor, it is true, are reduced; but then flour and beef,
and perhaps clothing, all of which you buy, are reduced also. What, then, can be your objections?
Why, said he, it is true that flour is now low; but then
it is an article that may rise suddenly, by means of a
scanty crop, in England, or at home; and if it should
rise from five dollars to ten, I do not know for certain
that it should fetch the price of my labor up with it.
But while wages are high, then I am safe, and if produce chances to fall, so much the better for me. But
there is another thing. I have but one thing to sell,
that is my labor; but I must buy many things—not
only flour, and meat and clothing, but also some arti-

cles that come from other countries; a little sugar, a
a little coffee, a little tea, a little of common spices, and
such like.

Now, I do not see how these foreign articles will be
brought down by reducing wages at home; and before the price is brought down of the only thing I have
to sell, I want to be sure that the prices will fall, also,
not of a part, but of all the things which I must buy.

Now, gentlemen, though he will be astonished, or
amused, that I should tell the story before such a vast
and respectable assemblage as this, I will place this
argument of Seth Peterson, sometimes farmer and
sometimes fisherman on the coast of Massachusetts,
stated to me while pulling an oar with each hand, and
with the sleeves of his red shirt rolled up above his el-
bows, against the arguments, the theories, and the
speeches of the administration and all its friends, in or
out of Congress, and take the verdict of the country,
and of the civilized world, whether he has not the best
side of the question.

Since I have adverted to this conversation, gentlemen, allow me to say, that this neighbor of mine is a
man of fifty, one of several sons of a poor man; that by
his labor he has obtained some few acres, his own un-
incumbered freehold, has a comfortable dwelling, and
plenty of the poor man's blessings. Of these I have
known six, decently and cleanly clad, each with the
book, the slate and the map, proper to its age, all going at the same time daily to enjoy the blessings of
that which is the great glory of New England, the
common free school. Who can contemplate this and
thousands of other cases like it, not as pictures but as
common facts, without feeling how much our free institutions, and the policy hitherto pursued have done
for the comfort and happiness of the great mass of our
citizens! Where in Europe, where in any part of the
world out of our country, shall we find labor thus
rewarded, and the general condition of the people so
good? Nowhere! Away, then, with the injustice and the
folly of reducing the cost of productions with us to what
is called the common standard of the world. Away,

then, away at once and forever, with the miserable
policy which would bring the condition of a laborer in
the United States to that of a laborer in Russia or
Sweden, in France or Germany, in Italy or Corsica.
Instead of following these examples, let us hold up our
own which all nations may well envy, and which unhap-
pily in most parts of the earth it is easier to envy than
to imitate.

But it is the cry and effort of the times to stimulate
those who are called poor against those who are called
rich; and yet among those who urge this cry and seek
to profit by it, there is betrayed sometimes an occasional sneer at whatever savors of humble life. Witness the reproach against a candidate now before the
people for their highest honors, that a log cabin and
plenty of hard cider is good enough for him.

It appears to some persons that a great deal too
much use is made of the symbol of the log cabin. No
man of sense supposes, certainly, that the having lived
in a log cabin is any further proof of qualification for
the Presidency than as it creates a presumption that
any one who, from humble condition or under un-
favorable circumstances, has been able to attract a considerable degree of public attention, is possessed of
reputable qualities, moral and intellectual.

But it is to be remembered that this matter of the
log cabin originated, not with the friends of the Whig
candidate, but with his enemies. Soon after his nomination at Harrisburg, a writer for one of the leading
administration papers spoke of this log cabin and his
use of hard cider by way of sneer and reproach. As
might have been expected, for pretenders are generally
false, his taunt at humble life proceeded from the party
which claims for itself the character of the purest Democracy. The whole party appeared to enjoy it, or at
least they countenanced it by silent acquiescence; for I
do not know that to this day any eminent individual
or any leading newspaper attached to the aministra-
tion, has rebuked this scornful jeering at the supposed
humble condition or circumstances in life, past or present, of a worthy man and a war-worn soldier. But it

touched a tender point in the public feeling. It naturally roused indignation. What was intended as reproach was immediately seized on as merit. "Be it so,
be it so," was the instant burst of the public voice.
"Let him be the log-cabin candidate. What you say in
scorn we will shout with all our lungs; from this day,
we have our cry of rally, and we shall see whether he,
who has dwelt in one of the rude abodes of the West,
may not become the best housed in the country."

All this is natural, and springs from sources of just
feeling. Other things, gentlemen, have had a similar
origin. We all know that the term "Whig," was
bestowed in derision, two hundred years ago, on those
who were thought too fond of liberty; and our national
air of Yankee Doodle was composed by British officers, in ridicule of the American troops. Yet, ere
long, the last of the British armies laid down its arms
at Yorktown, while this same air was playing in the
ears of officers and men. Gentlemen, it is only shal-
low-minded pretenders, who either make distinguished
origin matter of personal merit, or obscure origin
matter of personal reproach. Taunt and scoffing at
the humble condition of early life affect nobody in
this country but those who are foolish enough to
indulge in them, and they are generally sufficiently
punished by public rebuke. A man who is not
ashamed of himself need not be ashamed of his early
condition.

Gentlemen, it did not happen to me to be born in a
log cabin; but my elder brothers and sisters were born in
a log-cabin, raised amid the snow-drifts of New Hampshire, at a period so early, as that when the smoke first
rose from its rude chimney, and curled over the frozen
hills, there was no similar evidence of a white man's
habitation between it and the settlements on the rivers
of Canada. Its remains still exist. I make to it an
annual visit. I carry my children to it, to inspire like
sentiments in them, and to teach them the hardships
endured by the generations which have gone before
them. I love to dwell on the tender recollections, the
kindred ties, the early affections, and the touching nar-

ratives and incidents, which mingle with all I know of
this humble primitive family abode. I weep to think
that none of those who inhabited it are now among
the living; and if ever I am ashamed of it, or if I ever
fail in affectionate veneration for HIM who reared it
and defended it against savage violence and destruction,
cherished all the domestic virtues beneath its roof, and
through the fire and blood of a seven-years Revolutionary War, shrunk from no danger, no toil, no sacrifice, to serve his country, and to raise his children to a
condition better than his own, may my name, and the
name of my posterity, be blotted for ever from the
memory of mankind!

[Mr. Webster then reviewed the expenditures of the
Government, but just at the last moment, we find with
regret that the sheet containing this portion of the
speech has been mislaid or lost. We supply therefore
from memory a very brief, and we are aware, a very
inadequate outline of the argument.]

The expenditures of this administration have been
eminently wasteful and extravagant. Over and above
the ordinary revenue of the country, Mr. Van Buren
has spent more than *twenty millions*, that reached the
Treasury from other sources. I specify:

Reserved under the deposit act	$6,000,000
Fourth installment of surplus kept back	9,000,000
Payment by the Bank of United States on its bonds.	5,000,000
	20,000,000

But even this has been found insufficient for the prod-
igality of the administration, and we had not been long
assembled in Congress before a demand was made
upon it, notwithstanding the flattering representations of
the message and the Treasury report, for authority to
issue *five millions* more of Treasury notes; and this, we
were assured, if Congress would only keep within the
estimates submitted by the departments, would be
ample. Congress did keep within the estimates; and
yet, before we broke up, intimations came from the
Treasury that they must have authority to borrow, or
issue Treasury notes for four and a half millions more.

This time even the friends of the administration demurred, and finally refused to grant this new aid; and
what then was the alternative? Why, after having
voted appropriations for the various branches of the
public service, all within the estimates, and all of which
they were told were indispensable, they conferred on
the President, by a special section, authority to withhold these appropriations from such objects as he
pleased, and to select at his discretion the objects upon
which money should be expended. Entire authority
was thus given to the President over all these expenditures, in direct contravention of that provision of
the Constitution forbidding all expenditure except by
virtue of appropriations, which if it mean anything,
must mean the specification of distinct sums for distinct purposes.

In this way, then, it is proposed to keep back from
indispensable works four and a half millions, which are,
nevertheless, appropriated, and which, with the five
millions of Treasury notes already issued, will constitute
a debt of from nine to ten millions.

So, then, when General Harrison shall succeed in
March next to the Presidential chair, all that he will
inherit from his predecessors, besides their brilliant example, will be these Treasury vaults and safes, without
a dollar in them, and a debt of ten millions of dollars.

The whole revenue policy of this administration
has been founded in error. While duties are laid on
articles of daily use and necessity, articles of luxury are
admitted free of duty. Look at the custom-house returns, 20 000,000 dollars worth of silks imported in one
year free of duty; and other articles of luxury in proportion, that should be made to contribute to the revenue.

We have, in my judgment, imported *excessively*,
and yet the President urges it as an objection to
works of public improvement, to railroads and canals,
that they diminish our importations, and thereby interfere with the comforts of the people! His message
says:

"Our people will not long be insensible to the extent of the burdens entailed upon them by the false system that has been operating on their sanguine, energetic, and industrious character; nor to the means necessary to extricate themselves from these embarrassments. The weight which presses upon a large portion of the people, and the States, is an enormous debt, foreign and domestic. The foreign debt of our States, corporations, and men of business, can scarcely be less than two hundred millions of dollars, requiring more than ten millions of dollars a year to pay the interest. This sum has to be paid out of the exports of the country, and must of necessity cut off imports to that extent, or plunge the country more deeply in debt from year to year. It is easy to see that the increase of this foreign debt must augment the annual demand on the exports to pay the interest, and to the same extent diminish the imports; and in proportion to the enlargement of the foreign debt, and the consequent increase of interest must be the decrease of the import trade. In lieu of the comforts which it now brings us, we might have one gigantic banking institution, and splendid, but in many instances profitless, railroads and canals, absorbing to a great extent, in interest upon the capital borrowed to construct them, the surplus fruits of national industry for years to come, and securing to posterity no adequate return for the comforts which the labors of their hands might otherwise have secured."

What are these comforts that we are to get so much more of if we will only stop our railroads and canals? Foreign goods, loss of employment at home or European wages, and lastly direct taxation.

One of the gentlemen of the South, of that nullifying State-Rights party that has absorbed the administration, or been absorbed by it, comes boldly out with the declaration that the period is arrived for a direct tax on land, and among the reasons assigned for this project is this one, that it will bring the North to the grindstone. We shall see, before this contest is over, who will be the parties ground, and who the grinders. It is, however, but just to add that thus far, this is only an expression of individual opinion, and I do not charge it to be otherwise.

I had proposed to say something of the militia bill, but it is already so late that I must forego this topic. [No, no; go on, go on; from the crowd.]

Mr. Webster resumed, and briefly analyzed the bill.

Owing, however, to the lateness of the hour he did not go largely into the discussion. He did not, he said, mean to charge Mr. Van Buren with any purpose to play the part of a Cæsar or a Cromwell, but he did say that in his judgment, the plan as recommended by the President in his message, and of which the annual report of the Secretary of War accompanying the message developed the leading features would, if carried into operation, be expensive, burdensome, in derogation of the Constitution and dangerous to our liberities. Mr. W. referred rapidly to the President's recent letter to some gentleman in Virginia endeavoring to exculpate himself for the recommendation in the message, by endeavoring to show a difference between the plan then so strongly commended, and that submitted in detail some months afterwards by the Secretary of War to Congress. Mr. W. pronounced this attempt wholly unsatisfactory.

Mr. Webster then went on to say: I have now frankly stated my opinions as to the nature of the present excitement, and have answered the question I propounded as to the causes of the revolution in public sentiment now in progress. Will this revolution succeed? Does it move the masses, or is it an ebullition merely on the surface? And who is it that opposes the change which seems to be going forward? [Here some one in the crowd cried out, "None hardly but the office-holders oppose it."] Mr. Webster continued: I hear one say that the office-holders oppose it, and that is true. If they were quiet, in my opinion, a change would take place almost by common consent. I have heard of an anecdote, perhaps hardly suited to the sobriety and dignity of this occasion, but which confirms the answer which my friend in the crowd has given to my question. It happened to a farmer's son;

that his load of hay was blown over by a sudden gust on an exposed plain. Those near him seeing him manifest a degree of distress which such an accident would not usually occasion, asked him the reason; he said he should not *take on* so much about it, only father was under the load. I think it very probable, gentlemen, that there are many now very active and zealous friends, who would not care much whether the wagon of the administration were blown over or not, if it were not for the fear that father, or son, or uncle, or brother, might be found under the load. Indeed it is remarkable how fervently the fire of patriotism glows in the breasts of the holders of office. A thousand favored contractors fear lest the proposed change should put the interests of the public in great danger. Ten thousand post-offices, moved by the same apprehension, join in the cry of alarm, while a perfect earthquake of disinterested remonstrances proceeds from the custom-houses. Patronage and favoritism tremble and quake, through every limb and every nerve, lest the people should be found in favor of a change which might endanger the liberties of the country, or at least break down its present eminent and distinguished prosperity by abandoning the measures, so wise, so beneficent, so successful, and so popular, which the present administration has pursued!

Fellow-citizens, we have all sober and important duties to perform. I have not addressed you today for the purpose of joining in a premature note of triumph, or raising a shout for anticipated victories. We are in the controversy, not through it. It is our duty to spare no pains to circulate information, and to spread the truth far and wide. Let us persuade those who differ from us, if we can, to hear both sides. Let us remind them that we are all embarked together, with a common interest and a common fate; and let us, without rebuke or unkindness, beseech them to consider what the good of the whole requires, what is best for them and for us. There are two causes which keep back thousands of honest men from joining those who wish for a change.

The first of these is the fear of reproach from former associates, and the pain which party denunciation is capable of inflicting. But, surely, the manliness of the American character is superior to this! Surely, no American citizen will feel himself chained to the wheels of any party, nor bound to follow it, against his conscience and his sense of the interest of the country. Resolution and decision ought to dissipate such restraints, and to leave men free at once to act upon their own convictions. Unless this can be done, party has entailed upon us a miserable slavery by compelling us to act against our consciences on questions of the greatest importance.

The other cause is the constant cry that the party of the administration is the true Democratic party, or the more popular party in the Government and in the country. The falsity of this claim has not been sufficiently exposed. It should have been met, and should be now met, not only by denial, but by proof. If they mean the new Democracy, the cry against credit, against industry, against labor, against a man's right to leave his own earnings to his own children—why, then, doubtless, they are right; all this sort of Democracy is theirs. But if by Democracy they mean a conscientious and stern adherence to the true popular principles of the Constitution and the Government, then I think they have very little claim to it. Is the augmentation of executive power a Democratic principle? Is the separation of the currency of Government from the currency of the people a Democratic principle? Is the embodying of a large military force, in time of peace, a Democratic principle?

Let us entreat honest men not to take names for things, nor pretences for proofs. If Democracy, in any constitutional sense belongs to our adversaries, let them show their title, and produce their evidence. Let the question be examined, and let not intelligent and well-meaning citizens be kept to the support of measures, which in their hearts and consciences they disapprove, because their authors put forth such loud claims to the sole profession of regard for the people.

Fellow-citizens of the county of Saratoga, in taking leave of you, I cannot but remind you how distinguished a place your county occupies in the history of the country. I cannot be ignorant that in the midst of you are many, at this moment, who saw in this neighborhood the triumph of Republican arms in the surrender of General Burgoyne. I cannot doubt that a fervent spirit of patriotism burns in their breasts and in the breasts of their children. They helped to save their country amidst the storms of war; they will help to save it I am fully persuaded, in the present severe civil crisis. Fellow-citizens, I verily believe it is true, that of all that are left to us from the Revolution, nine-tenths are with us in the existing contest. If there be living a Revolutionary officer or soldier who has joined in the attacks upon General Harrison's military character, I have not met with him. It is not, therefore, in the county of Saratoga that a cause sustained by such means is likely to prevail.

Fellow-citizens, the great question is now before the country. If with the experience of the past the American people think proper to confirm power in the hands which now hold it, and thereby sanction the leading policy of the administration, it will be your duty and mine to bow with submission to the public will; but, for myself, I shall not believe it possible for me to be of service to the country in any department of public life. I shall look on, with no less love of country than ever, but with fearful forebodings of what may be near at hand.

But, fellow-citizens, I do not at all expect that result. I fully believe that change is coming. If we all do our duty, we shall restore the Government to its former policy, and the country to its former prosperity. And let us here, today, fellow-citizens, with full resolution and patriotic purpose of heart, give and take pledges, that until this great controversy be ended, our time, our talents, our efforts, are all due and shall all be faithfully given, to OUR COUNTRY.

PRENTISS' SPEECH.

An Eloquent Extract from the Speech of Hon. S. S. Prentiss, Delivered at Portland, Me., August 21, 1840.

" Fellow-citizens," continued Mr. Prentiss, " victory is before you; but, as good soldiers, every man must gird on his armor for the fight. Although victory may be certain, yet shame alone will keep every man from being listless and inactive in the contest. Let every man recollect his own strength and responsibility. The mighty ocean is made up of drops; and were the drops of water to say to the majestic rivers, I will not run from this hill, or flow from this mountain, or pass along this stream, you might pass along their extensive beds dry-shod. It is your right and your duty, fellow-citizens, to act. At Bunker Hill nothing would have restrained you from taking part in the battle. There is as much at stake here as there was there. Your ballot now is your bullet, and the one may do as much good here as the other did there. Go forth then and rescue your country from the hands of the spoilers—from the bad men in power. Behold your father looking down from the bright skies above you. They appeal to you, as posterity would, could they speak through the womb of time.

" Be united, then, and let no local difficulties separate you. It is not when the vessel is grating upon the coral reefs that men quarrel. Then they fly to the pumps and the ropes, and after the ship is safe and life secure, they sit down and talk over their little difficulties. Many a battle has been lost because men have not gone forth to battle with one heart and one mind, and if the Whigs do not gain this battle, we shall lose all and have no little differences to quarrel about. There never was such a necessity for union as there is now, and I am happy to believe there never was such unanimity as there is now. I have traveled from one end of the Union to the other, and everywhere I have heard the Whigs using the same arguments and governed by the same hopes. The meetings everywhere are enthusiastic, and the enthusiasm is seen everywhere where the people are seen. The people are resolved to raise themselves from the muddy pools of Loco Focoism. I have seen enough in traveling through the country to make me believe that the vestal flame of liberty will not be extinguished in our land. If not for interest, for honor men will unite to drive forth the usurpers from the places they have usurped. If they do not fight the battle before them for themselves, they will for their wives and children, for their mothers, their sisters and their sweethearts.

"We are," continued Mr. Prentiss, "men, coarse, hardy men, who can buffet the storms of life, but we have kindred and friends to protect, who appeal to us by the strongest of all human ties—the ties of blood. If ever there was a flower that needed protection from the pestilential effluvia of Loco Focoism, that flower—the fairest and lovliest of creation—is woman. If there is any one thing in our free institutions which we boast of over another, it is the respect they vouchsafe to womankind.

"In this country we may thank God that female beauty and female character has a greater value—a higher reward than in all the earth besides. But let Loco Focoism prevail, and what will be the result? The war which is going on against society destroys that which protects and sustains female character. It is one of the distinguishing features of a republican government that elevates female character to its own proper and noble dignity. If not then for yourselves, for the honor and protection and name of those so dear to you, I call upon you, men, to shield the fairest flower that blooms, by staying the hand and by resisting the blow that would destroy its sweetness and its beauty. You should feel every honorable sensation—and if not as a patriot aloud—as a man—as a Whig—to exert yourselves in protecting all of womankind.

"Permit me," said Mr. Prentiss, in conclusion—addressing himself to the hundreds of mothers and daughters scattered arouud him—" permit me to thank you, as most heartily I do in my own name, and in the name of every Whig here, for your presence and for the attention you have vouchsafed to-night. It is pleasant thus to meet and hold communion together, and especially here in the delightful city of Portland. Amid all my wanderings I have seen no city more beautiful. The bay that lies at her feet, is the fairest dimple on the cheek of the ocean, and the city that rises from its waters is the brightest jewel that sparkles in the diadem that adorns old ocean's brows.

" When you, fair daughters, come forth to encourage us by your smiles and your presence, we feel ourselves doubly armed, and though it be out of the common course for you to take part in the political strife which engages the sterner sex, yet it is your right and your duty to come forward in a time like this, and say by the interest your presence manifests, how much you have at stake in a contest like that to come. This is the time, and the occasion when we meet to discuss the principles of our fathers of the Revolution—yes, and of the mothers of the Revolution, too—for in our fiercest struggles for independence it was the stronger and more courageous heart of woman that gave to man hope and sympathy, the promises of affection and of love.

"Yes, our revered mothers and grandmothers were as much engaged in olden time in the cause of liberty as were their fathers, their husbands and their brothers. I have read until my heart thrilled within me of the generous sacrifices which woman has made in all ages, in the Old World and the New, for the accomplisment of every good and noble work. Our own mothers, who, though poor in this world's goods, were not poor in spirit, gave their little all for the cause of liberty. They had no jewels to give, but what they had they gave. Their pewter spoons were melted into bullets by their own hands, and conveyed to the camp of the army. As in Poland, the mothers and daughters gave their caskets of jewels, their bracelets and their rings into the common treasury, so in our land our mothers added their mite in the cause of freedom.

"It is time that I should close," said Mr. Prentiss. "This night I shall ever remember as one of the happiest of my life, not only for the privilege I have enjoyed of taking counsel with my old and new friends, but for seeing in wreathed smiles and bright glances the halo which has been spread around us by the ladies of Portland. I wish you all that happiness which belongs to morality, to virtue and intelligence. I trust that we men shall not become so deteriorated as to be unworthy sons of the fathers and mothers of the Revolution. I must apologize for having detained you so long.

"I commenced by shaking hands with you all in my heart, and trusting that we may often be permitted to meet together, I close, by bidding you an affectionate good night."

It was nearly 10 o'clock when Mr. Prentiss closed. The audience heard him for more than three hours and without a single sign of impatience. All were delighted, and with one heart united at the close of his eloquent address, in giving the distinguished speaker twelve cheers. The welkin rung with applause, and after a brief address from Mr. Kinsman, the chairman of the meeting, three cheers for Mississippi, three cheers for Maine and three others for Sargeant S. Prentiss, the multitude separated.

HARRISON AT FORT GREENVILLE.

THE OLD PATRIOT SPEAKS TO THE PEOPLE ON OLD TIMES AND PUBLIC AFFAIRS.

The celebration at Fort Greenville drew to that historic spot an immense concourse of Buckeyes and Hoosiers—who had gathered together expecting to meet the brave defender of the log cabins in the war of 1812. This gathering of people was the largest ever seen in this locality and the speech of welcome and the reply of General Harrison are given in the following words in the Eaton Register of August, 1840.

After Hiram Bell, Esq., had delivered an eloquent address of welcome, General Harrison replied as follows:

FRIENDS AND FELLOW-CITIZENS: It is with no slight emotion that I undertake to address you on this occasion. Nor am I a little embarrassed for words wherein to express my deep sense of your kindness towards me, manifested by the friendliness and magnanimity of your greeting. I must receive a different nature, becoming more or less than what I am, than what any man whlie living can be, before I can cease to remember and appreciate the too favorable regard and the kind demonstration of respect for me of my fellow-citizens here present. My heart yields up to you the homage of its deepest gratitude, though my tongue expresses it not.

Fellow-citizens, you are all aware of the position that I occupy before the American people—being a candidate of a portion of them for the Presidency of the United States. It will doubtless be said by some that I am here for the purpose of electioneering for myself; that I have come to solicit your votes; but believe me gentlemen, this is not the case. I am present on this occasion but as an invited guest of the citizens of Darke. It is my deliberate opinion and sincere desire that the bestowment of office should be the free act of the people, and I have no wish to bias their judgment unjustly in my favor. But, notwithstanding my wish and determination not to engage as a politician in the pending canvass for officers to administer the General Government, although I would have preferred to remain with my family in *the peace and quiet of our log cabin at the Bend*, rather than become engaged in political or other disputes as the advocate of my own rectitude of conduct, yet, from the continued torrent of calumny that has been poured upon me, from the slanders, abuses, and obloquy which have been promulgated and circulated to my discredit, designed to asperse and blacken my character, and from the villainous and false charges urged against me by the pensioned presses of this administration, my attendance at this celebration appeared to have been made an act of necessity, a step which I was compelled to take for self-defense. Chiefly for this purpose have I come among you, and trusting you will all perceive the propriety of its course, it seems superfluous to add any further reasons for its adoption.

Years ago, fellow-citizens, when I left this spot—for aught I knew, for the last time—I had little idea of the surprising change which would be wrought in its appearance during the time which has supervened. Never did I expect to stand here and behold such a scene as this. It resembles somewhat the recent *siege* of "Old Fort Meigs." I am now sixty-seven years of age. I have therefore lived to behold much of the glory of my country; I have seen the palmy days of this Republic; and especially have I witnessed many of the brilliant events which have characterized the growing greatness of the lovely West; but this very day and its incidents mark an epoch in my own history the like of which I have seldom experienced. It is now twenty-five years since I was at Fort Greenville —then surrounded by a dense forest, dark and drear. At that period there was scarce a log cabin between Greenville and Cincinnati—all between was one entire, unbroken wilderness. How wonderfully and how speedily have the giant woods bowed their stately tops to the industry and enterprise of Western pioneers, as if some magic power had cleaved them from the earth ! And now in their stead what do we behold ? Broad, cultivated fields, flowery gardens, and happy homes. Delightful picture—gratifying change ! Proud reflection ! that this transition of things is the result of the handiwork of Westers people—of American freemen.

Fellow-citizens, you have undoubtedly seen it often-times stated in a certain class of newspapers that I am a very decrepit old man, obliged to hobble about on crutches; that I was caged up, and that I could not speak loud enough to be heard more than four or five feet distant, in cousequence of which last misfortune I am stigmatized with the cognomen of "General Mum." You now perceive, however, that these stories are false. But there are some more serious matters charged against me, which I shall take the liberty to prove untrue. You know it has been said by some that I have no principles; that I dare not avow any principles; and that I am kept under the surveillance of a "committee." All this is false—unconditionally false. The charge of my being in the keeping of a committee is the only one that seems to merit a moment's consideration, and that barely to indicate its origin. A few months past almost every mail that has come to the post-offices at which I receive my letters and papers has brought me a greater or less number of letters, all of which I have opened and examined. Some of them have proved abusive and contemptible, designed especially to taunt and insult; and such were, of course, consigned to the flames. But, on the other hand, letters decorously written, for the purpose of eliciting information, have been uniformly replied to either by myself personally, or by some one acting under my authority and obeying my instructions —communicating my opinions, and not his own. Is there anything criminal or improper in this mode of doing business? Surely, my friends, I trow not.

Now, with regard to the political condition of our common country, I trust there is no impropriety in my addressing you upon subjects concerning the public weal. What means this "great commotion" among the people of this great nation? What are the insufferable grievances which have driven so many thousands, nay, millions, of the American people into the council for the purpose of devising measures for their mutual relief? Wherefore do they cry aloud as with one voice, Reform! Our country is in peril! The public morals are corrupted. How has it been done? "To the victors belong the spoils," say our rulers. What are the consequences? Ask the hundred public defaulters throughout the land! Ask the hirelings of corruption who are proffering "power and place" as bribes to secure votes! Ask the subsidized press what governs its op-

erations, and it will open its iron jaws and answer you
in a voice loud enough to shake the Pyramids—Money!
Money! I speak not at random—facts bear me testimony. The principle is boldly avowed, as well as put
in practice by men in high places, that falsehood is
justifiable in order to accomplish their purposes. Why
this laxity in the morals of our rulers and their followers? Did they inherit depravity from their ancestors?
How does it come that such recklessness of truth and
justice is manifested of late by some individuals among
us? Why, some of the causes which produce these
evils I have already intimated? There are others. Intense party spirit destroys patriotism.

A celebrated Grecian commander once said, and
said truly: " Where virtue is best rewarded, there will
virtue most prevail." It is even so, a wise and true saying. But how has the practice of your Government of
late accorded with this maxim? It is proverbial with
the advocates of monarchy in the Old World that republics are ungrateful. How does your experience for
the last few years give the lie to this proposition?
Nay, fellow-citizens, I fear that this Government
affords many examples which tend but too strongly to
verify the proverb. Among other instances of manifest ingratitude, to only one will I here recur. I mean
the removal from office, without cause or provocation,
save a difference of opinion with the President, of Gen.
Solomon Van Rensselaer, of New York. He was a
noble friend of ours in the "winter of our discontent." I
became acquainted with him when, like myself, he was
a young officer in General Wayne's army. I found
him an agreeable, social companion, as well as a brave
and magnanimous soldier. He assisted in fighting the
battles of his country; aye, for your behoof, my countrymen, his blood has been poured out upon the soil of
Ohio. The bullets of your enemies have pierced his
body while fighting in defense of your interests. And
not only on the plains of Ohio has he stood between
danger and his country, but in other places likewise.
In the sanguinary battle of Queenstown he received
six wounds from his country's foes. Well, what is

his reward? After having spent the flower of his
youth and the vigor of his manly prime in the service
of his country as a soldier, he was called by the American people to serve them in a civil capacity. He
obeyed the call with thankfulness of heart. But he
has been cruelly driven out of the service by the
administration, and why? Because, fellow-citizens,
he was the friend of the companion of his youth; because he would not forsake a fellow-soldier; because
he was my incorruptible friend; and because the emoluments of his office were wanted to reward the partisan services of a supporter of my political competitor.
"Ah, there's the rub!" But you, my friends, I am confident, will not long permit such wrong to the men
who "righted your wrongs" in olden times.

Fellow-citizens, you know that my opponents call
me a Federalist. But I deny the charge: I am not—
I never was a Federalist. Federalists are in favor of
concentrating power in the hands of the executive;
Democrats are in favor of the retention of power by
the people. I am, and ever have been, a Democratic
Republican. My former practices will bear me out in
what I say. When I was governor of Indiana Territory, I was vested with despotic power, and had I
chosen to exercise it, I might have governed that people with a rod of iron. But being a child of the Revolution, and bred to its principles, I believed in the right
and the ability of the people to govern themselves;
and they were always permitted to enjoy that high
privilege. I had the power to prorogue, adjourn and
dissolve the legislature, to lay off the new counties and
establish seats of justice; to appoint sheriffs and other
officers. But never did I interpose my prerogative to
defeat the wishes of a majority of the people. The
people chose their own officers, and I invariably confirmed their choice; where they preferred to have their
county seats, there I located them; they made their own
laws and I ratified them. *I never vetoed a bill in my
life.*

But I have been denounced as a bank man. Well,
let it go. I am so far a bank man as I believe every

rational Republican ought to be, and no further.   The
Constitution of the United States makes it the duty of
the Government to provide ways and means for the
collection and disbursement of the public revenue.   If
the people deem it necessary to the proper discharge
of the functions of their Government to create a national
bank, properly guarded and regulated, I shall be the
last man, if elected President, to set up my authority
against that of the millions of American freemen.   It
is needful to have a larger money circulation in a land
of liberty than in an empire of despotism.   Destroy the
poor man's credit and you destroy his capital.   The
peasant who toils incessantly to maintain his famish-
ing household, in the hard money countries of Europe,
rarely if ever becomes the noble lord who pastures his
"flocks upon a thousand hills."   There are necessarily
difficulties connected with every form and system of
the Government, but it should be the aim and object of
the statesman to form the best institutions within his
power to make for the good of his country.

Fellow-citizens, I cannot forbear inviting your attention to the concerns of your Government, in the welfare of which all good citizens feel a deep interest.   I
warn you to watch your rulers.   Remember, "Eternal
vigilance is the price of liberty."   When I looked
around upon the dangers which seem to be suspended
as by a hair over this people, I tremble for the safety of
this Republic.   In an evil hour has the Chief Magistrate
of this nation been transformed into a monarch and
despot at pleasure !   To show that this is the case I
need but refer you to the profound and philosophical
historian, Gibbon, who says, "The obvious definition
of monarchy seems to be that of a State in which a
single person, by whatsoever name he may be distinguished, *is intrusted with the execution of the law,
the management of the revenue, and the command of the
army.*"   Is not Martin Van Buren intrusted with these
functions ?   Most assuredly he is.   Call him by whatsoever title you choose, President, executive, chief
magistrate, consul, king, stadtholder, it does not alter
the nature of his power; that remains the same, un-

changed, and the President, therefore, possesses all the
functions necessary to constitute a monarch. You
have often heard of the "moneyed influence of the
country" denounced while it yet remained in the hands
of the people, as dangerous to public liberty.

Have you, then, no apprehension, no fear of a
moneyed influence, equal to that of half the nation,
concentrated in the hands of a single individual, at
the same time possessing two other of the most potent
powers that belong to our Government? The great
Julius Cæsar—the conquering Julius has said, "Give
me soldiers and I will get money: give me money and
I will get soldiers." The public purse is already confided to the hands of the President; a respectable army
is also under his control, and it is in contemplation by
the administration to add to the present military force
of the United States an army of 200,000 men. American freemen, pause and reflect. Meditate before you
act. Matters of the highest moment depend upon
your action and await your decision. There may be
no ambitious Cæsar among us who will dare to use the
ample means now combined in the hands of the President for the subversion of our liberties, but the excep-
tions to ambitious men so inclined are so few that they
but fortify the rule. Look around you, fellow-citizens.
Are you girt with your armor or have you surrendered
it to another? The "sentinels upon the watch tower
of freedom"—have they been true to their trusts, or
have they slept? I warn you, my countrymen, against
the danger of neglecting your duty. Power is always
stealing from the many to the few. Beware how you
intrust your rights to the keeping of any man. They
are never so secure as when protected by your own
shield and defended by yourselves with your own
weapons.

General Harrison adverted to the interference of
the officers of Government with elections, and pointed
out its impropriety in a clear manner. If (said he,
in conclusion upon that subject) I should be so fortunate as to be elected President, I would deem it my
duty to prevent, as far as possible, the practice of

Government officers using their official influence and patronage for electioneering purposes, but, at the same time, those officers should be allowed the freest exercise of the elective franchise— at perfect liberty to vote for and against whomsoever they pleased, without the fear of being proscribed or removed from office on account of their political preferences.

In conclusion fellow-citizens, indulge me in a few remarks in regard to my old fellow-soldiers. A small number of them are here by my side. They stood by me in battle, firm and invincible, in by-gone days. Some of them are remnants of the Revolution—soldiers with whom I served under the gallant Wayne. Where, my brethren, are our companions in danger on the field of strife ? Alas ! many of them are taking their final repose in the calm and peace of death !

> " Let them sleep on, sleep on
>   In the grave to which kindred have borne them,
> And blest be the braves who are gone,
> And the friends who survive but to mourn them ! "

The old soldiers, one by one, are dwindling away— gliding as it were down the river of time into the haven of long-sought rest. But a few of them even now are remaining to sorrow in gladness for the ingratitude of their country. When this country was a dismal howling wilderness those warriors were exposing themselves to danger and disease in the unwholesome swamps and morasses of the West, by guarding and defending our frontiers. Many of them became present victims to the malaria of the marshes and the insalubrity of the climate, others returned to their houses with disease engendered in their systems, but to linger for a time, and perhaps waste away with consumption; while yet smaller portions still remain among us, though generally shattered in constitution and feeble in health. Why is it, fellow-citizens, that these old soldiers of General Wayne's army have never been repaid for their services, or been allowed pensions by our Government ? The nation is much indebted to them, and justice requires that the debt should be paid,

and I could never die in peace, and feel no sting of re-
morse, if I were to permit their claims to pass unnoticed, and without making an effort, when opportunity
offered, to have them satisfied.

Fellow-citizens, my character has been most grossly
and wantonly assailed by the dangerous demagogues
of the administration party. They have falsely charged
me with the commission of almost every crime which
is denominated such that man can be guilty of. My
character, which I had fondly hoped to preserve unsullied as a boon and an example for my family, has been
much more traduced and belied within the few months
past, and, for this reason I have sometimes regretted
that your predilection had made me a candidate for
office; but, nevertheless, I claim no sympathy of the
public on that score. I only desire you to examine my
past conduct, to read the history of your country and
ascertain my political course heretofore, and the principles on which I have ever acted, and if you find that
my doctrines are unsound and unworthy of your support, it is your sacred duty to reject them. I ask not
your sympathy or favor. I want but common justice.
Let me have a fair trial, and, whatever may be your
verdict, I shall be satisfied. Investigate matters fairly
and honestly; compare the doctrines and practices of
my adversaries with mine, and then decide as you
shall think right and proper. Cast aside your prejudices and predilections, and vote only from principle.
It is your duty to do so. Heed not the censure of
knavish politicians who reproach you with the name
of "turn coat," etc. *It is not opprobrious to turn
from a party to your country.* We should despise the
odium sought to be heaped upon us by designing men,
from their selfish motives, as they despise truth and
honesty.

Hoping that the right may prevail and make our
country prosperous, I will only add the wish that you
may long enjoy its blessings, maintain its free institutions, and rejoice in the independence of happy freemen.

NASHVILLE CONVENTION.

Nashville, August 15, 1840.

DEAR SIR : We reached here in safety, after a fatiguing journey over heavy roads, made so by rains. From Louisville to Nashville everything is political; there is great enthusiasm along the whole road in favor of Harrison. Even on " Salt River" we found many hard-cider boys ready to transport the spoilers to its head-waters. Kentucky is proud of her recent victory, and well she may be. We saw a log cabin built on the top of a tree, with its cider barrels, latch strings, etc., etc. Great changes are taking place; even postmasters are coming over. One at whose door the stage stopped, inquired if Mr. Clay would be along saying, "I have done that man great injustice, and wish to take him by the hand and tell him so."

This has been a proud day for Mr. Clay—one of the proudest of his life. His entry into the city this afternoon was truly magnificent. Met a mile or more from town by several military companies and citizens on horseback and in carriages, in all about 1,500, he entered amidst the sound of martial music, the roar of cannon, the ringing of bells, and the shouts of many thousands.

At the mayor's house this afternoon a most beautiful flag, with a good likeness of General Harrison on one side and a log cabin being built on the other, was presented to the Harrison Guards of the city by a young lady. She addressed the company in a manner highly creditable to herself and the ladies she represented. The ceremony was interesting.

About sunset, the great Ohio ball arrived in a steamboat. An immense crowd flocked to the wharf to receive the present. It is an object of great curiosity—and much anxiety had been expressed to see it.

The city is already crowded with strangers. Large delegations are here from Louisiana, Mississippi, Alabama, Illinois, Missouri, Indiana, Kentucky, East

Tennessee, etc. By Monday morning the adjoining counties will pour in their thousands! What a change is here! Ten years ago it was hardly safe to name Clay, Harrison or Webster, except in terms of abuse. Now, at the hour of midnight, I hear the sound of the drum, the cannon, and the loud and repeated hurrah for Old Tip and for Clay. and nothing is thought of the "second section."

Mr. Clay staid at the Springs last night. He inquired of Dr. McNary what Felix Grundy was about. "Traveling through East Tennessee defending the Administration," was the reply. "Ah," says Mr. Clay, "Felix is at his old business—defending criminals."

GREAT MEETING AT NASHVILLE.

We copy from the Nashville *Whig*, the following notice of the meeting at Nashville. It acquires the more importance from the letters of General Jackson and Mr. Clay, in relation to it:

"At 10 o'clock, the immense procession moved, amidst the most deafening shouts of the multitude, from the head of Broad street, through Union street to Walnut Grove. The convention was temporarily organized by Dr. Thomas R. Jenning, the chairman of the nominating committee from the States, who announced the following nominations for officers of the convention:

For president, Hon. E. H. Foster, of Tennessee; vice-presidents, W. McPherson, Esq., of Arkansas, Hon. John Gayle, of Alabama, S. A. Bowen, Esq., of Missouri, Garret Duncan, Esq., of Kentucky, Hon. James Rucks, of Mississippi, John Hogan, of Illinois, C. L. Ash, Esq., of Pennsylvania, P. P. Erkine, Esq., of Maryland, Hon. B. Storer, of Ohio, A. C. Bullitt, of Louisiana, J. White, of Indiana.

Secretaries, W. Snethen, of Louisiana, R. Scott, of

Pennsylvania, C. Scott, of Mississippi, C. C. Norvell, of Tennessee, A. A. Hall, of Tennessee, C. G. Wintersmith, of Kentucky, W. W. Ferguson, of Arkansas, S. S. L'Hommedieu, of Ohio, J. R. Blocker, of Alabama, J. H. Matheeyn, of Illinois.

After an invocation of the Divine blessing from the Rev. J. W. Ogden,

Mr. Foster, the president of the day, rose and asked why this vast and magnificent multitute? Why this coming up from the valley and the rivers, from the plains, from the hills and hollows, from the counties near and the States far off? The people, the real people, he said, were before and round about him. They had come together, because the mechanic arts had received a severe blow, because commerce was prostrate, because trade flourishes not, because industry has not its reward! They were the great grand jury of the country, not a picked or packed grand jury, but an honest one that would render a verdict the thunder whereof would peal through the whole length and breadth of the land and stop not until it reached the White House at Washington, and cause its presiding inmate to cry out even in his midnight dreams, like the Roman chief, for the power which he has lost through his presumptive and overleaping ambition—until indeed, it caused him to cry out to *Chapman to crow* with more vehemence and terror than ever.

Mr. Foster said he had been an old Jackson man—but he had turned his coat inside out—though not a single *principle* had he abandoned—no, not one. He had no master but his God and the people. To the will of the people he would bow in submission at all times, but not to the *dictation* of the cohorts of modern Democracy, who pronounce every man a Federalist, no matter how many battles he has fought in, who refuses to support Martin Van Buren. Why, sir, said he, pointing to an old soldier of the Revolution, on the speaking stand before him, you fought gallantly and gloriously for your country—you were a Whig of '76, and you are a Whig of '40—and yet they call you a Federalist!

Mr. Foster referred to the sacrifice of Judge White, in compliance with the wish at headquarters. He pointed to the full-length and very striking likeness of that departed sage, which was borne aloft upon one of the banners near the stand, and bore testimony to his many sterling virtues, to his Roman firmness, to his intelligence, to his stern honesty and goodness of heart, and then called upon the vast multitude there assembled to remember Hugh Lawson White, and those through whose instrumentality Tennessee, aye, the whole country, has been deprived of a continuation of his most valuable services. Great, he proclaimed him to have been ! Not great like Cæsar, with his hands drenched in blood—but great in the councils of the nation, great in his virtues, great in his honesty and purity of heart.

Mr. Foster said, in his denunciations of Democracy, he made no allusion to the rank and file of the party, but to those demagogues who assume its lead. The rank and file were part and parcel of that body of the people, alike honest and sincere, and virtuous and upright with the rank and file of the Whigs. But the leaders of the Democracy were, generally speaking, a vastly different set of persons. They claimed to be Democrats. It was an old and true proverb that a man was best known by the company he kept. He asked who were the true Republicans, and who the true Federalists ? He referred in glowing terms to the many brilliant services rendered to the Republican cause, when Republicanism, as well as Federalism, meant something, by his distinguished friend then present, [pointing to Henry Clay. The very allusion made the air resound with the grateful shouts of ten thousand freemen.] He asked if that great statesman was not a true Republican. The multitude shouted, "Yes, he is." He asked if that Republican's colleague, also present [pointing to John J. Crittenden] was not a true Republican. The hearty affirmative response rose quickly upon the breeze. Well, then, said he, let us look at the other side of the picture. Go with me to the Senate Chamber in the Capitol, at Washington,

17

and behold Senator Buchanan, a fine looking gentleman and a leading Democrat, so called. He opposed
the last war, and was a furious Federalist. To the
left of him behold Senator Wall, an old gentleman,
dressed in the very extreme fashion, *en militaire.* He is a
modern Democrat, but boasted in the Senate in 1836
that he was a Federalist so long as Federalism was
known by its proper name. Now turn your eyes still
further to the left and behold my cousin of Bucking-
ham, Senator Hubbard, a modern Democrat, who was
so violent a Federalist during the last war that he got
up a meeting to send delegates from his section of
New Hampshire to the Hartford convention! Still
further on, you behold Senator Williams, of Maine, a
great Van Buren Democrat, but a notorious Federalist
during the whole of the last war. But Democracy of
the present day made all these men Democrats. He
was happy to say that he was no such Democrat himself.

Mr. Foster referred to the great civil revolution going on— to the ball so gloriously put in motion in Connecticut—which was handsomely accelerated by gallant Rhode Island, and which Virginia received and
sent rolling on so nobly and with such power! Why,
he said, he was on the top of Cumberland Mountain
when the news reached him, and he opened his mouth
and shouted at the top of his voice, Old Virginia never
tire!"

Next, he said, 'Louisiana gave the ball a turn with
a force that sent it rolling into Kentucky and Indiana, where it seems to have nearly annihilated the
whole of the Loco Foco party. The cohorts of power
were putting their ears to the ground to catch the
sound of the hoofs of the express horses that were to
bring them glad tidings from Louisiana! But lo and
behold the result! See Kentucky, too, a gain from
13,000 to near 20,000 of a majority! And nearly
the same gain in Indiana! Tennessee, he said, was
also coming. She would come with a power that
would make little Martin Van Buren wish himself out
of the White House as speedily as possible. This, he

said, was no vain boast, but sober reality. The work, the good and glorious work, was going on.

Mr. Foster thanked the vast multitude for the attention which had been paid him, and said he would give place for others to address them.

Mr. Clay was called for with an enthusiasm which seemed to contain no bounds, and when he came forward, with those characteristic smiles playing all over his remarkable countenance, the air was rent with nine such cheers as it has seldom fallen to the lot of any man to receive. When these had subsided he commenced.

THE UTICA CONVENTION.

[From the New York Star.]

We publish the following letter with great pleasure, not only as it exhibits the entire harmony and unanimity of the Whig convention at Utica in the nomination of State officers, but from finding the old and tried friends of Harrison and Clay, Peter R. Livingston, Judge Burt, of Orange, and P. B. Porter, of Erie, were chosen as presiding officers and State electors:

August 12, 1840.

DEAR SIR: This has been a great day for Utica. The convention met at the Mechanics' Exchange; called General Root pro tem. to the chair; appointed a committee to select officers for the meeting. Peter R. Livingston of Dutchess, was appointed, assisted by one vice-president from each district, and the same number of secretaries. Mr. Francis Hall was elected to fill the vacancy occasioned by the resignation of Mr. Ruggles.

The convention then went into an informal ballot; 115 delegates were present. Wm. H. Seward and Luther Bradish received the vote of the whole delegation without a single dissenting voice. We then adjourned to meet at 12 o'clock, in order to give the delegates an opportunity to look at one of the greatest assemblages ever witnessed. I intend to give you a sketch of it, and before I proceed, allow me to say, it numbered, from what I could see and learn, at least eighteen thousand persons. N. P. Talmadge, Stanley, Ketchum, and others, are now addressing the multitude. Perhaps it would be well to state that you would be perfectly astonished at the ease a convert can be made. The workingmen in opposition to us are ready and almost anxious for some plea by which they could release themselves from all further connection with the Loco Foco party. They cannot bear the name.

If we could circulate ten thousand copies of Buchanan's speech in this neighborhood it would help us at least a thousand votes. For example, I fell in with three coopers. I opened my conversation with them after this wise, " Well, friends, what procession have you here?" " Oh, nothing, sir, but a few Federalists parading the streets." " But, see here, I am a Democrat; I am in favor of equal laws and protection for the poor man's rights; I go for plenty of work and fair prices; are these men opposed to these principles? if so, I say down with them. I go for the country, and not for Van Buren or Harrison, but the man who will carry out these views." " Well, now, friend," said they, "you are a stranger to us; but we like these opinions of yours." " Well, then, let us support men of our cast, canvass their opinions carefully, look into the sub-treasury bill—see who are your friends—mark them, and remember when the election comes your children will hold you responsible for the vote you cast!" " But is not Mr. Van Buren the poor man's friend?" " Well, my friends, I will give you facts, and you can mature them yourselves." I then handed them a copy of Buchanan's speech which I found in the porter's room at Baggs'. I read a few extracts, told them Van Buren believed it; the sub-treasury was passed for the purpose of carrying out their views to reduce labor to fifteen cents a day; that he, Buchanan, was a bosom friend of Van Buren, and they acted together in all things. They took me by the hand, thanked me, and declared they would go home and use their influence for General Harrison, and vote for him.

Now, for the procession; it was acknowledged by all to be NINE MILES LONG—it was headed by one hundred and ten horsemen, dressed as farmers, with a hunting shirt and red sash round the middle—then music—then *four hundred and seventeen large double wagons*, drawn by horses and some by oxen. The first I noticed, was drawn by six horses—it was a car, upon which was erected a magnificent throne, with all the drapery, etc. Upon the throne was seated a boy, bareheaded! with a crown by his side—dressed like King George, in purple velvet and fine linen; by his side he had a splendid sword, the same as worn by one of the knights of old—and around his neck a diamond chain, to which was connected a large gold key, one hand strongly grasping and holding a key of the treasury—the other the sword; immediately behind the throne came the contrast—there sat old Tip, by the side of his log cabin, with flail in hand, the very picture of comfort and kindness, his right hand extended to some wornout soldiers. The next drawn by horses, with the motto, "One Fire More;" and "The Day is Ours;" "New York State Redeemed;" "We Are Young!—But We Will Be Old;" "American Youth—None Have a Deeper Interest in the Country." A log cabin drawn by four horses. Hung outside with coon skins, etc., beneath was, "Trenton is Eager for the Contest;" "When She Will Atone for Her past Follies." The next was a very large wagon drawn by twelve pair of oxen, with twenty-six farmers to represent the various States. The next was a car drawn by eight horses, with box sides, covered with American carpet, with this motto: "Domestic Carpet is Good Enough for the White House in 1841."

This letter is drawn up in a hurry, while hundreds and thousands are passing the door; all kinds of music and confusion, and a great haste to get back to the convention, which meets at 12 o'clock.

THE NASHVILLE CONVENTION.

In the Nashville *Whig* we find a sketch of the convention in that city. As the assembly was computed on the best authority to have exceeded in numbers the great Baltimore convention, we deem it of sufficient interest to warrant a further description of the delegations composing it, and of the proceedings. We transfer, therefore, the annexed matter from the Nashville *Whig*, recalling the sentiments of Mr. Webster, in the exordium of his speech at Saratoga: No one, said the eminent orator, can deny that an extraordinary excitement exists in this country, such as has not been witnessed for more than half a century; not local, nor confined to two or three or ten States, but pervading the whole from North to South, and from East to West, with equal force and intensity. For an effect so general, a cause of equal extent must exist. No cause, local or partial, can produce consequences so universal The immense assemblage in Tennessee is another proof of the justice of these remarks. At last the effects of the Federal policy have attained to an insufferable pitch of mischief. The people of every class assemble, not by hundreds, but by tens of thousands:

THE GREAT SOUTHWESTERN CONVENTION.

We present to our distant friends some account of this day's great work in Nashville, of the mighty ingathering of the real people and of their boundless enthusiasm in the cause of Constitutional liberty, on the occasion of the great Southwestern convention.

On approaching this most interesting task, we feel that our powers of description are wholly inadequate to anything like an impression to the life, of the scenes which have this day passed before our almost bewildered vision. The richness and grandeur of the pageant and the variety of incidents to which it gave rise; the fervid zeal of the people and the burning eloquence of the champion of liberty, whose fortune it was to occupy their attention; the meeting of the extremes of the Union, and the commingling of hundreds of kindred spirits from distant portions of the great valley of the Mississippi; the presence of the illustrious statesman of Kentucky and his distinguished colaborers in the Whig cause, together with the almost cloudless beauty of the day, all, all conspired to lend an interest to the occasion, which it would be vain to attempt to portray.

It would be equally futile to undertake a close estimate of the extent of this immense concourse. We have no data upon which to base a calculation of numbers, beyond the long line of procession which extended from the southern extremity of the city at the intersection of Franklin road and Broad street, from which point the line moved, to the western line of the corporation on lower College street. This, it will at once be seen, would be by no means a correct criterion, in view of the fact that countless thousands made their way to the convention ground both in advance of and subsequent to the entree of the procession. Mr. Clay remarked, incidentally, in his speech this morning, that the meeting of the 17th of August, 1840, might be regarded, as *par excellence*, the memorable convention of 1840, since it exceeded both in extent of numbers and the magnificence of its procession, the great convention of the 4th of May at Baltimore. Our own opinion is that considering the relative location and population of the two cities, the crowd today deserved to be held as a much more striking evidence of the extraordinary zeal that now pervades the friends of executive reform throughout the country than the Baltimore meeting. It has been our good fortune to witness both pageants, and we speak it with pride when we say that the free valley of Mississippi has this day followed in bold and generous rivalry the example of her sister States on the seaboard.

The morning was ushered in by "a glorious summer's sun," thus giving early promise of a day as bright with the smiles of beneficent nature as it is destined to be memorable for the scenes which have marked this triumphal movement of a free people.

At daylight three guns were fired from an eminence above the city, known, since the celebration of the triumph of the Whigs of New York in 1837, as Whig hill. At sunrise a gun was fired from the log cabin on lower Market street, the signal for meeting of the different delegations, clubs and military companies. At 10 o'clock two guns were fired as the note for preparation for the formation of the procession. The Straight Outs, Capt. Tanneyhill, were then marched into Broad street, in pursuance of the programme of the chief marshal, and as the base of the line of the procession. Between the hours of 7 and 9 o'clock, the line was formed, ready to move from the intersection of Broad and Spruce streets.

On riding up Broad street just before the procession moved out of that street, we discovered that as many as 14 States were represented, some of them quite largely, the delegation from each preceded by a general State banner, besides the insignia of the various town and county clubs and delegations, an infinite variety of which decorated the line and imparted unspeakable interest to the pageant.

The base of the line, as we before noticed, was the Straight Outs, and a more appropriate band of pioneers we dare venture could not have been selected. The dress, discipline, and origin of the Straight Outs, we have heretofore had occasion to describe. They are the representatives of a hardy race of honest log-cabin freemen, who, however ridiculed for their primitive manners by the advocates of power, never fail to make their influence felt and appreciated at the ballot-box. The banners borne by this corps were plain but expressive—the first, with a plain white ground, inscribed, "One Presidential Term, and Fair Wages for Labor." The second, a spread-eagle on white ground bearing in its talons, "Harrison and Reform," and underneath the celebrated watchwords of the Emperor Constantine, "*In Hoc Signo Vinces.*" The third, a game-looking chanticleer, on blue muslin ground, with the inscription, "A Loud Crow Chapman—4th March, 1841."

The Straight Outs were followed by the general committee of arrangements, with their invited guests, on foot and in carriages. These were succeeded by a division composed of the delegates from Arkansas, Missouri and Alabama. The Arkansas banner was inscribed with the motto of the lamented Crockett, "Be Sure You're Right; Then Go Ahead!" with an eagle in the center. The Missouri banner represented a buffalo, with the inscription expressive of the part borne by the illustrious Harrison in the admission of that State into the Union, "Roused to the Claims of an Early Friend!"

Our Alabama friends numbered three or four different delegations, headed by a general banner bearing the inscription, "Four Years Long Enough for a Good President; Too Long for a Bad One." The Madison county delegation displayed a beautiful fancy banner, representing the goddess of liberty looking down on old Tip's cabin, with the inscription (expressive of the recent immense gain in our sister commonwealth), "Day is Dawning" Our attention was especially attracted to the standard-bearer of this delegation, an ingenious artisan, we are told, of Huntsville, who wore in his bosom a log cabin breast-pin, representing by means of miniature springs, both the interior and exterior of a cabin, with the door, latch-strings, etc., all perfect, and a miniature canoe on the comb of the roof.

Next followed a delegation from Illinois, with a magnificent satin banner, representing the great seal of the State.

The Mississippi delegation came next in order, with the State banner, inscribed, " 'Tis Ours to Rectify: Not to Overthrow." The delegation from Yallabusha county carried a rich satin banner, wrought with fine taste and inscribed, "Mississippi—She Beat the Spoilers Once and Can Do It Again."

Indiana followed our Southern sister. Her banner represented a huge ball, inscribed, "The Ball in Motion

—Indiana 10,000 Majority." The New Albany delegation bore a handsome satin banner, representing a log
cabin "with the string of the latch hanging out."

Louisiana succeeded. Her State banner represented
the ballot-box —"The Freemen's Sword and Shield—
Louisiana 25,000 Majority." A separate banner was
borne by the Tippecanoe Club of New Orleans.

Ohio was represented by a spirited delegation, chiefly
from Cincinnati. Her banner represented a spread
eagle, bearing in its taions, "For President, the Farmer
of North Bend." with the inscription above—"Ohio—
Tip, Tom and Tyler."

Kentucky was strongly represented. Nearly all the
southern counties had their separate delegations, besides two handsomely equipped military companies
from Hopkinsville and Bowling Green. We noticed a
delegation from Mercer, one of the upper counties of
the State, with a handsome satin banner, representing
among other things, "Little Matty" scampering out of
the White House. The State banner was inscribed in
just compliment to her recent signal triumph at the
ballot-box, "Kentucky, She Speaks Not by Thousands,
but by Tens of Thousands." The Louisville delegation
was headed by a beautiful silk banner, representing.
we believe, a scene at the battle of the Thames.

The Livingston county delegation (Smithland) displayed two remarkably neat satin banners, one of which
represented a golden ball in motion. The Caldwell
banner bore the portrait, in military dress, of General
Harrison.

The banners of the District of Columbia, of Virginia,
of Delaware, of New Jersey, of New York and New
England were borne by small delegations from each
State. That of the District of Columbia was inscribed,
"Let His Days be Few and Let Another Take His
Place." That of Virginia, "The Blood of Our Fathers,
Let It Not Have Been Shed in Vain. Independence
Now and Independence Forever." That of Delaware,
"Our Cause It Is Just." That of New Jersey, "Her
Great Seat Shall Be Respected." That of New York
represented a pair of scales, with "M. V. B." in one

end and "Old Tip" in the other, the former "kicking the beam," the inscription, "Weighed in the
Balance and Found Wanting." That of New England —

> "From hill and from valley,
> From mountain and plain,
> We come to the rescue
> Of our country again."

The Pennsylvania delegation numbered two or three
sections, preceded by a banner representing a fox
trailing a lion, with the inscription, "This Won't Do,
Matty."

The Tennessee delegation formed, of course, much
the largest division of the procession. The county delegations bore a large number of flags and banners,
some of which excelled in grandeur of design, richness of material and beauty of execution anything of
the sort it has ever been our fortune to see displayed.
In this respect, indeed, we feel assured that the Columbus, Baltimore and Fort Meigs conventions were
thrown completely in the background. We must
necessarily, for the want of time and space, reserve a
more particular description of the various county devices for our next paper. The front banner of the delegation represented, on blue ground, a magnificent,
full-rigged seventy-four, her head pointed to the White
House and Capitol, which are seen in the distance.
The "Constitution" is the name of this truly national
vessel, and she bears on her topmast signal the initials,
" T. and T." The State banner bore a beautifully
wrought device (on satin, fringed with crape), representing the tomb of the lamented White.

The great ball, from Zanesville, Ohio, which came
safe to hand on the steamer Rochester on Saturday
night, occupied a conspicuous place in the procession.
It was given in charge of the Kentucky delegation, and
was hauled on four wheels under the immediate care
of Porter, the Kentucky giant. The ball is in the form
of a hemisphere, moving upon its axis and representing each of the individual States of the Union, with
the inscriptions, as heretofore copied from the Ohio

papers. Porter appeared as a delegate from Louisville, and it was really difficult to determine which of
the two lions attracted the most attention.

The military brought up the rear and made a rich
and beautiful display. This division of the line was
composed of the independent infantry companies from
Hopkinsville and Bowling Green, Ky., Franklin and
Clarksville, Tenn., and the Harrison Guards, Cadets
and Lancers, of this city.

At 10 o'clock the immense procession moved amidst
the most deafening shouts of the multitude, from the
head of Broad street, through Spruce to Spring, down
Spring to Summer, down Summer to Cedar, down
Cedar to the Square, round the Square to West College street, and through that street to Walnut Grove,
the country seat of Dr. D. T. McGavock. The convention was temporarily organized by Dr. Thomas R.
Jenning, the chairman of the nominating committee
from the States, who announced the following nominations for officers of the convention.

For president: Hon. E. H. Foster, of Tennessee.

Vice-presidents: W. M McPherson, of Arkansas;
Hon. John Gayle, of Alabama; S. A. Bowen, Esq., of
Missouri; Garnet Duncan, Esq., of Kentucky; Hon.
James Bucks, of Mississippi; John Hogan, of Illinois;
C. L. Ash, Esq., of Pennsylvania; J. P. Erskine, Esq.,
of Maryland; Hon. B. Storer, of Ohio; A. C. Bullitt, of
Louisiana; J. White, of Indiana.

Secretaries: W. Sneethen, of Louisiana; R. Scott, of
Pennsylvania; C. Scott, of Mississippi; C. C. Norvell,
of Tennessee; A. A. Hall, Tennessee; C. G. Winter-
smith, of Kentucky; W. W, Ferguson, of Arkansas; S.
S. L'Hommedieu, of Ohio; J. R. Blocker, of Alabama;
J. H. Matheney, of Illinois.

After an invocation of the Divine blessing from the
Rev. J. W. Ogden, the assemblage was addressed by
Mr. Foster, the president of the day.

The foregoing sketch of the preliminary proceedings
is followed in the Nashville *Whig* by a brief outline of
Mr. Clay's speech. The Kentucky Senator was received by the audience with a whirlwind of affection-

ate cheers. A friend has just handed us a letter written in Nashville the day before the organization of the convention, in which we note this passage:

"Twelve years ago Henry Clay was burnt in effigy in this place, and he had less than one hundred votes. Now, he has been welcomed as a conqueror, and receives as much homage as the most ambitious man could desire. I feel it will be utterly impossible to give anything like an adequate description of the glorious scene of tomorrow. The sights I have seen today convince me how vain would be the attempt. All is excitement and the most ardent enthusiasm. I and my companions each have a badge on the left breast, Pennsylvania, printed on white satin. We have excited much curiosity; we are from so far off that the people are surprised and delighted. A Tennesseean seeing the badge, exclaimed, " Pennsylvania! hurrah! the Dutch have come!" One of us has an appropriate banner which we shall carry in the procession."

More than one thousand ladies were seated in front of the principal stand and gave inspiration to the speakers.

The effect of Mr. Clay's speech was mighty among his hearers and the great cause received an impetus in Tennessee and the Mississippi valley which made the partisans of the administration tremble. In the course of the day addresses of power were delivered by Messrs. Hopkins and Underwood, of Kentucky, White, of Indiana, Storer, of Ohio, Hogan, of Illinois, Judge Gayle, of Alabama, and others. There was a grand barbecue for the delegates and other strangers provided by the farmers of Davidson county.

On the second day Hon. J. J. Crittenden, of Kentucky, Bailie Peyton, of Tennessee, and many other eloquent speakers from various States addressed the convention. Throughout the entire two days the great attendance of ladies and gentlemen seemed unbroken. They were loath to leave the place.

CLAY AT NASHVILLE.

SPEECH OF HENRY CLAY AT NASHVILLE, TENNESSEE, AUG. 17, 1840.

Mr. President. delegates of the convention, ladies, friends and fellow-citizens:

Our humble and profound thanks are due to the goodness of Providence for the bright, glorious and genial sun that now shines upon us. The firmament above is not unlike the surface of our country. Clouds are flitting over it, but the sun of truth is struggling to burst through them and dissipate the darkness which hangs over us. Before the month of November shall be numbered with the past, all the dark spots which now obscure our political sky shall disappear forever. [An old soldier on the stand here cried, amen!]

I congratulate you, friends and fellow-citizens, on the glorious prospect which the cause of our country presents, more glorious and more estimable because the movements throughout the land are the movements of the people enlisted in support of the Constitution and devoted to constitutional liberty.

· Fellow-citizens, may I not, without incurring the imputation of egotism. advert to some of the circumstances under which I appear before you? [Cries of yes, yes, yes.]

During a long and arduous struggle in political life for fifteen or twenty years, I would wrong myself if I did not confess that there were moments of discouragement; that there were periods in which my heart sank within me; but armed by the consciousness of the rectitude which governed my thoughts and actions, knowing my devotion to constitutional liberty, a devotion exceeded by that of no man living or dead, and believing the principles which I had always avowed and acted up to were founded on the rock of truth, I bore up amidst the difficulties that surrounded me, I stood dauntless and erect. [Shouts of applause.]

Had I come here some years ago, I should have deemed it a duty to disabuse your minds of the calumnies of which I was so unremittingly the object; but that necessity has passed away. In 1825 it was considered as a crime in me that I did not vote for your favorite fellow-citizen for the high office to which he aspired. If it was a crime I but obeyed the instructions of my own constituents, and was I not justified in obeying them ? [Cries of yes, yes.] It is true, I was accused of violating the instructions of the Kentucky legislature, but I deny the right of that body to instruct me. I represented the counties of Fayette, Jessamine and Woodford. They approved of my conduct in that matter, and in this approval do I justfy myself as the responsible agent of the people. [Shouts of applause.]

Of the motives which actuated me in voting as I did I shall not descend here to make any defense. They are known only to myself and to that God by whose justice, tempered by his mercy, I am willing to be tried.

Amidst all my trials, I have never doubted for a moment, that a generous and a just people would approve my course in this matter, if not during life, at least after death. I have never doubted for a moment that just and generous Tennesseeans would be the first to do me honor for that vote. But I am precluded from referring to myself, even had I a wish to do so. Last Saturday's procession, the roar of the cannon as I approached your city, the ringing of the bells, the gladdened shout of freemen saluting me on every side, and last though not least, the bright eyes of the ladies of Nashville, speaking me welcome, and their fair hands waving their handkerchiefs in token of their feelings, are sure proof that the verdict has been rendered. [Three cheers.] And yet, I made this visit with some reluctance, I am free to confess. I had, I thought, resisted all the influence that could be brought to bear upon me to make me leave my home, but there was an influence to which I could not be insensible and to which I yielded with more than ordinary pleasure—that was the influence of the ladies of Nashville. [Cheering long and loud.] I said that I had made this visit with some reluctance, a reluctance that grew out of the relations which I bore to the illustrious captain, your neighbor and your friend. I feared lest the idea might be entertained that I came to this city in the spirit of exultation and defiance to him you were wont to honor. If any man thinks that such is my feeling he does me great injustice. In all the various conditions in life I have been governed, not by the principle of retaliation, but by that of "what it is proper for one's-self to do." Toward the illustrious individual in question, I feel no resentment, no passion, and if he could see the bottom of my heart, he would bear me this testimony. [Loud cheering.] His signal military services to this country deserve the gratitude of all men, and my prayer to heaven is that his last days may be those of peace and tranquillity, and that when he leaves us forever, his home may be that bright and happy one promised by the Son of the Everlasting Father to him who shall perform His will while on earth. [Great sensation among his auditory.]

In addressing the primary assemblies of the people so frequently as I have had occasion to do, I find, my fellow-citizens, a great difficulty in the selection of topics which have not been worn threadbare. In this embarrassing position shall I speak to you of the troubles without example, of ruined commerce, of paralyzed industry, of the rapid accession of authority to the executive, of the dangers which threaten our institutions, of the wonderful expenditures of the Government for the last few years! Since my arrival here this paper has been put in my hands. I never saw it till now. It is a chart of the expenditures and squanderings of the public money. This little altitude of the expenditures under the administration of Washington is scarcely equal to the base of the column whose height marks the extreme of the expenditure under the administration of Mr. Van Buren. This humble spot overshadowed by the surrounding shafts which tower so loftily, exhibits the expenditures of John

Quincy Adams' administration, which were so much denounced at the time, and which called out in a remarkable degree, the energy of the nation to correct the seeming evil. But here are the figures. The eight years of Washington's administration cost the nation $15,000,000; while Mr. Adams the younger was in power it cost us $50,000,000; in General Jackson's time there were expended $145,000,000; and in the first three years of Mr. Van Buren's administration the people's money has been poured out to the sum of $111,500,000 dollars. [A voice in the crowd, "Take him from the throne."] The cheap government, therefore, promised by the present incumbent, has cost the nation, for three years, within one third as much as the eight years of Gen. Jackson's administration! The average daily expenditure of the Government under Washington was $7,000 a day, that under Madison during a perilous war $49,000, under Adams $37,000, while under Mr. Van Buren it amounts to the enormous sum of $110,000 per diem!

But passing this subject, there are two points on which I would speak, especially, to that portion of the audience composed of my old Democratic friends.

The dominant party profess to be the friends of State rights. How are they the friends of State rights? Without going far back for examples of their professed friendship to the States, every year has of late furnished just topics of complaint against those in power. The last session of Congress is peculiarly rich in instances of pretended friendship to the rights of the States from these men. You have already heard of the measure which has too little excited the just animadversion of the people, introduced at the beginning of the session by Senator Benton, and in which the extraordinary proposition was made that the General Government ought not to assume the payment of the debts contracted by the States! No mortal man in the Senate ever dreamed of proposing such an assumption. That proposition was brought in by the Senator in the most unprovoked and wanton manner. The General Government ought not to assume the payment of these debts!

18

The very proposition carried ridicule on its face.   There was a bankrupt Government with a paper circulation, busily engaged in denouncing that circulation and crying out for specie, declaring that it ought not to pay the State debts, and that too at a time when the States were embarrassed and trying to find out means to pay the interest on their loans for works of internal improvement, works which General Jackson's administration had promoted.   The Government, in fact, proclaimed to all Europe that these State debts were so bad that it would be imprudent to meddle with them.   Of the report making this declaration there were 30,000 copies printed, and all to prove the propriety of not doing that which no one had ever proposed to do.

This report was prepared by a fellow-citizen of yours.   With him I have served a long time in public life, and I had hoped to meet him on my arrival here, but when I asked after Mr. Grundy, they told me he was in Eastern Tennessee making speeches in support of Mr. Van Buren.   What!—at his old vocation—defending criminals!"   [Immense cheering and laughter.] There is one difference, however, between his present position and his accustomed practice.   He is now defending State criminals before the grand inquest of the country, and not before a packed jury, and my life on it, he will hear such a verdict as he never heard before in the tribunals of authority.   [Shout of applause.]

But the party in power are friends of State rights! are they?   Does that odious, loathsome theme, the subtreasury project, prove it?   You know the merits of that measure—I will not discuss it—but I tell you, the Presidential party *stocked the cards* twice upon us in the Senate in the matter of this bill and once in the House of Representatives. [Roars of laughter.] Yes, they marked them before they dealt them.   If Senators had been faithful to the will of their constituents and the Senate had been full, that bill never could have passed.   It was hastened through the Senate in January last, despite of entreaties to wait till the Chamber was full, to wait till the entry of the only Senator from New York representing the constituency of that State! But how was it carried in the lower House? At the beginning of the session it was determined to procure a majority to force it through. The admission of the five New Jersey claimants to seats on the floor of the House became necessary, and the measure was resolved upon. Was there any love of State rights displayed upon this occasion? The rightful possessors of their places, the five Whig Representatives, appeared before the House with credentials of the highest known credit. No representative either from Tennessee or Kentucky could appear with higher claims, yet these five claimants were rejected by the absence of one member, detained by sickness. The subject was referred to a committee. It would take a whole day to discuss the principles on which that committee acted. If any Whig has looked into the matter, he has doubtless found that alienage has been no bar to the admission of administration votes, while it was made to exclude Whig votes; that minority does not disqualify an administration voter, while it prevents a Whig from exercising the right of suffrage. In truth there was no rule adopted by the committee save that which went to secure to the five administration claimants their seats.

These are not the only instances which prove the insincerity of the professions made by the ruling party in favor of State rights. There was an occasion during the past session, on which they could have put beyond doubt their devotion to State rights—the passage of the bankrupt bill. But while that measure was before the Senate, they introduced into it a provision to subject to its operation all the banks of the States furnishing a paper circulation. The effect of this proposition was to withdraw from the jurisdiction of the States and consign to the General Government the power over nine hundred State banks, over five hundred millions of dollars of property, over several of the great State works now in a state of prosecution by means of charters or State credit.

I feel, fellow-citizens, that my strength will not justify my going further into the description of the

professed friendship but real enmity to State rights on
the part of the Presidential party ; so that with your
leave, I will hasten to another part of my subject.

The Executive party claims to be the exclusive Democrats of the country. All who do not belong to their
ranks are either Federalists or Tories. Of all their
usurpations there is none more flagrant than this usurpation of the name of Democracy. Democracy, as I
understand it, and as I was taught it in the school of
'98, is: respect of the people's representatives to the
people's wishes, the prosecution of measures which
secure the interests of the people, the promotion of a
nation's happiness and prosperity. Is this the Democracy of Mr. Van Buren ? Hear what he says. Read
it on your banners, "The people expect too much from
the Government. They must take care of themselves
and the Government must take care of itself." Is this
the dictate of Democracy, of the Democracy of the ancient time ? No ! No ! Democracy demands the acquiescence of the representative in the will of the people, when that will is properly expressed, when that
will is known to be the deliberate resolve of the constituent. Not under the Czar, not under the Sultan,
are the people entirely without power. But in this
country, at the present moment, allegiance to the
powers that be is substituted for allegiance to the people. If a candidate for governorship of any of the
States be rejected by the people, he is sure of advancement at Washington. There is my old acquaintance,
the Senator from Tennessee, who was no sooner rejected by the people than he went into the Cabinet of
Mr. Van Buren. Mr. Niles was defeated by a majority
of 4,500 votes, as a candidate for the governorship of
Connecticut. Did this defeat prevent his promotion?
No. It was a passport to office. In less than two
months thereafter he was advanced to the Cabinet of
the President. Bye the bye, the seat to which he was
lifted is the last in the gift of the Government to be
sought as a post of honor under the present administration, seeing that it had been occupied previously by
the greatest reptile that ever crept on the face of the

earth. It is seldom that I permit my lips to be polluted by the utterance of his name, or by reference to him, but they who are from New England may easily guess to whom I allude. [Shouts of applause.]

These instances show that power at Washington is different from and superior and paramount to the will of the people. It is not devoted to the country's happiness. Serious attention should, fellow citizens, be paid to the basis of republicanism! Bad measures pass away. A single false step in government, made undesignedly, may lead to no permanent mischief. War itself is of transient duration. The calamities of disease and pestilence which befall the human species, inflicting extreme agony and pain, pass from the memory, and after a lapse of time no traces are left of their ravages. But there is one truth founded in human nature, verified by the history of the past, strengthened by our own experience as a people, and that truth is—A REPUBLIC CAN ONLY EXIST UPON THE FOUNDATION OF VIRTUE AND GOOD MORALS. This great principle is eternal, is unchangeable. A corrupt people may have the forms of a republic, but their government is dead to good works, its vitality is gone. We need only go back to Rome, to Greece, to republican France, for proof of this thing. Nor can any power save us from the same fate, but the ballot-box. That is the physician to heal us. We have not only suffered from the sub-treasury policy, the specie circular system, the destruction of the United States bank, but far greater evils than these have befallen us. The attempt has been made to corrupt the morals of the people, to corrupt the right of suffrage. When before in private life have we ever witnessed such a deplorable want of confidence? Go to desolate Mississippi—go wherever you please and you will find that violation of solemn contracts characterizes every part of our country. *When before were sixty-three out of sixty-seven receivers of public moneys defaulters?* There must be a cause for all this. The good old Jeffersonian interrogatories have not been put to those seeking office. "Is he honest—is he capable, is he faithful to the Constitution"—have not been asked, but a new rule has been adopted. "Is he boisterous at the polls—is he devoted to my interest and party—what number of votes can he give?" These are the ques, tions now asked. It is this system which has disfigured our country with a want of moral rectitude truly alarming.

It was in the time of General Jackson's administration that this policy was introduced into the Government. He appointed to the Department of State a man who had been a defaulter for $100,000—I mean Edward Livingston—the ornament of the bar of this country and a jurist for whose memory I have the most profound respect. In this appointment the President virtually and in effect proclaimed to the nation the fact that defalcation in the administration of the public moneys constituted no barrier to office. Perhaps the illustrious captain, then at the head of affairs, did not intend that such should be the construction of his course of conduct, but every man who knows the law of cause and effect must agree with me that such an appointment tended to this result. The elevation of Edward Livingston, the advancement to high office of Samuel Swartwout, a man known to the whole country as having been concerned with Aaron Burr in treasonable designs against these United States, are evidences enough that honor, fidelity, and trustworthiness were not the only passports to Presidential favor, even in those days, but that other qualifications were requisite, qualifications which tended to sap the foundations of our institutions. When before have been given so many fraudulent votes ? When before have we seen men regardless of their oaths multiplying their votes and receiving bribes equally disgraceful to the recipient and to the instigator, equally disgraceful to the times in which we live and the country in which such scenes are enacted. Take the case of Letcher. It is a reproach to the parties concerned, and they should be marked as false to the country and the Constitution. Yet Hocker, the sheriff, received for his conduct in that affair the best office in this country in the gift of the Postmaster General. I have heard, though I do not state it as a fact known to me, that this man afterwards ran away, a defaulter to the Government. Thus, when vice is rewarded, when corruption receives reward instead of reproof, the example cannot fail to exert a pernicious influence on the country. The case of New Jersey Representatives proves beyond a doubt that the party in power would disfranchise the Union itself, if they dared do it, to secure to themselves power.

I shall now proceed to address myself particularly to my Democratic friends, to those, as I have said before, who have worked and toiled in the old Democratic army. Not as an enemy do I approach them, but as their friend and countryman. You are equally honest with me in your preferences. You have the same stake with me in the prosperity of the Union. You are equally devoted with me to the happiness and glory of our common country. I believe that the mass of all political parties are patriotic, honest and devoted to the good of the nation, but it is natural that we should differ about measures and men, though that difference of opinion does not make us enemies. You elevated to power the last and present administrations, hoping therefrom the most glorious results. Have your hopes been fulfilled? Have their pledges been redeemed? Have their promises been kept? Have the expectations excited by them been realized? Take the pledge of one term, has it been redeemed? When the illustrious captain of Tennessee was elected to the Presidency, he held out the idea of one term; did he carry it out? Has the promise of economy been kept? [No, no, no.] That lofty column on this chart [showing the chart of public expenditures] will answer. Has the promise of retrenchment and reform been in any way fulfilled? [Loud cries of no, no, no.] Did he redeem his pledges not to appoint members of Congress to office? [No.] What pledge has he redeemed, what promise fulfilled? [None, none, none.] What has ensued? Has harmony among the different parts of the Union been promoted? Has concord increased? Have the fra-

ternal relations which ought to exist in these United
States been advanced? Let this convention answer—
this convention, far exceeding in point of numbers, in
banners and in display of every kind, the great Baltimore convention. [Shouts of applause.] What has
brought you here, my fellow-citizens? A deep and
profound feeling that the country has been wronged, a
lively sense of injury to the people, a full persuasion
that an immediate change is necessary in the General
Government. Do not be deceived, fellow-citizens, by a
name. A blue light has been held out. Go below the
surface of things. Wipe off the colors which assail
your eye with their glare. Look at things as they are,
and tell me whether true Democracy prevails in the
land. [Loud and long shouts of no.] My friend on
my left has said that he was no Democrat [alluding to
Mr. Foster]. I am a Democrat! [Immense cheering];
was born a Democrat, have lived and shall die a Democrat, in the true and genuine sense of the term; but I
am not one of those selfish Democrats whose practice
is to disregard the true interests of the people, to seize
upon their offices as the spoils of victory. No, I am a
Democrat who looks to the interests of the whole people, and to the glory of his country [cheers], and I have
no doubt that my friend near me is a Democrat in this
its legitimate sense.

Mr. Foster here rose and said that he was a Democrat too in this sense of the word, but that he was not
a modern Democrat.

Mr. Clay proceeded:

Delegates of the convention, friends and fellow-
citizens, a great victory is at hand, a glorious victory;
but you should remember that as much judgment is
requisite in the use of triumph as there is still required
to achieve it. The day is near when you shall be
called on to decide how you will use your victory.
Suffer me to say to you, let there be no unkindness in
your course to our Democratic friends who may be
supporting the party in power—to the mass on the
other side. Who are to be the victors and who the
vanquished in the approaching contest? Do we con-

quer aliens, who have come among us with blood on
their feet? No. We fight but against our brothers.
They are all part and parcel of the crew of the great
State ship, all our brethren. Never forget in the flush
of victory this sacred relation. Let us unite with
them in one harmonious union. They as well as we
are interested in a proper administration of public affairs. But there are some classes of the opposite party
to whom the same indulgence ought not to be extended.
There are leaders of the party in power who cannot
be hung too high! [Tremendous cheering.] Drive
these leaders back to their den of demagogism
whence they have emerged but to deceive you. Let
the frown of your indignation visit them, and refuse
to them any longer the opportunity of imposing on
your confidence. They are not a numerous class.
They preach Democracy with the lips, but in heart
their hatred of the people is only equaled by their
tyrannical disposition. They deserve any condemnation
that a generous people may see proper to pronounce
upon them.

There is yet another class, which, in the administration of State justice, should not be unnoticed. I mean
the boisterous office-holders, the Prætorian guard, I
was going to say, of Mr. Van Buren. [Laughter.]
Only imagine such a monarch over such a people, such
a king over such subjects! [Great laughter.] Mr.
Van Buren a ruler of these brave Tennesseeans with
their brawny arms as free as air! [Cries of derision.]

I trust I may be excused in making an appeal to you,
Tennesseeans? [Yes, yes.] In former days the military of Kentucky and Tennessee fought side by side and
won a great and glorious battle. That occasion and
this present one exhibit many strong points of resem-
blance. When Jackson led our brave troops against
the myrmidons of Great Britain, a glorious victory was
achieved by that gallant captain, the victory of New
Orleans. Of that victory I shall always speak as my
heart prompts, for it was one which shed the brightest
luster on our arms. But what is the contest now?
Not between the hirelings of a foreign king and Amer-

ican troops, but between a miserable being engaged in
stealing power by encroachments of the executive on
the Constitution between an American king supported
by his janissaries [Down with him] and the people
commanded by a gallant and noble captain [cheers,
three times three.] They say that this captain is a
coward, an old woman, a caged animal, and yet he
fought more battles than any other general during the
late war, and won them, too. [Cheering for several
seconds.] No general? General Jackson rolled back
from the shores of the Mexican gulf the wave of foreign invasion, and for flogging the British troops alone
received the highest honors a nation could bestow, yet
they call General Harrison no general, in the face of
the fact that he conquered in many battles the combined forces of Great Britain and the American savages! As a statesman, he has served in more civil employments than any man living, from the lowest office
in the land to the highest, in the great wigwam of the
people, the Senate of the United States. [Applause.
Some one here cried out, "Give us some of Van Buren's
fights."] Ah! fellow-citizens, some of Mr. Van Buren's
battles! [Great laughter.]

My colleague (Mr. Crittenden) has just reminded
me of the heroism of the President. He, no hero?
How ignorant you are of the history of your country,
says my colleague. He is the hero of three memorable
wars. There is his war against the commerce of the
country. He has triumphed, and the enemy lies at
his feet. [Applause]. There is his war against the
currency. In this too he has proved the conqueror,
and his opponent is destroyed. [Applause.] There
is his last war, though not least, his campaign against
the Seminoles, in which he was aided by his allies and
auxiliaries from Cuba. [Great applause.] I am sorry
to say in this instance that the Seminoles have maintained their ground. [Laughter.] But to return to
our captain. There is one qualification for public office, fellow-citizens, which our candidate does not
possess, and for this reason he is condemned by the
office-holders—he has no capacity for pocketing the

people's money and running away with it. [Cheering.] He has handled millions of the public treasure, and not a cent ever polluted his hands. Where is now this honest public officer? He is poor and derided by those who have rioted on the speculations of the people's money.

Fellow-citizens of Tennessee, I have said that the present struggle for liberty is not unlike that of 1812. Then it was a fight for liberty on the high seas now it is a contest for freedom on the land. At New Orleans, you Tennesseeans had the advantage of us Kentuckians a little, and that was on the right bank of the river, where, being badly posted and badly armed, we did not fully sustain the character of our State. It is true, we fought with you, side by side, on the left bank, and there you found us ever at our post. But do you intend to repose on your laurels gained in that battle? Do you intend to let us beat you in November? [One general shout,—No. no.] Is it possible that brave, gallant Tennessee, Tennessee devoted to constitutional rights, will not be found abreast with Kentucky, 17,000 strong? You must be up and doing, for in November our majority will reach 25,000. [Applause.]

A few words more and I have done. Our success in this contest I have never doubted. In a spirit of unbounded liberality, I gave, some time since, to Mr. Van Buren, six out of the twenty-six States, but I have had occasion to review that estimate, and the result at which I have arrived is, that if the Whigs do their duty, if they fight to conquer and save the country, the President will not even get these six. Alabama I assigned to him, but she scorns such an association. [Shouts of applause.] Even of Missouri I do not despair. Her gallant sons are in the field, and if they conquer, it will be indeed a victory. Arkansas, too, if I know her, she will not abandon the heath till the fight is over. She will do her duty. South Carolina! [Here Mr. Clay bowed his head in silence; great laughter.] I look back upon the gallant stand she made in the Revolutionary struggle, with feelings of the warmest admiration for her chivalry, and it is with pain that I pass her by in this glorious contest, but while I do so, it is with profound detestation for her present leaders. She will probably throw a blank vote or go with Isaac Hill's State. As for Maine, whom I had put down for Mr. Van Buren, she too is coming—if not in November, she will soon after be admitted into the great Whig family.

Fellow-citizens, the cause in which we are engaged is the cause of the people. The people are moving to victory, and treading upon the heels of the leaders in power. We cannot fail. It is a contest between the log cabin and the palace, between hard cider and champagne, and the issue will be that the office-holders will take to their heels with more rapidity than the popping of the corks from the necks of their favorite bottles.

In repeating to you my acknowledgments for the kindness with which I have been received by my fellow-citizens of Tennessee, and more especially by the ladies of Nashville, I pray that the talismanic influence of their power, which alone brought me here, will contribute to rescue the country from the dangers which now threaten it, and help to preserve and transmit to posterity the liberty won for us by our forefathers. [Nine cheers].

THE PEOPLE AROUSED.

SOME OF THE HARRISON RALLIES IN GEORGIA, VIRGINIA, PENNSYLVANIA, MARYLAND, OHIO, VERMONT, NEW YORK, KENTUCKY AND LOUISIANA.

The Georgia convention was the grandest affair ever known in the State. Twelve thousand eight hundred and forty-eight delegates reported themselves at Macon on the 13th of August, besides several thousands of Whig and administration men were there. Every county in Georgia was represented, and several in

Alabama. The convention organized by calling John McPherson Berrila to the chair, and all the Revolutionary patriots present, nine in number, were by motion made vice-presidents, and five secretaries were appointed. Hon. William C. Preston, of South Carolina, delivered an indescribably eloquent and convincing address. After his speech, the people, in procession, proceeded through the principal streets to the barbecue prepared in the immense cotton sheds. The tables were filled many times and it seemed as though half of Georgia was being fed.

The Whigs of Wheeling, Virginia, on the 10th of August erected a Harrison pole 230 feet high, and threw an American flag to the breeze from its top.

At Washington, Pennsylvania, over six thousand people with great enthusiasm held a grand Tippecanoe rally on the 28th of August.

There was a grand gathering of the friends of Harrison at Middletown, Frederick county, Maryland, on the 14th of August, whereat thousands of people partook of an old-fashioned barbecue.

A large meeting at Warner's factory, in Cockey's district, Baltimore county, Maryland, on October 10, was addressed by S. H. Taggart, J. N. Steele and others.

Tom Corwin, the wagon boy, began his canvass of Ohio at Chillicothe on the 15th of August, and spoke every other day till election to rousing crowds in various counties of Ohio.

On the 14th of August, 15,000 of the Whigs of Vermont assembled at Bennington and were addressed by a Whig of the Revolution, General Wilson, of New York ; Senator Tallmadge and Colonel Stone, of New York, and others.

John W. Baer, the Buckeye blacksmith, on the 15th of August, addressed the Whigs of the Ninth Ward of New York, at the Whig rendezvous, and on the 17th spoke at the central log cabin, on Broadway—"The star that never set shines with redoubled lustre and brightness."

The Whig Harvest Home in Walton, Delaware

county, on the 22d, was attended by over three thousand people. The "old Delaware chief," General Post introduced Hon. G. P. Tallmadge, who spoke one of his clear and forcible speeches for more than two hours. Hon. Geo. W. Bruen and Hon. Aaron Clark, the late mayor of New York, followed.

The Whigs of Louisville, Ky., had a grand revival on the 9th of August, the services being led by Messrs. Clay and Crittenden. The Louisville *Journal* says: Mr. Clay arose amid the hurrahs of the assembled thousands and exhorted them to the further discharge of their duty in a strain of eloquence that made the blood of every person present rush in a warmer and quickened current through their veins, etc. Mr. Crittenden came forth and spoke about half an hour in that style of chaste, felicitous and powerful eloquence for which he is so distinguished throughout the nation.

The Whigs of Louisiana had a large meeting at New Orleans on the 3d, which was addressed by Prentiss, of Mississippi; Gen. G. Edward Sparrow, Barrow, White and others.

The New York State convention at Utica on the 10th was addressed by General Van Rensselaer Stanley, of North Carolina; Alfred Kelley, of Ohio; H. Ketcham, of New York; Fletcher Webster, of Illinois; South and others. James Burt and Peter B. Porter were chosen senatorial electors, and J. P. Phenix, B. Davis Noxon, Philo Orton and twenty-nine others, district electors. It was a huge meeting.

HARRISON'S TASTE FOR HARD CIDER.

[From the Pittsburgh Intelligencer.]

It appears that General Harrison's taste for "hard cider" has not been imbibed since his residence in Ohio, but originated in the family of his ancestors, who have been famous for the excellent cider which they manufactured. Some years ago John Randolph and Dr. Parrish, of Philadelphia, were in conversation about the relative amount of good things of this life which were produced in the different States of the Union. Mr. Randolph took the ground that his own State, Virginia, produced more than any other. After enumerating a good many excellent things for which Virginia was famous, he was interrupted by Dr. Parrish, who said, "Surely, Mr. Randolph, you will admit that you have never seen any cider in Virginia equal to the Jersey cider which you have just been drinking." "I beg your pardon," replied Mr. Randolph, "I have drank cider at Berkeley, which was superior to any Jersey cider I ever drank, and will procure some for you in order that you may judge for yourself." Dr. Parrish accepted the offer, and Mr. Randolph addressed the following letter to Mr. Harrison, of Berkeley:

DEAR SIR: I take the liberty to remind you of a promise which you were so good as to make me, to send a few bottles (half a dozen) of your fine cider to my friend "David Parrish, Esq., York buildings, Philadelphia." Left with Messrs. Tompkins & Murray, Richmond, and addressed to the care of Thomas P. Cope, Philadelphia, it will (the dangers of the seas excepted) go safe.

I am, sir, yours with great respect,

BENJAMIN HARRISON, Esq., Berkeley, Charles City.

March 22, 1816. J. R.

HARRISON AT DAYTON.

GENERAL HARRISON'S SPEECH AT DAYTON, OHIO,
SEPT. 10, 1840.

One hundred thousand people had answered the call
of the log-cabin boys of the Miami Valley, and the assemblage was one of the most magnificent ever held in
America.

The convention was organized by calling to the chair
"Old Stone Hammer," Ex-Governor Metcalf, of Ken-
tucky, and appointing nineteen vice-presidents, among
whom were Preston W .Faner, of Louisiana; Major A.
Miller, of Mississippi; Governor Bigger, of Indiana;
Ex-Governor Vance, of Ohio, and others, and W.
Snethen, of Louisiana, secretary.

After a brief and happy address, welcoming the Old
Chief to Dayton, from Judge Crane, General Harrison
rose, and in a clear, sonorous voice that was heard by
every man of the immense multitude before him, addressed the convention for nearly two hours. The appearance of the old hero was hailed by the mighty
shouts of thousands for several minutes. He was in
excellent health and spoke with a fervor and animation
belonging rather to youth than to age. The fire of his
eye was undimmed by time, nor had the strength of his
manly intellect suffered in the least. The people were
impressed with the belief that he would go into the
Presidential chair a veteran in wisdom and experience,
and grasp the helm of state with a steady hand and
firm resolution, ready to administer the people's government after the people's will.

The following verbatim report of his speech was
made by W. Snethen, Esq., secretary of the convention:

I rise, fellow-citizens [the multitude was here agitated as the sea when the wild wind blows upon it,
and it was full five minutes before the tumult of joy at
seeing and hearing the next President of the United
States could be calmed]—I rise, fellow-citizens, to ex-

press to you from the bottom of a grateful heart my warmest thanks for the kind and flattering manner in which I have been received by the representatives of the valley of Miami. I rise to say to you that however magnificent my reception has been on this occasion, I am not so vain as to presume that it was intended for me, that this glorious triumphal entry was designed for one individual. No, I know too well that person's imperfections to believe that this vast assemblage has come up here to do him honor. It is the glorious cause of Democratic rights that brought them here. [Immense cheering.] It is the proud anniversary of one of the brightest victories that glows on the pages of our country's history, which hath summoned this multitude together. [Tremendous cheering.]

Fellow-citizens, it was about this time of the day, 27 years ago, this very hour, this very minute, that your speaker, as commander-in-chief of the North-western army, was plunged into an agony of feeling when the cannonading from our gallant fleet announced an action with the enemy. His hopes, his fears, were destined to be soon quieted, for the tiding of victory were brought to him on the wings of the wind. With the eagle of triumph perching upon our banners on the lake, I moved on to complete the overthrow of the foreign foe. The anniversary of that day can never be forgotten, for every American has cause to rejoice at the triumph of our arms on that momentous occasion; but the brave and gallant hero of that victory is gone, gone to that home whither we are all hurrying, and to his memory let us do that reverence due to the deeds of so illustrious a patriot. From Heaven does his soul look down upon us and gladden at the virtues which still animate his generous countrymen recurring to his noble and glorious career while on earth. [Great sensation for several seconds.]

I am fully aware, my fellow-citizens, that you expect from me some opinion upon the various questions which now agitate our country, from center to circumference, with such fierce contention. Calumny, ever seeking to destroy all that is good in this world, hath

19

proclaimed that I am averse to declaring my opinions on matters so interesting to you; but nothing can
be more false. [Cheers.]

Have I not declared over and often, that the President of this Union does not constitute any part or portion of the legislative body? [Cries from every quarter, You have, you have.] Have I not said over and
often, that the executive should not by any act of his
forestall the action of the National Legislature? [You
have, you have.]

Have I not time out of mind proclaimed my opposition to a citizen's going forward among the people
and soliciting votes for the Presidency? Have I not
many a time and often said, that in my opinion no man
ought to aspire to the Presidency of the United States
unless he is designated as a candidate for that high office by the unbought wishes of the people? [Cheering.]
If the candidate for so high an office be designated by
the will of a portion or majority of the people, they
will have come to the determination of sustaining such
a man, from a review of his past actions and life, and
they will not exact pledges from him of what he will
do or what he will not do, for their selection of him is
proof enough that he will carry out the doctrines of his
party. This plan of choosing a candidate for the Presidency is a much surer bar against corruption than the
system of requiring promises. If the pledging plan is
pursued the effect will be to offer the Presidential
chair to the man who will make the most promises.
[Laughter.] He who would pledge most, he who
would promise most, would be the man to be voted for;
and I have no hesitation in declaring my belief that he
who would subject his course to be thus tied up by
promises and pledges would not stop to break them
when once in office. [Cheering.] Are my views on
this topic correct or are they not? [With one voice
the multitude indicted they were.]

If, fellow-citizens, we examine the history of all
republics, we shall find as they receded from the purity
of representative government, the condition of obtaining office was the making promises. He who bid the

highest in promises was the favored candidate, and the higher the bids, the more marked and certain the corruption. Look at the progress of this thing in our own Republic. Were any pledges required of your Washington or your Adams? Adams was the candidate of the Federal party, and as a statesman was bound to carry out the principles of his party. Was his successor, Thomas Jefferson, the high priest of Constitutional Democracy, called on for pledges? No. His whole life was a pledge of what he would do. And if we go back to this old system of selecting men for the Presidency whose past career shall be a guarantee of their conduct when elected to the Chief Magistracy of the Republic, the nation would advance safely, rapidly and surely in the path of prosperity. But of late years the corrupting system of requiring pledges hath been adopted. The Presidency hath been put up to the highest bidder in promises, and we see the result. It remains for you, my fellow-citizens, to arrest this course of things. [Cries of "We will, we will."]

While, then, fellow-citizens, I have never hesitated to declare my opinions on proper occasions upon the great questions before the nation, I cannot consent to make mere promises the condition of obtaining the office which you kindly wish to bestow upon me. My opinions I am free to express, but you already have them, sustained and supported by the acts of a long and arduous life. That life is a pledge of my future course, if I am elevated by your suffrages to the highest office in your gift. [Immense cheering for several seconds.]

It has been charged against me, fellow-citizens, that I am a Federalist. While I acknowledge that the original Federal party of this country was actuated in its course by no improper motives, I deny that I ever belonged to that class of politicians. [Tremendous cheering.] How could I belong to that party? I was educated in the school of anti-Federalism, and though too young to take an active part in the politics of the country when, at the erection of the Constitution, the nation was divided into two great parties, my honored father

had inducted me into the principles of Constitutional
Democracy, and my teachers were the Henrys and the
Mason's of that period.   He who declared that the seeds
of monarchy were sown in the soil of the Constitution
was a leader in my school of politics.   He, who said
that "if this Government be not a monarchy, it has an
awful squinting towards a monarchy," was my mentor.
[Immense applause.   Some time elapsed before order
could be restored, at hearing these emphatic declarations of the general.]   If I know my own feelings, if
I know my own judgment, I believe now as I did
then, with the patriarchs of the Jeffersonian school, that
the seeds of monarchy were indeed sown in the fertile
soil of our Federal Constitution; and that though for
nearly fifty years they lay dormant, they at last sprouted
and shot forth into strong and thriving plants, bearing blossoms and producing ripe fruit.   This Government is now a practical monarchy! [Loud and long cheering, indicating that the people felt the full force of his
declaration.]   Power is power, it matters not by what
name it is called.   The head of the Government exercising monarchical power may be named king, emperor, president, or Imaum [great laughter], still he is
a monarch.   But this is not all.   The President of these
United States exercises a power superior to that vested
in the hands of nearly all the European kings.   It is a
power far greater than that ever dreamed of by the
old Federal party.
   It is an ultra Federal power, it is despotism!
[Cheering.]   And I may here advert to an objection
that has been made against me.   It has been said, that
if I ever should arrive at the dignified station occupied
by my opponent, I would be glad and eager to retain
the power enjoyed by the President of the United
States.   Never, never.   [Tremendous cheering.]
Though averse from pledges of every sort, I here
openly and before the world declare that I will use all
the power and influence vested in the office of President of the Union to abridge the power and influence
of the National Executive! [It is impossible to
describe the sensation produced by this declaration.]

Is this Federalism ? [Cries of no, no, for several
seconds.] In the Constitution, that glorious charter of
our liberties, there is a defect, and that defect is, the
term of service of the President was not limited.
This omission is the source of all the evil under which
the country is laboring. If the privilege of being
President of the United States had been limited to
one term the incumbent would devote all his time to
the public interest, and there would be no cause to
misrule the country. I shall not animadvert on the
present administration, lest you may in that case conceive that I am aiming for the Presidency, to use it for
selfish purposes. I should be an interested witness if
I entered into the subject. But I pledge myself before
Heaven and earth, if elected President of these United
States, to lay down at the end of the term faithfully
that high trust at the feet of the people ! [Here the
multitude was so excited as to defy description.]

I go farther. I here declare before this vast assembly of the Miami Tribe [great laughter] that if I am
elected, no human being shall ever know upon whom
I would prefer to see the people's mantle fall; but I
shall surrender this glorious badge of their authority
into their own hands to bestow it as they please!
[Nine cheers.] Is this Federalism? [No, no, no.]
Again, in relation to the charge of being a Federalist,
I can refer to the doings previous to, and during the
late war. The Federal party took ground against that
war, and as a party there never existed a purer band
of patriots, for when the note of strife was sounded,
they rallied under the banner of their country. But
patriots as they were, I do know *that I was not one of
them!* [Cheering.] I was denounced in unmeasured
terms as one of the authors of that war, and was held
up by the Federal papers of the day as the marked
object of the party. I could here name the man who
came to me, and a more worthy man never lived, to
say that he was mistaken in his views of my policy as
governor of Indiana, when I was charged by the Federalists as uselessly involving the country in an Indian
war. He told me that I acted rightly in that matter,

and that the war was brought on by me as a matter of necessity. [Cries of name him, name him.] It was Mr. Gaston, of North Carolina. [Three cheers.] Is this a proof that I was a Federalist? [No, no, no.]

I have now got rid, my fellow-citizens, of this baseless charge—no, I have not. There are a few more allegations to notice. I am not a professional speaker, not a studied orator, but I am an old soldier and a farmer. and as my sole object is to speak what I think, you will excuse me if I do it in my own way. [Shouts of applause, and cries of "the old soldier and farmer for us."]

I have said that there were other allegations to notice. To prove that I was a Federalist, they assert that I supported the alien and sedition laws, and in doing so, violated the principles and express words of the Constitution. I did not, fellow-citizens, ever participate in this measure. When those laws passed, I was a soldier in the Army of the United States! [Applause.]

Again, they censure me for my course in Congress, when I served you in that body as a Representative of the Northwest Territory. And here I will advert to the fact that I represented, at the time, a territory comprising now the States of Indiana, Ohio, Illinois and Michigan. I was the sole representative of that immense extent of country. [A voice here cried, "And you are going to be again!" Tremendous cheering.] As I understand Federalism to be in its origin, so I unstand it to be now. It was and is the accumulation of power in the executive to be used and exercised for its own benefit. Was my conduct in Congress then such as to entitle me to the appellation of Federalist? [Cries of no, no, and cheering.]

I had the honor, as chairman of a committee in the year 1800, to devise a bill which had for its object to snatch from the grasp of speculators all this glorious country which now teems with rich harvests under the hands of the honest, industrious and virtuous husbandmen. [Immense cheering.] Was I a Federalist then? [Cries of no, no, no.] When I was governor of Indiana, ask how the unlimited power bestowed

upon me was exercised—a power as high as that exercised by the present President of the United States!
I was the sole monarch of the Northwest Territory!
[Laughter.] Did I discharge my duties as governor
of that vast territory in such a way as to show that I
was in love with the tremendous powers invested in
me? [Here some 4,000 persons in one quarter of the
crowd raised their hats in the air and rent it with shouts
of No, no, no. They were the delegation from Indiana.
This prompt response from so many persons produced
great sensation.] There is an essential difference between the President of the United States and me.
When he was in the convention which remodeled the
Constitution of New York he was for investing the
governor with the appointment of the sheriffs. When
I was governor of Indiana, and possessed the power of
appointing all officers, I gave it up to the people!
[Intense excitement and great cheering.] I never appointed any officer whatever while governor of In-
d.ana, whether sheriff, coroner, judge, justice of the
peace, or ought else, without first consulting and obtaining the wishes of the people. [Shouts of applause.]
Was this an evidence that I was a Federalist? [No,
no, no.]

I think I have now shown you, fellow-citizens, con-
clusively that my actions do not constitute me a Federalist, and it is to them I proudly point as the shield
against which the arrows of my calumniators will fall
in vain. [Immense cheering.]

Methinks I hear a soft voice asking: Are you in favor
of paper money? I am. [Shouts of applause.] If
you would know why I am in favor of the credit system, I can only say it is because I am a Democrat.
[Immense cheering.] The two systems are the only
means under heaven by which a poor, industrious man
may become a rich man without bowing to colossal
wealth. [Cheers.] But with all this I am not a bank
man. Once in my life I was, and then they cheated
me out of every dollar I placed in their hands. [Shouts
of laughter.] And I shall never indulge in this way
again, for it is more than probable that I shall never

again have money beyond the day's wants. But I am
in favor of a correct banking system, for the simple
reason that the share of the precious metals which, in
the course of trade, falls to our lot, is much less than
the circulating medium which our internal and external
commerce demands, to raise our prices to a level with
the prices of Europe, where the credit system does
prevail. There must be some plan to multiply the gold
and silver which our industry commands; and there is
no other way to do this but by a safe banking system.
[Great applause.] I do not pretend to say that a perfect system of banking can be devised. There is nothing
in the offspring of the human mind that does not savor
of imperfection. No plan of government or finance
can be devised free from defect. After long deliberation I have no hopes that this country can ever go on
to prosper under a pure specie currency. Such a currency but makes the poor poorer, and the rich richer.
A properly devised banking system alone possesses
the capability of bringing the poor to a level with the
rich. [Tremendous cheering.]

I have peculiar notions of government. Perhaps I
may err. I am no statesman by profession, but as I
have already said, I am a half soldier and a half farmer,
and it may be, that if I am elected to the first office in
your gift, my fellow-citizens will be deceived in me;
but I can assure them, that if in carrying out their
wishes, the head shall err, the heart is true. [Great
huzzaing.]

My opinion of the power of Congress to charter a
national bank remains unchanged. There is not in
the Constitution any express grant of power for such
purpose, and it could never be Constitutional to exercise that power, save in the event the powers granted
to Congress could not be carried into effect, without
resorting to such an institution. [Applause.] Mr.
Madison signed the law creating a national bank because he thought that the revenue of the country could
not be collected or disbursed to the best advantage without the interposition of such an establishment. I said
in my letter to Sherrod Williams, that if it was plain

that if the revenues of the Union could only be collected and disbursed in the most effectual way by
means of a bank, and if I was clearly of opinion that
the majority of the people of the United States desired such an institution, then, and then only, would I
sign a bill going to charter a bank. [Shouts of applause.] I have never regarded the office of Chief
Magistrate as conferring upon the incumbent the
power of mastery over the popular will, but as granting him the power to execute the properly expressed
will of the people and not to resist it. With my
mother's milk did I suck in the principles on which the
Declaration of Independence was founded. [Cheer-
ing.] That declaration complained that the king
would not let the people make such laws as they
wished. Shall a president or an executive officer undertake, at this late time of day, to control the
people in the exercise of their supreme will? No.
The people are the best guardians of their own rights
[applause], and it is the duty of their executive to abstain from interfering in or thwarting the sacred exercise of the law-making functions of their Government.

In this view of the matter, I defend my having
signed a well-known bill which passed the legislature
while I was governor of Indiana. It is true, my opponents have attempted to cast odium upon me for having done so, but while they are engaged in such an
effort, they impugn the honor and honesty of the
inmates of the log cabins, who demanded the passage
and signature of that bill. The men who now dare to
arraign the people of Indiana for having exercised
their rights as they pleased, were in their nurse's arms
when that bill passed the legislature. What do they
know of the pioneers of that vast wilderness? I tell
them, that in the legislature which passed the bill
exciting so much their horror, there were men as pure
in heart and as distinguished for their common sense
and high integrity as any who set themselves up for
models in these days. [Immense cheering.] I glory
in carrying out their views, for in doing so, I submitted

to the law-making powers in accordance witl. the
Declaration of Independence; I did not prevent the
people from making what laws they pleased! [Cheer-
ing.]

If the Augean stable is to be cleansed, it will be
necessary to go back to the principles of Jefferson.
[Cheers.] It has been said by the Henrys, the Madi-
sons, the Graysons, and others, that one of the great
dangers in our Government is, that the powers vested
in the General Government would overshadow the
government of the States. There is truth in this, and
long since and often have I expressed the opinion that
the interference of the General Government with the
elective franchise in the States would be the signal for
the downfall of liberty. That interference has taken
place, and while the mouths of professed Democrats
appeal to Jefferson, and declare they are governed by
his principles, they are urging at the same time 100,000
office-holders to meddle in the State elections! And
if the rude hand of power be not removed from the
elective franchise, there will soon be an end to the
Government of the Union. [Cries of assent.] It is a
truth in Government ethics, that when a larger power
comes in contact with a smaller power, the latter is
speedily destroyed or swallowed up by the former. So
in regard to the General Government and the State governments. Should I ever be placed in the Chief Magistrate's seat, I will carry out the principles of Jackson,
and never permit the interference of office-holders in
the elections. [Immense applause.] I will do no
more. While I will forbid their interference in elections, I will never do aught to prevent their going
quietly to the polls and voting, even against me or my
measures. *No American citizen should be deprived of
his power of voting as he pleases.*

I have detained you, fellow-citizens, longer than I
intended, but you now see that I am not the old man
on crutches, nor the imbecile they say I am [cheer-
ing]—not the prey to disease—[a voice cried here, Nor
the bear in a cage] nor the caged animal they wittily
described me to be [great laughter and cheering.]

But before I conclude, there are two or three other topics I must touch upon.

The violence of party spirit, as of late exhibited, is a serious mischief to the political welfare of the country. Party feeling is necessary in a certain degree to the health and stability of a republic, but when pushed to too great an extent, it is detrimental to the body politic; it is the rock upon which many a republic has been dashed to pieces. An old farmer told me the other day that he did not believe one of the stories circulated against me, and he would support me if I were only a Democrat. [Laughter.] But if I support and sustain Democratic principles, what matters it how I'm called? It matters a good deal, said he; you don't belong to the Democratic party! [Laughter.] Can anything be more ruinous in its tendency to our institutions than this high party spirit, which looks to the shadow and not to the substance of things? Nothing, nothing. This running after names, after imaginings, is ominous of dangerous results. In the blessed Book we are told that the pretension of false Christs shall be in future times so specious that even the elect will be deceived. And is it not so now with Democracy? The name does not constitute the Democrat. It is the vilest imposture ever attempted upon the credulity of the public mind to array the poor of the country under the name of Democrats, against the rich, and style them aristocrats. This is dealing in fables. The natural antagonist of Democracy is not aristocracy. It is monarchy. There is no instance on record of a republic like ours running into an aristocracy. It can hurry into a pure Democracy, and the confidence of that Democracy being once obtained by a Marius or a Cæsar, by a Bolivar or a Bonaparte, he strides rapidly from professions of love for the people to usurpation of their rights, and steps from that high eminence to a throne! [Cheering.] And thus in the name of Democracy the boldest crimes are committed. Who forgets the square in Paris, where ran rivers of the people's blood, shed in the name of Democracy at the foot of the statue of liberty! Cherish not the man, then, who under the guise and name of

Democracy, tries to overthrow the principles of Republicanism as professed and acted upon by Jefferson
and Madison. [Immense cheering.]

General Harrison here adverted to the calumnies put
forth against his military fame by that noble pair of
brothers, Allen and Duncan, and in severe but just
terms exposed the falsehoods of these vilifiers. He
proved they were guilty of falsifying the records of the
country, and in a brief and lucid manner vindicated
himself and the honor of the nation from the aspersions
of these and other reckless politicians. He showed that
the received history of his brilliant career in the Northwest had been stamped by the impress of truth, and he
will soon find that a generous and grateful people will
testify their admiration of his glorious services in their
cause by raising the brave old soldier to the highest office in their gift.

A precious inheritance, continued the general, has
been handed down to you by your forefathers. In
Rome, the sacred fire of fabled gods was kept alive by
vestal virgins, and they watched over the gift with
eager eyes. In America, a glorious fire has been lighted
upon the altar of liberty, and to you, my fellow-citizens,
has it been intrusted in safe keeping to be nourished
with care and fostered forever. Keep it burning, and
let the sparks that continually go up from it fall on
other altars and light up in distant lands the fire of freedom. The Turk busies himself no longer with his harem
or his bow string. To licentiousness have succeeded
the rights of man, and constitutions are given to the
people by once despotic rulers. Whence the light that
now shines in that land of darkness? It was a brand
snatched from your own proud altar, and thrust into
the pyre of Turkish oppression. Shall then the far-
seen light upon the shrine of American liberty ever be
extinguished? [No, no, no.] It would not be your loss
only; it would be the loss of the whole world. The
enemies of freedom in Europe are watching you with
intense anxiety; and your friends, few as the planets of
heaven, are praying for your success. Deceive them
not, but keep the sacred fire burning steadily upon

your altars, and the Ohio farmer, whom you design to make your Chief Magistrate, will, at the end of four years, cheerfully lay down the authority which you may intrust him with free from all ambition. It will be glory enough for me to be honored as those pure and honest Republicans, Washington, Jefferson and Madison, were honored with the high confidence of a great, noble, just and generous people! [The excitement and cheering continued for several minutes, and the multitude were swayed to and fro as the leaves of the forest in a wind storm.]

While General Harrison was delivering this address the mail arrived with a letter for a leading Whig in the crowd, giving the particulars of the glorious victory in Vermont. Old Tippecanoe paused in the midst of his eloquence, and the letter was read in a loud tone from one of the speakers' stands. Mighty beyond description was the shout that followed when one hundred thousand voices mingled in one long and startling thunder peal, as when the whirlwind rends the ash it burst the years of the Loco Foco's and crushed their hopes and bruised their hearts.

IN MASSACHUSETTS.

The Bunker Hill Convention at Boston, Thursday, September 10, 1840.

I arrived here yesterday morning at 8 o'clock, and found the city already full in anticipation of the great Whig convention which is to take place on Bunker Hill to-day. Although I had taken the precaution to send for an apartment at the Tremont House ten days in advance I was not sufficiently early. Every hotel and every boarding-house of which I could hear was full, and, with thousands of others, I was thrown upon the hospitality of the people, a hospitality always pro-

verbial, and certainly, on the present occasion. exercised
without stint. Even in the forenoon of yesterday the
city was so full of strangers, the streets of people from
abroad in motion, that the inhabitants were almost
puzzled to know whether they were themselves at
home or not. The mighty influx gathered strength
through the day, and what it will be at 10 o'clock this
morning, I am utterly unable to form a conjecture.

The house of every Whig in the city, where there
was not sickness to prevent, was cheerfully thrown
open; every extra bed was taken, and nearly a thousand new beds were made by contracts, under the direction of the committee, and before dark last evening all
were distributed in vacant rooms throughout the city
and made up for use; so that by 11 o'clock last night,
as one of the committee, who has been charged specially with this branch of the commissariat, informed me
on closing his day of arduous labor, it was believed that
every stranger who had reported himself to the central
committee at Fanueil Hall was comfortably housed.

The proceedings of the occasion were in fact commenced yesterday, by various preliminary meetings.
The citizens of Roxbury took it upon themselves to
provide for the people gathering in from the adjacent
towns of the county of Suffolk; as did the inhabitants
of Charlestown for those from the country to which
it appertains. Large meetings were held in both places
yesterday afternoon. Who were the speakers at
Charlestown I have not learned. Those at Roxbury
were the Hon. Benjamin Watkins Leigh, of Virginia,
and the Hon. George Evans, of Maine. There were
several large meetings in different quarters of the city
last evening. The Marlborough Chapel was thronged
until 11 o'clock, to hear Reverdy Johnson, of Baltimore, and a very able man from Ohio, whose name
I have not learned. At the log cabin, which is in the
Sixth ward, there was a large gathering in the street,
which was addressed by Colonel Kinsman, of Maine,
and Colonel Frank Johnson, of Kentucky, and by
your humble servant.

Among the distinguished gentlemen from a distance,

who had arrived last evening, are Mr. Leigh, of Virginia; Mr. Reverdy Johnson, of Baltimore; Governor Penington, of New Jersey; Governor Ellsworth, of Connecticut; Mr. Phelps, Senator in Congress from Vermont; Mr. Huntington, Senator, and Mr. Williams, Representative in Congress from Connecticut; Mr. Evans, member of Congress from Maine; Mr. Chinn, from Louisiana; Mr. Hoffman, member of Congress, and Philip Hone, from New York, Mr. F. Johnson, from Kentucky; Mr. Tillinghast, Senator Robbins, and Mr. Whipple, Rhode Island; Mr. William King, from Maine; General Kimberly, of New Haven, and many others. Several members of Congress from Massachusetts are, or will be present, among whom are Governor Lincoln, Mr. Saltonstall, Caleb Cushing and others.

The delegation from abroad will be very numerous. It is believed that there will be ten thousand people here from Essex county. Mr. Robbins assures me that the delegation from Rhode Island will be fourteen hundred. The delegations from New York, New Jersey, Pennsylvania and Maryland have already arrived, but I have not yet had time to see them.

The proceedings of the day are to commence at 10 o'clock, by the formation of the procession on the mall. The executive committee with guests by particular invitation, meet at the State House at nine o'clock. The line of march to Bunker Hill is about five miles, and it will not probably reach the place before 2 P. M. There is not to be any speaking there save a few remarks by Mr. Webster, who is to preside, introductory to a declaration from his pen, which will be printed for the public by a printing press which is to move in the procession.

There are to be five meetings at different places this evening, viz: One at Faneuil Hall, over which Mr. Webster is to preside; at the Odeon, where Franklin Dexter is to preside; at the Marlborough Chapel, where Mr. Winthrop will preside; at the City Hall, under the direction of James T. Austin; and at the Republican Whig Hall, under Stephen Fairbanks.

When all is over I will endeavor to give you as good an account as I can, though from the scattering of the meetings, the observations of any one spectator must necessarily be very inadequate.

There was a great crowd on board the noble steamer Massachusetts, from New York, on Tuesday evening- five hundred at least. All were full of ardor and enthusiasm, and such was the feeling that it could only be expressed through a meeting and such speaking as was to be had on the occasion.

There is another great subject of attraction here in Boston now—the great fair for which the ladies have been so long preparing, in order to raise funds for the completion of the Bunker Hill Monument. The work will be done.

HALF PAST THREE O'CLOCK.

The great pageant of the day is over. Such a pageant before I have never seen. Such a pageant again I never expect to see. The spectacle of the mighty gathering upon the mall was animating beyond any other movement of the people that I ever beheld. The procession when formed, and the appearance of the city along all the great streets through which it moved, the thousand gay and streaming banners, the triumphal arches, the decorations of public and private buildings, the twice-ten-thousand ladies at their windows and upon piazzas, balustrades and galleries, saluting the immense procession with myriads of snow-white handkerchiefs, and ten thousand children with their gay little banners, all, all formed the most brilliant exhibition that can be imagined. And it must only be pictured in the imagination, for it cannot be described.

It was a few minutes past one o'clock before the head of the procession reached the consecrated ground, and a full hour elapsed before the whole of this magnificent procession came up. Indeed, it did not all come upon the ground, for it could not. At 2 o'clock Mr. Webster took the chair, amid the loud acclamations of a greater assemblage of men than any of us had ever gazed upon. His address on the occasion was short and impressive, the hallowed cause which had brought the mighty throng together, and the consecrated spot on which he stood, gave solemnity to his manner and inspiration to his thoughts. He spoke of the declaration to which I referred as being in preparation in my first letter this morning; and, on concluding, he introduced Mr. Winthrop, speaker of the House of Representatives, who read it. It was then adopted by the unanimous shout of aye, which almost shook the hill to its base; and no wonder, for the shout was the united voice of seventy-five thousand freemen, and it sounded like what Byron calls "The earthquake voice of victory."

After the adoption of the declaration, Mr. Webster rose, and successively introduced to the multitudinous assembly a number of the distinguished guests present on the occasion, each of whom delivered a brief and pertinent speech in response to the cheers with which they were received. The first of them was Governor Pennington, of New Jersey; the second, Governor Ellsworth, of Connecticut; next, Mr. Senator Phelps, of Vermont, was introduced; next General Kimberly, late Senator from Connecticut, next was Benjamin Watkins Leigh, of Virginia; next, George Evans, of Main. While the last was speaking I left the ground for the purpose of preparing this brief dispatch, and inclosing a copy of the noble declaration adopted as I have already stated.

The morning opened upon us beautifully, and until half-past three a finer day for the occasion could not have been vouchsafed by Providence. About half-past one o'clock the clouds gathered blackness and strength in the West, and one or two heavy showers went round us to the North. At half-past three, however, a gust of rain and wind suddenly broke over the meeting, which caused a quick dispersion, though considering the circumstances, and the masses collected, the breaking up was not disorderly. While I am writing it is clearing away, and the skies afford cheerful promise for the evening.

20

THE PROCESSION.

The following was the order of the procession: Cavalcade; music; chief marshals and aides; Whig State central committee; soldiers of the Revolution, and other invited guests; officers who served in the last war; committee of reception and arrangement, for Suffolk and Charlestown; delegates from States out of New England, in the order of their adoption of the Constitution and admission into the Union. Whigs of New England, in the following order: Maine, New Hampshire, Vermont, Rhode Island, Connecticut, Massachusetts, by counties.

Among the banners were the following:

Ward 1: Banner, The mechanic's arm, with a hammer in hand—inscription over it, "In This Good Right Arm We Place Our Trust." Underneath, "The First Ward—The Home of Paul Revere." On the reverse, "The Laborer Is Worthy of his Hire"—surrounding, "Ward 1."

Ward 5: An eagle with a scroll in its mouth, bearing the inscription,

"To save the ship of state from wreck,
We'll place a patriot on her deck."

Underneath is a vessel representing the ship of state in distress and storm. Motto, "We Love Our Liberties, we Venerate the Constitution; We Hold in Grateful Remembrance its Founders; we will Honor and Sustain Its Defenders." Reverse, A copy of Stuart's Washington; motto, "The Rulers of a Republic Elected to Serve the People, Not Tyrannize Over Them."

Ward 6: A correct picture of the log cabin which is the Whig headquarters of this ward, with the motto, "Shall the People or the Office-holders Prevail?" On the reverse, Ward 6—"Harrison and Tyler, the Men of the People."

Ward 10: Steam engine. Over it, "The People's Engine." Underneath, "1775—Our Whole Country is our Track—1840."

East Boston: "The Log Cabin Which Sheltered Our

Fathers while Achieving Our Freedom, is Our Emblem in Its Defense." Reverse. " We Come to Protect Our Interests—Commerce, Fisheries, Mechanic Arts, Labor." A representation of the barracks that Washington gave Williams, owner of East Boston.

Boston Harrison Club: The banner of the Harrison Club represents Diogenes in search of an honest man. He is represented as looking at a guide-board which points in two directions, on one is inscribed the " White House," and the other, " North Bend." The old fellow, of course, is about taking the North Bend road. On one side is inscribed " Boston Harrison Club," and " Diogenes in Search of an Honest Man." On the other side is the motto from Pope, " An Honest Man's the Noblest Work of God," and the painting represents Diogenes giving " Old Tip" a hearty shake at the door of a log cabin, and pouring the rays of his lamp full upon his honest face. The inscription below is, " Diogenes Successful in his Search."

Bristol county banner: A beautiful painting, representing the crew of a whale boat in the act of harpooning a whale—ship in the distance. Motto, " Harrison and Tyler." Inscription, " Fortune Has Buckled Honors on our Backs, which We Would Fain Throw Off' (referring to Governor Morton's residence in that county.) On the reverse—a painting representing the different interests of the country, with the inscription, " From Our Work Shops, Our Ships and Our Farms, We Come to the Rescue."

Beverly : Upon one side a ship under full sail, but apparently in great confusion, her top-gallant sheets gone, and many of the crew leaving her in boats— Van Buren at the helm, and steering directly on the rocks. In the foreground, Amos with his chin just under water, hugging a life-buoy nearly sunk, labeled, " Extra Globe," and crying " I'm Sick " On the reverse, a ship in fine order, Harrison at the helm, and going off with a flowing sheet. Motto—" Beverly Goes for Harrison and Davis."

Dukes County : " No Duties at the Custom House —Full Duties at the Ballot Box."

Taunton : " We Form to Reform."

Providence Tippecanoe Club : Arms of State, " In God We Hope. " On the reverse, painting of Perry's Victory on Lake Erie. " We have Met the Enemy and They are Ours. "

Every county and every town in old Massachusetts, was well represented on this occasion. Each town had its banner and other emblems, generally ingeniously devised, and containing some local or political allusion of an appropriate character. The Nantucket and New Bedford delegations were accompanied by whale boats; elegantly built for the occasion, and neatly trimmed, and manned by stout and stalwart, thorough-going Whigs. The delegates from Lynn brought with them the màmmoth shoe, drawn by white horses, and containing twenty-five or thirty good Whigs—real working men. Several log cabins were also in the procession, and other emblems expressive of simplicity, industry, honesty and patriotism,

The cavalcade was very numerous, and among them was a large body of truckmen, who, with their white frocks, and mounted on large and powerful horses, attracted great attention. Mr. Eastburn's printing press, mounted on a car drawn by five horses, and appropriately embellished and in full operation, was also an object of great curiosity.

A band of noble-looking sailors also mingled in the procession, preceded by Captain Hunt, of the ship Switzerland, bearing a large American ensign. A ship, full rigged, and attended by a band of gallant sailors, from Essex county, was regarded with much interest. Arches, beautifully decorated, were thrown across the streets in this city in several places. And we must not forget to mention the great Whig ball, covered with inscriptions, rolled along by the Whigs of Concord, which formed quite a conspicuous object.

In Charlestown, across the Warren avenue, a beautiful triumphal arch was erected, beneath which the procession passed.

The delegation from Middlesex, consisting of some thousands, assembled at 8 o'clock in the public square in Charlestown, and marched in procession over Warren bridge to the common. They made a splendid appearance.

The American ensign and pennants were seen flying in every direction, extending across the streets of Boston and Charlestown, waving from flag staffs erected for the occasion, and in some cases from the tops of trees.

SARGENT JOEL DOWNING TO GEN. JACKSON.

Downingville, away down East,
in the State of Maine, July, 1840.

DEAR GINERAL: In respect of your letter, dated at the Hermitage, 23d of June, and sent to the editor of the Nashville *Union,* I think down along here it's all working 'tother way from what you meant it; and it seems to me our cause and Mr. Van Buren's is getting along about as fast as a crab would run, and pretty much the same way.

Go where you will it's all log cabin and hard cider and there's no stopping on't. I found it so all the way from the Hermitage here, and it's been so here ever since I got here. It aint now as 'twas a few years ago when I and my cousin, the Major, used to be fighting for you. Then we could carry everything jest as we'd a mind to. All we had to do was to hurrah for old Hickory, and folks would turn out and give us a lift, and carry any election we wanted to all over the country. But folks down this way say they've got tired of Mr. Van Buren. They don't think he's sich a great President as you've cracked him up to be. Uncle Joshua says he don't come up to Mr. Jefferson or Mr. Madison, no touch to it.

I had a serious talk with Uncle Joshua last night about matters. You know he always went for you through thick and thin, all weathers, and we had a tight pull here in Maine, he was commonly the main spoke in the wheel for us. So when I see him chairman of the log cabin meeting the day I got here, and see him swinging his hat with the rest of 'em, I began to feel a little streaked, and was afraid we was a going to lose him. So I got a chance to get him alone last night, and had a long talk with him. I went right at him in what I thought would be his sorest pint, in the first place; and says I:

" Uncle, you'll lose the post-office as sure as your name is Joshua Downing, if you go to wavering about and giving up Mr. Van Buren, and taking sides with old Tippecanoe."

At that he snapped his fingers at me, and, says he, "Joel, you needn't think to come here to teach me politics. I knew politics before you was born. I was a Republican of the old stamp, and was the first one in Dowingville that come out for Jefferson against old John Adams. Then was the days, Joel, to larn politics. We used to have it hot and heavy, up hill and down. I went right into the front of the battle and fit it out, till I brought over three-quarters of Downingville to my side. So 'twas pretty much all over the country. When we begun the battle, most everybody was for Adams. He come in under Washington, you know, and everybody thought of course he must sarve eight years jest as Washington did. But when he begun to have his alien and sedition laws, and gag laws, and I don't know what all, why, by jings, the Democratic-Republican blood of the country was right up. You could hear the rumbling of the young earthquake clear from the District of Maine to Georgia; and, after fighting like tigers, we brought Jefferson in."

" Well, now," says I, " Uncle Joshua, what does all this rigmarole about Jefferson and Adams amount to? I want you to stick to Mr. Van Buren, so as not to lose your post-office."

At that he snapped his fingers in my face again, and says he:

" I tell you, Joel, I don't care that for the post-office, compared with the good of the country. We are fight-

ing over almost jest sich a battle as we did in the days
of Jefferson and Adams. Here's Van Buren, you
know, come in under old Hickory, and in the first on't
he had most all the country in his favor, and if he had
done as he ought to, he might a stood his eight years.
But only see what a pickle he's got us into. He's turned
the whole country topsy-turvy, capsized everybody's
business, and made us all bankrupt. And I think its
high time to have a change. And I tell you what 'tis,
Joel, the Democratic-Republican blood of the country
has got roused, and if it don't put things straight again,
I'm mistaken. There's been little kind of flustrations
in politics a good many times in this country since
we've been a government; but there has'nt been only
three times when the Republican blood fairly biled
over. The first time was when it turned out old John
Adams and put in Jefferson; and the second time was
when it turned out John Quincy Adams and put in old
Hickory; and 'tother time is now, when it is biling
over to turn out Van Buren and put in the old hero of
Tippecanoe. And it'll do it, Joel, and no mistake."

"Well, now, uncle," says I, "what fault do you find
with Mr. Van Buren? It isn't he that's brought on
all these difficulties. Biddle's bank has done all the
mischief."

At that Uncle Joshua rolled up his eyes at me, and
puckered the corners of his mouth as if he was half
laughin, and says he,

"Joel, a man that's been about the country as much
as you have ought to have more sense than that.
Squire Biddle's bank has been out of the Government
this long time, but things has kept growing worse and
worse all the time, and it's quite too late now to
shoulder it off onto Biddle's bank."

"Well," says I, "uncle, after all your talk, you haven't
brought up a single thing yet against Mr. Van Buren
or his government, and until you can do that, I think
you ought to be in better business than to be coming
out against h'm."

"There's one fact alone," says Uncle Joshua, "that's
enough to satisfy me that things ain't right at head-

quarters, and that is, the expenses of carrying on the Government. About a dozen years ago, our Government expenses was only thirteen or fourteen millions of dollars a year, and now they've got up to *between thirty and forty millions a year.* Now, Joel, you can't make me believe that things is all right when money is squandered away at that rate, and the people know nothing about where it goes to."

Uncle Joshua run on in this way, and talked about the Florida war and the sub-treasury, and sich like, and said he thought it was time to try to have honest men in the Government, till I begun to feel satisfied we mustn't expect any more help from Uncle Joshua. And, to be honest about it, Gineral, I'm really afraid the jig is up with us; for I find Uncle Joshua ain't alone in turning against the Government and coming out for old Tip. I find sich ones all around in every quarter. I was out electioneering 'tother day, and coming along through Baldwin, the 4th of July, I met a great crowd of people out a celebratin'. The road was full of 'em, marching along with their banners and their mottoes, and one of 'em was in large printed letters, "Isaac Dyer and Forty-two Others." And I asked a chap what that meant, and he said Isaac Dyer and forty-two others there used to be Jackson and Van Buren men, but now had come out for old Tip.

You may depend upon it, Gineral, Dowingville is gone as slick as a whistle, and I'm pesky afraid the State of Maine is gone tou. I think I shall be off soon in some of the other States, and try my luck at electioneering there. I wish you would write to me and let me know how you get along out West, and whether the tide is going against us there too, but I wouldn't send any more letters to the printers to publish, for I don't think it helps us a long a mite.

I remain your old friend,

SARGENT JOEL DOWNING.

As showing how catching was the feeling to go for Old Tippecanoe, it may be mentioned that three hundred original Jackson men signed their names to a call for a public meeting of the "Democratic" citizens of

Fairfield county, Ohio, which appeared in the Lancaster
Gazette of August 19, now before us, and at the great
gathering on the 10th of September they marched under
a " Straight Out " banner, with many others of the same
sort. At Cleveland, one hundred and fifty-eight voters
in the *Herald* renounced Van Burenism between the
first and the fifteenth of the month, and thus "the ball
went rolling on for Tippecanoe and Tyler too," and
the influence of Jackson and all other men could not
stay the torrent of condemnation of the Loco Foco
party.

WHIG MEETING.

GOVERNOR CALL, OF FLORIDA, AND J. L. SMITH, OF
ILLINOIS, AT PHILADELPHIA.

A portion of the Whigs of the city and county of
Philadelphia, amounting to about two thousand, assembled at the Whig reading room, corner of Chest-
nut and Fifth streets, to hear that distinguished advocate of our cause, General Call, ex-Governor of Florida.

Josiah Randall, Esq., was called to the chair.

It being expected that Captain Stockton would address the meeting, Mr. Randall read the following
letter:

To the Chairman of Executive Committee:

GENTLEMEN: I am flattered by your invitation to address the meeting to be held this evening, because there
is no portion of our fellow-citizens out of my own beloved State that it would give me more pleasure to
speak to.

No one can be more desirous to lend his aid than I
am to bring back the Government to the pure principles of Democracy, to regulate the banks, to restore a
sound mixed currency to the people as well as to the
Government, to protect our home industry, to give to

the poor man the power of supporting his family, and to enforce that noble doctrine of Mr. Jefferson, that a man's claim for office should rest entirely upon the answers to these questions: "Is he fit? Is he faithful?" I must, however, be excused when I say that I cannot attend your meeting. The unhappy condition of New Jersey is such that I have no spirit to speak to any other people but her own, or to do anything except within her territory. To speak to freemen, one ought to be free himself—and I will not rest either tongue or pen, or the sole of my feet, till New Jersey is redeemed and disenthralled and restored to her former freedom. Your obedient servant,

R. F. STOCKTON.

Mr. Randall, in a brief speech, presented Governor Call to the expectant crowd. The governor commenced by referring to General Harrison's letter to Vance, in which that hero and statesman avows the principles by which, if elected, he will be governed! 1st. That he will serve but one term. 2d. That he will exercise no control over the public treasury, except to apply the appropriations as directed by Congress. 3d. That his rule of appointments to office shall be: "Is he honest? Is he capable!" 4th. That in his dismissals from office, the reasons, in all cases, shall be assigned. 5th. That he will not use his office for party purposes, and will consider the interference of officers in elections sufficient ground for removal. 6th. That the exercise of the veto power will be confined to three classes of bills; those evidently unconstitutional, those infringing the rights of citizens, and those doubtful bills whose vast importance will render a reference to the people necessary. 7th and last, though not the least, of these cardinal maxims, that he will not interfere in the deliberations of Congress. General Harrison guarantees the faithful execution of these promises by pointing to his past life. If, said General Call, there be a man present (and I doubt not there are many Van Buren men as well as Whigs) who can point to any unconstitutional act by General Harrison during his long public life, let that man step forward and proclaim it;

but if he is silent now, let him forever hold his peace. Now, my countrymen, fellow-citizens, measure Mr. Van Buren by the same rule. Is he not directly opposed to every one of these glorious principles? Is he not electioneering for a second term? Is he not grasping the public purse and exercising his discretion in applying the appropriations? Examine each of these principles and see if Mr. Van Buren is not in direct opposition to them. And yet General Harrison is denounced as a Federalist, and Mr. Van Buren applauded as a Democrat.

When I charge the administration with interfering in the elections, I am ready with the proof. During the last summer the commanding general of the United States Army was sent to Florida, not to make war upon the savage foe, but to negotiate a peace. The treaty was signed and a proclamation was issued that the war was over, and that the inhabitants might return to their desolate homes. The post-boy was yet bearing this proclamation through the country, when the tomahawk and scalping knife of the savages were employed in butchering their unsuspecting enemies. Ten miles from the Capital of the Territory the foe burnt the houses and massacred the bodies of their defenseless victims. I dispatched a committee of the most respectable citizens to implore the President to give us his assistance, or at least to allow me to lead an army against our enemies. [Here the governor was interrupted with the most deafening applause.] But the President and the Secretary were absent from Washington. They were in New York attending to [to them] more important enemies. The committee pursued them, and at last caught them [laughter and cheers] at Saratoga, amidst an admiring crowd.

The President said he had no time to talk about Florida—come to Whitehall. To Whitehall the committee went—come to Plattsburg. He was at last cornered, and in reply to the entreaties of the committee, referred them to the Secretary of War. That convenient reference said no! they would carry on the war in their own way. In what way, my countrymen, that war has been carried on, let the wretched survivors of Indian Key bear testimony.

It is impossible to give the language of the eloquent orator, there being no regular reporter present, but the effect was irresistible. The audience applauded, and were silenced by an instant hush, so anxious were they to catch every word. In conclusion, said Governor Call, what is the great argument that Mr. Van Buren addresses to the South? He is a Northern man with Southern principles. The South needs no Northern man to sustain her principles, and she disdains a Chief Magistrate who avows himself to be governed by any sectional principles. Her principles are Constitutional principles. If ever that dread day should come, when she will be called upon to sustain her rights, she will yield her life with the Constitution in one hand and her arms in the other. A Northern man with Southern principles! Southern principles are American principles. Who attacks the North attacks the South. Should our country be called upon to sustain her rights upon the Northwestern boundary question, the South will battle for the Northern boundary beside the North. Yes, if not as much soil is taken from our country as will cover the bones of our dead, she will pour out her dearest blood in its defense. If that territory be but barren rocks, she will leave her bones to bleach upon them rather than yield an inch to foreign aggression. The governor continued in a most eloquent strain for an hour and a half, frequently interrupted by the loudest applause. After he was seated, Mr. Randall introduced Mr. J. L. Smith, of Illinois, formerly of Philadelphia, who exhorted the Whigs to imitate the son of Carthagenian Hamilcar, who swore on the altar of his country to oppose the enemies of his country until he or they should be no more. Mr. Naylor being called upon, expressed his gratification at the proceedings, and thanked Governor Call for the instruction imparted in his eloquent speech.— *United States Gazette.*

NEW YORK MERCHANTS' MEETING.

IMMENSE MEETING OF THE NEW YORK MERCHANTS, IN FAVOR OF WHIG TICKETS AND PRINCIPLES.

One of the most important meetings of the campaign, that of the business men of the great metropolis, is worthy of being remembered as well by reason of the prominent names connected with it as of its size and effect upon the popular mind. We condense from a lengthy report in the New York *Express:*

The number of persons present was variously estimated, some going as high as 40,000, who took their accounts when Mr. Webster first opened his address. A count was made from the portico of the Exchange at a quarter before 4 o'clock and 11,000 were counted. At 10 minutes before 3 o'clock, and a quarter after, the same person states three times as many were present.

We have never before seen Wall street quite as much decorated with beauty as it was on this occasion. The stage from which Mr. Webster spoke was placed at the corner of Wall and William streets. The crowd of men stood up and down William and Wall streets in a dense throng, as far as Mr. Webster's voice could be heard. Almost every window was crowded with ladies waving their handkerchiefs. The tops of building were full of spectators.

The shipping presented a beautiful appearance. From the forest of masts for miles in extent flags of every nation floated to the breeze. The day was delightful.

This was a merchants' meeting, and what a contrast in numbers, appearance, and every other thing of importance did it present, when set off either with the meager call of administration men, first published in the *Journal of Commerce,* or when assembled on the Exchange.

Mr. Webster spoke about two hours and a half. Our readers will find a very full and accurate report of his remarks. He was listened to with profound attention throughout.

At a meeting of the merchants and traders of the city of New York, disapproving the leading measures of the administration, and opposed to the re-election of Martin Van Buren, and in favor of the election of Harrison and Tyler, held in pursuance of public notice, in front of the Merchants' Exchange, on Monday, the 28th of September,

W. W. Todd, Esq., called the meeting to order, and on his motion, the following officers were chosen:

President: Jonathan Goodhue.

Vice-Presidents : Benjamin Strong, James Brown, Edward G. Faile, David Lee, Jonathan Sturges, Stephen Whitney, James G. King, John Haggerty, John Rathbone, Jr., G. P. Disosway, Charles H. Russell, John W. Harris, John D. Wolfe, Abraham Fardon, William Scott, Hugh Archineloss, James J. Van Alen, D. A. Cushman, Thomas Brooks, D. W. C. Olyphant, John P. Stagg, John A. Underwood, Henry A. Bogert, R. H. Nevins, Peter I. Nevins, John Van Nostrand.

Secretaries: William H. Aspinwall, Augustin Averill, Thomas Williams, Jr., John Steward, Jr., E. P. Heyer.

The Hon. Moses H. Grinnell then presented the following resolutions, which he enforced in a brief address:

1. *Resolved*, That in the opinion of the merchants and traders of New York here assembled, the existing derangement in the financial and commercial affairs of the country may be directly traced to the measure of the National Government in its experiments, blindly commenced and recklessly prosecuted, with the promise of a better currency, to the lamentable failure of those experiments; and to the catastrophe which compelled the repudiation of its legitimate powers, as the only excuse to the people for the abandonment of its Constitutional responsibilities.

2. *Resolved*, That a mixed currency, partly paper and partly metallic, and the use of credit are essential to the prosperity of all commercial nations; and that to

these causes are due, in no small degree, the rapid progress which this country has made, altogether unexampled in the history of mankind.

3. *Resolved*, That the power to regulate the currency is granted by the Constitution of the United States to the General Government; and that this power having been recognized and exercised by successive administrations from that of General Washington to that of General Jackson, and confirmed by the Supreme Court of the United States, its constitutionality cannot now be questioned or denied.

4. *Resolved*, That the recommendation in Congress, in a special message, by Mr. Van Buren, to subject all banking incorporations to a national bankrupt law, and thereby to regulate the currency, is an admission of the constitutionality of the power and of the duty of Government to exercise it

5. *Resolved*, That the use of the State deposit banks, under a law passed during General Jackson's administration, with a professed view, among other things, of regulating the currency of the country, is also a direct admission of the duty of Government in this respect.

6. *Resolved*, That it is a most important duty imposed upon the National Government, and a fundamental principle derived from the Constitution in the use of the necessary power, that it shall so regulate the currency that it shall be safe, stable and uniform; not only thereby to secure the collection. safekeeping and convenient disbursement of the public revenues, but from the vital necessity of such currency to the prosperity of commerce, manufactures, agriculture, the mechanic arts and the daily transactions of life.

7. *Resolved*, That the sub-treasury scheme tends to concentrate the whole money power in the hands of the executive, and that it may be used, by a weak and wicked executive, to break down all sound banking institutions, and the commerce and trade of any and every part of the country at its will.

13. *Resolved*, That the merchants and traders of New York continue an unabated, hearty opposition to the present administration, to its war upon State credit, to

its sub-treasury, to its financial schemes, to its conduct
of the Florida war, to its plan for an unconstitutional
standing army, to its increase of patronage, to its fearful proscription for opinions sake, to its squandering of
the public revenue, to its defaulting agents, to its
attempt to array the poor against the rich, to its encouragement given to the avowers of agrarian and
other disorganizing doctrines, to its reduction of the
price of labor, to its neglect of the currency, and finally
to its general incompetency at home and abroad; and
we, therefore, pledge ourselves to use every honorable
exertion to secure the election of William Henry Harrison and John Tyler, as President and Vice-President
of these United States.

14. *Resolved,* That we cordially respond to the
unanimous nomination of those tried servants of the
people, William H. Seward and Luther Bradish, and
that we will contribute by our strenuous efforts to their
re-election, and are confident of an overwhelming majority, and,

15. *Whereas,* during the administration of Washington, commerce was fostered and protected, the
rights of property carefully guarded, the currency
wisely regulated, and the foundations broadyl laid of
national prosperity; and, whereas the merchants and
traders of New York yield to none in admiration
of his character, therefore,

Resolved, That we look with indignation and scorn
on the late and present administration to disparage the
fame and dishonor the character, by questioning the
motives of the Father of his country. "His is that
name which an American may utter with pride in every part of the world; and which, wherever uttered, is
shouted to the skies by every true lover of liberty; and,
until time shall be no more, a test of progress, which
the human race has made in wisdom and virtue, will
be derived from the veneration paid to the immortal
name of Washington."

Resolved, That the following persons, viz : Robert
B. Minturn, Pelatiah Perit, Henry R. Bogart, George
S. Robbins and Daniel S. Miller be appointed a com-

mittee on behalf of this meeting to carry out the foregoing resolutions, with power to add to their number.

The resolutions being read, the Hon. Daniel Webster addressed the meeting.

The question being put on the resolutions, they were unanimously adopted, and the proceedings, signed by the president and secretary, were ordered to be printed, and the meeting adjourned.

WEBSTER IN NEW YORK.

DANIEL WEBSTER REPELS SLANDER AT THE GREAT MERCHANTS' MEETING.

You'll be addressed to-morrow by a gentleman of high talent, a distinguished supporter of the administration, one of the most distinguished, certainly, in that portion of the councils of the nation to which I belong. He'll not say, but others will say for him—it will be said—and all the papers, friendly to the administration, will say, "Don't believe Webster, that old aristocrat; you can't believe anything that he says."

Now, my friends, it would be very strange if I, who have grown up among the people, and, as it were, of the people, should at any time of life take a fancy to aristocracy! I have plowed, and sowed, and reaped the acres that were my father's, and that now are mine. By the aid of those valuable institutions, public schools, and the guidance and assistance of the best of parents, I was enabled to get such an education as fitted me to come to the bar; I have been some time in public life, I never held an office in the course of that life, except such an one as came directly from the bestowment of the people; I have had no money out of the public Treasury, except the pay as a member of Congress; I have no family relations—no one in any way

21

or shape—nothing with blood of mine flowing in their veins that ever held an office or touched a cent of the public money. [Cheers.]

After all this I shall still be told that I am an aristocrat. Very well. Prove it. If I am one I am quite false to my origin and connections as well as to my nature. But I ask for the proof. Look at my votes in Congress. What right of the people have I voted away? By what vote of mine in the people's councils of the country am I to be proved an aristocrat?

I do not come here, however, to speak of men, (much less of myself), but of principles, and therefore what such men as I am are is comparatively unimportant. It has indeed happened to me to be in Congress for many years. If in the course of that time I have done anything that is worthy of approbation it was done in the exigency of peculiar events, when I thought the Constitution was in danger, and when I thought it was my duty to uphold it.

My prejudices for one set of men and another set of men never made me cease to defend that glorious Constitution which our fathers obtained by a miracle and which has flourished by a miracle ever since.

And yet I shall go for a very bad aristocrat. And echo will tell in a thousand ways, from Brooklyn to Montauk Point, that Mr. Webster is a sad old aristocrat and knows nothing of Democracy, and particularly of the Democracy of this country.

On the other hand, our opponents know Suffolk well; they study it; they know that it was distinguished in the Revolution for its stern Democracy, tried and proved. They remember that it produced the L'Hommedieus and the Floyds, and the Smiths and Joneses, and they'll all come down here to-morrow as the Pharisees came of old with their phylacteries, and the garbs of Democracy, and the word "Democracy," "Democracy," "Democracy," which occurs as often among them as "ditto," "ditto," "ditto," in a tradesman's bill. [Laughter and cheers.]

Now all I have to say to you, my friends, is, look at

facts! Words are cheap—promises are easy and cost
nothing. But there is an old adage among the farmers
that "fine words butter no parsnips." [Laughter.]

I claim no more patriotism than others, but I claim
just as much. Have I no stake in this fair inheritance
of our common country? Don't I wish to go down to
my grave with my full share of its honors and its
glories? Have I no interest or desire to protect what
I have, that it may descend unblemished to my children
and to my children's children? [Here Mr. Webster's
voice changed very perceptibly, and he was much affected and labored with strong feelings.] The man
that says that I am an aristocrat, *is a liar!* [Tremen-
dous cheering.]

I may be mistaken. I may err. I submit to the judgment of those who can see more clearly than myself
when I am at fault. But the man that will not meet
me fairly with argument, and uses idle and abusive
declamation instead, and then will not come within
the reach of my arm, is not only a liar but a coward !
In common with many others, I think it necessary to
change the administration. I don't mean to call names.
It is not my habit to attack persons. I leave that to
those who feel ill-natured. I discuss principles; and
at this moment [alluding to the news from Maine]
I feel particularly good natured.

I have no galled withers. I have nothing to fear;
but, on the contrary, am hopeful of everything.
[Cheers.] I don't want to triumph in what is called
the prospects of our party in the coming election.
That election is settled already.

I desire to put it upon this issue—that if the measures
of the present administration have been Democratic,
support them; if not, do not do so. But do not take
names for things, and professions for principles. By
Democratic measures, I mean such as the good old
Democrats of past times would have supported. Such
measures as Chancellor Livingston would have supported; such as Mr. Jefferson would have supported;
such as Virginia, the old pure school of Democracy,
would have supported. Such measures I advise you

to support. But examine and inquire well for yourselves, and decide as you find.

The Democratic head of this Democratic Government passed the sub-treasury bill. Was this by a law
of Congress or a law of the executive? In 1837 when
Mr. Van Buren proposed this measure, there was no
one in Congress in favor of it. It was not liked, and
got very little support. Well, he held out four successive sessions of Congress; his measure belongs to
the important question of how best to keep all the
public money; and yet with this important subject,
and executive influence, and the fatiguing drill of four
sessions, it only at last got into the House of Representatives. And what was done then? It lay there
for three months; at last it passed; and out of 250
members (I believe that's the number) who voted for
it, they didn't alter a word or syllable—they didn't, as
we say in common parlance, dot an *i* or cross a *t*.

Well, it was passed. And I'll venture to say that
even the Parliament of Paris, in the ten years that preceded the Revolution, never passed an edict so completely submissive to royal authority as did the House
of Representatives' by passing the sub-treasury bill
conform to executive authority.

How very Democratic this conduct was! The people choose members of Congress to make laws; as
they pass just as the President wishes them to pass.
And I, who complain of this course of procedure, am
an aristocrat, and not to be believed!

Now, if the regular increase of executive influence
be Democratic, then by all means go for a renewal of
Mr. Van Buren's term. He'll give you enough of that,
[Laughter.] Why, as things are now, the office-holders can't live or breathe but as they conform to the
desires of their superiors. And yet the Constitution
under which we live says that he has no superior. Is
not this, then, a gross attempt to fetter the free minds
of a free people? They give a man an office and say
he is no longer a free agent. What shameful perversion of Democracy.

And now let us see how it is with respect to the

augmentation of the number of office-holders. Is it the present administration that extends the number? Take the custom-house of the city of New York as a criterion. I won't go to Illinois or to Michigan to the land offices there, because you can't easily see and examine for yourselves. But take your own great city, and take the published official documents and you'll see that the custom-house officers are double in number to what they used to be. Where there were 100, now there are 200; for 200 there are 1,000. And what is all this increase for? It can't be because they are wanted to attend to the legitimate business of the custom-house; because there were not half the number when the duties were much greater. Very well, then, they must be wanted for an illegitimate purpose. [Laughter.]

Now, as to the expenses of the Government, we all know that in Adams' time $13,000,000 a year was the most that was spent. The expenses then never averaged that sum. Now, at the close of 1837, they were run up to $39,000,000! I don't say that this is conclusive that the Government has been wasteful and extravagant. There has been occasion this year for extraordinary expenditures. We have a Florida war which Adams had not. And in my opinion, if he had been in office, we never should have had it.

Here, then, are the facts. They complain that Adams' administration was wasteful and profligate, because it spent nearly $13,000,000. Now, then, call on them to say why they spend nearly $39,000,000. It's a case that calls for an account—a strict and correct one —and they ought to render it.

To recur a moment to the custom-house of New York. The expenses now are three-fold more than they were in Jonathan Thompson's time. Inquire how this is, and obtain a full and satisfactory answer, and then ponder over it. It does not appear like that truly stern economy which should characterize a Democratic Government.

A recent governor of this commonwealth, in his place in the Senate, expressed the true feelings of his heart and those of his party when, flushed with the triumphs of victory, he was justifying the removal of every one from office that was opposed to his party and measures. He then made use of that remarkably characteristic expression, " Do not the spoils of victory belong to the conqueror?"

This is applied to the party that seizes on all the offices and turns out all that differ from them when they obtain the victory. Is that Democratic? Are the offices merely made to be sported with in this way? Are offices made for mere adventurers? Is that the spirit of the Constitution of this free country?

In a word, is that Democratic? Stick to the old text. Is not the Government instituted for the good of the people? Should not a government be checked so as to possess no more power than good people require? Should a government have any more money at command than is absolutely necessary for its simplest wants? All this used to be Democratic.

But take a view of what the present Government calls Democracy. Why you may look for a description of it in all the books from the primer to the English reader, run the range of the whole vocabulary, and you'll not find a word about it in all the good old Democratic schools.

Then keep to this. Are the measures of the present administration Democratic? Why, the leading measure and the only measure is the sub-treasury. From alpha to omega it's all " sub-treasury," " sub-treasury," " sub-treasury." And its echoes have not ceased and will not cease till the administration go out of office. It puts one in mind of Orpheus going to seek Eurydice, " Eurydice the woods, Eurydice the floods, Eurydice, the rocks and hollow mountains rang." With our Government it is, " Sub-treasury the woods, sub-treasury the floods, sub-treasury the rocks and hollow mountains ring." [Immense cheering and tumultuous laughter.]

MEETINGS IN SEPTEMBER.

FROM THE GRANITE MOUNTAINS TO THE GULF ALL
TIP'S BOYS IN MOTION.

The battle of Lake Erie was celebrated in grand style on the 10th of September, at Erie, Pennsylvania, by the Keystone Tippecanoes. September 6 there was another grand rally at Monument Square, Baltimore, Maryland.

The friends of Harrison and Tyler had a huge convention at Harrisburg, Pa., on the 13th of September. Over seventy-five thousand freemen assembled at Syracuse, N. Y., on the 16th, who were addressed by General Wilson, of New Hampshire, and Tallmadge and Hoffman, of New York, greatly to the delight of the people.

A State convention and festival of the friends of Harrison and reform was held at Hagerstown, Md., on the 16th, which was a regular love feast.

The three days' meeting at Dayton, Ohio, commencing on the 10th of September, the anniversary of Perry's victory, will long be remembered as one of the grandest conventions ever assembled in Ohio. The one hundred thousand people were addressed by General Harrison, Henry Clay, Tom Corwin, " The Wagon Boy," Harry Southgate, and many other distinguished orators.

On the 18th of September, at Lancaster, Pa., was the greatest gathering of people that had ever been known in that hospitable city. Such processions, with banners and streamers, and canoes, and log cabins and other devices, surpassed anything in this part of the country. Charles Stephens, Penrose and Reed, and many other eminent speakers addressed the vast concourse.

At the great Harrison and reform convention at Wheeling, W. Va., on the 3d of September, the extreme right of the procession was occupied by over three hundred who had denounced Van Buren and marched under the banner—"Straightouts ! "

At Staunton Va., on the 30th, there was a grand convention, which was eloquently addressed by B. W. Leigh, James Lyon, Bailee Peyton, John H. Pleasants, H. Rhodes, W. Robertson, J. M. Wickham, H. L. Brook. S. S. Baxter, L. W. Chamberlayne, W. R. Gratton.

At Salsbury, Somerset county, Md., there was a rousing Whig meeting on September 23.

The Whig State convention at Baton Rouge, Louisiana, on the 28th, was addressed by Hon. Sergeant S. Prentiss and others. The Tippecanoe club of Mississippi was there in great numbers. The enthusiasm was great.

WEBSTER IN VIRGINIA.

THE VIRGINIA CONVENTION AT RICHMOND, OCTOBER 5, 1840—MR. WEBSTER'S SPEECH BEFORE THE CONVENTION AND THE LADIES IN THE LOG CABIN.

The convention held at Richmond on Monday last, — the never-to-be-forgotten fifth of October — will take a place in the foremost rank of those great gatherings of the people which have distinguished the present year

The day—the memorable anniversary of the battle of the Thames—was ushered in by a national salute from artillery in the Capitol square; and as early as sunrise the stir and bustle of preparation began. The different delegations with their flags, banners, and insignia, marched to their respective places of rendezvous, and, accompanied by fine bands playing martial or patriotic airs, gave great animation to the streets. The procession formed in Maine street and it extended about a mile and a half. This wide and continuous street was admirably fitted to show the procession to advantage, and the houses consequently were filled with those who were eager to enjoy the splendid spectacle. Throughout the whole line of march the procession was hailed with demonstrations of the most fervent enthusiasm on all sides. All seemed to enter into the spirit of the hour, and if there were those who did not sympathize heartily with the scene they kept their sentiments to their own bosoms, or were carried beyond themselves and participated for the time in the general feeling. Every window, every doorway, every point that commanded a view of the procession, was occupied by ladies, who showed by their plaudits and waving of handkerchiefs, and miniature banners, that their whole souls too were in the holy cause of the people against the opposers of the people, and if they had suffrages they would be given on the side of "Harrison and reform," and in opposition to this corrupt, imbecile and blundering administration. A triumphal arch of shrubs and flowers had been thrown quite across the street, having at each end a pendent flag bearing some appropriate inscriptions; and as the delegates passed under, the most rapturous and inspiring cheers arose from bevies of beauties on either side.

The spot selected for the meeting of the convention was the noble and extensive area, on old Shockoe Hill, in front of the Capitol; and no city in the world can present a place better suited for such purposes. The facade of the Capitol was tastefully adorned with flowers and evergreens; elegant wreaths hung from every pillar, and in the midst names of those glorious fields in which Harrison had won so much renown while his achievements shed so much luster on his country's arms, shone 'out conspicuously "Tippecanoe," "The Thames," etc. Over all the national ensign floated to the breeze. The most excellent arrangements had been made for the accommodation of the speakers, the invited guests, the ladies and the public generally. About 12 o'clock the procession entered the square, and the different delegations were conducted to the

places assigned to them with an order and harmony
which reflected the highest credit on the marshals, as it
called out the approbation of all who witnessed the admirable results of their skill and efficiency. The banners of the different counties and States were successively hoisted up to the colonnade of the Capitol, and
placed in full view of the assemblage, who hailed the
sight of them with loud cheering. When that of Maine
was recognized, the applause was peculiarly long and
loud, but it was nothing to the earnest enthusiasm with
which the old time-worn banner that had been borne
by Captain Spencer's company at the battle of the
Maumee, pierced with many a bullet, and slashed by
the tomahawk, was presented to the gaze of the meeting. Several other old banners and ensigns, associated
with the Revolutionary events, and with the triumphs
of our countrymen in the War of Independence, were
hoisted, and among them a banner of 1776, belonging
to the old Alexandria Rifle Corps.

The spectacle presented to us on the pavilion that
had been fitted up for the officers and speakers, was
one of the most magnificent that can be imagined. In
the area below there were at least ten thousand—some
say fifteen thousand persons—assembled. The dense
mass of good Whigs of our own sex in the center was
flanked by galleries of beauty, and of true, sincere, and
devoted Whigism, too, of the fairer portion of our
species. Then there was the town between us and the
shining river; and a lovely, rich, undulating country
beyond, extending as far as the eye could reach—bask-
ing under bright skies and a clear and inspiring atmosphere—and over the whole thrown a halo of poetic,
historical and patriotic associations, with the glory and
freshness of the scenes, which were then to be enacted
before us. It is but feeble and halting praise that we
can, by any words of ours, bestow on our fair allies of
Richmond, but we are sure that the impression produced
by the lovely forms, the bright eyes, and charming
faces that gave such luster to the Capitol and its pre-
cincts, will not soon pass away from the men of sense
and feeling, who composed the convention.

The convention was organized by the appointment of Ex-Governor James Barbour, of Orange, as president, the Whig electors who happend to be present, as vice-presidents, and Beverly Tucker, Esq., and James M. Garnett, Esq., as secretaries. Governor Barbour on taking the chair, addressed the convention in the easy, flowing, and felicitous manner for which he is distinguished.

I compliance with the invitation of the committee of arrangements, a meeting of the clergy of Richmond had been held in the Capitol, in the morning. These reverend gentlemen had appointed two of their number to perform their sacred offices, when required, during the sitting of the convention. Accordingly, after the president's address, the Rev. Mr. Palmer came forward and offered a brief but earnest and appropriate prayer to the Divine Benignity.

Benjamin Watkins Leigh, Esq., then appeared, and, after a few eloquent remarks, read an address to the people of Virginia, which was unanimously adopted.

The cry now arose on all sides, " Webster, Webster!" It had been the wish of Mr. Webster and his friends that he should not be called on to speak until Tuesday. He had undergone great exertion for weeks previous, and was suffering from the effects of a severe cold. But the impatience of the people to see and hear him could not be controlled. The call was loud and universal. He answered it with promptness, and with the spirit and energy which he seems to have ever at command to meet any emergency, however unexpected.

He appeared and was introduced by the president amidst the loudest and most enthusiastic acclamations, the buzzes being mingled with cries of " Welcome! welcome!" " Three cheers again for him!" "God bless you!" etc.

When the applause subsided, Mr. Webster began a speech, which, considering the time and circumstances, will be regarded as one of the best judged and most admirably conceived and most exquisitely finished productions of his great mind. It was characterized throughout by a dignity of tone, a power of thought, and

beauty and force of diction, which won the reluctant admiration even of his political opponents, and more than
justified all that his most encomiastic friends had led
the public to expect. It was, from beginning to end,
the very opposite of rhetorical sophistry—solid, substantial and energetic; and even in those passages
where the high argumentation was enlivened and enforced by passionate and overwhelming eloquence, a
manifest and profound feeling of truth, sincerity and
honesty, forked the fulminations of his oratory. If we
are to judge from the impressions made upon his audience, never was there a more successful speech. The
philosophic statesmen of Virginia, and the plainest and
most untutored denizens of that State, equally admitted
that they never were more instructed, delighted, or animated to patriotic, steady, and perserving exertion,
by any speech from any public man.

We have not room for a full report. We cannot,
however, pass over some of the most striking passages.
His allusion to those amiable persons who are so very
considerate of their reputation and his reputation as to
think it a great breach of propriety in him to have gone
•to Richmond, or to be invited there, was received with
loud laughter and cheering and cries of "Welcome!
welcome!" "If," said he, "there be any question or
questions on which you and I differ in opinion, those
questions are not to be the topics of discussion to-day.
No! We are not quite soft enough for such an operation as that. [Laughter.] We are battling together
in the face of a common enemy; we are armed to the
teeth, putting forth as many hands as Briareus, and
with each hand dealing him all the blows we can; and
does he imagine that at such a moment we shall be
carrying on our family controversies? That we are going to give ourselves those blows which are due to him?
No; he is the enemy of our country; we mean to pursue him till we bring him to capitulation or to flight;
and when we have done that, if there are any differences of opinion among us, we will try to settle them
ourselves, without his advice or assistance [laughter],
and we will settle them in a spirit of conciliation and

mutual kindness. If we do differ in any of our views we must settle that difference not in a spirit of exasperation, but with moderations, with forbearance, in a spirit of amity and brotherhood."

The most striking passage in his speech, unquestionably, was that in which he referred to the subject which so deeply interests the whole South. "There is," said Mr. Webster, "one perpetual outcry in all the administration papers from Baltimore south, admonishing the people of the South, that their own State governments and the property they hold under them, are not secure if they admit a Northern man to any considerable share in the administration of the Government. You all know that that is the general cry. Now I have spoken my sentiments in the neighborhood of Virginia, though not actually within the State, in June last, and again in the heart of Massachusetts in July, so that it is not now that I proclaim them for the first time; but ten years ago, when obliged to speak on the same subject, I uttered the same sentiment in regard to slavery and to the absence of all power in Congress to interfere, in any manner whatever, with that subject. I delivered my sentiments fully in Alexandria in the month of June, and in July at Worcester, in Massachusetts. I shall ask some friend connected with the press to circulate in Virginia what I said on this subject in the Senate of the United States on the 30th of January last. I have nothing to add or subtract from what I then said. I commend it to your attention, or rather I desire you to read it. I hold that Congress is absolutely precluded from interfering in any manner, direct or indirect, with this, as with any other of the institutions of the South."

Now the cheering was so loud and long continued that Mr. Webster was interrupted for several minutes. One sonorous voice was heard above the other expressions of approbation, exclaiming, "We are here from Maryland to Louisiana; repeat that sentiment and we will tell it to our neighbors at home! Repeat! Repeat!"

" Well," exclaimed Mr. Webster, in trumpet notes that seemed to be echoed back from the whole country around, "I do repeat—proclaim it on the wings of the winds—tell it to all your friends. [Cries of " We will ! we will !"] Tell it, I say, that, standing here in the Capitol of Virginia, beneath an October sun, in the midst of this assemblage, before the entire country and upon all the responsibility which belongs to me, I say that there is no power directly or indirectly in Congress or the General Government to interfere in the slightest degree with the institutions of the South."

The cheering was renewed, and several voices cried and repeated, " That gives two thousands votes more for Harrison."

" And now," added Mr. Webster, " I ask you to do me only one favor. Carry that paper home. Read it; read it to your neighbors, and when you hear the question, " Shall Daniel Webster, the Abolitionist, profane the soil of Virginia." Here the orator was interrupted by the most cordial shouts of applause that we ever heard. Every hat and every handkerchief was waved in the air—the chorus of cheering being led by the most distinguished men of Virginia, who seemed to vie with each other in reprobating the foul and infamous slander. " Welcome! welcome! Heaven bless you, Webster! Huzza! We scorn their abuse of you! " etc., etc., etc., burst from the thousands before him. A more exciting scene was never presented; and his choking voice, and burning tear drop that gathered in his eye, and trickled slowly down his pale cheek, showed how deeply the orator himself was moved.

We add two important passages as reported by the Richmond *Whig*, to give our readers some notion of this masterly speech.

After Mr. Webster finished, the convention took a temporary adjournment for dinner. A bountiful lunch had been prepared in the Capitol for those who did not choose to retire, and all were made freely welcome. Every house of every Whig was, besides, thrown widely open, and all the luxuries of the season were presented to the visitors in the greatest profusion.

At 4 o'clock the people—emphatically, we say—the people assembled again after rational and moderate enjoyment. A platform had been erected on the north side of the Capitol; and there Mr. Archer and Mr. John Campbell, late Treasurer of the United States, addressed the people in speeches which engaged their attention to the last. Some of the crowd, too, who had not heard Mr. Webster in the morning, felt their disappointment so keenly that they could not rest till they had him out again, and hearing he was within hail they called for him. He obeyed the call, and addressed them briefly with wonderful power and eloquence.

In other parts of the square Mr. John Hill, a high-spirited and talented representative of the old commonwealth, and other gentlemen, addressed the people in the course of the afternoon.

When the shades of the evening fell, the Capitol facade was illuminated, and the speaking was continued. Mr. Botts made a most instructive and powerful speech, which was listened to with the closest attention. He was followed by several gentlemen; among them Mr. Skinner, late postmaster at Baltimore; Mr. Snowden, of Alexandria; and Mr. Duncan, of Louisiana.

In the meantime meetings were held at other places. The log cabin was filled to overflowing, and Mr. Leigh made a speech of singular ability and eloquence. In different parts of the city little squads were assembled and if we could collect all the flowers of fancy and all the corruscations of wit, and sallies of humor, which were produced even in our presence, our paper would indeed be to-day a most brilliant and valuable one.

On Tuesday, at 10 o'clock, the convention reassembled in the area on the south side of the Capitol, and Mr. Wm. C. Rives addressed the people in a speech of more than three hours' length, with all the eloquence and spirit which make him so interesting and power ful as a public speaker. After he had finished, there was a short recess; and again the people met, and were addressed by Governor Barbour. He was followed by a number of other gentlemen, and the speaking was continued until after midnight.

While these proceedings were going on in the Capitol square, some of the delegations that had been detained on their way to the convention arrived; and having been deprived of the opportunity of hearing Mr. Webster, they waited on him at the house of a distinguished gentleman, whose hospitality he was enjoying. He promptly appeared, and responded to their hearty greetings, in one of the most fervent, impassioned, and effective speeches that ever fell from human lips. He concluded with a promise that he would meet them in the log cabin in the evening. He did so; and there again he made a speech, which is represented by many who heard it, in whose judgment we confide, to have been fully equal to his speech at the Capitol, for the intellectual power it displayed, and peculiarly distinguished for that faculty of high, earnest and pathetic eloquence which he can so readily command.

MR. WEBSTER'S SPEECH TO THE LADIES IN THE
LOG CABIN.

LADIES: I am very sure I owe the pleasure I now enjoy to your kind disposition, which has given me the opportunity to present my thanks and my respects to you thus collectively, since the shortness of my stay in the city does not allow me the happiness of calling upon you severally and individually. And, in the first place, I wish to express to you my deep and hearty thanks, as I have endeavored to do to your fathers, your husbands, and your brothers, for the unbounded hospitality I have received ever since I came among you. It is registered, I assure you, on a grateful heart in chapters of an enduring nature. The rough contests of the political world are not suited to the dignity and to the delicacy of your sex; but you possess the intelligence to know how much of that happiness which you are entitled to hope for, both for yourselves and for your children, depends on the right administration of good government, and a proper tone of public

morals. That is a subject on which the moral percep-
tions of woman are both quicker and juster than those
of the other sex. I do not now speak of the administration of government whose object is merely the
protection of industry, the preservation of civil liberty
and the securing of enterprise its due reward. I speak
of government in a somewhat higher point of view.
We live in an age distinguished for great benevolent
exertion, in which the affluent are consecrating the
means they possess by endowing colleges and acad-
emies, by uniting to build churches and support the
cause of religion, and by establishing athenæums, ly-
ceums, and all other modes of popular instruction.
This is all well; it is admirable; it augurs well for the
prospect of ensuing generations. But I have sometimes thought that there is a point of view in which government is to be considered; I mean in its power and
its duty to augment the morals of the community and
to inspire it with just sentiments of religion, which is
too often overlooked.

A popular government is more powerful than any
other influence (and I have sometimes feared than all
other influences put together) in its action on the morals of the community for good or for evil. Its example,
its tone, whether of respect or of disrespect to moral obligation, is most important to human happiness, because
it is among those things which most affect the political
morals of mankind, and hence their general morals
also. I advert to this, because there has been put forth
in modern times the false maxim that there is one morality for politics and another morality for other things;
that in their political conduct to their opponents men
may say and do that which they would never think of
saying or doing in the personal relations of a private
life. There has been openly announced a maxim
which I consider as the very concrete of false morality,
which declares that "all is fair in politics." If a man
speaks falsely or calumniously of his neighbor and is
reproached for the offense, the ready excuse is this: It
was in relation to public and political matters; I cherished no personal ill-will whatever against that indi-

22

vidual, but quite the contrary; I spoke of my adversary merely as a political man. In my opinion the day is coming when falsehood will stand for falsehood and calumny will be treated as a breach of the commandment, whether it be committed politically or in the concerns of private life. It is by the promulgation of sound morals in the community, and more especially by the training and instructions of the young that woman performs her part towards the preservation of a free government. It is now generally admitted that public liberty, the perpetuity of a free constitution, rests on the virtue and intelligence of the community which enjoys it. How is that virtue to be inspired, and how is that intelligence to be communicated? Bonaparte once asked Madam De Stael in what manner he could most promote the happiness of France. Her reply was full of political wisdom. She said, " Instruct the mothers of the French people." Because the mothers are the affectionate and effective teachers of the human race.

The mother begins this process of training with the infant in her arms. It is she who directs, so to speak, its first mental and spiritual pulsations. She conducts it along the impressible years of childhood and of youth; and hopes to deliver it to the rough contests and tumultuous scenes of life, armed by those good principles which her child has first received from maternal care and love.

If we draw within the circle of our contemplation the mothers of a civilized nation, what do we see? We behold so many artificers working, not on frail and perishable matter, but on the immortal mind, molding and fashioning beings who are to exist forever. We applaud the artist whose skill and genius present the mimic man upon the canvas; we admire and celebrate the sculptor who works out that same image in enduring marble; but how insignificant are these achievements, though the highest and fairest in all the departments of art, in comparison with the great vocation of human mothers. They work not upon the canvas that shall fail, or the marble that shall crumble into dust; but upon mind, upon spirit which is to last forever, and which is to bear, for good or for evil, throughout its duration, the impress of a mother's plastic hand.

I have already expressed the opinion, which all allow to be correct, that our security for the duration of the free institutions which bless our country depends upon the habits of virtue and the prevalence of knowledge and of education. The feelings are to be disciplined, the passions are to be restrained, true and worthy motives are to be inspired, a profound religious feeling is to be instilled, and pure morality inculcated under all circumstances. All this is comprised in education. Mothers who are faithful to this great duty will tell their children that neither in political nor in any other concerns of life can man ever withdraw himself from the perpetual obligations of conscience and of duty; that in every act, whether public or private, he incurs a just responsibility, and that in no condition is he warranted in trifling with important rights and obligations. They will impress upon their children the truth, that the exercise of the elective franchise is a social duty of as solemn a nature as man can be called to perform; that a man may not innocently trifle with his vote, that every true elector is a trustee as well for others as himself, and that every man and every measure he supports has an important bearing on the interests of others as well as his own. It is in the inculcation of high and pure morals such as these that in a free republic woman performs her sacred duty and fulfills her destiny The French, as you know, are remarkable for their fondness of sententious phrases, in which much meaning is condensed into a small space. I noticed lately on the title page of one of the books of popular instruction in France, this motto: "Pour instruction on the heads of the people; you owe them that baptism." And certainly, if there be any duty which may be described by a reference to that great institute of religion, a duty approaching it in importance, perhaps next to it in obligation, it is this.

I know you hardly expect me to address you on the popular political topics of the day. You read enough —you hear quite enough on those subjects. You expect me only to meet you and to tender my profound thanks for this marked proof of your regard, and will kindly receive the assurances with which I tender to you, on parting, my affectionate respects and best wishes.

MEETING AT AUBURN, N. Y.

Hon. William C. Rives, of Virginia, and Hon. Hugh S. Legare, of South Carolina, Eloquently Address the People of New York, at Auburn, on the 5th of October.

The following is the notice of the organization of the convention:

At 11 o'clock on Thursday morning, the convention met at the Baptist chapel. General Tallmadge was appointed president *pro tem.*; Mr. Romeyn, of Ulster county, made a good and appropriate speech, pointing out the propriety and beauty of the attendance of ladies at these meetings. Gen. Pierre Van Cortlandt (one of Jefferson's electors) was chosen president of the convention, and the meeting adjourned to a good dinner at the American hotel, which was washed down with champagne, and the convention met again on the green in front of the Theological Seminary, at half past one.

This seminary is situated at one extremity of the village on a beautiful knoll of rising ground, with a very large green before it. At the extremity of the green, and facing the college, a large platform was erected for the Revolutionary soldiers (many of whom were there), the officers of the meeting, the speakers and the reporters. About forty long benches were constructed

out of rough planks for the ladies, all of which were
filled with some of the most lovely women in the country. All the trees around the green were filled, and in
every window of the college there were dozens of
young ladies, all anxious to see and to hear Mr. Rives
and Mr. Legare. There must have been, at half past
one o'clock, not less than 5,000 persons present.

GEN. VAN CORTLANDT.

We have assembled to discuss those principles of
government—principles which have been subverted to
the purposes of the present administration. We have
assembled as our Revolutionary fathers did, to discuss
the merits of the stamp act and tea tax; and have assembled to present these principles of our faith which
should be held sacred—and I have risen here to present
to you our distinguished fellow-citizens from another
State.

We have seen the effect of some of the measures of
the administration at Washington, and it is high time,
my fellow-citizens, that the Augean stable there was
cleansed. Augean, King of Elis, you know, kept a
large number of oxen for nine years in his stable without having it cleaned out; and it was one of the labors
of Hercules to cleanse it. The Augean stable at Washington has had a number of animals in it for nearly
twelve years, without being cleaned out. [Laughter.]
Hercules performed his immense task by turning the
river Alpheus through it, and thus cleansed it through.
Now, we'll turn the great current of public opinion
(that is rushing all over the land) through the Augean
stable at Washington; and we'll not only clear out the
litter and filth, but we'll clear out the cattle along with
it. [Immense cheering and laughter.]

But I have not risen to speak, but to introduce to
you a man who stood up for the defense of his country, in the very worst of times, in the times that tried
men's souls. [Loud cheering.] I have risen to introduce to you that noblest work of God, an honest man.
[Cheers.] One who stood up in his place on the floor
of the Senate and declared in the presence of the min-

ions of executive power, that he had a country to serve
as well as a party to obey ! [Immense cheering.] I
have the honor to introduce to you the Hon. William
C. Rives, of Virginia.

Here a voice in the crowd called out, "Nine cheers
for old Virginia," and nine cheers were given.

The Hon. W. C. Rives then came forward and was
received with tumultuous shouts of welcome.

He spoke for two hours, and his remarks stirred the
hearts of the people to their inmost depths. Then
came Legare and others, thrilling the hearts of the
people by their eloquence.

HARRISON AT LANCASTER, OHIO.

General Harrison spoke at Lancaster, Ohio, on the
21st of October, to an immense concourse, large numbers of whom were foreign born, and his attention being
called to a report extensively circulated by his enemies
that he was unfriendly to immigrants from the Old
World, and unwilling that they should enjoy the privileges of citizens, he replied to the charge in the following eloquent words:

" I am accused, fellow-citizens, of entertaining unfriendly feelings towards foreigners who emigrate to
this country with a view of becoming citizens, and of
a design to throw obstructions in the way of their
naturalization. Nothing can be more false than this
charge. Indeed, it has become the custom of my political opponents to ascribe to me opinions and feelings
the very reverse of those that I entertain, and, without
a shadow of proof, on their naked, unsupported assertion put me upon my defense. What, my fellow-citizens, can be more cruel and unjust than this? I have
been more than forty years before my country, most
of the time engaged in active public service; and my
votes, and my speeches which are upon record and be-

fore the public, are a true index to my opinions on this
as well as other important subjects. And if those who
thus accuse me will point to a single vote, or any expression of mine, which can in the least support their
assertion, then I will agree that I am bound to come
forward and explain or admit its truth. But they cannot do this. No such vote was ever given by me, and
no such opinion ever expressed. On the contrary, I have
ever felt the warmest sympathy for the victims of tyranny and oppression in the Old World who have fled
here for refuge, and I have, on all occasions. given my
support, whether in the national councils or as a private
citizen, to all the laws which have been passed to
render their condition better or their naturalization
more easy. Nay, more: I have, on several special occasions, lent my aid to bands of oppressed foreigners
exiled from their homes, when the general laws of our
country were not effectual for their relief.

"When Ireland was crushed in the attempt to throw
off the British yoke, and when her enthusiastic sons,
the united Irishmen, were defeated and driven into ex-
ile, and as exiles sought our shore—they came poor and
without a home—I was one who sympathized in their
sufferings, and advocated a law for their relief—a law
setting apart to them a tract of land sufficient for their
wants, to be given them on long credit and on most
moderate terms. I advocated, too, a like grant of land
to the French exiles, on which they proposed to cultivate the vine and olive. In short, whether in or out
of public station, I have always done whatsoever was
in my power to relieve the burdens and add to the
comforts of the foreign emigrant—and where I could
not serve them more efficiently, I have given them my
counsel and my sympathy, and they have rewarded
me with the strongest marks of their gratitude and affection.

"In the last struggle of Poland for liberty, and in the
last battle fought under the walls of Warsaw, in which
the fate of that gallant nation was sealed, there was an
eminence immediately under the walls, obstinately contested, and three times lost and won by the contend-

ing armies. The spot was overgrown with small alder shrubs, and every bush was steeped in the blood of the patriot Poles. When the contest was over, and Poland had sunk into a Russian province, her people, who mingle a strong degree of religious devotion with patriotic enthusiasm, flocked to the spot to cut and preserve as holy relics those shrubs stained with the blood of their countrymen, who fell as martyrs in the cause of liberty and their country.

"The Russian Government, fearing the effect of this feeling, ordered the hill to be cleared and the bushes burned, so that no more of these relics could be procured; hence those already gathered became, in the estimation of the Poles, a treasure above all price. Only one of them, perhaps, has found its way to America, and that was presented to me but three days ago by a delegate of the exiled Poles, as a token of their gratitude for some services which I was able to render them, and for the kind feelings which they knew I entertained for them and their country. It is, as you see, a cross made of small stems of the alder, and beautifully wrought with silver. These unfortunate men esteemed it the most precious gift they could bestow on one whom they knew to be their friend, and I prize it as they prized it."

IN BOSTON.

GREAT GATHERING OF THE PEOPLE AT THE NORTH END.

The meeting of the Whigs of the three northern wards in the Bennett street school-house, on October 25, was throughout a most successful affair. Although no attempts were made to get any numbers together, the room was thronged at an early hour, and many, in the early part of the evening went away unable to

obtain an entrance. We never witnessed any public
assemblage that was better conducted or where there
was a more universal satisfaction on the part of the
audience. There was no attempt to arouse the passions
on the part of the speakers. Everything was addressed
to the reason alone. There was no idle and ridiculous
declamation and naked assertion on their part about
British gold, nor any sneers against the laboring classes
who live in "log cabins" and drink "hard cider,"
which mark all the harangues of the hirelings of the
custom-house. All was as it should be, plain, sober,
common sense, such as the intelligent and patriotic
mechanics and laborers of the North End can understand and appreciate; and we were glad to see that
not a few of those who last year were opponents of
the Whigs, because they had been led by the misrepresentations of the paid partisans of the administration
to believe the Whigs were inimical to the interests of
the people, and anti-Democratic in their principles,
were present on this occasion, and manifested by the interest they took in the proceedings, as well as by their
repeated expressions of applause, that they had at
length found out who were the real friends of the
people.

The meeting was called to order by Simon W. Rob-
inson, Esq. Hon. Nathaniel Gurney, of Ward one, was
appointed president; Benson Leavitt, Esq., of Ward
two, and David Tillson, Esq., of Ward three, vice-
presidents; and Richard G. Wait, Esq., and Henry L.
Gurney, Esq., secretaries. After the organization of
the meeting, Dr. T. M. Brewer offered a preamble and
series of resolutions, which will be found below. They
were received with great applause, and at the close of
the meeting were adopted by acclamation.

The chairman then introduced to the meeting Hon.
Samuel G. Goodrich, of Roxbury, who was warmly
and enthusiastically received, and who addressed the
audience about an hour in his best and happiest style.
He exposed in a strong light the abuses of the administration, and displayed in the clearest colors how inimical it had shown itself by all its measures to the in-

terests of the laboring portion of the community. The
operation of the sub-treasury—its effects in reducing
wages and in lessening the value of property, while the
debts of the poor man were not diminished, and while
at the same time the wages of Van Buren, Bancroft,
and the whole tribe of office-holders, were increased in
proportion to the fall in the price of labor and produce—
was shown in a masterly, forcible and most convincing
manner. Mr. Goodrich closed his remarks amidst the
most urgent calls to go on, and the most evident and
real reluctance on the part of the audience to have him
stop. His remarks were interspersed with a great
variety of anecdotes and interesting illustrations of his
topics, which rendered him even more than usually entertaining.

The general doctrine that he sought to establish and
enforce was that of American labor. American industry being the great source of our wealth and happiness, demands encouragement at the hands of the
administration. Take care of the laborer, take care of
the poor, and the rich will take care of themselves.
This, said Mr. Goodrich, is sound policy and everybody
can see it. When the pockets of the mass of the people are well lined, the dependent classes as the lawyers,
doctors, ministers and merchants, will do well enough.
Take care of the people, then. This is a first duty of
government; yet it has been neglected by the present
administration. Their measures tend to clean out the
poor man's pocket and put the contents into the rich
man's purse. The sub-treasury is a measure of con-
spiracy against the working-classes. It reduces wages;
it destroys the currency; it annihilates credit; it takes
out of the poor man's hands the only means of placing
himself on a level with the rich man; it makes the people without cash necessarily the servants of the rich;
it sacrifices the poor debtor to the rich creditor. It
tends to run all the business of the country into the
control of mere capitalists; it is a measure imported
from Europe and tends to reduce us to the standard of
Europe; it would make our workmen slaves, and our
women drudges in the field and in the street; it would

change the whole inducement to labor, substituting the fear of poverty for the hope and expectation of success in life.

We have not space to notice Mr. Goodrich's remarks in detail; we can only offer a sketch of a story which he introduced, and which was nearly as follows:

THE MORTGAGE AND THE SUB-TREASURY.

Let us suppose a case. Of a Saturday evening a mechanic of one of our Norfolk towns sits down with his wife for a comfortable chat The children are all in bed, the week's work is done, its cares are laid aside. The husband has just returned from the Springfield convention; his heart is full of Democracy. He can think of nothing else, he can speak of nothing else; in the fullness of his heart he calls his youngest child Democracy, and as he kisses his wife on his return, he calls her Democracy also. Everything he loves is Democracy, everything he hates is Hartford convention Blue Lights Federalism.

The conversation of the mechanic and his wife on the occasion supposed naturally turns upon politics, and the following conversation ensues:

Wife. Well, husband, you talk a great deal about Democracy: now I am a woman and know nothing about politics, but pray tell me what Democracy is?

Mechanic. Why, Democracy is —— Democracy!

W. Indeed! who told you so?

M. Bancroft told me so. I have heard him say so more than fifty times, and Hallett says so, and Rantoul and Everett; they all say so.

W. Well, if they say so, it must be true. But what does Democracy mean?

M. Pshaw! You women can never understand politics; you have no head for it. Now I'll read to you out of the Boston *Post* what it means. Here are the resolutions of the Democratic convention, prepared at Boston last fall. They were written by Brownson, or some of the great guns. Here it is. "Democracy is the supremacy of man over his accidents."

W. Whew! Democracy is the supremacy of man

over his accidents! What a critter it must be. But to tell the truth I don't understand any more about Democracy than I did before; I suppose it's because I'm a woman. But look, here husband — I want to talk to you about that mortgage of Squire Graball's upon the house and land. He called here while you were gone and he said a part of it must be paid or he'd sue for it, and then the house and land would all go.

M. Why did'nt you tell me of this before?

W. Because your head was so full of Democracy and the Springfield convention that you would'nt listen to me. I've mentioned it three times, and it went in at one ear and out of the other. Now, husband, I've been thinking about the mortgage, and it worries me; your wages have fallen off of late, and some of the time you have no employment. When your wages were a dollar and a half a day, and you had full work, you could support the family well, and pay a hundred dollars a year towards clearing the mortgage. It was a pleasant thing to work and be economical and saving when we had the prospect of having a house of our own, without Squire Graball's clutches upon it. Now you can hardly support the family, and when I ask for money you say you are running in debt. This is a bad prospect if we are to lose the house and land after all.

M. Oh, never fear, wife; times will be better soon. They've got a sub-treasury now which is to make us all rich except the aristocrats.

W. I don't know about that. The times have been getting worse and worse. It's four or five years since you talked of having better times, and now that they have really got a sub-treasury they say it is going to reduce wages to fifty cents a day.

M. Well, that's true, but everything we buy is to come down at the same rate.

W. And what advantage is that? Beside, some people say that sugar, and tea and coffee, and spices and all foreign things will be as high as ever because the sub-treasury don't work in those countries where these things come from. But if wages are to come down how are you to pay the mortgage of $600 to Squire Graball?

M. How am I going to pay the mortgage?

W. Yes, if your wages go down to fifty cents a day how can you ever pay it? It will cost all that you can earn to support the family.

M. Well, I must sell the cow and the garden lot.

W. Yes, but these have gone down half price, and they won't go far toward reducing the mortgage.

M. Well, I must sell the house.

W. But that has gone down half price too! so that all the property you have got won't pay Squire Graball's mortgage. We must be turned out of house and home, and still you are in debt. You are a ruined man if the sub-treasury goes into full operation.

M. I never thought of all this before. There's something wrong somewhere.

W. There is, indeed, husband. When they made the sub-treasury to reduce the poor man's wages and the poor man's property, why didn't they make it reduce the poor man's debt? Answer me that. When they reduced a man's means of paying his debt, why didn't they reduce the debt too?

M. I can't say, upon my word.

W. Well, these men who made the sub-treasury, pretend to be the poor man's friend; but it seems to me that they are the rich man's friend, and the poor man's enemy. You agree, to give Squire Graball $800 for the house and land. Now you have paid $200, and after you have paid $200 more he will get it back for $400. So Squire Graball gets $400 out of you for nothing, just because we must have a sub-treasury; and you must be ruined to make him rich. Seems to me, this is grinding the poor to fatten the rich. It is making the poor man poorer and the rich man richer.

M. Well, really, wife, all that sounds true; but Bancroft and Brownson did not tell us that.

W. No, no; they didn't tell you, though they knew it well. They filled your head with fantastic ideas of Democracy and liberty. They blindfolded you with names and words, and led you with prejudices and passions.

M. But why should they deceive us?

W. Why? Does'nt Bancroft get $6,000 a year so long as Van Buren is in, and the sub-treasury supported? Does'nt Brownson get $1,600 a year, so long . as his master, Van Buren, reigns? Now, you have a vote, and the voters can say who shall be President. The way for Bancroft to keep his place, therefore, is to throw dust in your eyes, and then he'll lead you up to the ballot-box to vote for Van Buren, who supports him, though he ruins you and your family.

M. Really, wife, you seem to be a politician after all.

W. No, husband, I am no politician; but sometimes a looker-on sees more of the game than they who play it—I judge of government by its effects on our home. Formerly, before this cry of Democracy—before these Halletts, and Rantouls, and Bancrofts filled your head with their humbugs, everything went well with us. You were then a happy man, and I a happy wife. Our children were then well fed and well clothed. Every year we added a little to our furniture; if I wanted a new gown you always gave it to me, and you paid $100 a year to reduce the mortgage. You were industrious and cheerful; your face was always pleasant to me; your voice was always kind to the children. Those days are gone. I mourn, husband, but I do not reproach you. You have your cares and I know your heart is right. But how has this change come about?

M. I think I must ask you.

W. Well, then, I will tell you my opinion. I think you, with too many others in the country, have been grossly cheated and deceived. A set of men, who only wished to enjoy power, and office, and spoils, have been intrusted with the reigns of Government, and they have driven us over a precipice. We only suffer with the rest of the country—thousands and thousands are as bad off as we.

M. Well, wife, I am afraid you are right; but what can I do?

W. You can do two things. The first is to forsake those who have cheated you—to withdraw your confidence from a set of false prophets and false guides—men who use you only to abuse you.

M. And what next shall I do?

W. First tell me whether you will do as I request?

M. I never buy a pig in a poke. Tell me what it is you propose, and if it's reasonable, I'll do it.

W. Vote for old Tip!

M. I thought it was coming to that! Well, there's no danger in trying the change. Here it goes: Hurrah for Harrison and better times!

"Such, my friends," said Mr. Goodrich, "is my story, and who will say it is not probable? Who will say that the wife, whose happiness is directly and perhaps fatally influenced by political measures, has no right to use her influence in relation to this subject. The Boston *Post* may indeed deny it, and, if wives reason it as well as the heroine of our story, the *Post* may fear it. We wonder not that men who fear the truth should scoff at the influence of clear-headed and true-hearted woman. You may beguile men with humbug names, but woman brushes these cobwebs of delusion away with common sense. She tests things by results; she asks herself whether the reign of Loco Focoism makes home happier: whether it brings peace to the pillow and comfort to the fireside? The wives of the country have been applying this test, and their decision is that the humbug Democracy of your Bancrofts, and Buchanans, and Van Burens is an imposition of half-wages to the working man and full salaries to the office-holder. It is a reduction of all the wages and property, and all the means of payment to the poor debtor and no reduction of debts; it is a system of pretended benefit, but real ruin to the poor. It is a pretended war upon the rich, but an effective and powerful promotion of their interests. It is a reverse of the measures upon which our Government should be administered, to encourage the interests of the working classes of the poor, and the rich will take care of themselves. It is a system of fattening the rich at the expense of the poor. It is not strange that such injustice in the administration should make all good wives good Whigs. It is not strange that Loco Foco editors should try to ridicule woman out of the field of political influence. where that influence tends to substitute truth for falsehood. prosperity for ruin, the reign of reason for the dominion of party, and the adoption of sound and stable policy in place of juggling tricks and fatal experiments.

A WET BLANKET.

Governor Lewis occasioned no little consternation at the Loco Foco Poughkeepsie convention, of which he was chairman, by denouncing the sub-treasury. The following sketch from the Albany *Evening Jour-nal*, gives the details of the affair. The scene must have been rich.

General Lewis began by saying that he felt grateful for the compliment bestowed upon him; that he was an old man of eighty-seven; that he had been all his life an observer of public affairs and probably knew more of the history of the sub-treasurers than most present; that the first sub-treasurer with whose history he was acquainted was Lord ——, under the Colonial Government, who turned out to be a large defaulter! [Here there was much whispering on the stage, and Mr. Vanderpool stepped behind] That the second was —— [giving the name] who was also a defaulter! [Here the confusion increased, and General Maison and Richard D. Davis moved forward]; and that in fine, he had never known but one man, and he lived next door, who could settle his accounts with the Government as a sub-treasurer, and he was enabled to do so only by the charity of his neighbors, who brought him the gold and silver in little bags as a loan, that he might seem to have it to secure his reappointment, and the next day it went back where it came from. That for these

reasons he had been opposed to the sub-treasury.
[Here the alarm and confusion on the stage became immense.] D—n the old man, said D—— to M——; he
don't know when to stop! He'll talk all day, said
another; call for Wright. General Maison stepped up
to the speaker, and saying to the audience in an undertone (the General is very deaf) "Don't you want to
hear Wright?" and on their calling out for Wright, he put
his hand on the speaker's shoulder and yelled in his
ear, "Don't you hear, General, they call for Wright!"
"I am just about giving my reasons why I think it
may do. If the bill makes it felony to abstract the
money," persevered the General——. Mortification and
chagrin was now marked upon every countenance
upon the stage. "Choke him off," muttered one. "Let us
drown him with cheers," said Senator Maison, who
came to the front of the stage, and threw his cap three
times round his head, bawling hurrah at each swing.
The three cheers, however, were faint and forced; and
the deaf man did not hear them and was going on with
his reasons, etc., when Senator Maison gave the signal for three more. These were gotten up in better
style, and the speaker was again reminded to give his
reasons. When Senator Maison gave the signal, the
band on the stage struck up Yankee Doodle, a grand
hubbub ensued, and in the midst of it Vanderpool
pulled the old veteran into the chair by his coat tail.

MEETINGS IN OCTOBER.

ONE FIRE MORE—DEAR FRIENDS, ONCE MORE TO
THE BREACH.

The battle of the Thames was grandly celebrated at
Detroit on the 5th day of October, by the Wolverenes.

In Ohio at the county seat of each county, the Buckeyes met and celebrated the battle of the Thames, on
the 5th, and was preparatory to two more signal victories of old Tippecanoe.

On the 5th of October there were thirty-four acres of
people at a great Whig rally near Norris' woods, about
three miles north of Philadelphia. They came together
in their strength to celebrate the anniversary of the
battle of the Thames, one of the most brilliant of American engagements, in which the army, under Harrison's
command gave final peace to all the great Western territory which was for twenty years the field of his arduous labor as soldier and civilian. About twenty thousand
people were said to have been under the management of
Col. C. G. Childs, chief marshal, and his numerous aides.
The city procession, augmented by the delegations
from Germantown, Frankford, Bristol, Oxford and
other places was huge in its proportions. Alexander
Ferguson presided, and gave an interesting account of
the fight, he having been a captain under Harrison.
From their stands, speaking was carried on by John
Sargeant, Morton McMichael, W. B. Reed and others.
As the crowd was in the procession returning to the
city the infuriated Loco Foco bullies assaulted it with
clubs, stones and missiles, but they were repulsed.

At Wilmington, Delaware, there was an enormous
crowd on the 5th of October. Doctor Naudain presided, and the thousands were eloquently and ably addressed by Daniel Webster, John M. Clayton and
Hiram Ketcham. Great was the enthusiasm created
by these grand orators.

The Loudon, Virginia, Whig festival on the 12th of
October was a splendid affair. The Leesburg *Genius
of Liberty* says the procession numbered 6,000 footmen,
and there was a brilliant assemblage of 1,000 ladies
adding life and animation to the scene. Eloquent
speeches were made by C. C. Washington, of Maryland; L. Chillon, of Fauquier county; J. S. Pendleton
and others.

On the 18th of October, a great meeting was held at
Bridgetown, N. J., which was addressed by Senator
Southard, Governor Call, of Florida, and other distin-
guished orators.

The glorious anniversary of the 9th of October was
grandly commemorated by noble Whigs from far and

near on the plains of Yorktown, Va., who were addressed by electors from North Carolina, Maryland
and Virginia in inspiring speeches for Harrison and
Tyler.

COOLNESS ON THE FIELD OF BAT-TLE.

Connected with the movements of the Northwestern armies, in 1838 and previously, are many incidents
which, though too unimportant for the pages of general history, are nevertheless highly interesting and
well worthy of preservation. Some of these have
been related by General Tipton and other brave officers; several are recorded in the narratives of Dawson
and Hall; a few may be found in the newspapers of
the times in which they occurred; but the greater
number of them dwell merely in the recollections of
the surviving soldiers who witnessed them. Some of
them display an intrepidity unsurpassed in the history
of warfare; others exhibit a coolness, in the moment
of imminent danger, indicative of the most determined
resolution and the most extraordinary nerve. Of this
latter character are the two incidents mentioned below. We find them related in a letter from Col. John
Speed Smith (a prominent friend of the administration, in Kentucky) to a gentleman of this city. Colonel Smith, it will be recollected, was one of the aides
of General Harrison in the battle of the Thames:

The writer states that a moment before the battle
commenced, General Harrison rode up to a majestic
Seneca chief, and took his powder-horn to reprime his
pistols. Upon witnessing this, Lieutenant Smith asked
him if he expected to come in personal contact with
the enemy; to which the general replied that it was
proper to be prepared for any event; that he commanded
an army of better materials than Proctor's, and

that he was determined not to survive a defeat; adding with a smile, to Lieutenant Smith, "You had better fresh prime, too, as I shall expect my aides to die around me!"

Whilst at the crochet, after the left wing had recovered from its momentary confusion, and was joining the front, General Harrison ordered Lieutenant Smith to bring down Chilles's command to support it. While he was giving this order, the necks of the two horses were interlocked; and some twigs of a tree above them, which had gathered and retained a cluster of leaves, and around which the aide had to look at his commander, were cut down by the enemy's balls. Near the spot, at the same moment, a soldier was shot through the thigh, and seeing the commander-in-chief as he swung arouud and fell, he cried out: "Did you see that, General? they have shot me again."

This man had been wounded the day before at the bridge. General Harrison directed him to be taken back to have his wounds dressed, but finding that his thigh was not broken, the brave fellow bandaged it with his handkerchief to stop the bleeding, clutched up his gun, swore he meant to have satisfaction, and continued to fight. A few moments afterwards, a young man dashed up to the commander, holding a scalp in his hand, and sung out, "Look here, General, I've got it! My father was an old Kentucky Indian fighter, and when I left home, he made me promise to bring the scalp of a red skin killed by myself. And here it is—this is for the old man. Now I want one for myself." And away he sprang in search of another enemy.

These two anecdotes, Colonel Smith says, greatly amused Commodore Perry, when he related them to him at the close of the battle; and the gallant sailor truly said that an army of such men could not be conquered. And he frequently afterwards, on meeting with the officers of the army, would repeat the brave soldier's exclamation with great zeal, " Do you see that, General? They have shot me again!"

THE LADIES IN THE CANVASS.

On the 14th of August the Whig ladies of Dover, Delaware, presented the Dover Hundred Tippecanoe Association a beautiful banner wrought by them. Several young ladies in the West promised to marry their lover provided Harrison was elected, and many young men who had been Loco Focos took the stump in earnest for "Tip and Ty."

The following, from the Providence *Journal*, is one of the pleasing signs of the times. When the ladies are for us, we are certain of two things, that our cause is just and that it will prevail:

"The ladies of Maine are, almost without exception, all Whigs. In the town of Bristol, a young girl who was engaged to a young fisherman in the island of Mowhegan, which is attached to that town, and who was suspected of Loco Focoism, told him that she would banish him from her favor unless he voted the Whig ticket. The young man, who, by the way, was just twenty-one, and had consequently never voted before, demurred, but his lady-love was inexorable, and very justly insisted that not to be a Whig in these times argued either a lack of intelligence and discernment, or a want of principle and true patriotism. Neither deficiency was to be overlooked by her, and he need never come and see her again, therefore, if he did not vote the Harrison ticket. Love and prejudice had a hard contest, but the former triumphed. The young man voted the entire Whig ticket, and Thorpes, the Whig candidate, was chosen by one majority. The damsel is surely deserving the thanks, not only of the young man whom she thus saved from the sin of Loco Focoism, but of every true Republican in the State."

From the Connecticut *Courant*, of August 13, 1777: "Williamsburg, Virginia, July 4. We hear that the young ladies of Amelia county, considering the situation of our country in particular and the United States in general, have entered into a resolution not to permit the addresses of any person, be his circumstances or condition in life what they will, unless he has served in the American Army long enough to prove by his valor that he is deserving of their love."

Such were the daughters of America, when our sires were struggling in the War of Independence against a foreign foe; and such the daughters of America are still, and ever will be, admirers of bravery and honor, and devoted to their country. We have before taken notice of the enthusiasm of the fair children of our land in the present contest between a people, zealous of their liberty and royalty, with its stately palace, its better currency, and its standing armies. We have now another instance to give of their Roman virtue. We learn that, at the Whig meeting in Alexandria, the ladies were at the windows as the Whig procession paraded the streets, encouraging them with their sweet smiles, waving their handkerchiefs, and breathing the pure and grateful prayer of woman for their success in the coming struggle. A few hours passed, and the Loco Foco procession came in its turn. No bright eye beamed upon their path; no sweet smile shone upon them, but the closed blinds, and the black flags, which hung from the windows where these fair forms stood two hours before, showed how the good and virtuous mourned o'er the trampled liberties of their country.

> If ought on earth can toil beguile,
> 'Tis lovely woman's cheering smile;
> Its sweetest meed, its best reward
> Is smiling woman's kind regard.

EFFECT OF A NATIONAL SONG.

The last Nashville *Whig* contains a letter from Rogersville, East Tennessee, which gives an account of a promiscuous political meeting at Greenville, where Mr. Grundy and Turney addressed the people in reply to General Arnold. Grundy and Turney then adjourned over to this place, not expecting that Arnold would be there—but hear the writer in his own words:

"Well, when we arrived, say about 12 o'clock, Grundy was addressing some three hundred persons in the large new court-house. They had no idea Arnold would be here; and having invited Mr. Senter to attend and reply to them, who was sick and unable to speak at all, as they well knew, just as Grundy was lamenting that there was no gentlemen of the opposite party present to advocate the Whig cause, Arnold stepped in, and making his bow to the old gentleman, told him he had come in good time. Nothing was more manifest than that Grundy and his whole party were very much confused. On he went, however, making all manner of statements, for near five hours, evidently with a view to prevent a reply. He became angry upon seeing Arnold enter the house, and denounced the Whigs as 'a miserable pie-bald party,' having no principles, but little honor, and a candidate destitute of talent—one, too, whom he declared they were trying to elect by singing, and by the exhibition of log cabins and coon-skins!

"When he sat down, the redoubtable Colonel McClelland attempted to introduce Turney, but the crowd called out for Arnold, long and loud, though they refused to let him speak at all. Arnold asked them for one hour only—for the hour they had offered his sick colleague, Mr. Senter, but they refused to let him say one word. The crowd then called to Arnold to go with them into the street, and answer Grundy's speech, which he did, and did, too, in a masterly manner—leaving but sixty persons in the house, as I was told by those who afterwards counted them!

"At the close of Arnold's speech, Turney having been forced to close for the want of hearers, Senator Anderson attempted to speak, but the Tippecanoe club struck up a fine Harrison song, and took the whole assembly from them. I never saw a set more completely used up. Their countenances told the tale of their souls, horror. I view it as the best day's work the Whigs have ever done in Hawkins."

GOOD REASONS FOR TURNING ONE'S COAT.

The following dialogue from the *Pilot* is reproduced as indicative of the feeling of the workingmen:

I was sitting at my window some evenings ago, when two mechanics met each other and began to talk just below me. Being pleased with the good sense of their conversation, I took up my pen, and as well as I can recollect, wrote it down: here it is:

"Good morning, John; have you found any work yet? I have not."

"No," said John, "not one stroke; nobody's doing anything."

"What," said his companion, "are things coming to, if they keep on at this rate?"

"I don't know, indeed," said John, "I can't live on one day's work in a week and support my family; Bill, I hate to go home and see my poor children, for God only knows how long it will be before they are crying to me for bread; it's all owing to the currency, and our rulers should better it; they have the power."

"They are going to, John."

"Yes," replied he, "and their attempts are like the man who undertook to make his horse live on one straw a day; his experiment went on bravely with this exception, that before he had reduced him to the one straw diet he was dead."

"Why, John, you talk like a Whig."

"So I am."

"You a Whig?"

"Yes, you need'nt stare; the story is short; I had nothing to do, so got the papers and read both sides, and now I mean to go it strong for Tippecanoe."

"Well!——"

"Yes, it's very well indeed."

"But, John, the boys will laugh at you and call you 'turn-coat.'"

"Let them; and those of them I can't thrash I'll try to! I know my own business best, and I know who is my friend; Old Tip *is*, and Martin Van Buren *is not*. Tip's a brave old soldier, and AN HONEST MAN; and what is still better, a working-man like myself. As regards the coat, I'll tell you how it is: I got up in the morning, half asleep, and put it on *wrong side out*, and that was the Van Buren side, all threads, seams and linings; when I awoke, well I, like a sensible fellow, took it off, brushed it, and then put it on *right*. Now the *Tip side is out;* and I consider that man a fool who takes an exception at the change, but him a greater fool who is ashamed to turn his coat right; but would, because he put it on wrong in the morning, wear it so all day."

"But, John, what's your reason ?"

"For these: Van Buren's experiments have played the d——l with the currency, and I am consequently out of work; he has, therefore, virtually taken my wages from me, and I mean to charge him in my book for every day I am out of work, and consider the sum total so many good reasons for not voting for him. When his party came into office, they found the best of currencies, and I found work plenty; both are gone to Davy Jones' locker; he promised us a gold and silver currency. Where'st? Why, here is one of the ghosts of the humbug;" and he took out a shin-plaster levy.

"But, John, 'twas the Whigs and the banks."

"Pshaw, nonsense! nobody in his senses believes that. What have the Whigs to do with our financial affairs? They are not at the head of the Government. They were in the minority (but don't intend to be any longer); but, admitting this falsehood, a party that would permit a minority to do as they please with our moneys, is not fit to pretend to rule, and should be turned out. And, again, I should be a fool, indeed, to vote for a party who goes the whole hog for reducing my wages; and that, by-the-bye, I think is very useless, for just let them tinker and cobble away as usual, and the mechanic won't have any wages to be reduced at

all. And Mr. Van Buren is not the choice of the people; he was smuggled into the Presidential chair under
the old general's popularity. We want no such bastard
politicians foisted upon us. Let a man's own worth,
talents, merit and popularity, father him—not another's.
And, again, this party has proposed and acted upon
this curious proposition, 'a small rogue's a big rogue,
and a big rogue is no rogue at all,' he is only a defaulter—an absquatulator, but no rogue. Steal a five
dollar note and you will be sent to jail; steal (don't
steal, oh, no! only take) a million and a half, and you
are a fine fellow—very much surprised you did'nt take
more; and, in one case, they actually applied the old
fable of the fox and the flies to some rodguing, thiev-
ing rascal out West."

"Well, John, I have no work to do; I will go and
read both sides. May be my old jacket is on wrong,
too; so good-bye."

"Good-bye, Bill; tell all your friends to read both
sides, too;" and they departed.

WILLIAM WILKINS AND THE MAN-
UFACTURERS.

On Friday evening last, at the Porter meeting, at the
Exchange, William Wilkins contended that the sub-
treasury scheme, with cash duties on foreign products,
would be better for the manufacturers than the best
tariff. He then called by name on the Messrs. Bakewells, and other manufacturers, to express their opinions on the subject. The following is their response
to his call. We ask the attention of Mr. Wilkins, and
of our farmers, manufacturers and working men to it.
It gives an admirable summing up of the truth of the
whole matter in a very small compass. — *Pittsburgh
Gazette.*

To the Hon. Judge Wilkins:

SIR: Having heard that in your address from the Exchange steps, on Friday evening last, you appealed to our firm, amongst others, whether the sub-treasury scheme, with cash payments of duties, would not be better for the manufacturers than the " best protective tariff," and not doubting your desire to have every erroneous impression corrected, we beg leave to observe that, although the latter would, as far as it went, be favorable, the operations of the former will be highly injurious to them.

It will paralyze the enterprise of the manufacturer, and the ingenuity of the mechanic by diminishing the demand for their products. It will oppress the industrious farmer by greatly reducing the prices of his produce, and it will bring down the wages of the laboring man so low as to deprive him of the means of obtaining many of the comforts he has been accustomed to enjoy.

Manufacturers flourish best when the farmer, the mechanic and the working man are doing well!

In no country with which we are acquainted, possessing only a metallic currency, does labor meet its just reward; and the inevitable tendency of the sub-treasury law is to bring into operation the anti-Democratic principle of making the "poor poorer and the rich richer;" and is totally opposed to that of " promoting the greatest good to the greatest number."

We remain, sir, respectfully yours,
August 16, 1840. BAKEWELLS & CO.

INCIDENTS AND HUMOROUS FACTS WORTH REMEMBERING.

Mr. Webster, at the great log-cabin gathering in Vermont, was introduced to a member of the Boston Tea Party, an old veteran, 94 years of age, who pushed the tea from the gunwale of the ship into the water. Mr. Webster, on his return to Brattleboro, called on the hero at his dwelling among the mountains in July, 1840, and he avowed himself ready to push Matty Van Buren from the gunwale of our national ship into the briny deep.

NO CROWING.

We are sorry to hear that the very Chapman who received orders to crow is "cooped up," his comb cut and his gaffs off, for the Indianapolis *Journal*, of July 4, said, "Chapman, the Loco Foco editor of the Wabash *Enquirer*, stands indicted in the court of Vigo county for perjury."

FEDERAL OUTRAGE.

Three students of Dartmouth college, New Hampshire, have been expelled from that institution, and seventeen fined $3 each for attending a Harrison convention.

At Dayton, Ohio, at the great convention in a log cabin, was a live wolf with a sheep-skin on him, labeled "Van Buren."

Another picture, Van Buren running down hill, his locks and coat-tail streaming in the wind and a barrel of hard cider rolling after him; he was crying out, "Stop that barrel."

REVOLUTIONARY ARMY.

We find the following in an old Vermont paper: The number of regulars furnished to the Revolutionary army were, by New England, 147,441; by the Middle States, 56,571; by the Southern States, 56,997. It appears by the above that New England, consisting of New Hampshire, Massachusetts, Rhode Island and Connecticut, furnished more troops for the defense of the country than the other nine States by 3,872. The number of troops furnished by South Carolina was 6,448; Massachusetts, 67,907; Georgia, 2,697; Connecticut, 31,939.

Wm. L. Crandell, editor of the Onondaga, N. Y., *Standard*, publicly asserted in a speech at Brockway's, in the town of Camillus, that " with the sub-treasury in full operation, the farmer could hire ten men to labor for the sum that he now has to pay five."

FACTS TO BE REMEMBERED.

That four votes, given in the Fifth ward of New York, made Thomas Jefferson President of the United States.

That one vote made Marcus Morton Governor of Massachusetts in 1839.

That six votes, given in the Fourteenth ward of New York, in 1837, gave the Whig party the majority in the common council.

That in 1839 a merchant from the Eighth Senatorial district of New York, being in the city on business, returned home to vote, by which the Whigs elected a State senator.

At a loafers' meeting on the island opposite Wheeling, Va., on the 10th of August, Richard M. Johnson was one of the speakers, and upon being asked whether General Harrison was a coward, he replied: "You might as well ask me whether I was a coward, for in the battle of the Thames there were no cowards — every man did his duty from the general down." He also said he never heard his bravery questioned until the present canvass.

An anecdote illustrating an important fact is the following : Mr Williams, the State senator, was addressing a meeting at Alexandria, Westmoreland county, and remarked that on the administration side the contest was maintained by office-holders, and that without their opposition Harrison would be elected by universal acclamation. Some one in the crowd exclaimed : "That's not true !" Mr. Williams promptly replied, "I know that voice; it is the voice of Mr. Moorhead, our postmaster at Pittsburg, and this is another evidence of the truth of my remarks."

Log-cabin carpets were brought into use, and inkstands, cane heads and quilts and various other emblems and devices were to be met with in the homes of Harrison men in all the States.

The Louisville *Journal* states that Capt. John Fowler, who certifies that, in 1798-99, General Harrison wore the black cockade, presided at a public dinner in Lexington, in November, 1813, at which, among toasts to Jefferson, Shelby, Colonel Johnson, etc, the following was drank to Harrison:

"The commander-in-chief of the Northwestern Army; the favorite son of the Western country."

On one of the steamboats going from New York to Albany, on July 3, a party of office-holders were drinking toasts to Mr. Van Buren and the administration, and called upon an Irishman who was present for his toast with the promptness characteristic of his native isle, he said:

> " Here's to our fathers and mothers,
> Likewise to ould Ireland too;
> Down with Martin Van Buren,
> And up with Old Tippecanoe."

GEN. HARRISON'S REPLY TO POINDEXTER.

ELOQUENCE OF THE OLD TIPPECANOE CHIEF—EXTRACT FROM GENERAL HARRISON'S REMARKS IN THE HOUSE OF REPRESENTATIVES ON THE SEMINOLE WAR.

No public man seemed ever to have been so much underestimated as General Harrison. At least no one's abilities have been so assailed by his adversaries. There never has been a candidate who was so often called upon for expositions of his nerve. No one has so frankly, freely and fully given his opinions in letters and speeches, as these pages will bear witness. His letters were plain and direct, his speeches practical and to the point, and elicited unbounded applause. Notwithstanding his life from boyhood had been upon the frontier, and much of the time in the army, yet he had read much and possessed a well cultivated mind and retentive memory. He had read and thoroughly studied ancient history, and seemed to have in great part regulated his conduct by illustrious examples in Grecian and Roman history. His allusions were ever apt, and his sentiments appropriate. Where will anything more excellent be found than the following extract from his reply to Governor Poindexter, on the subject of General Jackson's invasion of Florida. It is well worthy of preservation among the gems of eloquence by American statesmen:

"A Republican Government should make no distinctions between men, and should never relax its maxims of security for any individual, however distinguished. No man should be allowed to say that he could do that with impunity which another could not do. If the father of his country were alive and in the administration of the Government, and had authorized the taking of the Spanish posts, I would declare my disapprobation of it as readily as I do now. Nay, more, because the more distinguished the individual, the more salutary the example. No one can tell how soon such an example would be beneficial. General Jackson will be faithful to his country; but I recollect that the virtues and patriotism of Fabio and Scipio were soon followed by the crimes of Marius and the usurpation of Sylla. I am sure, sir, that it is not the intention of any gentleman upon this floor to rob General Jackson of a single ray of glory, much less to wound his feelings or injure his reputation. And, while I thank my friend from Mississippi (Mr. Poindexter), in the name of those who agree with me that General Jackson has done wrong, I must be permitted to decline the use of the address which he has so obligingly prepared for us, and substitute the following as more consonant to our views and opinions. If the resolutions pass, I would address him thus: 'In the performance of a sacred duty imposed by their construction of the Constitution, the representatives of the people have found it necessary to disapprove a single act

of your brilliant career; they have done it in the full
conviction that the hero who has guarded her rights in
the field will bow with reverence to the civil institutions of his country, that he has admitted as his
creed that the character of the soldier can never be
complete without eternal deference to the character of
the citizen.　Your country has done for you all that a
republic can do for the most favored of her sons.　The
age of deification is past; it was an age of tyranny and
barbarism; the adoration of man should be addressed
to his Creator alone.　You have been feasted in the
pritanes of the cities.　Your statue shall be placed in
the Capitol, and your name be found in the songs of the
virgins.　Go, gallant chief, and bear, with you the gratitude of your country.　Go, under the full conviction
that, as her glory is identified with yours, she has
nothing more dear to her but her laws, nothing more
sacred but her Constitution.　Even an unintentional
error shall be sanctified to her service.　It will teach
posterity that the Government which could disapprove
the conduct of a Marcellus, will have the fortitude to
crush the vices of a Marius.'　These sentiments, sir,
lead to results in which all must unite.　General
Jackson will still live in the hearts of his fellow-citizens, and the Constitution of our country will be immortal."

PEACE HATH ITS VICTORIES AS WELL AS WAR.

The great Revolution was not made in peace, but
through storm and bloodshed; the people favoring
Harrison had to walk in many localities.　There were
deeds of violence such as no other political campaign
in the Union had known.　From the time when
Thomas Laughlin, the honest carpenter, marching

with the procession of Whig young men at Baltimore, the 5th of May, was killed, there were hundreds of supporters of Tippecanoe assaulted, battered, bruised beaten, and very many killed in various parts of the country. These outrageous attacks were applauded unblushingly by that class of papers that believed with the *Globe* that "rivers of blood should flow before Van Buren should be removed from the executive office." Blair and Kendall, with brutal indecency, insolent bluster and savage bullyism, did all in their power to incite desporadoism and make violence. Attacks by ruffians and bullies were made upon men going to and returning from conventions, and upon processions and meetings in various parts of the country. Public speakers like John W. Bear, the Buckeye blacksmith, were pelted with eggs, brickbats and stones, and the man of the people the bullies sought to murder at Huntington, Pennsylvania, and other places. From many accounts of like character, the following extract of a letter, dated Cincinnati, October 1, 1840, is taken as showing the malicious and vindictive spirit of the times:

A tremendous excitement prevails in the city in regard to a disturbance which took place about an hour ago (ten o'clock at night). The Whigs seemingly of all creation held a meeting here to-day. All places of business were closed, and an immense procession, which commenced in the morning at eight o'clock, was held. Old Tip, Governors Metcalf, Poindexter, Wickliffe, Moorehead, etc., were the speakers. This evening an immense crowd of ladies and gentlemen assembled in front of the Huron House, where I stop. While Mr. Graves, of Kentucky, was speaking from the portico, the meeting was broken up by a number of Loco Focos, and ended in a general fight. Brickbats, clubs, sword-canes, bowie knives, pistols, etc., were used. Several have been badly hurt, some of whom have just been brought into the house, and there are all sorts of reports flying. I saw several pistols fired from my room window in the third story.

24

Old Tip takes the stage for Pennsylvania to morrow morning. So it is likely he will be with you before the election.— *U. S. Gazette.*

The *Examiner* thus describes a like outrageous scene at Lancaster, Pennsylvania, on the 5th of October:

As usual with them for the past few weeks, the Loco Focos issued a call for a meeting on Saturday evening last, knowing that we had called a meeting on the same evening. Coming down East King, from the place where we keep our big ball, we were met by the Van Buren men; some of them threw stones and broke several holes into the ball, and came near hitting the boy inside! Our friends passed on, determined to suffer rather than resent the outrage. Returning from the place of meeting, the same outrage was attempted to be repeated; but was prevented by one of our friends. After the ball was put away our procession was dismissed in front of Levi Swope's (late Sharp's) tavern; some few went into the tavern, but the greater number returned to their homes. After this, a number of Van Buren bullies, headed by John Boot, George Huffnagle, Neal Donnelly, Cooney Plitt, Bill Haines, —— Fraley and others, armed with clubs, stones, pistols, etc., rushed into the house, and, before our friends were aware of their object, beat and bruised several of our most worthy citizens. Our friends rallied and put them out of the house, when they commenced throwing stones through the door and windows, injuring several persons inside, and shattering the door and windows to pieces! The sheriff interfered, but was also knocked down! The mayor was prevailed upon to restore order, but complied in such a manner as to create dissatisfaction among some of those who assisted him, time after time, into his present office! It is said, he even declared on the ground that the Whigs should never be suffered to obtain the ascendency in this city! If this be true, is it not seconding the declaration of Reah Frazer, that "the Democrats should maintain their ascendency, even if they had to do it at the point of a bayonet!"

Order was at length restored, but several of our friends were afterwards waylaid and beaten on their return home !

The *National Gazette*, of Philadelphia, speaking of the attacks upon the procession of October 5, when it was passing through the northern part of the city, and was broken in upon by gangs of Van Buren roughs and bullies, says: "They cannot see an assembly of their political opponents without commencing an assault upon it. And their conduct, instigated by the spirit of their journals, is then palliated or justified by the same authorities. We speak of what we know. We witnessed on Monday several unprovoked sallies by Van Buren pugilists upon persons in the Whig procession. We saw missiles thrown, and a banner dragged from the hands of a bearer, which has simply this inscription: 'One Presidential Term and No Sub-Treasury,' certainly nothing to give just offense. That was just what they were mad at. They could not bare the thought that their party should be routed from power. The Democratic party are always opposed to going out of office, while to get in they may profess to be in favor of 'one term.' No sooner does their President become seated than he begins wise working and manipulating for another term."

This book could be filled with accounts of mobocratic acts of Loco Foco ruffians in Virginia, Kentucky, Missouri, Mississippi, Louisiana and other States, where, by inaugurating a reign of terror, they tried to intimidate men and prevent them from voting. The old veterans in Ohio will remember the assaults upon their processions and the meetings in Jefferson, Licking, Fairfield, Knox, Richland, and other counties. The writer of these reminiscences has been on the speakers' stand, with others, pelted with eggs, in procession dragged from his horse, and has personally witnessed wanton and unprovoked attacks upon carriages and wagons filled with men, women and children, driving in processions or going home from conventions. Nearly every town of size had its bullies and beastly ruffians, who, ready to do the bidding of ad-

ministration leaders, set upon and grievously hurt
their fellow-citizens, who dared to exercise the rights
of freemen. By domineering and brute force they endeavored to maintain their ascendency. But, unfor-
tunately for them, the followers of Harrison were of
sterner stuff than to yield. They remembered their
gallant leader's words: "The people can do their own
voting as well as their own fighting." They stood up
manfully for their rights and privileges as American
citizens, and another victory was scored for " Old Tippecanoe."

THE GRAND TRIUMPH.

Harrison's Creed Approved by the People— Reflections and General Summing Up.

It will be seen from the foregoing that General Harrison's canvass was hotly contested. He was the subject of more misrepresentation than any candidate in
the history of the country. He was catechised from
all sections and by all manner of men. His answers
were plain and were models of epistolary correspondence. His views were presented upon slavery, duel-
ing, immigration, treatment of the Indians, and other
questions of moral and political character. His letters
of acceptance and to Hon. John MacPherson Berrier,
of Georgia, Thomas Sloo, Jr., of Louisiana, Sherrod
Williams, Mr. Owen, Harmor Denny and various
others, were republished in all the papers of the United
States.

His creed, briefly summed up was as follows:

To serve one term and to be President of the United
States, and not of a party.

To communicate to Congress the affairs of the
nation truly.

That Congress shall make the laws, and not the President.

To use the veto power but seldom, and then only for the preservation of the Constitution.

That Congress had no right to interfere with slavery in any way.

That right is reserved to the States where slavery exists.

That no man shall be appointed to office but such as is known to be capable and honest.

No man shall be dismissed from office without proper reasons being given.

That office-holders shall not interfere in elections.

That the people's money shall be under the immediate control of Congress, and not to be kept in boxes, to be Swartwouted whenever the sub-treasury may deem necessary.

The protection of American labor by the Clay tariff.

The rights of the people.

The freedom and purity of elections.

The people had faith in Harrison and believed in the principles he avowed. They elected him by an overwhelming majority of the electoral and popular votes. Scarcely a county in the United States increased its Democratic majority. Van Buren Democracy was routed "horse, foot and dragoons," and the people were victorious. The result proving that—

> " Easier were it
> To hurl the rooted mountain from its base,
> Than to force the yoke of slavery upon men
> Determined to be free."

This is the moral to be impressed upon the mind. The many thousands of meetings throughout the Union we could not mention, nor the names of all the gallant speakers and workers in the great campaign. Those given are simply as samples illustrative of the way the work was done. Every man did his duty, and nobly, too. As to the effect of the cyclone upon the opposition, we will let the oldest Democratic editor of Ohio, Hon. Lecky Harper, of the Democratic *Ban-*

ner, tell how it struck him, by extracting from his communication to the *Graphic:*

"The campaign opened at Columbus on the 22d of February, 1840, when the greatest mass-meeting ever witnessed in this country took place, to which the writer was an eye-witness. Being then engaged as a legislative reporter on Medary's *Statesman*, I was detailed, with others, to write up the grand pageant. But no imagination could paint and no pen could describe it. The fifty thousand or more people who dropped into Columbus on that memorable morning, came from every nook and corner in the State. They came in log cabins, dressed as old pioneers; and coon-skins and gourds, and barrels of 'good old hard cider,' were conspicuous objects inside and outside of every cabin. Some of these cabins were fifty feet long, and were fitted up like boarding-houses, with cooking and sleeping apartments, and were drawn by ten or twenty horses, and each horse carried a rider, dressed to suit the momentous occasion. There was no organization and no speaking to amount to anything, the whole day being taken up in marching, hurrahing and singing. It was this singing that did the work. Some of the songs I shall never forget. They rang in my ears wherever I went, morning, noon and night, during the whole of that campaign. Men, women and children did nothing but sing. It worried, annoyed, dumbfounded, crushed the Democrats, but there was no use trying to escape. It was a ceaseless torrent of music; still beginning, never ending. If a Democrat tried to speak, argue, or answer anything that was said or done, he was only saluted with a fresh deluge of music. If a Democrat would say that John Tyler was no Whig, the Whigs would join in a derisive laugh and a song, which ended with the chorus:

> 'And we'll vote for Tyler, therefore,
> Without a why or wherefore.'

"When compelled to listen to such arguments, many of the old hard-shell Democrats would become angry: but this only pleased the Whigs, and they 'rubbed it in' the harder. The most popular song of the day was one about 'Tippecanoe and Tyler, too,' one verse of which I shall quote from memory:

'Oh, what has caused this great commotion, 'motion, 'motion, the country through?
It is the ball a rollin' on
 For Tippecanoe and Tyler, too,
 For Tippecanoe and Tyler, too, .
And with them we'll beat little Van.
Van, Van, Van is a used up man,
And with them we'll beat little Van.'

"Well, the *bawl*, that was thus started at Columbus, kept 'rollin' on' all over the country. Van Buren was badly beaten, and Harrison and Tyler were elected by an overwhelming majority of the popular as well as the electoral vote of the country."

Was it not burning as with a red hot iron when Whig songs were so riveted upon the mind of hardshell Democrats, that they can correctly "quote from memory," that which was so distasteful after a lapse of forty-eight years? When men, women, and children did nothing but sing, our hoary-headed old friend, under the inspiration, joined the choir. The writer can remember of many wives and daughters of Democrats joining in the singing, and how mad the husbands and fathers were, and what fantastic tricks some of them cut in their rage, and all to no purpose; the singing still went on. We know of daughters being locked up to prevent their singing Whig songs, and of their company being unceremoniously turned out of houses to which they had been invited by irate parents. And among those who flew into such passion were many of the most prominent and respectable Democrats of the country. It has seemed strange to us that nothing should in all these years have been written to perpetuate the incidents of 1840, when the whole people may be said to have gone wild for Tippecanoe. We have collected by considerable effort many of the best songs of the campaign. Some of them are of a high order of merit, descriptive of the men and times. In eloquence they have never been equaled in any

subsequent campaign. Well might A. Fletcher say:
"G.ve me the making of the ballads of a nation, and
I care not who makes the laws."

This work is done. With all its imperfections, and
they are many, it goes forth to awaken old memories.
It has been prepared and compiled while in much suffering from "poison oak," and a virulent attack from
coming under the influence of the cursed ivy that is
foolishly let grow upon walls and in yards as an adorn-
ment, has put us to bed and closed our eyes so that
we could give no attention to copy or reading proof.
Harrison and Tyler, Van Buren and Johnson, and
nearly all their supporters have been consigned to the
tomb, and over their ashes a new generation busily
moves on to other contests of rivals for popular honors.

> "Now is the stately column broke,
>   The beacon light is quenched in smoke;
>   The trumpet's silver sound is still,
>   The warder silent on the hill."

TIPPECANOE SONGS

OF THE

Log Cabin Boys and Girls

OF 1840.

EDITED BY

A. B. NORTON.

A. B. NORTON & CO.:
MOUNT VERNON, O., AND DALLAS, TEXAS.

1888.

Werner Ptg. & Litho. Co.

AKRON O.

PREFACE.

The songs waked the people up in 1840, and played a very important part in the great Revolution. In the cabins, upon the roads, in the towns and cities, everywhere, sweet voices were singing the songs for "Tippecanoe and Tyler too." Those in this book have been collected from all portions of the Union, and were the most popular in the days of log cabins, hard cider and coons. The Whigs sang them loudly. Every Harrison man loved a good song.

"The songs of old, they come to us, and take possession
  of our heart;
The words are rude, the measure strange, devoid of ornament or art,
And yet they touch a deeper depth- bring warmer tears
  to fill the eyes —
And hold a sweeter, stronger charm than finer songs in
  finer guise.

.   .   .   .   .   .

"These Old Tippecanoe songs were made by men who
  knew the midnight foe;
Who caught the arrow on the shield, and swung the
  sharp sword's fatal blow;
Who held the helm of rolling ship, and steered their
  course by ice cliffs bare;
Who hunted wolves upon the hills or 'fronted lions in
  their lair.

And some were writ by women whose white hands were
    wet with salt tears' rain,

Keeping a drear sad watch at home for those that never
    came again;

Who broke their hearts in dungeons deep of gloomy
    castles closely pent,

Or withered slow in foreign lands, doomed to a life-long
    banishment.

" And those old songs have in them now the spirit of the
    writers' days:

Each word a well of their old life which rises as the tune
    we raise;

And lo! there flows from them to us the feeling, be it stern
    or sweet,

And with its added volume makes our smaller, shallower
    lives complete."

TIPPECANOE SONGS.

WHIG SONG.

Tune, "*Marseillaise Hymn.*"

Rise! rise! ye freemen! Once 'twas glory
  For man t' oppose a tyrant's power,
And who resisted lived in story.
  Oh, seize, then, seize the present hour!
Say, shall we slumber, while around us
  Oppression's galling chains are cast?
  Say, will they lighter hang at last,
To call them gold when they have bound us?
    No, no! no, no!   Then rise
      For our forefathers' laws;
    March on, march on! resolved to win
      Our favorite hero's cause.

Will flatt'ring tales of coming pleasures,
  When plenteousness and peace shall reign,
And all be rich in glittering treasures,
  The poor man's present wishes gain?
Will it stay the tide of desolation
  That sweeps so strongly o'er our land,
  To gorge an office-holding band
And rob the pockets of the nation?
    No, no, etc.

O, freemen, up!   Let widely flowing
  Your banners to the breeze be thrown,
Your love of worth and valor showing;
  Your scorn for tyrant knaves make known!
Shall men believe the voices telling
  In syren tones, your ship of state
  Is safe, when all around dark fate
Frowns out in ev'ry wave that's swelling?
    No, no, etc.

That statesman chief who led undaunted
  And cheered in strife his warlike band;
Whose praise a grateful nation chaunted;
  Who tills, a farmer bold, his land—

Shall we neglect for one, who scorning
  Our rights, the people's cause;
  Who dares to trample on our laws,
Nor list their prayers their threats, nor warning?
  No, no, etc.

DA CAPO CHORUS.

Then rise, rise all for one,
  Who ev'ry suffrage claims;
Huzza for him! a loud huzza!
  Who conquered at the Thames.

SHOULD BRAVE SOLDIERS BE FORGOT.

AIR, "*Auld Lang Syne.*"

Should brave old soldiers be forgot?
  Should patriots fail to twine
Wreaths, glorious wreaths, for those who fought
  In days of old lang syne?
No! long as life endures will we
  Deep in our hearts enshrine
The names of those who made us free
  In days of old lang syne.

Proud England, gloating o'er her Crown,
  And King, and "rights divine,"
Sent forth her slaves to chain us down,
  In days of old lang syne;
But Freedom's champions averr'd
  They'd make her lion whine,
And nobly did they keep their word,
  In days of old lang syne.

They drew a charter, strong and full,
  Nor did they fear to sign
The bulletin that pricked John Bull
  And cut in every line.
Among those hearts of flint, whose fire
  Lit up the flame benign,
Was Harrison—Tip's sainted sire—
  A Whig of old lang syne.

But not the father's fame alone
  Exalts the soldier son—
He has bright laurels of his own
  In hard-fought battles won!

The Wabash banks, Fort Meigs, the Thames;
 Their tributes all combine
To rank him high with those whose names
 Were dear in old lang syne.

And who's Van Buren? Where and when
 Did he lead on the brave,
Or raise his voice or wield his pen
 Or ope his purse to save?
While Tip gave fight he styled the war
 "Disastrous and malign,"
And richly earned a coat of tar,
 As Tories did lang syne.

Let those who love sub-treasury charms,
 Hard work and little pay,
Closed working shops and mortgaged farms,
 Extol King Martin's sway.
But we have solemnly affirm'd
 We will not rest supine
Till Van shall squirm as Croswell squirm'd
 And wriggl'd—not lang syne.

The knapsack pillow'd Harry's head,
 The hard ground eas'd his toils;
While Martin on his downy bed
 Could dream of naught but spoils.
And shall the Blue-light rule the free?
 Shall Freedom's star decline?
Forbid it, Heaven! Forbid it ye
 Who bled in old lang syne.

Is Harrison one whit the worse
 Because he'd not secure,
As Martin did, a long full purse,
 But went from office poor!
And does the low " log cabin " hearth
 Unfit Old Tip to shine?
Did no log house give nobles birth
 In days of old lang syne?

What though the hero's hard " huge paws,"
 Were wont to plow and sow!
Does that disgrace our sacred cause!
 Does that degrade him? No!
Whig farmers are our nation's nerve,
 Its bone, its very spine!
They'll never swerve—they did not swerve
 In days of old lang syne.

No ruffled shirt, no silken hose
  No airs does Tip display;
But like "the pith of worth," he goes
  In home-spun "hodden-gray."
Upon his board there ne'er appear'd
  The costly sparkling wine,
But plain hard cider, such as cheer'd
  In days of old lang syne.

Connecticut has raised the heel
  Tip's Tory foes to bruise;
And keenly do their vitals feel
  The tread of Jersey Blues."
November's ides will give the stroke—
  Hard, final and condign—
A blow like that which snapped the yoke
  In days of old lang syne.

Yes, Tip must grace the White House!
  (Alas for groom and cook)
And Van on kabbitch-stocks must brouse,
  At home, sweet home—the 'hook!
Thrice hail, Old Tip! "Log Cabin" Tip!
  "Hard-cider Tip!" To you
The helm we give! Hail, noble ship!
  Land, ho! The port's in view!
Huzza! huzza! Kind heaven be praised—
  The star, the star benign,
Shines bright!—'tis Freedom's star that blaz'd
  In days of old lang syne!

THE SOLDIER OF TIPPECANOE.

DIRGE, "*Not a Drum Was Heard.*"

The stars are bright, and our steps are light
  As we sweep to our camping ground,
And well we know, as we forward go,
  That the foe fills the greenwood round;
But we know no fear, though the foe be near,
  As we tramp the greenwood through,
For oh! have we not for our leader got
  The soldier of Tippecanoe.

Now the deep green grass is our soft mattress
  Till the beating of reveille;

No light's in our camp but the fire-fly lamp,
  No roof but the greenwood tree.
Brief slumber we snatch, till the morning watch,
  But one eye no slumber knew!
One eye was awake for his soldiers' sake,
  'Twas the soldier of Tippecanoe!

The faint dawn is breaking, our bugles are speaking,
  Quick rouses our lengthened line.
Sweet dreams are departing, the soldier is starting
  And welcomes the morning shine.
But, hark! 'tis the drum! the foe is come
  Their yells ring the dark wood through;
But see mounted, ready, brave cautious, and steady,
  The soldier of Tippecanoe!

Now nigher and nigher, tho' hot in their fire,
  And ceaseless the volleying sound.
We press down the hollow, and dauntlessly follow,
  Then tramp up the rising ground.
With dealing ardor we press them yet harder,
  And still as they come into view,
"Now steady, boys, steady; be quick and be ready!"
  Cries the soldier of Tippecanoe!

Down, down drop the foe, and still on we go,
  And each thicket and dingle explore;
Loud our shrill bugle sing, till the wild woods ring,
  And their rifles are heard no more.
Now weave the green crown of undying renown
  For the patriot hero's brow,
And write his name with the halo of fame,
  The soldier of Tippecanoe!

THE HARRISON CAUSE.

Air, "*Bonnets o' Blue.*"

Here's a health to him that's just,
  Here's a health to him that's true,
And who could not wish success to the man
  Who conquered at Tippecanoe?
It is good to be noble and firm,
  It is good to be honest and true,
It is good to support our Harrison's cause.
  Who stuck to the "red, white and blue."
  Huzza for the brave and the true

'Who battled at Tippecanoe.
And the heroes whose names
On the bank of the Thames,
   Were written in " red, white and blue "

Here's success to him that's firm,
   Here's success to him that is wise,
And tho' aged and poor, will give from his store,
   When misery ever applies!
Here's a health to the sage of North Bend,
   Here's success to the man of the plow,
Here's a health to the man who sticks to his friend,
   And lives by the sweat of his brow!
     Huzza for the just and the true,
     And the hero of Tippecanoe,
     And the star-spangled " red, white and blue."

A SONG OF AN OLD SOLDIER.

TUNE, "*Old Oaken Bucket.*"

Oh, dear to my soul are the days of our glory,
   The time-honored days of our national pride,
When heroes and statesmen enobled our story,
   And boldly the foes of our country defied,
When victory hung o'er our flag proudly waving
   And the battle was fought by the valiant and true,
For our homes and our loved ones the enemy braving,
   Oh, then stood the soldier of Tippecanoe.
     The iron-armed soldier, the true-hearted soldier,
     The gallant old soldier of Tippecanoe.

When dark was the tempest and hovering o'er us,
   The clouds of destruction seemed gathering fast,
Like a ray of bright sunshine he stood out before us,
   And the clouds passed away with the hurrying blast.
When the Indian's loud yell and his tomahawk flashing,
   Spread terror around us, and hope was with few,
Oh, then, through the ranks of the enemy dashing,
   Sprang forth to the rescue old Tippecanoe.
     The iron-armed soldier, the true-hearted soldier,
     The gallant old soldier of Tippecanoe.

When cannons were pealing and brave men were reeling
   In the cold arms of death from the fire of the foe,
Where balls flew the thickest and blows fell the quickest
   In front of the battle bold Harry did go.

The force of the enemy trembled before him,
  And soon from the field of his glory withdrew.
And his warm-hearted comrades in triumph cried o'er him,
  God bless the bold soldier of Tippecanoe!
    The iron-armed soldier, the true-hearted soldier,
    The gallant old soldier of Tippecanoe.

And now since the men have so long held the nation
  Who trampled our rights in their scorn to the ground,
We will fill their cold hearts with a new trepidation
  And shout in their ears this most terrible sound:
The people are coming, resistless and fearless,
  To sweep from the White House the reckless old crew;
For the woes of our land, since its rulers are tearless
  We look for relief to old Tippecanoe.
    The iron-armed soldier, the true-hearted soldier,
    The gallant old soldier of Tippecanoe.

OLD TIPPECANOE.

Hurrah for the Father of all the green West!
  For the Buckeye who follows the plow!
The foeman in terror his valor confest,
  And we'll honor the conqueror now.

His country assailed in the darkest of days,
  To her rescue impatient he flew;
The war whoop's fell blast, and the rifle's red blaze,
  But awakened old Tippecanoe!

On Maumee's dark waters, along with brave Wayne,
  Green laurels he glean'd with his sword.
But when peace on the country came smiling again,
  His steel to the scabbard restored.

But wise in the council, as brave in the field,
  His country still asked for his aid;
And the birth of young empires his wisdom revealed
  The sage and the statesman displayed.

But the red torch of war, the tomahawk's gleam
  To the battle again called the true;
And there where the stars and the stripes brightly stream,
  Rushed the hero of Tippecanoe.

Now hark! from the far frozen winds of the North
  What battle shouts burden the gale?

The hosts of Old England ride gallantly forth,
  And the captive and conquered bewailt.

His country recalls the bold chieftain she loves,
  The sword of Old Tip she reclaims;
And victory heralds wherever he moves
  The path of the hero of Thames!

/ Hurrah for the hero of Tippecanoe—
  The farmer who plows at North Bend!
A soldier so brave, and a patriot so true,
  Will find in each freeman a friend.

Hurrah for the log-cabin chief of our choice!
  For the old Indian fighter hurrah!
Hurrah! and from mountain and valley the voice
  Of the people re-echoes—hurrah!

Then come to the ballot-box—boys come along,
  He never lost battle for you;
Let's down with oppression and tyranny's throng,
  And up with Old Tippecanoe.

———

TO THE AMERICAN FLAG AND HARRISON.

Air, "*Sparkling and Bright.*"

See in the light of glory bright,
  Each star and stripe proudly beaming,
Our flag once more unfurled to the war,
  To the breeze of reform now streaming.

CHORUS.

Your goblets fill with a free good will,
  To the chief renowned in story;
Pledge your faith to him on the beaker's brim
  To speed him onward to glory.

Oh! that he might arrest the blight
  Destroying our dominions,
Yet first awhile he must beguile
  The spoiler of his minions.

  Chorus—Your goblets fill, etc.

Our hero bright will stop the wight,
  And all his friends shall leave him,

And every one, for our Harrison,
  With loud huzza's shall grieve him.

  Chorus—Your goblets fill, etc.

When high in state we'll place elate,
  By his side our flag unwaved;
Loud be our cheers, when the hero for years,
  Plants that flag o'er a Union saved.

  Chorus—Your goblets fill, etc.

SONG FOR JIM CROW.

Tune, "*Tell Chapman He Must Crow.*"

Let all de British Tory,
  Who feel very low,
Keep stiff de upper lip,
  And give a loud crow.
    Brag about and bet about—
      And grin just so;
    And every time you meet a Whig,
      Give a loud crow.

Massa Kendall give de order,
  "Charge on de foe!"
Se neber be down-hearted,
  But give a loud crow!
    Brag about, etc.

Old Missus Grundy,
  Who eberything do know,
He tell de loco,
  "Give a loud crow!"
    Brag, etc.

Old Massa Ritchie—
  He say just so—
Stick to de dunghill,
  And give a loud crow!
    Brag, etc.

Dere is Louisiana,
  No matter how she go—
Only claim the battle,
  And give a loud crow!
    Brag, etc.

Massa Van be frightened,
  Everybody know,
Still he scold at Amos
  'Cause he doesn't crow!
    Brag about and boast about—
      And strut just so,
    And never lose de spirits,
      But give a loud crow!

GENERAL HARRISON.

Air, *"Pizen Sarpient."*

When the British foemen swarmed around,
And burnt our cabins to the ground,
          Ri tu ral, etc.

A gallant boy, brave Harrison,
By noble deeds bright laurels won,
          Ri tu ral, etc.

He fought by Wayne, where brave men bled,
And where the ground was strown with dead,
          Ri tu ral, etc.

And where the battle fiercest seemed
His ready blade to combat gleamed,
          Ri tu ral, etc.

He spent long years in hardy fight,
And always kept his laurels bright,
          Ri tu ral, etc.

And when with peace our land was blest,
We find him on his farm at rest,
          Ri tu ral, etc.

No prying demagogue was he,
But honest, noble, brave and free,
          Ri tu ral, etc.

He would not barter truth for gold—
His mind was never bought and sold,
          Ri tu ral, etc.

To great men's skirts he never hung,
As Martin to brave Jackson's clung,
          Ri tu ral, etc.

But all alone he trod the way,
Where honors thick around him lay.
Ri tu ral, etc.

The White House will by him be filled,
For so the yeomanry have willed,
Ri tu ral, etc.

HURRAH FOR OLD TIP.

Old Tip's the boy to swing the flail,
 Hurrah, hurrah, hurrah!
And make the locos all turn pale,
 Hurrah, hurrah, hurrah!
He'll give them all a tarnal switchin',
When he begins to " clare de kitchen!"
 Hurrah, hurrah, hurrah.

Plowboys! though he leads in battle,
He's a team in raisin' cattle,
And tho' old Proctor at him kicked,
He is the chap that ne'er was licked,
 Hurrah, hurrah, hurrah.

His latch-string hangs outside the door,
As it has always done before;
The people vow he shall be sent
To Washington as President,
 Hurrah, hurrah, hurrah.

In all the States no door stands wider,
To ask you in to drink hard cider,
But any man's "given to grabbin',"
Ne'er can enter his log cabin,
 Hurrah, hurrah, hurrah.

For such as Swartwout, Price and Boyd,
His honest soul will e'er avoid,
And poverty the thinks no crime,
But welcomes it at dinner time,
 Hurrah, hurrah, hurrah.

So here's three cheers for honest Tip,
We've got the locos on the hip—
We'll row them all far up Salt river,
There let them stand to shake and shiver,
 Hurrah, hurrah, hurrah!

LOG CABIN LYRICS.

AIR, "*There's Nae Luck About the House.*"

Come let us join with heart and voice,
  And hail the people's friend,
And send to Washington our choice—
  The hero of North Bend.
    For there's no luck at the White House,
      There will be none at a'
    Till Martin and his myrmidons,
      Are driven far awa'.   .

The cabinet assembled there,
  While thousands in each State
Have not wherewith to purchase food,
  They dine off golden plate.
    O! there's no luck at the White House.

Then let us vote for Harrison,
  And turn out scheming Van;
Capsize his kitchen cabinet,
  And rout the loco clan.
    For there's no luck at the White House.

AN INVITATION TO THE LOG CABIN BOYS
TO OLD TIPPECANOE'S RAISIN'.

TUNE, "*The Good Old Days of Adam and Eve.*"

Come all you log-cabin boys, we're going to have a raisin',
We've got a job on hand that we think will pe pleasin',
We'll turn out and build Old Tip a new cabin,
And finish it off with chinkin' and daubin'.
We want all the log-cabin boys in the nation,
To be on the ground when we lay the foundation;
And we'll make all the office holders think its amazin'
To see how we work at Old Tippecanoe's raisin'

On the thirtieth day of next October,
We'll take some hard cider, but we'll all keep sober;
We'll shoulder our axes and cut down the timber
And have our cabin done by the second of December,
We'll have it well chink'd and we'll have on the cover,
Of good sound clapboards, with the weight poles over,
And a good wide chimney for the fire to blaze in,
So come on, boys, to Old Tippecanoe's raisin'.

Ohio will find the house-log timber,
And old Virginia, as you'll remember,
Will find the timber for the clapboards and chinkin',
'Twill all be first rate stuff, I'm thinkin'.
And when we want to daub it, it happens very lucky,
That we have got the best of clay in old Kentucky,
For there's no other State has such good clays in,
To make the mortar for Old Tippecanoe's raisin'.

For the hauling of the logs we'll call on Pennsylvania,
For their Conestoga teams will pull as well as any,
And the Yankee States and York State and all of the
    others,
Will come and help us lift like so many brothers.
The Hoosiers and the Suckers and the Wolverine Farmers,
They all know the right way to carry up the corners,
And every one's a good enough carpenter and mason,
To do a little work at Old Tippecanoe's raisin'.

We'll cut out a window and have a wide door in,
We'll lay a good loft and a first rate floor in,
We'll fix it all complete, for Old Tip to see his friends in,
And we know that the latch-string will never have its
    end in.
On the fourth day of March Old Tip will move in it,
And then little Martin will have to shin it;
So hurrah boys, there's no two ways in
The fun we'll have at Old Tippecanoe's raisin'.

YE SOLDIERS OF FREEDOM.

TUNE, "*Bonaparte's Return from Russia.*"

Ye soldiers of freedom, pray stand to your arms,
Prepare for the battle, our freedom alarms:
The trumpets are sounding, come soldiers and see
The standard and colors of sweet liberty.

Though Van's black organ is sounding so near,
Take courage, brave soldiers, his powers don't fear;
In the strength of our freedom, we dare him to fight.
We'll put his black powers of aliens to flight.

As the great Alexander, Van Buren shall fall;
With the emblem of freedom we'll conquer them all;
We'll leave no oppressor alive on the field,
By the strength of the patriots we'll force them to yield.

2*

Through Harrison our leader we'll battle their rage;
My heart beats for freedom, come soldiers engage;
The drums are sounding, the armies appear,
We'll not leave one standing from front to rear.

Old Tip, he is riding, the fort on before,
With a keg of hard cider to treat us once more,
Some shouting, some singing, for Harrison they cry,
In the great cause of freedom all gags we defy.

WHAT HAS CAUSED THIS GREAT COM-MOTION ?

TUNE, *"Little Pig's Tail."*

What has caused the great commotion, motion, motion,
    Our country through ?
    It is the ball a roiling on, on.

CHORUS.

For Tippecanoe and Tyler too—Tippecanoe and Tyler too,
And with them we'll beat little Van, Van, Van,
Van is a used up man,
And with them we'll beat little Van.
Like the rushing of mighty waters, waters, waters,
    On it will go,
    And in its course will clear the way
        For Tippecanoe, etc.

See the loco standard tottering, tottering, tottering,
    Down it must go,
    And in it's place we'll rear the flag
        Of Tippecanoe, etc.

Don't you hear from every quarter, quarter, quarter,
    Good news and true,
    That swift the ball is rolling on
        For Tippecanoe, etc.

The Buckeye boys turned out in thousands, thousands,
    Not long ago,
    And at Columbus set their seals,
        To Tippecanoe, etc.

Now you hear the Van Jacks talking, talking, talking,
    Things look quite blue,
    For all the world seems turning round,
        For Tippecanoe, etc.

Let them talk about hard cider, cider, cider,
    And log cabins too,
      'Twill only help to speed the ball
              For Tippecanoe, etc.

The latch-string hangs outside the door, door, door,
    And is never pulled through,
      For it never was the custom of
              Old Tippecanoe, etc.

He always has his table set, set, set,
    For all honest and true,
      And invites them in to take a bite
              With Tippecanoe, etc.

See the spoilsmen and leg treasurers, treas, treas,
    All in a stew,
      For well they know they stand no chance
              With Tippecanoe, etc.

Little Matty's days are number'd, number'd, number'd,
    Out he must go,
      And in the chair we'll place the good
              Old Tippecanoe, etc.

Now who shall we have for our governor, governor,
    Who, tell me who?
      Let's have Tom Corwin, for he's a team
For Tippecanoe and Tyler too--Tippecanoe and Tyler too,
And with him we'll beat Wilson Shannon, Shannon,
Shannon is a used up man,
And with him we'll beat Wilson Shannon!

———

OLD TIP'S BROOM.

TUNE, *"Buy a Broom."*

Come, patriots, come, and let's clare out the kitchen,
Let's sweep out the parlor and clean the east room,
Drive out the magician, who long has been witching,
His schemes to dissolve, let us try a new broom:
Take a broom—Old Tip's broom!
Come, every true Whig, and help handle the broom.

To nullify subs that so long have annoyed us
And have fattened themselves from the treasury spoils,

Will be the best exercise that ever employed us,
And well will reward us for all of our toils:
Take a broom--Old Tip's broom?
Come, all ye true Democrats, take Old Tip's broom.

We all know our rights, let us dare to maintain them,
And sign the death warrant of Martin's downfall:
He reads not the signs, let our Daniel explain them,
Interpret the writing that's writ on the wall:
Take a broom—Old Tip's broom?
Come, lovers of freedom, come take Old Tip's broom.

When the contest shall come, let us all do our duty,
And make a clean sweep of our twenty-six rooms;
We'll send the experiments' crew and their booty
To south seas exploring, with lots of old brooms:
Take a broom—Old Tip's broom?
Come, patriot sweepers, and use a new broom.

Reform the reformers and sweep out corruption,
Let tyrants and spoilsmen, with faces of gloom
Hear the rumbling and throes of the earthquake's eruption,
The voice of a nation deciding their doom:
Take a broom—Old Tip's broom?
To sweep out corruption, come take a new broom.

The new broom of him whom they call Old Granny,
Shall sweep out the suckers of treasury pap;
The vampires that lived on the blood of the many,
While we, the dear people, were taking a nap:
Take a broom—Old Tip's broom?
Wake, Democrats, wake! and let's try a new broom.

When we were deceived by a Hickory hero,
Our credit was wither'd at his fatal touch;
Now we are insulted by this modern Nero,
Who says we are looking to him for too much:
Take a broom—Old Tip's broom?
No longer be slaves, come and try a new broom.

And when little Matty is out of employment,
With bloodhounds and broomstick, far south he might go;
In the everglade wars, he might find some enjoyment,
And end a long contest by flogging the foe;
Take a broom—take a broom?
[*Spoken.* Take Tip's broom?]
[*Spoken.* In the everglade swamps, among the frogs
with his dogs, don't you think he'd find Sam Jones?]
Come, patriots, come, let us try a new broom.

To end all this warring, defaulting and scheming.
This war upon labor, and credit, and banks,
On commerce and trading, a new light is gleaming,
The people will soon put an end to their pranks,
With a broom—Old Tip's broom,
They'll drive out the spoilers by using Tip's broom.

THE LOG CABIN AND HARD CIDER CANDIDATE.

TUNE, "*Auld Lang Syne.*"

Should good old cider be despised,
    And ne'er regarded more?
Should plain log cabins be despised,
    Our fathers built of yore?
For the true old style, my boys!
    For the true old style?
Let's take a mug of cider, now,
    For the true old style.

We've tried experiments enough
    Of fashions new and vain,
And now we long to settle down
    To good old times again.
For the good old ways, my boys!
    For the good old ways,
Let's take a mug of cider, now,
    For the good old ways.

We've tried your purse-proud lords, who love
    In palaces to shine;
But we'll have a plowman President
    Of the Cincinnatus line.
For old North Bend, my boys!
    For old North Bend,
We'll take a mug of cider, yet,
    For old North Bend.

We've tried the "greatest and the best,"
    And found him bad enough;
And he who "in the footsteps treads"
    Is yet more sorry stuff.
For the brave old Thames, my boys!
    For the brave old Thames,
We'll take a mug of cider, yet,
    For the brave old Thames.

Then give 's a hand, my boys!
  And here's a hand for you,
And we'll quaff the good old cider yet
  For Old Tippecanoe.
For Old Tippecanoe, my boys!
  For Old Tippecanoe,
We'll take a mug of cider, yet.
  For Old Tippecanoe.

And surely you'll give your good vote,
  And surely I will, too;
And we'll clear the way to the White House, yet,
  For Old Tippecanoe.
For Tip-pe-canoe, my boys,
  For Tip-pe-canoe,
We'll take a mug of cider, yet,
  For Tippecanoe.

"ANOTHER SONG."

The Whigs they are rising all over the land,
  And resolving, as brethren should do,
To bury dissensions, and join hand in hand
  In the cause of Old Tippecanoe.

The voice of their country now calls them, and they,
  As patriots faithful and true,
Can never refuse her commands to obey,
  While led by Old Tippecanoe.

Then rally, brave boys, with your banners on high,
  And the motto unfolded to view,
"For our country to conquer, or in battle to die,"
  By the side of Old Tippecanoe.

The Tories full long have triumphant appeared,
  But now they begin to feel blue,
For they know that a tyrant has never yet dared,
  To stand before Tippecanoe.

His cabin is built up, of logs all unhewn,
  (They say, and we grant it is true,)
But "another guess" house they'll discover full soon,
  Is destined for Tippecanoe.

His "cider's too hard" for our stomachs, say they,
  And admit it we readily do,

But harder, by far, on their shoulders will lay,
   The lash of Old Tippecanoe.

" He is old," they exclaim, but for that we don't care,
   For so was Old Hickory too,
The older, the tougher to them will appear
   The arm of Old Tippecanoe.

But, besides, " he is poor," and can never withstand
   The gold of Van Buren & Co.;
But poor as he is, all the wealth of the land,
   Can't "buy up " Old Tippecanoe.

And tho' the base minions of power may sneer,
   As their master compels them to do,
They cannot regard without quaking and fear,
   The march of Old Tippecanoe.

For the chaps that surround him are "just of the sort,"
   To " lick up " a Tory or two;
A keen set of fellows, so runs the report,
   Are the soldiers of Tippecanoe.

Then rally, brave boys, with your banners on high,
   And the motto unfolded to view,
For our country to conquer, or in battle to die,
   By the side of " Old Tippecanoe."

YOU REMEMBER THE TIME.

TUNE, "*You Remember It, Don't You.*"

You remember the time when our sires sought the West,
To find a safe home for the friends they loved best—
How each hill and each valley a foeman concealed,
And each plain the red warrior in armor revealed?
     You remember it, don't you ?
     Oh! think of it, won't you ?
Yes, yes, of all this the remembrance shall last
Long after the present fades into the past.

You remember the era, when Wayne with his legion,
Drove the merciless foe from this blood-sprinkled region,
The gallant young soldier the foremost in fight,
Who pursued the wild foe in his perilous flight ?
     You remember it, don't you ?
     Oh! think of it, won't you ?

Yes, yes, of all this the remembrance shall last
Long after the present fades into the past.

You remember, years after, in the progress of time.
How this same gallant soldier, who was then in his prime.
Drove far from our border the wild savage foe,
And the Briton, at Thames, Meigs, and Tippecanoe?
        You remember it, don't you?
        Oh! think of it, won't you?
Yes, yes, of all this the remembrance shall last
Long after the present fades into the past.

You remember the man who, when war's dread commotion,
Spread over the land, and the fathomless ocean—
Or when peace cast her blessings our wide country o'er.
Who was ever a father and a friend to the poor?
        You remember him, don't you?
        Oh! think of him, won't you?
Yes, yes, of this man, the remembrance shall last
Long after the present fades into the past.

When tyrant oppression walks abroad in the land,
And spreads want and disaster with a merciless hand
Who boldly steps forward her hope to renew?
'Tis the gallant old soldier of Tippecanoe!
        You remember him, don't you?
        You will think of him, won't you?
Oh, yes, of all this, the remembrance will last.
Long after the present fades into the past.

And when the oppressors are scattered afar,
Their forces all vanquished and sunken their star—
The drama then ended, our hopes bright and true,
He will join in a concert to Tippecanoe.
        And we'll remember each blunder,
        While he's flying with plunder
Of the wily magician caught napping at last.
Long after the spoilers from pow'r are cast.

THE TIMES ARE GROWING HOT.

TUNE, "*Yankee Doodle*."

The times are growing hot, they say,
    Van Burenites are few, sir;
Old Tip and Tyler take the day,
    As such good Whigs should do, sir.

The people think of other days,
　　When Indian yells were loud, sir;
They call'd the General far away,
　　From out the youthful crowd, sir.

'Twas Washington, with soldier's eye,
　　Who saw the hero plain, sir,
And bade him march to do or die,
　　Triumphant o'er the slain, sir.

He march'd into the distant West,
　　With patriot heart and hand, sir;
'Tis useless now to tell the rest,
　　He thrash'd the Indian band, sir.

His country free, her warriors sav'd,
　　He seeks his much lov'd home, sir,
But soon he hears the cry again,
　　Our enemies are come, sir.

He seeks again the tented field,
　　And lands on British soil, sir;
Where Proctor went it with a rush,
　　And Thames records the toil, sir.

They could'nt come it over Tip,
　　He's always wide awake, sir,
He only wanted half a chance,
　　His enemies to take, sir.

He ruled the land his valor won
　　With laws both good and right, sir,
And proved himself a glorious son
　　Of one who swore he'd fight, sir.

In Congress next we see Old Tip,
　　The soldiers' cause he plead, sir;
The living there a pension got,
　　And honor for the dead, sir.

The western lands he portion'd out
　　In farms that all might buy, sir;
The honest poor their portion took,
　　And now they're 'mong the high, sir.

The ship of State's in trouble now,
　　There's war upon her border,
Old Tip, they say, must take the helm,
　　The people give the order.

Come swell the shout, ye noble hearts,
  Like Tip, we fear no yell, sir;
Let all who hear me act their parts,
  The locos to expel, sir.

The dandy Mat shall stand aside,
  Perhaps in Eaton's room, sir;
'Neath petticoats he there may hide,
  Or act the part of groom, sir.

One shout for Tip, long, loud and high,
  And then my song is o'er, sirs;
Ye locos bid your spoils good-bye,
  Ye'll get them now no more, sirs.

OLD TIPPECANOE.

TUNE, "*Rosin the Bow.*"

A bumper around, now, my hearties.
  I'll sing you a song that is new;
I'll please to the buttons, all parties.
  And sing of old Tippecanoe.

When first near the Thames' gentle waters.
  My sword for my country I drew,
I fought for America's daughters,
  Long side of Old Tippecanoe.

Ere this, too, when danger assailed us,
  And Indians their dread missiles threw,
His counsel and courage availed us.
  We conquered at Tippecanoe.

And when all the troubles were ended,
  I flew to the girls that I knew,
They promptly declared they intended
  To kiss me for Old Tippecanoe.

And now that the good of the nation
  Requires that something we do,
We'll hurl little Van from his station,
  And elevate Tippecanoe.

Again and again fill your glasses,
  Bid Martin Van Buren adieu,
We'll please ourselves and the lasses,
  And vote for Old Tippecanoe.

OLD TIPPECANOE.

TUNE, "*Rosin the Bow.*"

Ye Vanites of wide Pennsylvania,
  Of every old State and each new;
Take warning, come out with the many,
  And vote for Old Tippecanoe!
    And vote for Old Tippecanoe;
    Take warning, come out with the many,
    And vote for Old Tippecanoe!

We've multiplied here past endurin',
  Blair and Rives begin to look blue,
They see there's no chance for Van Buren,
  In a fight with Old Tippecanoe.
    In a fight with, etc.

The little Magician, he sickens
  At the sight of Delaware, too;
When the blue hen calls her game chickens,
  To fight for Old Tippecanoe!
    To fight for, etc.

Both New York and New Jersey are ours,
  Massachusetts, Conneeticut, too;
And Vermont with her green mountain flow'rs
  Will flourish for Tippecanoe!
    Will flourish, etc.

We'd a brush in Rhode Island lately,
  To show them what Yankees could do;
And we flog'd 'em all most completely,
  In the name of Old Tippecanoe!
    In the name, etc.

And in old never tire Virginny,
  They've found of good Whigs, not a few;
A State, sirs! I'll hold you a guinea,
  Goes hollow for Tippecanoe!
    Goes hollow, etc.

Who flies to the rescue ? Kentucky,
  With hearts, gallant, loyal and true;
We'll beat them with brave men and lucky
  Harry Clay and Tippecanoe!
    Harry Clay, etc.

Illinois, Indiana, Ohio,
  Their towns and green prairies go thro',

You'll hear from each nook of the trio,
  Loud shouts for Old Tippecanoe.
    Loud shouts, **etc.**

On Michigan's shores and Missouri,
  The ball is in motion, 'tis true;
But Benton cries out in a fury,
  'Tis rolling tow'rds Tippecanoe.
    'Tis rolling, etc.

Mississippi, Louisiana,
  Tennessee, Al'bama here view,
They send from each hill and savanna,
  Their voices for Tippecanoe.
    Their voices, **etc.**

Should I name all those who are for us,
  'Tis plain I should never get through;
Rejoice in the prospect before us,
  Huzza! for Old Tippecanoe.
    Huzza! for, etc.

But before I finish my ditty,
  I'll claim patriot Maryland, too;
And hail! noble monument city,
  Where we gather for Tippecanoe!
    Where we gather, etc.

THE ROUGH LOG CABIN.

I love the rough log cabin
  It tells of olden time,
When a hardy and an honest class
  Of freemen in their prime,
First left their fathers' peaceful home   /
  Where all was joy and rest
With their axes on their shoulders,
  And sallied for the West.

Of logs they built a sturdy pile,
  With slabs they roofed it o'er;
With wooden latch and hinges rude
  They hung the clumsy door.
And for the little window lights,
  In size two feet by two,
They used such sash as could be got
  In regions that were new.

The chimney was composed of slats
  Well interlaid with clay,
Forming a sight we seldom see
  In this a later day;
And here, on stones for fire-dogs,
  A rousing fire was made;
While round it sat a hardy crew
  " With none to make afraid."

I love the old log cabin—
  For here, in early days,
Long dwelt the honest Harrison,
  As every loco says;
And when he is our President,
  Which one year more will see,
In good hard cider we will toast
  And cheer him three times three.

THE FARMER OF NORTH BEND.

TUNE, "*Auld Lang Syne.*"

Can grateful freemen slight his claims
  Who bravely did defend,
Their lives and fortunes on the Thames,
  The farmer of North Bend ?
      The farmer of North Bend, my boys,
      The farmer of North Bend,
      We'll give a right good hearty vote
      To the farmer of North Bend.

The trump of fame in storied song
  The patriot's deeds shall tell,
And freedom's voice the strain prolong,
  The gladsome chorus swell.
      The gladsome chorus swell, my boys,
      The gladsome chorus swell,
      We'll join to-night in merry song,
      The gladsome chorus swell.

The chieftain heard the stirring drum,
  And bent his soldier's bow,
But victor soon—he hastened home,
  His farming fields to mow,
      His farming fields to mow, my boys,
      His farming fields to mow,
      Exchanged the saber for the scythe,
      His farming fields to mow.

Though youthful valor bravely won
  The laurel for his brow,
Yet victory's own triumphant son
  Now holds the yeoman's plow.
     Now holds the yeoman's plow, my boys,
     Now holds the yeoman's plow,
     And soon we'll try his trusty hand
     To hold the nation's plow.

Now hear the note, his country's call,
  From the hill-tops and the shore,
It comes from camp, and cot, and hall,
  And all the valleys o'er.
     And all the valleys o'er, my boys,
     And all the valleys o'er,
     It calls him to the rescue, boys,
     From all the valleys o'er.

The hero who, long years ago,
  Once wore the warrior's mail,
Now comes to beat the yeoman's foe,
  A farmer with his flail.
     A farmer with his flail, my boys,
     A farmer with his flail,
     And they'll get a right gude threshing, yet,
     From the farmer with his flail.

Then cheer we up, my boys, to-night,
  A helping hand we lend,
And pledge the old Keystone to-night,
  To the farmer of North Bend.
     To the farmer of North Bend, my boys,
     To the farmer of North Bend,
     We'll pledge the old Keystone to-night,
     To the farmer of North Bend.

HARRISON SONG.

TUNE, "*Star-Spangled Banner.*"

Oh say have you heard how in days that are past,
Bold sons of the West with brave Harrison leading,
At the bugle's shrill call and the trumpet's loud blast,
To the battle-field rush'd where our frontiers lay bleeding;
    Hark! with the loud acclaim,
    How they shout at the name,
Of the hero predestin'd to guide them to fame!

Oh! the name of our Harrison, long may it stand
The boast of our country, the pride of our land!

Hark! loud rings the war-whoop o'er forest and plain,
And the savage and Briton in bloody alliance
Bringing havoc and death in their murderous train,
To the brave sons of Freedom are bidding defiance;
      But when Harrison came,
      At the sound of his name,
They trembled and fled in confusion and shame;
Oh! the name of brave Harrison, long may it stand
The boast of our country, the pride of our land!

Unmov'd and serene the brave Harrison stood
'Mid the din of the strife and the cannon's dead rattle,
And Tecumseh and Proctor, twin monsters of blood,
By their death or their flight prov'd his prowess in battle,
      And victory flew,
      To his flag ever true,
At Fort Meigs and the Thames and at Tippecanoe!
Oh! the name of the brave Harrison, long may it stand
The boast of our country, the pride of our land!

Oh, long as the fame of our country endures
Be the names of her heroes embalmed in her story,
How her Jackson defended, her Washington saved,
And her Harrison fill'd up her measured glory;
      Then long may the men
      Of the "Log Cabin" strain,
Stand true to the cause of the pupil of Wayne;
Oh! the name of Harrison, long may it stand
The boast of our country, the pride of our land!

THE UNITED STATES.

TUNE, "*Bay of Biscay, O.*"

Van Buren on the weather tack,
Our gallant ship did sail,
When she was struck aback,
By a wild and sweeping gale.
      For a long time drear and dark,
      Was the Constitution bark,
          Tossed by tides,
          Till on the ides.
In Loco Foco Bay.

Her topsails in ribbons fly,
And her yards were blown away
As the waves roll'd mountain high,
For many a stormy day.
No vessel can we spy,
And no harbor now is nigh,
Till on the ides,
Toss'd by tides,
In Loco Foco Bay.

And the stormy petrels flew
Thro' the feathery ocean's foam,
As the bark and her poor crew
On the raging seas do roam,
While the spirits of the clouds,
Peal'd their war-notes on her shrouds,
Till on the ides,
Toss'd by tides,
In Loco Foco Bay.

But a gallant boat's in view,
Dancing lightly o'er the wave,
'Tis pilot Tippecanoe,
Bearing down the ship to save.
Hurrah! give him three cheers,
As upon deck he appears:
For now we sail.
With the gale,
From Loco Foco Bay.

A SONG.

TUNE, "*Hail Columbia.*"

Immortal patriot bright in arms,
Whose breast the fire of freedom warms.
Defender of our hearths and homes,
Defender of our hearths and homes.
The scalping knife fell from the hand,
That raised it o'er our boasted land.
The savage yell'd and conquered fled,
Britain lowered her plumed head;
Proctor yielded to thy skill—
Victor then, victorious still.
Firmly to our standard flock,
Freemen stand like solid rock,
Tides of slander cannot shake,
Traitors' hearts alone shall quake.

Then rise above the servile dust,
To deeds of glory pure and just;
    Our hero's fame still fadeless blooms,
    Our hero's fame still fadeless blooms,
Let slander hide her dastard head,
The ground is safe on which we tread;
So rally to the standard on,
Sons of sires like Washington;
Let the battle well be fought,
Glory's best when dearest bought.
      Firmly to our standard flock,
      Freemen stand like solid rock,
      Tides of slander cannot shake,
      Traitors' hearts alone shall quake.

Lo, now a grateful people rise,
With cheers exulting rend the skies,
    Brave Harrison in loud huzzas,
    Brave Harrison in loud huzzas,
From East to West the echo rings,
And Freedom flaps her airy wings,
Rejoiced to see her reign prolonged,
By millions round the hero throng'd;
Hoist the banners high in air,
Grateful hearts are everywhere.
      Firmly to our standard flock,
      Freemen stand like solid rock,
      Tides of slander cannot shake,
      Traitors' hearts alone shall quake.

HAVE YOU HEARD THE GOOD NEWS.

Tune, *"Rosin the Bow."*

Have you heard the good news from Virgin'a,
  That makes all the locos look blue?
She has hauled down the flag of Van Buren,
  And hoisted Old Tippecanoe.

Old Ritchie & Co. told "the party"
  That the State for Van Buren was true;
But the log-cabin boys gave them battle,
  And conquered for Tippecanoe.

The locos they worked like all nature,
  And told all their lies old and new;
But the cabin boys said you can't come it,
  We are going for Tippecanoe.

3*

Rhode Island we've got and Virginia,
  And we've taken Connecticut too;
In '36 each was for Martin,
  But now they're for Tippecanoe.

Ten cheers for the ancient dominion;
  Ten cheers for our triumph in view;
We will beat them as bad in October,
  As Old Tip did at Tippecanoe.

Huzza for the rest of the Union;
  Huzza for our cause good and true;
Huzza for John Tyler, Tom Corwin,
  And huzza for Old Tippecanoe.

GENERAL HARRISON.

TUNE, "*The Lament.*"

Hark! with shouts, the air is rending,
  Of the white man's savage foe;
Now their cruel course is bending
  To the work of death and woe.

Hear the cries of widows weeping
  For a murdered husband, son;
Low in death forever sleeping,
  Did they spare them? No, not one.

Now their savage bosoms swelling;
  To destroy, their only aim;
See! they burn the lowly dwelling;
  See destruction in their train.

They, with stealthy steps are treading,
  To secure their feeble prey;
Now, in fear, the white man dreading,
  Unpursued they flee away.

Hear! the trump of war is sounding;
  See an injured people come;
See the red man's host surrounding;
  See the gallant Harrison.

He, his country's rights defending,
  Has no cause but that alone;
He, the foe's proud power rending,
  Ranks on ranks, has overthrown.

Now the cannon loudly roaring,
   In destruction on the foe;
Now in vengeance death is pouring,
   Lays the haughty chieftain low.

Now from battle he's returning
   With the spoils his valor won;
See, with joy his bosom burning;
   See our own, our Harrison.

Now in safety he's returning;
   Joy to those who lived in dread;
They, in silence, now imploring
   Choicest blessings on his head.

Now once more his way is wending
   To his pleasant rural home;
Now his golden fields is 'tending,
   In domestic pleasures roam.

Now in life he's fast declining,
   Yet in wisdom holds his sway;
Round his head he's fast entwining
   Sages' counsel, brightest ray.

Now ye people—now ye nation,
   Ere life's feeble course is run,
To the high exalted station,
   Raise your own, your Harrison.

HARK TO THE WARNING.

TUNE, "*All the Blue Bonnets.*"

All praise to the hero, the statesman, the farmer,
As threefold his title, be threefold his fame;
The strong arm is stronger, the warm heart is warmer
When touched by the magic of Harrison's name.

CHORUS.

Hark! to the warning a nation has spoken—
It rolls from the mountain, it springs from the plain,
Down with the spoilers, their trust who have broken,
And up with the standard of freedom again!

He calls on the wealthy, whose store he protected,
The poor man whose pittance he labored to save;

The patriot, who frowns not on merit neglected,
The soldier, who honors the noble and brave.
                    Hark! to the warning, etc.

By the toils and the dangers that sadden his story,
By the blood that he poured with the blood of the foe,
By the homes that he fought for, his triumphs his glory
He calls us to aid him, to strike the last blow.
                    Hark! to the warning, etc.

Then up at his call—speed the plow my good neighbors,
To the fields so long barren, all eagerly come;
Soon autumn shall yield the rewards of our labors,
And the land shall be glad with its new harvest-home.
                    Hark! to the warning, etc.

Then shout to the hero, and forth swell the chorus,
More loud than the war-whoop that died at his voice;
Will the agent of ruin fly trembling before us,
And the country, redeemed at their downfall, rejoice.
                    Hark! to the warning, etc.

NEW NATIONAL WHIG SONG. *

AIR, *"Hail to the Chief Who in Triumph Advances."*

Hail to the chief, for whom triumph advances,
    Honored and blest by the people anew,
Long may the Buckeye's green o'erspreading branches
    Shelter the hero of Tippecanoe!
            North, send it happy dew;
            South, send it sap anew;
        Firmly to flourish as broadly it grew
            Whilst every hill and plain
            Echoes, in joyful strain,
        Harrison! hero of Tippecanoe!

Our's is no dandy—no poor man's oppressor,
    Blooming in power—next winter to fade,
When the people shall point out to Martin's successor
    Oh! then shall our hero emerge from the shade,
            First in the nation's choice;
            Called by the people's voice;
        Proudly they'll welcome the veteran anew,
            Who at Fort Meigs and Thames
            Was his country's and fame's—
        Harrison! hero of Tippecanoe!

Loudly our tocsin was thrilled through the nation,
  With Harrison's banner unfurled o'er the land,
The proud Old Dominion has taken her station,
  The Empire and Keystone are taking their stand.
      The Buckeye and the Bay States
      We count on as first rates
  To carry the gallant old veteran through;
      For, tired of dallying
      The people are rallying
  For Harrison! hero of Tippecanoe!

Rise! freemen, rise! for the hope of the nation,
  Vote for the hero and pride of the West,
Whose fitness to fill so exalted a station
  His virtues both private and public attest,
      Firm to his country's cause;
      True to her outraged laws,
  Keeping her honor and glory in view,
      Triumph will grace him
      Wherever we place him—
  Harrison! hero of Tippecanoe!

DYING GROANS OF THE TIN-PAN.

(Sung at the great Ohio Convention, held at Columbus, February 22, 1840.)

We have had a hard time on account of the road,
But we looked not behind, for we knew our cause was
    good,
The object of our journey was plain to discover,
'Tis to row Mat Van Buren way up Salt River,
    Ching ring a ching, O ching ring a ching.

When this grand delegation will arrive at the convention,
Then we'll learn more fully General Harrison's intention,
We'll compose such a body that the Locos will look sour,
For they well know we come for to witness their last hour.
        O ching, etc., etc.

The brig General Harrison is just on before
With a band of Northern Whigs ten thousand or more,
Representing when this nation was as fair as any realm—
Till little Mat Van Buren the magician took the helm.
        O ching, etc., etc.

And broadside and broadside into him we send
Until he strikes his colors to the hero of North Bend,

And yields up command to the people again,
And then success to commerce and fair prices for our
grain.
O ching, etc., etc.

The Vans of Mount Vernon thought the Whigs would
give o'er
On account of the rain on the roads, but O never;
For we yield not the spirit which is roused all around
Till the great hydra monster is driven from our land.
O ching, etc., etc.

The Loco Foco party at Mt. Vernon down did look—
When they failed to steal the brig, and showed their
cloven foot,
When the Whig bugle sound and in triumph we set sail,
For a more honest party at Columbus to hail!
O ching, etc., etc.

He has taught to wean attention from the general theme,
That it's bad policy when our country's not serene;
So Medary was instructed to spread the reason far,
They never had settled the Northwestern boundary war.
O ching, etc., etc.

The spirit of our nation is now all on fire,
But they can pay their way without stealing Quasi Quire;
We are coming from the South and the far distant Maine,
For to rally 'neath the banner of our Harrison again.
O ching, etc., etc.

The people now are coming, little Matty will be routed,
For their patience is exhausted and all Swartwouted,
Sam Medary typed a lie against Mr. Lloyd up,
But their testimony failed, and used Payne and Wilson up.
O ching, etc., etc.

Andrew Jackson recommended his dear little Van
For to follow in his footsteps and try to be a man;
But his administration has proved to his scorn,
That he is a barren stalk of great baden corn.
O ching, etc., etc.

When arriving, shouts came from the whole reform nation.
It roll'd o'er our land, then arose up to heaven;
But from a distant silent house, there came a sound of
booming,
And we soon learnt with joy 'twas the tin pan a groaning.
O ching, etc., etc.

Now we join happy thousands at the close of our journey,
At our proud Capitol all is free as milk and honey;
Now we point up aloft, where our nation's banners flying,
And this shall be the requiem for the Vans while they're
    dying.

                  Ching a ring a ching.

VAN BUREN'S LAMENT.

Air. "*O. No, I'll Never Mention Her.*"

Oh, no, I never mention'd it,
    I never said a word;
I lent Swartwout a lot of cash,
    Of which I've never heard.
He said he only borrow'd it,
    To pay another debt,
And since I've never mention'd it.
    He thinks that I forget.

And Price, and others like himself,
    Have borrow'd money too,
And since I've never mention'd it,
    They think it is not due.
I fear the money was not mine,
    And I must pay the debt.
For though I've never mention'd it,
    The people wont forget.

HARRISON SONG.

Tune, "*Gaily the Troubadour.*"

Truly did Harrison come from his home,
Whilst he was yet a youth not twenty-one,
He joined our gallant band on the frontiers,
Harrison, Harrison—give him three cheers.

Hark, all ye gallant Whigs, firm, brave and true,
After he'd joined the band what did he do ?
He led to victory, free from all fears—
Harrison, Harrison—give him three cheers.

Huzza for Harrison—success to him,
He makes the Vanocrats look rather slim,

He is the people's man, away with our fears—
Harrison, Harrison—give him three cheers.

Then let us stick to him, young, old, and all.
And, like old Proctor's men, Matty must fall;
Turn, then, ye Vanocrats, fear not their sneers,
Harrison, Harrison—give him three cheers.

OHIO WHIG CONVENTION, 1840.

TUNE, "*The Son of Alknomook.*"

'Twas on Washington's birthday, the Whigs of the State.
In Columbus assembled—their numbers were great;
From the North, from the South, from the East and the
        West,
By ten thousands they came, at their country's behest.

They were freemen assembled their rights to maintain
And to rescue their land from corruption's foul stain,
To consult on the means their lov'd country to save,
And to drive from high places base traitors and knaves.

There was old Cuyahoga, the pride of the North,
By her sons, which the country in scores had sent forth,
With their brig newly rigged, and a fine hearty crew
All resolved to do battle for Tippecanoe.

There was Portage, Medina, Geauga, Lorain,
Ashtabula, and Trumbull, and western Champaign,
And Muskingum, and Guernsey, and Green, and Monroe,
And Franklin, and Licking, and old Scioto.

There was Richland, and Warren, and Union, and Stark,
There was Mercy and Franklin, Montgomery and Clark,
There was Erie, and Henry, and Paulding, and Wood,
All poured forth their thousands of Whigs stanch and
        good.

There was Morgan, and Clermont, and Highland, and
        Brown,
Swelled the ranks of the Whigs to put tyranny down,
While Belmont, and Hamilton, Preble, and Ross,
With their thousands on thousands made Locos look cross.

There were farmers, mechanics, and hunters, and tars,
Proudly o'er their heads waved the stripes and the stars.

While the soul-stirring music poured forth by the bands,
Cheered their hearts, while the Tories in grief wrung
their hands.

Yes, those plunder-stained hands, then in sorrow were
wrung.
While the Whigs the loud chorus of liberty sung:
'Twas the death knell of knavery, hearty and loud,
'Twas the song of which freemen shall ever be proud.

There was Washington's life-guard, a relic of times,
That tried brave men's souls in our own happy climes,
And he led a white charger along through the street,
On his back was the saddle—great Washington's seat.

And next came the patriot of Tippecanoe,
The hero who fought for his country when new;
These banners were met with shouts of applause,
From the houses devoted to liberty's cause.

Assembled at length and in liberty's name,
For President—Harrison loud they proclaim:
For Governor—Corwin, a friend of the free,
Huzza, shout huzza, shout huzza, three times three.

The days of the spoilsmen are numbered and told;
In March, '41, shall the hero be rolled
In triumph to Washington, there to restore,
His country, now fallen, to glory once more.

THE SPOILSMEN.

The spoilsmen came down like the wolf on the fold,
And their train bands were rev'ling in ill-gotten gold,
And Benton's hoarse howl on the gale did resound
Like the deep deadly yell of the blood-scenting-hound.

Like leaves of the forest when summer is green,
In the year '39 their *bought* banners were seen,
Like the leaves of the forest when autumn hath blown
In March '41 they lay withered and strown.

For Freedom's proud bird spread his wings on the blast,
And the breath of his wrath laid them low as they passed,
And the eyes of the Vanites grew deadly and chill,
And Sub-Treasurers' legs forever grew still.

And there lay sad Amos distorted and pale,
With a curse on his lip and his grip on the mail,
And there lay Calhoun with his nostrils all wide,
And the "galvanized corpse" lay dark by his side.

And there lay "poor Pickin" and Duncan hard by,
With the Globe in his hand and a drop in his eye,
And the kitchen was silent, the Cabinet flown,
The cravat of the humbugger hung there "alone."

And the wail of the scullions is loud in their woe,
The "footstep" is vanished, the "follower" laid low,
And the popular might hath the spoiler expunged,
The might of the freeman hath freemen avenged.

THE LAST CABINET COUNCIL.

AIR, "*There's Nae Luck About the House.*"

Sly Matty's face was overcast,
His hopes began to lower,
His kitchen cabinet he called,
Besides the lawful four;
And bade them with a scolding tongue
That each should truly say,
If any chance remained for him
On next election day.

CHORUS.

> For it's Boyd and Harris, Linn and Price,
> And Swartwout they do say,
> Have toted off the nation's cash,
> As lawful Loco prey.

Then up steps Amos, grim and thin,
With sick and ghastly look,
You never would have thought that he
Was scullion and chief cook;
Now Matty dear, says he, I'm sure,
The game is up with us,
Those cursed Whigs will beat us now,
They kick up such a fuss.

CHORUS.

> About the outside quires and cash
> You'd think this nation's broke,
> And Blair, and I, and Calhoun think,
> This time they do not joke.

Says Blair to M— good President
I think it is unlucky,
That I must streak it back again
To teach school in Kentucky;
But go I must, for I am sure,
Our battles all are fought,
And New York's favorite son is beat
By sober second thought.

CHORUS.

Now Matty don't get sick, I'm sure
We may as well clear out,
And join the Loco Foco Price,
And honest Sam Swartwout.

And next, says Paulding, I do wish
To novels I had stuck,
For writing them would ne'er have made
Of me so lame a duck;
Dear Matty we must soon go back
To quiet Kinderhook,
And in your garret I will write
Another shilling book.

CHORUS.

Oh, dear! the times are very hard
When wheat's but fifty cents,
But I'm the man that's rich enough
If I collect my rents.

Come, Uncle Levi, tell us now
What think you of Whig votes?
Oh, dear! I fear they can't be bought
With my sub-treasury notes;
I've figured out my long reports
Arrayed in solid column,
But where's your cash, the Whigs cry out,
With faces long and solemn.

CHORUS.

The cash is gone and credit too
With our administration,
And we have ruined every man
Throughout the Yankee nation.

Now Poinsett can you cheer us up
With glad and cheerful sounds?
Oh, no! I can't, those cursed Whigs
Have tree'd me with bloodhounds;

We've got to quit the White House, now,
As fast as we can go;
I'll take my hat, and make my bow,
For I am D. I. O.

CHORUS.

The spoils are gone—there's nothing left
Of paper, blanks, and twine,
And every man is fortunate
Who knows where he can dine.

Perdition catch you all, says Mat,
Come, Forsythe, you're true blue,
And are so versed in politics
Can tell me what to do.
I wish I could, for I am sure
You'd hear it very soon;
But I will go and advise with
My friend J. C. Calhoun.

CHORUS.

For he's the man to jump Jim Crow,
And prove that black is white,
He will convince you its noonday,
When dark and pitchy night.

Now Harry Clay was passing by,
And hearing such a roar,
With hasty strides he mounted up
And opened wide the door—
Hallo! says he, what means this noise
Within this garrison?
You'd better all make tracks—here comes
The patriot Harrison.

CHORUS.

So off they ran with nimble legs,
As fast as they could lean;
As granny he took up the broom
And swept the White House clean.

WHIG ALARUM.

Whigs away, Whigs away, 'tis no time for delay,
    For the foeman's rude footsteps our temples degrading,
To the contest prepare, and by strong arm declare,
    That no tyrant survives who our rights are invading.

Fling the broad stripes on high, they shall float on the sky,
  As the beacons on the towers of liberty gleaming,
'Tis the banner of might, in the midst of the fight,
  For victory shouts where its bright folds are streaming.

And our eagle is nigh, with his fierce lightning eye,
  And his broad wings in the midst of the battle are
    dashing;
He has heard from afar, the loud tumult of war,
  Soon the Vanites shall quail where his wild glance is
    flashing.

Long our breezes shall fan the ensign of a land,
  Which ne'er shall be crushed by a tyrant's stern heel;
Then warriors awake and your bright sabers take;
  Let the foes of our freedom their keen edges feel.

Whigs away, Whigs away, 'tis no time for delay,
  For a tyrant's in the temples of sweet liberty;
Strike for freedom and laws, for our dear country's cause,
  From the wide western prairies to the shores of the sea.

THE VOICE OF COLUMBIA.

Lo! the seal of power is breaking,
Patriots, who have slept, are waking,
    And a tyrant's fall declare;
Freemen, arouse! a voice is singing,
In mount and vale, the peal is ringing;
See, the stars and stripes are flinging,
    Meteor-flashes on the sky.

Minstrelsy the land is filling,
In brave hearts its tones are thrilling,
    'Tis the harp of Liberty;
From her seraphic temple springing,
Swift on lightning pinions winging,
While her gallant sons are bringing,
    Vengeance on her enemy.

Hosts to battle now are dashing,
In the sun their blades are flashing,
    Hear ye not their battle cry?
Banners on the sky are gleaming,
And upon the breeze are streaming,
Leading, by their beacon beaming,
    Men resolved to do or die.

Tyrant, our sacred rights invading,
With miscreant slaves our soil degrading,
    In freedom's halls you dwell no more;
Tho' now against her laws rebelling,
Soon you'll hear on wild winds swelling,
Mighty shouts thy downfall knelling,
    Far along Atlantic's shore.

REPORT.

DIRGE, "*Burial of Sir John Moore.*"

Not a sigh was heard not a farewell groan
  Though he looked confoundedly flurried;
No patriots breast was heard to moan,
  As from the White House he was hurried,
He streaked it out darkly, at dead of night,
  The way with his grabbers feeling,
And he seemed, by the glare of lantern light,
  Like a rogue just caught a sheep stealing.

No useless carriage encircled his breast,
  Nor in ruffles, nor jewels we found him;
Yet he looked like a chap that had feathered his nest
  With the people's earnings around him;
Nor few, nor short, the maledictions said,
  And spoke more in anger than sorrow,
As the people they gritted their teeth in their head,
  And cursed the magician all hollow.

Startled and wild was his cat-like tread,
  (As Old Tip's name was rung o'er each hill, Oh!)
Like a hyena scared from his feast of the dead,
  As the red morning breaks over the billow;
Lightly they'll talk of the sprite that is gone,
  And o'er the sub-treasury upbraid him;
But little we'll reck, so we'll let him sneak on
  To the grave where the people have laid him.

But half our grateful task was done,
  When the clock toll'd the hour so desiring;
And we knew by the boom of a Harrison gun
  That the Whigs were merrily firing.
Down slowly and sadly the Locos come
  From the east room, in uppermost story;
In Virginia fence-line, they all reel'd home,
  And left Old Tip alone in his glory

LET FAME PUT HER TRUMP.

Let fame put her trump to the lip of the morn,
  And rouse up the slumbering day;
On the wings of the wind be the blast onward borne,
  Till it dies in the ether away;
But on the broad hills let it lay,
  And echo the green valley o'er,
That a chieftain exists, who, though aged and gray,
  Shall this country's lost luster restore.

From the North to the South, from the East to the West,
  From the center all round to the sea,
On the pinions of time, that are never at rest,
  It is borne to the ears of the free:
Then tremble the tyrants that be,
  For the moments of reckoning come,
More appalling than tempests that scourge the dark sea,
  Or the war-notes of trumpet and drum.

From the long dreary night of misrule and dismay,
  A whole people awake to the light,
While the dark clouds of error are breaking away,
  And the morning of truth dawning bright:
Again in her splendor and might,
  Fair Freedom unveils to the view,
And points to the chief, whose integrity's plight
  Shall the stars of her glory renew.

Betrayed by false statements, the sons of the soil
  Long in error and darkness did grope,
While the vampyres bore off the reward of their toil,
  And withered each promise of hope:
But a chieftain there is, who shall cope
  With the spoilers with Hercules' arm,
While the phalanx of freemen, unscathed and unbroke
  The abuses of power shall disarm.

He was tried in the battle, and ne'er known to yield,
  Lang syne, in the days of our pride;
A sage in the Senate, a chief in the field,
  On whom sages and warriors relied:
They will rally again to his side,
  As they did when the war-arrows flew;
And he'll lead them to conquest and glory beside,
  As he led them at Tippecanoe.

At the sound of the blast cheering onward amain,
  Prosperity lifts her pale head,

And looks, as her eye brightens up once again,
  Like a vestal arose from the dead:
Toward the chieftain her arms are outspread,
  Who her beauty and strength shall restore,
And robe her anew in the white blue and red.
  That so gracefully veiled her before.

Then pour a libation, and bear it on high,
  And let Fame give the word of command,
While the eagle of victory stoops from the sky,
  And hovers above the green land:
Round the altar of Freedom we stand,
  With the swords of our country in view,
And accoutred for battle, pledge heart and pledge hand,
  For the hero of Tippecanoe.

IT OFTTIMES HAS BEEN TOLD.

Tune, "*The Constitution and Gurriere.*"

  It ofttimes has been told,
  That British sailors bold,
Could flog the tars of France so neat and handy, O;
  But they never found their match,
  Till the Yankees did them catch,
Oh, the Yankee boys fighting are the dandy, O.

  The British now so bold,
  Hired just to fight for gold,
Commanded by proud Proctor, the grandee, O;
  With Indians by the score,
  A thousand too, or more,
They swore they'd flog the Yankees now so handy, O.

  Then Proctor loudly cries,
  Make this great field your prize,
You can in thirty minutes neat and handy, O;
  Thirty five's enough I'm sure,
  And if you'll do it in a score,
I'll treat you to a double share of brandy, O.

  The Indians with a yell,
  As if they came from h—ll,
Slashed round their tomahawks so neat and handy, O;
  Now says Harrison to his braves,
  Come on and whip these slaves,
If we take these savage boasters we're the dandy, O,

The first gun that was fired
Into their hearts inquired,
Which made the lofty Proctor look abandoned, O;
This Briton shook his head,
And to his officers said,
Lord, I didn't think old Harrison was so handy, O.

Our second told as well,
It made the Indians yell,
Which doused Tecumseh's hopes so very handy, O.
By George, they cried, we've done,
We'd better cut and run,
While the Yankees struck up Yankee doodle dandy, O.

The Indians now unarmed,
Because they were alarmed,
And buried all their tomahawks so handy, O;
But Harrison did not rest,
And on the battle press'd,
And tightly grasped his good old sword so handy, O.

Yet the brave old soldier said,
He wished not Proctor dead,
But meant to dress him in a petticoat so handy, O;
Then send him to the squaws,
The reason why, because
Among men he wasn't quite the dandy, O.

Now great success to him
Who does the work so trim,
As flog two great warriors so handy, O;
Our President he'll be,
Which you will shortly see,
And, fellow-citizens, wont that be the dandy, O!

THE PEOPLES' SONG.

TUNE, "*Gilderoy.*"

We long to see the season come
When we can vote for Harrison,
For there is nothing can prevent
His being the next President;
For he's the man that risk'd his life,
Against the savage scalping knife;
And Proctor thought he'd better run
Than measure swords with Harrison.

When some were in their cradles rock'd
Their fathers round the hero flock'd,
The fight was hard, but still they won,
Led on by General Harrison;
But now with double force they come,
The war-worn soldier, with his son,
They strike the time without the drum,
Both right and left, for Harrison.

Supporting General Harrison,
The people have no risk to run—
For he can first adjust their laws,
Then with his sword maintain their cause.
Then raise the banner till it floats,
While men are handing in their votes;
And may their ballots tell as one,
Success to General Harrison.

Then let this song, for one, be sung,
As clear as Indian rifles rung,
By middle-aged, old and young,
Without one jar or faltering tongue;
And let the spangled banner wave,
High on the breeze, above the brave,
While they proclaim the work is done,
We'll join for General Harrison.

The eagle with bright plumage dressed,
Directs her flight towards the West,
Where oft she'd heard the battle yell,
To drop a tear where Davies fell;
Now round the field her way she wings,
And with her notes the welkin rings,
She sings McArthur, Cass and Croghan,
Then tops her song with Harrison.

THE FLAG OF TIPPECANOE.

AIR, "*A Health Let Us Drink to the Hero and Sage.*"

The "Spoilsmen" are fretful and gloomy as night,
Their "Denmark is rotten" about,
The party's perplexed, and in horrible plight,
For Matty they know must go out:
   Our flag, like the sign to the Roman, I ween,
   Will lead us to glory—and who
   Would'nt stick to that flag while a star's to be seen
   The flag of Old Tippecanoe.

"The scepter and power from Judah must go;"
The days of Van Buren are told,
The people, refusing to take, as you know,
Shin-plasters, for promised gold:
    Then on to the rescue my hearties we move,
    Corruption must shrink if we do,
    Let's stick to Old Buckeye, the statesman we love,
    The Hero of Tippecanoe!

Our ship CONSTITUTION, though stanch in her hull,
Is marr'd by the Partisan storm;
But we safely will moor her by united pull,
In the haven of real reform:
    But the ship to be saved a new Master must own,
    And a new set of Tars for the crew;
    From the Ancient Domain the Lieutenant must come
    The Captain from Tippecanoe!

When war's deadly summons had led us to blows,
Where was Kinderhook Van to be found?
In the rear of all dangers, with Bluelights and foes,
He hated the battle's dread sound.
    Where was HARRISON then? on the field of his fame
    There, prov'd himself gallant and true,
    The roar of the cannon was music to him
    The Hero of Tippecanoe.

When peace by proud victories came again brief,
The Hero returned to his plow;
But the people are coming to make him their Chief,
With purpose inflexible now.
    Then fill up your wine cups and pass them around,
    Let's drink to the brave and the true,
    And this be our toast, The Brave Hero of Thames,
    The Hero of Tippecanoe!

THE HERO OF TIPPECANOE.

[The following song was sung at the convention held at Columbus, February 22, 23, '40.]

TUNE, "*Rosin the Bow.*"

Ye jolly young lads of Ohio,
    And all ye sick Vanocrats too,
Come out from amongst the foul party,
    And vote for old Tippecanoe, etc.
    And vote for old Tippecanoe, etc.

The great Twenty-Second is coming,
  And the Vanjacks begin to look blue,
They know there's no chance for poor Matty,
  If we'll stick to old Tippecanoe,
              If we'll stick, etc.

I therefore will give you a warning,
  Not that any good it will do,
For I'm certain you all are a going,
  To vote for old Tippecanoe,
              To vote, etc.

Then let us be up and doing,
  And cling to our cause brave and true,
I'll bet you a fortune we'll beat them,
  With the hero of Tippecanoe.
              With the hero, etc.

Good men from the Vanjacks are flying,
  Which makes them look kinder eskew,
For they see they are joining the standard,
  With the hero of Tippecanoe.
              With the hero, etc.   '

They say that he lived in a cabin,
  And lived on old hard cider too,
Well, what if he did, I'm certain,
  He's the hero of Tippecanoe.
              He's the hero, etc.

Then let us all go to Columbus,
  And form a procession or two,
And I tell you the Vanjacks will startle,
  At the sound of old Tippecanoe.
              At the sound, etc.

As for one I'm fully determined,
  To go, let it rain, hail or snow;
And do what we can in the battle,
  For the hero of Tippecanoe.
              For the hero, etc.

And if we get any ways thirsty,
  I'll tell you what we can do,
We'll bring down a keg of hard cider,
  And drink to old Tippecanoe.
              And drink, etc.

HURRAH SONG.

Old Tip's the boy to swing the flail,
          Hurrah, hurrah, hurrah!
And make the Locos all turn pale,
          Hurrah, hurrah, hurrah!
He'll give them all a tarnal switchin',
When he begins to " Clare de Kitchen."
          Hurrah, hurrah, hurrah, hurrah, hurrah!

Plowboys! though he leads in battle,
          Hurrah, hurrah, hurrah!
He's a team in raising cattle,
          Hurrah, hurrah, hurrah!
And though old Proctor at him kicked,
He is the chap that never was licked,
          Hurrah, hurrah, hurrah, etc.

His latch-string hangs outside the door,
          Hurrah, hurrah, hurrah!
As it has always done before,
          Hurrah, hurrah, hurrah!
We vowed, by Whigs he should be sent
To Washington as President,
          Hurrah, hurrah, hurrah, etc.

In all the States no door stands wider,
          Hurrah, hurrah, hurrah!
To ask you in to drink hard cider,
          Hurrah, hurrah, hurrah!
But any man that's fond of grabbin',
Ne'er can enter his log cabin,
          Hurrah, hurrah, hurrah!

For such as Swartwout, Price and Boyd,
          Hurrah, hurrah, hurrah!
His honest soul will e'er avoid,
          Hurrah, hurrah, hurrah!
And poverty he thinks no crime,
But welcomes it at dinner time,
          Hurrah, hurrah, hurrah, etc.

So here's three cheers for honest Tip,
          Hurrah, hurrah, hurrah!
We've got the Locos on the hip,
          Hurrah, hurrah, hurrah?
We'll row them all far up Salt River,
There let them stand to shake and shiver,
          Hurrah, hurrah, hurrah, etc.

THE HERO PLOWMAN.

TUNE, "*Yankee Doodle.*"

The hero plowman of North Bend,
　　According to my notion,
Who did our cabins long defend,
　　Is worthy of promotion.
　　　　Then for the plowman we'll array,
　　　　　Our gallant Buckeye forces—
　　　　Van Buren's collar men K K*
　　　　　They soon will fly their courses.

Van cannot bribe us with his Price,
　　Nor will we be Swartwouted;
We'll stick to Tip like any vise,
　　Until the foe is routed.
　　　　　　Then for, etc.

Come one come all, the spoilsmen clan,
　　Who jump at Matty's orders;
We'll clear his kitchen to a man,
　　And boost them from our borders.
　　　　　　Then for, etc.

The false magician long has play'd
　　His feats of hocus pocus;
Has congregated and array'd,
　　His rabid Loco Focos.
　　　　　　But for, etc.

Leg-treas'rers scent his old Dutch cheese,
　　The smell whereof so loud is;
It makes them jump and snuff and sneeze
The Loco Foco rowdies.
　　　　　　Then for, etc.

The treas'ry-Kraut is wholly spoil'd,
　　It never was half salted,
But spoilsmen gulp it down unboil'd,
　　But just a little scalded.
　　　　　　Then for, etc.

Our Buckeye hero, true and tried,
　　Is rightly nam'd old granny;
To deliver (is his pride)
　　The house of little Vanny.
　　　　　　Then for, etc.

---

*K K means can't come it.

But granny never works by halves,
  He's eke a famous doctor,
He'll ease the nation of her knaves,
  As he did Gen'ral Proctor.
          Then for, etc.

The spoilsmen will be forc'd to slope;
  To take unto their scrapers;
Old Tip will grant them, soon I hope,
  Authentic walking papers.
          So for, etc.

And then the famous Kinderhook,
  Sir Martin will reside in;
He'll find some cranny nook or crook,
  His infamy to hide in.
          Then for, etc.

Now here's a health to Harrison:
  His fame keeps circling wider;
Ohio's boast Virginia's son—
  We'll toast him on hard cider.
          Then for, etc.

THE BATTLE OF THE THAMES.

TUNE, "*The Battle of the Nile.*"

Arise! arise! sons of the West arise,
And join in the shouts of the patriotic throng;
Arise! arise! sons of the West arise,
And let Freedom's walls re-echo with your song.
    For he will lead us on
    Who did lead us years ago,
    When he trod a foreign soil,
    Wreaking vengeance on the foe.

CHORUS.

And the battle of the Thames, as every tongue proclaims,
And the battle of the Thames, as every tongue proclaims,
Shall live in history, in poetry and song.
  Huzza! huzza! huzza! huzza! huzza, boys,
  For him who fought for us, and never yet was known to
    yield,
  Huzza! huzza! huzza! huzza! huzza, boys,
  Our Harrison again will win the field.

Arise! arise! sons of the West arise,
Your brethren of the East are arousing in their might,
Arise! arise! sons of the West arise,
And be ready now to aid them in the fight.
      For he will be our chief,
        Who when danger was at hand,
      To our frontier brought relief,
        With his gallant western band.
    And the battle of the Thames, etc.

Arise! arise! sons of the West arise,
Your liberties maintaining, your country now befriend,
Arise! arise! sons of the West arise,
And gather 'round the farmer of North Bend.
      For he will bring us aid,
        Who was aide to gallant Wayne,
      When the Indian's yell was heard,
        From every hill and plain.
    And the battle of the Thames, etc.

LOG CABINS AND LOG CABIN BOYS.

[Sung at the Log Cabin "raisin'" at Annapolis, on Thursday, 25th ultimo.]

TUNE, "*Hunters of Kentucky.*"

Log Cabins now are all the go,
  My friends, suppose we rear one,
We're clumsy architects, I know,
  Yet still we can prepare one.
    Yankee Doodle keep it up,
      Yankee Doodle dandy,
    Old Tip's the chap to put things right,
    - In State affairs he's handy.

We owe it to each *Hoosier* friend;
  'Tis due to old Kentucky,
Who 'neath the Banner of North Bend,
  In war or peace is lucky.
    Yankee Doodle keep it up,
      Yankee Doodle dandy;
    In honor of the West we'll have
      A Cabin neat and handy.

When Proctor and our savage foes,
  With yells the West astounded,
Van Buren liv'd in soft repose,
  By luxury surrounded.

Yankee Doodle keep it up,
Yankee Doodle dandy;
'Twas then Old Tip that savage horde
Just beat and took so handy.

Log Cabin *Boys* are all the go,
The fool alone derides them,
Their hearts with manly feelings glow,
And honor ever guides them.
Yankee Doodle keep it up,
And 'bout the work be handy,
They've order'd Van to Kinderhook,
And that you know's the dandy.

Now, friends, a song I've given you,
Let some one sing another—
A courtesy that's always due
From one Whig to a brother.
Yankee Doodle keep it up,
Let's with our work be handy,
Old Tip will be the President,
And that will be the dandy.

THE "LOG CABIN" SONG.

[Composed and sung by the Clark county delegation at the great People's Convention of Ohio, on the 22d of February, 1840.]

TUNE, "*Highland Laddie.*"

Oh, where, tell me where, was your Buckeye Cabin made?
Oh, where, tell me where, was your Buckeye Cabin made?
'Twas built among the merry boys that wield the plow
    and spade,
Where the Log Cabins stand, in the bonnie Buckeye
    shade!
                    'Twas built, etc.

Oh, what, tell me what, is to be your Cabin's fate?
Oh, what, tell me what, is to be your Cabin's fate?
We'll wheel it to the Capital, and place it there elate,
For a token or sign of the bonnie Buckeye State!
                    We'll wheel, etc.

Oh, why, tell me why, does your Buckeye Cabin go?
Oh, why, tell me why, does your Buckeye Cabin go?
It goes against the spoilsmen, for well its builders know
It was Harrison that fought for the cabins long ago.
                    It goes, etc.

Oh, what, tell me what, then, will little Martin do?
Oh, what, tell me what, then, will little Martin do?
He'll "follow in the footsteps" of Price and Swartwout too,
While the log cabins ring again with old Tippecanoe.
He'll follow, etc.

Oh, who fell before him in battle, tell me who?
Oh, who fell before him in battle, tell me who?
He drove the savage legions, and British armies too
At the Rapids, and the Thames, and old Tippecanoe!
He drove, etc.

By whom, tell me whom, will the battle next be won?
By whom, tell me whom, will the battle next be won?
The spoilsmen and leg treasurers will soon begin to run!
And the 'Log Cabin Candidate' will march to Washing-
ton!
The spoilsmen, etc.

———

THE HERO STATESMAN.

TUNE, "*The Campbell's Are Coming.*"

He comes from the West, in the strength of his name,
The favored of song, and a hero in fame;
He's the People's own choice, and his resting shall be
At the side of the brave, in the hearts of the free,
No more in the shade of retirement he's laid,
Where the warrior's plume rests with his chivalrous blade;
For his country demands his true service again,
To protect with his sword, and defend with his pen.
  He comes from the West in the strength of his name
  The favored of song, and a hero in fame;
  He's the people's own choice, and his resting shall be
  At the side of the brave, in the hearts of the free.

Though gray be his locks, there's a fire in his eye,
That flashes in scorn when a foeman is nigh;
To the poor and oppressed who his kindness implore,
He never in scorn shuts his hand nor his door.
Then hail to the hero who merits our thanks,
To the statesman who lives on Ohio's green banks;
For the banner of freedom that floats to the breeze,
Shall ne'er be dishonored on land nor on seas.
He comes from the West, etc.

When joined with the wise and engaged with the great
To act for his country in councils of state,

No traitor unscathed shall escape from his hand—
The boldest he'll sweep from a place in the land.
Though dastards revile, and though cowards defame,
They dim not the glory of Harrison's name;
And louder and broader our plaudits shall rise
For the hero so bold, for the statesman so wise.

      He comes from the West, etc.

NEW COMIC SONG.

TUNE, *"Hey, Come Along, Josey."*

Come listen to me and I'll sing you a song,
Which I promise you shall not be long;
And I know you'll say it's a first-rate thing
And dis is de tune dat I will sing:
    Hey, cum along, jim along, Josey,
    Hey, cum along, jim along, Jo.

I spose you know de Whigs next fall
Are gwoing to stop the Loco ball;
Gin'rawl Harr'sin he too strong for Martin,
And at de lexshun will beat him sartin:
    Hey, cum along, etc.

De spilers say dey will no hab him
Kase how he lib in a log cabin;
But de peeple say dey do not kere,
He shall hab de White House 'fore a year.
    Hey, cum along, etc.

De Locos say he drink hard cider,
But dey only spread his fame de wider
And dey may ober dere shampane
Make fun of him but it's all in wane:
    Hey, cum along, etc.

Yes, let um laf and call him granny,
But it's well for you my little Vanny,
Dat he draw de Injuns and British far
While you were talkin' 'gainst de war:
    Hey, cum along, etc.

And as de enemy den flew,
At Meigs, at Thames, at Tipp'canoe,
So he will make de hirelings run
When he is sent to Washington:
    Hey, cum along, etc.

De fox will den wid a sheepish look
Sneak back to de hole in Kinderhook;
And de leg treasurers will make tracks
As if de debil was at dere backs:
>   Hey, cum along, etc.

And he who at 'Cumsey pull de trigger
Whose wife was cousin to dis niggur;
Eben dat wont save him, for de nashun
Say dey not for amalgamation:
>   Hey, cum along, etc.

"White man, white man, werry unsartin,"
"How you off for soap," my darlin' Martin;
Next March de log cabin boys will shout,
"Does your anxious mammy know you're out?"
>   Hey, cum along, etc.

I swow I pity your condition,
For you were for de bobbolishoun,
And voted for darkies cum ob age
To hab de right ob free sufferage:
>   Hey, cum along, etc.

And now, gentle folks, I bid you good bye,
Don't let de Locos fro chalk in your eye;
And when to de city de Gin'rawl you bring,
Dis nigger will be dere all ready for to sing:
>   Hey, cum along, etc.

TIPPECANOE SONG.

AIR, "*Bonnets of Blue.*"

The voice of the nation has spoken,
  The tyrants all shake in their shoes—
The scepter of Martin is broken—
  He shrinks at the glorious news.

CHORUS.

All hail to the glorious West,
Log cabins and yeomen to you;
The land of the brave and the blest,
And home of old Tippecanoe.

The political valley of Death,
  Surround his vile minions of power,

Their slanderous, pestilent breath,
  Is hushed like the storm of an hour.
                    All hail, etc.

The *cooks* of the kitchen aghast,
  Hear their knell sound far from the West,
And fear that their dishes, at last,
  Will poison the "greatest and best."

Then hail to the glorious West,
  Log cabins and yeomen to you;
The land of the brave and the blest,
  And the home of old Tippecanoe.

CLEARING THE KITCHEN AND WHITE HOUSE.

[A song for the fourth of March, 1841.]

TUNE, "*Young Lochinvar.*"

Old Tippecanoe has come out of the West,
Through all the wide border his fame was best,
For save his log cabin, he station had none,
He came with his friends, with true hearts alone,
So dauntless in war, to his country so true,
Was ever there soul like Old Tippecanoe?

He staid not for break, he stopped not for stone,
He swam the Ohio where ford there was none,
But ere he alighted at Washington gate
The spoilers were scampering before 'twas too late,
For, laggard in heart, to his country untrue,
Had kept this fair place from Old Tippecanoe.

So boldly he entered the President's hall,
'Mong patriots and brothers and ladies and all,
That, to little Van, it politely occurred,
Unto the new-comers he must say a word.
"Oh, whence are you here?—what came you to do?
Must you take this White House for Old Tippecanoe?"

"He long served his country," the lovers replied,
"She wooed him to come, when her suit you denied,
But now is he here with friends from afar,
To fill up the measure of glory and war,
There are men in this country more fitting than you,
To rule this fair land with Old Tippecanoe."
They sat down the mug when Old Tip took it up,

And quaffed the hard cider, then proffered the cup,
Van looked down to blush, and then looked up to sigh
With a frown on his lip and a squint in his eye;
Then, bowing full low, says he, "Good-bye to you,
I surrender this house to Old Tippecanoe."

So good a form and so honest a face,
That never this hall such a farmer did grace;
While Kendall did fret and Levi did fuss,
And Benton stood dangling his yellow boy's purse,
And the ladies they whispered, "'twere 'tis true,
The country were governed by Tippecanoe."

One touch to Blair's hand and one word in his ear,
As Van reached the door, and his carriage was near,
"We are gone, we are gone, by hook or by crook,
I must wend my way back to my own Kinderhook;
My light English coach, though often it flew,
Couldn't match the hard gray of Old Tippecanoe."

There was mounting and tramping of Cabinet clan,
And the kitchen concern, some rode and some ran;
There was racing and chasing o'er Capital lea,
But the little Magician no more could they see!
So dauntless in war, to his country so true,
Who could clear the kitchen but Tippecanoe?

HARD CIDER.

[Composed by Dr. J. Kilbourne, and sung at the Log Cabin **Raisin'**, Columbus.]

TUNE, "*Old Rosin the Bow.*"

Come ye who, whatever betide her,
To freedom have sworn to be true,
Prime up with a cup of hard cider,
And drink to old Tippecanoe, etc.

On top I've a cask of as good, sir,
As man from the tap ever drew;
No poison to cut up your blood, sir,
But liquor as pure as the dew, etc.

No foreign potation we puff, sir,
In *free-land* the aple-tree grew;
Its juice is *exactly* the stuff, sir,
To quaff to brave Tippecanoe, etc.

Ye log-cabin monarchs, who reign o'er
The West, in your hunting-shirts blue;
A *brimmer* you surely can drain to
Your neighbor of Tippecanoe, etc.

Ye yeomen, so hardy and noble,
Who'll sup on a mess of parch'd corn,
And then make but light of the trouble
To fight the wild Indian till morn, etc.

One cup to the men who fell round you,
The gallant, the brave and the true;
Another, to him who inspir'd you,
To conquer at Tippecanoe, etc.

At Thames, too, he spurn'd ev'ry danger
And planted the flag of the free,
The star-lighted flag of the ranger,
Where subjects had bended the knee, etc.

When war, with his battles was over,
With peace, he retir'd to his farm,
Where the culture of wheat, corn and clover,
For the hero, had life-giving charm, etc.

And when with his toils growing weary,
He'll turn to his comrades and share
A cup of old cider, so cheery,
Dispelling both languor and care, etc.

Let Van sport his coach and outriders,
In liveries flaunting and gay,
And *sneer* at log cabins and cider,
But, woe, for the reckoning day! etc.

"Parch'd corn" men can't stand it much longer;
Enough, is as much as we'll bear:
With Tip at our head, in October,
We'll tumble him out of the Chair.

Then ho!—for March 4th, forty-one, boys,
We'll shout, till the heaven's arch blue
Shall echo, hard cider and fun, boys,
Drink, drink to old Tippecanoe.

    We'll drink to old Tippecanoe,
    We'll drink to brave Tippecanoe,
    Shall echo—Hard cider and fun, boys,
    Drink—drink, to Old Tippecanoe,

THE HERO OF OHIO.

[Written for the Log Cabin lads and ladies, by a Log Cabin poet.]

TUNE, "*The Hunter's of Kentucky.*"

Come listen, lads and ladies, now,
　To my immortal story;
And, while you wreathe around his brow
　The garland of his glory,
The troubadour will sound a name
　That none will dare deny O,
Was first upon the field of fame,
　The hero of Ohio.
　Oh! Ohio,
　The hero of Ohio.

Fair Freedom's Father, Washington,
　Gave Harrison a station,
And said: "My boy, your father won
　A name in this great nation;
Go, battle for the fair and free,
　And on thy God rely, O;
And future fame shall welcome thee,
　The hero of Ohio,
　Oh! Ohio, etc.

Beloved by all his soldiers brave,
　Nor terrified by trifles;
For glory or a hero's grave,
　He met the Indian rifles;
Into the fight he fearless flew,
　Resolv'd the foe should fly, O;
And Congress crown'd at Tippecanoe,
　The Hero of Ohio,
　Oh! Ohio, etc.

'Mid British bayonets and flame,
　And savage thrusts and thumps, he
Beside the foremost phalanx came,
　The terror of Tecumseh;
And Proctor's life but seldom names,
　Without a curse or cry, O,
The day he dared, upon the Thames,
　The hero of Ohio,
　Oh! Ohio, etc.

His country he has nobly served,
　Both in the field and forum;
From truth or trust he never swerv'd
　Nor from a just decorum.

Like Cincinnatus, to the plow
  He keeps a steady eye, O;
And every one will hail him now,
  The Farmer of Ohio.
  Oh! Ohio, etc.

Bring laurels, lovely ladies, now,
  For he will guide the nation;
Bring garlands for his glorious brow,
  When he shall hold his station,
And let us hear the wild hurrah,
  From all the Western sky, O;
Hail, boys, with many a loud huzza,
  The Farmer of Ohio,
  Oh! Ohio, etc.

———

A TIP-TOP SONG ABOUT TIPPECANOE.

'Tis the tip of the fashion for brave hearts and true
To join in the shout for brave Tippecanoe;
The soldier, the farmer, the statesman, the friend,
Who fought at the Thames, and who lives at North
    Bend;
Who gathered his laurels where bravely they grew,
'Mid the slaughter and carnage of Tippecanoe,
            Tippecanoe, Tippecanoe,
  An honest old soldier is Tippecanoe.

No parasite he at the footstool of power,
To flatter and fawn for the rule of an hour,
All honor and manliness basely to smother
And avow it his glory to follow another;
Oh, no, for our hero is honest and true,
And the tip-top of honor is Tippecanoe,
            Tippecanoe, Tippecanoe,
  The tip-top of honor is Tippecanoe.

Though the frosts of old age may have whitened his
    brow,
Yet the light of his deeds round his temples will glow
Like the sun on a mountain, whose head in the sky
Receives the first snow on its summit so high,
But will show forth in majesty, beauty and light,
When the valleys below are all shrouded in night—
            Tippecanoe, Tippecanoe—
  And thus stands the soldier, bold Tippecanoe.

5*

Then join in the shout that has so loud gone forth,
From the East and the West, from the South and the
        North,
From the prairies and lakes to the briny blue sea,
The shout of the mighty, the bold and the free—
From the cold Granite State to warm generous Lou-
        isiana,
The shout of Tippecanoe,
                Tippecanoe, Tippecanoe,
        The tip of all tips is brave Tippecanoe.

THE BEST THING WE CAN DO.

Tune, "*Malbrouk*."

The times are bad and want curing,
They are getting past all enduring;
Let us turn out Martin Van Buren,
        And put in old Tippecanoe;
            The best thing we can do,
            Is to put in old Tippecanoe;
It's a business we all can take part in,
So let us give notice to Martin,
That he must get ready for starting,
        For we'll put in old Tippecanoe.

A change of the Administration
Will be for the good of the nation,
For it is now in a bad situation,
        So we'll put in old Tippecanoe.
            The best thing we can do,
            Is to put in old Tippecanoe.
And send the whole posse a packing,
Van Buren and all of his backing;
For we've tried them and found them all lacking,
        And we'll put in old Tippecanoe.

We've had of their humbugs a plenty,
For now all our pockets are empty;
 We've a dollar now, where we had twenty,
        So we'll put in old Tippecanoe.
            The best thing that we can do,
            Is to put in old Tippecanoe;
For their roguery can't be defended,
And it's time that their reign should be ended,
We shall never see times mended,
        'Till we put in old Tippecanoe.

Uncle Sam han't a cent in his purse now,
And matters are still growing worse now;
There's only one thing left for us now,
    It's to put in old Tippecanoe.
        The best thing that we can do,
        Is to put in old Tippecanoe.
For we are all of us going to ruin,
As long as we keep such a crew in,
So let us be up and a doing,
        And put in old Tippecanoe.

A JACKSON MAN'S SONG.

Come listen my trusty old cronies,
    I'll sing you a short verse or two,
And I know you would not be offended,
    Should I sing of Old Tippecanoe.

His enemies call him a coward,
    And sneer at his poverty too,
But a true-hearted Jackson man, never
    Will slander the brave and the true.

But a true-hearted Democrat, ever
    Will honor the brave and the true,
And leave it to British and Tories
    To slander old Tippecanoe.

And who, pray, is Martin Van Buren,
    What wonders did he ever do?
Was he in the battle of Orleans,
    Meigs, Thames or Old Tippecanoe?

Oh, no! he had no taste for fighting,
    Such rough work he never could do;
He shirked it off on the brave Jackson,
    And the hero of Tippecanoe.

This larkey we once have elected,
    Not that any good he would do,
But because he had been recommended
    By Jackson the brave and the true.

And since for one term we're in favor,
    We think that this honor should do;
So good-bye to you, Mr. Van Buren—
    Here goes for Old Tippecanoe.

BUCKEYE BOYS.

Tune, "*Swiss Boy.*"

Come, arouse ye, arouse ye, my brave Buckeye boys,
 Take the axe and to labor, away;
The sun is up with ruddy beam,
The Buckeye blooms beside the stream:
    Come, arouse ye, etc.

Love ye not, love ye not, O, my brave Buckeye boys,
 To the rally with Tippecanoe;
For the hero, patriot, brave and free,
Waits to assert your liberty.
    Love ye not, etc.

To the polls, to the polls, then my brave Buckeye
 boys,
 To the rescue, then haste ye away.
The cup we fill—the hard cider pass,
In friendship round, until the last;
With a shout, with a shout, go the brave Buckeye
 boys,
With old Tip to the White House away.

————

SONG FOR THE BOYS.

Tune, "*I Want To Be a Nun.*"

Now is it not a pity such a pretty lad as I,
Should be a Loco Foco to pine away and die?
  But I won't be for Van,
  No, I can't go for Van,
For I so love my country that I cannot go for Van.

I'm sure I cannot see what is there in the man,
That my father often tells me I must be for Van,
  But I can't go for Van,
  No, I won't go for Van,
I dislike the Loco Focos, and I cannot go for Van.

With the Locos I can't stay, it will never do for me,
So I'll go among the Whigs just to see what I can see;
  Now I will be a Whig,
  Now I shall be a Whig,
They cheer so much for Harrison, I must be a Whig.

I see among the Whigs the bone and sinew too,
They all are going to vote for Old Tippecanoe;
  So I now go for Tip,
  Yes I must go for Tip,
The things are in my heart and I will go for Tip.

They said the Loco Foco boys would make fun of me,
But they've all turned to Harrison and none can I see;
  Yes they all go for Tip,
  And now I'll go for Tip,
For he's the Boys' Candidate, and we all go for Tip.

My mother says she doesn't care if I am only true,
If I do leave the Vans, for Old Tippecanoe;
  For I like a canoe,
  And like a canoe,
And we'll sail it safe to Washington, you'll see what
  we will do.

So father don't be angry, but let your sonny be,
For the Vanites would not like such a Loco as me;
  For I don't go for Van,
  No I shan't go for Van,
I shall go for Henry Harrison, so help it if you can.

OLD FORT MEIGS.

Air, "*Oh! Lonely is the Forest Shade.*"

Oh! lonely is our old green fort,
 Where oft in days of old,
Our gallant soldiers bravely fought,
 'Gainst savage allies bold.
But with the change of years have past
 That unrelenting foe,
Since we fought here with Harrison,
 A long time ago.

It seems but yesterday I heard,
 From yonder thicket nigh,
Th' unerring rifle's sharp report,
 The Indians startling cry.
Yon brooklet winding at our feet,
 With crimson gore did flow,
When we fought here with Harrison,
 A long time ago.

The river rolls between its banks,
  As when of old we came;
Each grassy path, each shady nook,
  Seems to me still the same.
But we are scattered now, whose faith
  Pledg'd here through weal or woe,
With Harrison our soil to guard,
  A long time ago.

But many a soldier's lip is mute,
  And clouded many a brow,
And hearts that beat for honor then,
  Have ceased their throbbing now.
We ne'er shall meet again in life,
  As then we met, I trow,
When we fought here with Harrison,
  A long time ago.

———

PATRIOTIC SONG.

Air, "Ye Mariners of England."

Ye brave tars of Columbia,
  Her glory and her pride,
Who bear the sacred flag of stars
  Triumphant o'er the tide,
A cheer for him, while you fought
  Our bloody naval fights,
Took his stand on the land,
  As defender of her rights.
On many a field the firm, the strong
  Defender of her rights.

Old soldiers of Columbia,
  Who lingering yet, may tell
The horrors of a border war,
  And how your brothers fell?
Come, rally round your leader now,
  For justice now implores,
And proclaim to their shame,
  That his enemies are yours,
And 'twill be echoed loud and long,
  His enemies are yours.

Ye farmers of Columbia,
  Who till this Western soil,
Your broad and goodly heritage,
  Was gained through blood and toil.

Will ye be backward to defend,
　The name we have espoused?
No! At length, in their strength,
　Like a lion when aroused,
They'll come.　Awake the farmer's wrath
　A lion is aroused.

Ye freemen of Columbia,
　Who still in faith esteem
The charter of your fathers' blood,
　Would ye that faith redeem?
In Macedonian phalanx form,
　In one unbroken band,
And they'll beat a retreat,
　The despoilers of the land—
Sub-treasurers, Levellers, and all
　The spoilers of the land.

The true son of Columbia!
　We bring him now before
The people, with his services
　Of forty years or more;
Unstain'd—untouch'd—to his reward,
　To save the country's fall.
Let us rise, for the prize
　Is the dearest right of all—
A free and healthy government,
　The dearest right of all.

————

TIPPECANOE AND JACKETS OF BLUE.

TUNE, "*Ye Sons of Columbia.*"

The good ship of State is driven ashore,
The thunder howls round us, and dark tempests low'r;
The sea is fast rising—and breaks in the bay,
And the hearts of the boldest are filled with dismay,
She will founder unless with true patriot zeal,
We get rid of the *lubber* who stands at the wheel!
And take a *new* pilot, whose heart is *true blue*—
And such we shall find in old Tippecanoe.

Old "Tip" is a hero, brave, honest and true,
Who deserves the esteem of the jackets of Blue.
His bosom so free from intrigue, guile or art,
Is the shrine of that treasure, a patriot's heart.
Besides, if we turn over his log we shall find
A foe to oppression—a friend to mankind.

What say ye then sailors—ye jackets of blue,
Shall we choose as our pilot, Old Tippecanoe?

He has fought for our rights, and in peace he has
       shown   .
That in State navigation he's second to none,
His soul with true " live oak grit " is imbued,
He is worth to stand where a Washington stood.
Then give him the tiller—when he steps on deck
His firmness and wisdom wlll save us from wreck.
Then summon him, tars! shout jackets of blue,
" Oh, haste to our rescue, Old Tippecanoe!"

Had he lived in a country where merit is known,
And rewarded by pensions and praise, or a throne,
Wealth, power and fame would have been his just
       meed,
And an humble "log hut" would have ne'er shel-
       tered his head.
But his nature is noble, his worth stands confessed,
The son of Virginia, the pride of the West.
Come on, then, my hearties, ye jackets of blue,
And salute with nine huzzas, Old Tippecanoe.

ON! TO VICTORY!!

Tune, "Scots We Wha."

Whigs! whose sires for freedom bled,
Whigs! whom patriots oft have led,
Whigs! by the " treasury spoils" unfed,
       On, to victory!

" Now's the day, and now's the hour,"
See approach the tyrant's power!
Shall we to the tyrants cower?
       Shall we turn and flee?

Hear the foe's insulting cry,
Hear him boast of triumph nigh;
Whigs! that boasting do defy,
       We shall still be free.

What care we though others yield,
Here's our chosen battle field;
Grasp the sword and brace the shield,
       On, to victory!

Rally, Whigs! in freedom's cause,
Fight for liberty and laws!
Falter not, nor turn, nor pause,
    Till each State is free.

Gallant Harrison leads us on,
America's accepted son;
Think of former triumphs won—
    On, to victory!

GOLD SPOONS vs. HARD CIDER.

In a cabin made of logs,
    By the river side,
There the Honest Farmer lives,
    Free from sloth and pride,
To the gorgeous palace turn,
    And his rival see,
In his robes of regal state
    Tinsell'd finery.

At the early morning light,
    Starting with the sun—
See the farmer hold the plow
    'Till the day is done.
In his silken bed of down
    Martin still must be;
Menial servants waiting 'round,
    Dress'd in livery,

See the farmer to his meal
    Joyfully repair;
Crackers, cheese, and cider too,
    A hard but homely fare.
Martin to his breakfast comes
    At the hour of noon;
Sipping from a china cup,
    With a golden spoon.

See the farmer pace his fields—
    Mark his lightsome foot;
Leaning now upon his staff
    To catch a songster's note.
Martin's steeds impatient wait
    At the palace door;
Outriders behind the coach
    And lackies on before.

OH, MATTY VAN, MY JO, MAT.

TUNE, "*John Anderson*," *etc.*

O, Matty Van, my Jo, Mat! I wonder what you mean,
By such a naughty act as that which lately has been seen?
What want you with an army, Mat? Ah, why do you do
      so?
'Twill march you back to Kinderhook! Oh, Matty Van,
      my Jo.

Oh, Van Buren, my Jo, Van, you've climb'd the hill o'
      State,
And monie a cunnin' trick, man, was fathered in your
      pate;
But now your tottering down, Van; how rapidly you go,
You'll soon be sprawling at the fit; oh, Matty Van, my
      Jo.

Oh, Matty Van, my Jo, Mat, when first we were acquaint,
'Tis true you were not slow, Mat, with sinner or with
      saint;
But now you have grown ould, Mat, you never seem to
      know
How fast you're goin' "bock agen," Oh, Matty Van, my Jo.

Oh, Van Buren, my Jo, Van, when Jackson ruled the hour,
And took you up behind him, Van, and left you with his
      power,
You promised us to follow in his footsteps, as you know,
And pit your fit in hero's tracks, Oh, Van Buren, my Jo.

Oh, Matty Van, my Jo, Mat, his faith you did abuse,
For it's not in your nature, Mat, to wear a hero's shoes;
So step you just aside, Mat, Old Tip is on your toe,
Old Tip, a hero ready made; Oh, Matty Van, my Jo.

YOUNG MEN'S NATIONAL CONVENTION.

Lo! as the gathering throng appear,
How huge the volume opened here
      Of human life!
Where'er the various banners lead,
Around them every heart we read
      With hope is rife.
All these of freemen's rights are proud,
And to redeem these rights this crowd
      Is borne along.

Oh, what shall stay them in their might,
When they do battle for the right,
  Confiding, strong!

Gay music floats upon the air,
And scarf and sash are flaunting there,
  And banners high;
Fair hands the snowy kerchief raise,
Bright eyes from hall and window gaze,
  And balcony.
No idle pomp they came to fill,
No sycophantic throng to swell
  Of pageantry;
Scepter and crown to none they yield,
For e'en the humbled in the field
  Was majesty.

The Monumental city led
Its honored guests, and next the head
  Followed the State.
Where, let the storm of ill that blows
Prostrate all else, yet virtue grows
  Beneath its weight;*
Now Bunker Hill, with fife and drum,
Moves on; yes, " Birnam wood has come
  To Dunsinane."   .
Ill-used, ill-gotten power take heed!
For thus the augury we read,
  Or read in vain.

Two victor States take up the word,
And then New York's deep voice is heard
  In thund'ring peal:
Mute in the ranks, but undismayed,
New Jersey sternly there displayed
  Her own broad seal.
Room! for the Keystone State draws near
Room! for unconquered Delaware,
  The Bayard's home.
Warm-hearted Maryland, we greet
Thee next—and mayst thou ever meet
  Thine own welcome!

Disfranchised, but not o'erborne,
Nor wholly from the Union torn,
  Triumvirate.
Though in no *vote*, thou can'st rejoice,

---

* "Crescit sub pondere virtas," was the New Hampshire motto.

Yet, in the contest let thy *voice*
        Still animate.
Birth-place of hero and of sage,
Which from the nation's earliest age
        Has borne command,
In thee, unless bright omens fail,
Another President shall hail
        His native land !

Here Georgia and the Carolinas
Send forth from out their sterling mines,
        A gallant band.
And mountaineers, a valiant train,
Follow their neighbors of the plain
        With ready hand.
Undaunted Tennessee draws near
With sable badges of the bier
        And mournful tread;
For Cincinnatus now her voice,
The second Roman of her choice—
        The first is dead.

A standard bears a single name!
No eulogy can swell the fame
        Of "Henry Clay"—*
That name exerts a magic part,
And over many a noble heart
        Holds silent sway.
No thought of self comes o'er his mind,
His only effort is to bind
        The broken laws.
And when at stake his country's weal,
He forwards with a gen'rous zeal,
        His rivals cause.

Still onward sweeps the vast array,
And onward holds its lengthened way,
        The hero's State.
His banner waving at their head,
They follow on with lightsome tread
        And hearts elate.
All, all are here—the West and South,
The hardy East, and rugged North,
        In numbers strong,
Nor will they lay in rest the spear
Until upon their lips we hear
        The victor's song.

---

*"Tanto nomine nullum par eulogium."

LONG LIVE THE KING.

Long live Van-Kinderhook!
Magician, wizard, witch, or spook!
      Long live King Martin!
May he triumphantly
Reign o'er such slaves as we,
The Tory's joy to be—
      Long live the King!

On! Kendall, Blair, arise!
Seatter his enemies,
      Long live King Martin!
Confound Whig politics,
Frustrate their trait'rous tricks,
On him our hopes we fix,
      Long live the King!

UNION COUNTY CABIN SONG.

TUNE, "*Pennsylvania Quick Step.*"

Our fathers in the days of yore
  Were resting in their wildwood home
When the trumpet's clang and the cannon's roar
  Came booming from the briny foam.
And many a stately bark and high,
  And many a gallant legion came;
And every soldier's battle-cry
  Was "Charge for glorious England's name."

But soon the seal of Freedom's trust,
  Her starry flag began to shine;
And many a Britom bit the dust
  At Bunker Hill and Brandywine;
And quickly passed the strife of death,
  And soon was victory's garland won,
And Freedom bound the glorious wreath
  Upon the brow of Washington.

Again they rested in their fame
  Till many a new State round them rose;
Again the host of England came,
  And the stormy sound of battle rose.
Again the wreath of victory
  On many a battle-field was won,
And Freedom bound it gloriously
  Upon the brow of Harrison.

And now this green and glorious land
  Is with distress and ruin fraught,
And desolation, by the hand
  Of its despotic ruler wrought.
And Freedom, by her falling fame,
  And by her scorned and broken laws,
Adjures her patriot sons again
  To rally in her sacred cause.

They come, they come, they will not stay,
  Their glorious march is just begun;
Around their flag the sunbeams play,
  And their leader's name is Harrison.
He calls his comrades true and tried,
  He calls them from their wilwood home;
He calls, and instant to his side
  The inmates of the cabins come.

And like the lawless king of old
  Who feasted in his gorgeous halls,
The oppressor's righteous doom is scrolled
  And 'graven on the palace walls.
His hour is come; his trembling throng
  Of paid and pensioned minions flee,
And many a wildwood cabin song
  Shall his resounding requiem be.

GEN. WILLIAM HENRY HARRISON.

'Tis not for martial glory,
  For battles bravely won,
Fit theme for song and story,
  We laud his name alone;
But for the noble and the pure,
  In *every station* tried,
And ever constant to endure
  A guardian and a guide.

True, that we feel as proudly
  Our *soldier's* honest fame,
True—we dare speak as loudly,
  All honor to the name.
But yet a closer tie must bind,
  When peace proclaims her reign,
The will to aid and bless mankind—
  And this *is his* gain.

What though with malice daring,
  Detraction's darts are cast;
His calm, sublime forbearing,
  Shall vindicate the past,
Those who'd thus *disgrace their land*,
  Are found in ev'ry age,
Not e'en our Washington, could stand
  Untouched by *party rage.*

His country's voice hath spoken
  Her gratitude and trust;
And his deeds have been a token
  That the confidence was just.
And when that voice again is heard,
  May its shouts of triumph be,
That the *people's friend* hath been preferred,
  And is *first among the free.*

WHEN BRITISH BANDS.

TUNE, "*Who'll Be King but Charley.*"

When British bands invade our land
And savage hosts so dreary,
Young Harrison, he was the man
To draw his sword so early.
    Come hither, come hither, around him gather,
    Come Whig and Democrat all together,
    Unite your bands and firmly stand
    For him who fought bravely.

With brave Kentucky's gallant sons,
With Owen and brave Davies;
He led the van 'gainst savage bands
And routed them so clearly.
    Come hither, etc.

And when proud Britain's cannon roar'd
He never beat a parley,
His sword and shield made Proctor yield,
And whipped him out so fairly,
    Come hither, etc.

There's Martin Van with all his clan
Of demagogues and knavery,
Old Tip can scan their secret plan
And ferret them out so clearly.
    Come hither, etc.

From sordid gold to him untold
He freed his hand so clearly,
His door-latch string he ne'er pulled in
The poor he fed most freely.
    Come hither, come hither, around him gather,
    Come Whig and Democrat altogether,
    Old Tip's the man who will defend
    The rights we bought so dearly.

GRAND NATIONAL WHIG SONG.

" In the strength of your might from each mountain and
    valley,"
    Sons of Freedom, arise! the time is at hand—
Around liberty's standard, we'll rally, we'll rally;
    The star-spangled banner floats over the land.

Then let the proud eagle spread his wings wide asunder,
    And burst from the trammels which strive to enchain
" If we rise in our strength, if we speak but in thunder"
    The bit of "strip'd bunting" will flourish again.

For our rights and our laws, we'll stand firm and united;
    The blood of our father's shall ne'er be forgot—
The faith and the honor they sacredly plighted,
    Shall never be tarnished by Anarchy's blot;
Around liberty's standard, we'll rally, we'll rally—
    Old Tippecanoe, boys, the watch-word shall be;
Its echo will thunder from each mountain and valley
    Of the home of the brave—the land of the free.

OLD TIP AND THE LOG-CABIN BOYS.

TUNE, "*Low Down in Old Virginy, Long Time Ago.*"

    When the frontier was in danger,
        Long time ago,
    Young Harrison, to fear a stranger,
        Long time ago,
    Left the scenes of ease and splendor,
        Long time ago,
    To the log cabins aid to render,
        Long time ago.

    With his hunting shirt and rifle,
    In his pocket but a trifle,

With Old Wayne he marched to the forest
And shared his wallet with the poorest.

At the Rapids they fought the savage band,
And whipped them tomahawk in hand,
Mad Anthony praised the gallant boy,
And the cabins rung with a shout of joy.

And when again the war-whoop rang
And the cabin boys to their rifles sprang,
They called again to lead them on
Their gallant leader Harrison.

They met the foe at Tippecanoe,
And again he made the savage rue.
Again with joy the cabins rung,
And his name with grateful praise they sung.

Then Britain dared our flag to assail,
And again the Indian took the trail,
Again the cabins were in mourning
And every eye to him was turning.

He drew once more his faithful sword
And gave the cabin boys the word,
At Thames they laid Tecumseh low
And captured Proctor's army too.

Then Britain saw and felt 'twas vain,
Her gallant soldiers' blood to drain;
Her treasures were in vain expended,
Whilst Old Tip the cabins defended.

Peace again its blessings spread
Beneath the humble cabins shed,
Danger no more its hopes alarm,
With gratitude all hearts were warm.

Old Tip shook hands with the boys once more,
And told them open stood his door,
That welcome they should always be,
And the latch-string always outside see.

Long years rolled round and the cabins flour-
ished,
Their liberties they dearly cherished,
No more alarmed by savage foes
The forest blossomed like the rose.

At length there rose up in the land
A numerous and thriving band,
They stole the fruits of honest toil,
And claimed them as their lawful spoil.

The office-holders stole the treasure,
And then absconded at their leisure,
The honest cabin boys they jeered at,
And their cabins and hard cider sneered at.

The cabins then became oppress'd,
Hard times the boys opprest.
They sought relief as they had done
From Government, but they found none.

Van Buren led the spoilers on
Against the cabins old Tip had won,
He rolled by in his English coach,
And told the boys "they asked too much."

Then from every hill, and every valley,
The cabin boys began to rally,
They raised one everlasting shout,
And swore the spoilsmen should turn out.

They called again their brave old chief,
Who had always sprung to their relief;
With him in command they feared no dangers,
For he and defeat were total strangers.

They knew he had whipped the Indian foe,
And he had licked the British too,
He could'nt be scared by the Treasury frogs,
And he'd whip Van Buren and his dogs.

Old Tip's in the field, and the boys around him,
The office-holders try to confound him,
But the shout of the boys does thunder resemble,
And Martin and his hirelings tremble.

On the fourth of March little Van will run,
And the cabin boys will laugh at the fun,
They'll place old Tip at the head of the nation,
And have a thundering jollification.

Three cheers for the old log cabin's friend!
The cabin boys on him depend,
In English coaches he's no rider,
But he could fight and drink hard cider.

HARK! THEY COME!

[Sung at the National Convention of Young Men in Baltimore.]

Hark! hark! from the west of the mountains,
  A voice from the log cabin crew,
Who drink at the hard cider fountain,
  And fought under Tippecanoe—
  And fought, etc.
Who cultivate orchards and cornfields,
Defended by Tippecanoe.
  Heretofore, all the money we needed,
    From pork, corn and flour we drew,
  All raised from the soil we defended,
    When under brave Tippecanoe—
    When under, etc.
  From soil we've subdu'd by our labor,
  Since led by Old Tippecanoe.

From this soil we've fed the lov'd Buckeye,
  And Hoosier, and Sucker babes too;
Rejoicing 'twas parceled to suit us,
  By schemes of Old Tippecanoe—
  By schemes, etc.
Parcel'd out to suit log cabin farmers;
By the efforts of Tippecanoe.
  But now at sub-treasury prices,
    Our taxes we'll never get through
  Till we call our friend to assist us,
    That led us at Tippecanoe—
    That led us, etc.
With whom we beat British and Indians,
At Thames, Meigs, and Tippecanoe.

He's good in the field and the council,
  The plow he wields skilfully too,
As well as to portion to farmers,
  And conquer at Tippecanoe—
  And conquer, etc.
In whom may we be so confiding,
As our friend, Old Tippecanoe.
  From Eastward, and Northward, and South-
    ward,
    Come join us in what we will do;
  We'll pull at the string of the cabin,
    That's knotted, by Tippecanoe—
    That's knotted, etc.
  Old soldiers will always be welcom'd
  By warm-hearted Tippecanoe.

Lo! Eastward, and Northward, and Southward,
  In thunder they echo—we, too,
Will call on the hard cider farmer,
  That conquer'd at Tippecanoe—
  That conquer'd, etc.
We'll greet the old log-cabin farmer,
And vote for brave Tippecanoe.
See! onward! en masse, they're moving
  In earthquake voice uttering halloo!
For the White House exchange the log cabin,
    Thou hero of Tippecanoe—
    Thou hero, etc.
For thee the White House we've determined
O hasten, Old Tippecanoe.

Hark! hark! how the American ladies,
  In cabins and palaces too,
Are joining in song with their lovers,
  Huzza for old Tippecanoe—
  Huzza for, etc.
They sing in sweet strains to their lovers,
Go vote for brave Tippecanoe.
  From city, and forest, and mountain,
    And likewise Western prairies too,
  Each man will respond to his mistress,
    And vote for old Tippecanoe—
    And vote, etc.
  Then send forth a tone like an earthquake,
  Huzza for Old Tippecanoe!

SONG.

Tune, *"Life Let Us Cherish."*

  For life let us cherish
The fame of honored Harrison,
  And never perish
    The laurels he won.

The spoils engrossing ravenous band
Have desolated all the land,
  They glean their spoils from all its soils,
    And honest labor foils.

    So let us cherish
  The fame of honored Harrison,
    And never perish
      The laurels he won.

Though clouds obscure the atmosphere,
And ruin threatens everywhere,
  Yet down the storm rides swift reform,
  And honest hearts grow warm.
      So let us cherish, etc.

New hopes inspire our hearts with glee,
Our offspring ever shall be free,
  For dread alarm, like magic's charm,
  Benumbs the spoiler's arm.
      So let us cherish, etc.

To rescue, now comes Harrison,
His strength's a mighty garrison,
  His growing weight in every State,
  Predicts Van Buren's fate.
      So let us cherish, etc.

WHEN THIS OLD HAT WAS NEW.

When this old hat was new, the people used to say,
The best among the Democrats were Harrison and Clay;
The Locos now assume the name, a title most untrue,
And most unlike their party name when my old hat was
    new.

When my old hat was new, Van Buren was a Fed,
An enemy to every man who labored for his bread;
And if the people of New York have kept their records
    true,
He voted 'gainst the poor man's rights, when my old hat
    was new.

When my old hat was new, Buchanan was the man
Best fitted in the Keystone State to lead the Federal clan,
He swore "if Democratic blood should make his veins look
    blue,
He'd cure them by phlebotomy," when my old hat was
    new.

When my old hat was new ('twas eighteen hundred eleven),
Charles Ingersoll did then declare by all his hopes of
    Heaven,
" Had he been able to reflect, he'd been a Tory true,
And ne'er have thought it a reproach," when my old hat
    was new.

When my old hat was new, of Richard Rush 'twas said,
To figure well among the Feds he wore a black cockade;
Deny this Locos, if you please, for every word is true,
I knew full well old Dicky Rush, when my old hat was
    new.

When my old hat was new, the Senator from Maine,
Destroyed by fire an effigy, to immortalize his name.
The effigy was Madison's, if common fame be true,
So Reuel Williams was a Fed, when my old hat was new.

When my old hat was new, 'twas in the Granite State,
That Henry Hubbard asked each town to send a delegate
To meet in council at the time when Federalism blue
Made Hartford look like Indigo, when my old hat was new.

When my old hat was new, Sam Cushman did declare
"That should a soldier cross the lines he hoped he'd perish
    there,
And leave his bones in Canada for enemies to view,"
So much for his Democracy, when my old hat was new.

When my old hat was new, old Governor Provost·
The States invaded at the head of numerous British hosts,
Then mark, ye Locos, what did Martin Chittenden then
    do?
Forbid Green Mountain boys to fight, when my old hat
    was new.

When this old hat was new, Woodbury and Van Ness,
E. Allen Brown, and Stephen Haight, were of the Federal
    mess,
A. H. Everett, Martin Field, and Sam C. Allen, too,
Now patent Democrats, were Feds, when my old hat was
    new.

When my old hat was new, these worthies did oppose
The cause, and friends of liberty, and stood among their
    foes,
Not so with "**Granny**" Harrison, for at Tippecanoe,
He bravely fought the savage foe, when my old hat was
    new.

When my old hat was new, the friends of liberty
Knew well the merits of Old Tip, while fighting at Mau-
    mee;
Come, now, huzza for Harrison, just as we used to do,
When first we heard of Proctor's fall, when my old hat
    was new.

LIBERTY CABIN RAISING.

[Sung at the Log Cabin Raising, Annapolis.]

TUNE, "*Rosin the Bow.*"

Come on, ye firm Whigs of old Crawford,
  And all ye true Democrats too;
Come up, for old Liberty's raising
  A cabin for Tippecanoe.

There you'll find many raisers from Whetstone
  And a few from Sandusky, too,
For the people's determined on raising
  A cabin for Tippecanoe.

Bucyrus will furnish her twenties,
  And Chatfield her dozen or two,
And Cranberry 'll help at the raising,
  A cabin for Tippecanoe.

Holmes claims a share in the building
  Which she has a good right to do;
And she'll send up her hands to the raising
  A cabin for Tippecanoe.

And when we have finish'd the building
  We'll call for one speech or two,
From those who have help'd at the raising
  A cabin for Tippecanoe.

———

A NEW SONG.

AIR, "*Star Spangled Banner.*"

[Sung at the annual election for Charter Officers in the city of Pittsburgh.]

Oh! who does not see, in this heart-cheering ray,
  That pierces the cloud of malign domination,
A sign, that foretells with precision, the day
  When Columbia shall rise from her low degradation,
When the spoil-hunting race shall be foiled in the chase,
The Kinderhook quack hide his head in disgrace,
  And the starry Whig banner triumphantly wave
  " O'er the land of the free and the home of the brave."

O'er the city of Pitt, 'mid the eagle's own hills,
  Where many a patriot bosom is burning,
What is that which gives Tories such horrible chills,
  And to which all Whig-eyes are in "fine frenzy" turn-
      ing?

Say, what is that sight which fills Van with affright,
And makes all his vassals the nether lip bite?
 'Tis the Harrison banner! and soon 'twill be waved
 O'er a whole State redeem'd, o'er a great nation saved.

All hail the proud Keystone—she fired the first gun
 For the old " Declaration " blood seal'd by the martyr;
And now she is first to declare for the son
 Of the sire, whose own hand sign'd that dear cherish'd
  charter.
Her first gun has roar'd for the hero, whose sword
Sprang quick from the scabbard and ne'er was restored
 Till victory smiled—for though brave men oft yield,
 He never surrender'd, he ne'er lost a field.

Let the Swartwouts and Prices, who, year after year,
 Have fed on " the spoils " and wax'd rich on our treas-
  ure,
At Harrison's " poverty " throw out the sneer,
 And heap on the vet'ran abuse without measure:
The wretch that defames, does but strengthen the claims
Of the hero of Tippecanoe and the Thames,
 And freshen the laurels, which none sought to bruise,
 'Till 'twas found that their greenness gave Martin the
  blues.

GRAND NATIONAL WHIG SONG.

[Written for Henry Russell, by Henry John Sharpe.—Dedicated to the
Whigs of the whole Republic.]

" In the strength of your might, from each mountain and
 valley,".
Sons of freedom, arise! the time is at hand—
Around liberty's standard, we'll rally, we'll rally,
The star-spangled banner floats over the land;
Then let the proud eagle spread his wings wide asunder,
And burst from the trammels which strive to enchain—
" If we rise in our strengh, if we speak but in thunder,"
The "bit of strip'd bunting" will flourish again.

For our rights and our laws we'll stand firm and united,
The blood of our father's shall ne'er be forgot—
The faith and the honor which they sacredly plighted,
Shall never be tarnished by anarchy's blot;
Around liberty's standard let ev'ry Whig rally.
" Old Tippecanoe " boys, the watchword shall be!
Its echo will thunder from each mountain and valley
Of the"home of the brave! the land of the free!"

OLD TIPPECANOE.

AIR, "*When Britain's Oppression, Her Laws,*" etc.

Come, rouse up! ye bold hearted Whigs of Kentucky,
 And show the nation what deeds you can do:
The high-road to victory lies open before ye.
 While led to the charge by old Tippecanoe.

When Indians were scalping our friends and our brothers,
 To Ohio's frontier he gallantly flew;
And thousands of innocent infants and mothers,
 Were saved by the valor of Tippecanoe.

When savage Tecumseh was rallying his forces,
 In innocents blood his hands to imbrue;
Our hero despis'd all his bloody associates,
 And won the proud name of "Old Tippecanoe."

And when this Tecumseh and his brother, Proctor,
 To capture Fort Meigs—their utmost did do;
Our gallant old hero again play'd the doctor,
 And gave them a dose like at Tippecanoe.

And then on the Thames, on the fifth of October,
 Where musket balls whizz'd as they flew;
He blasted their prospects, and rent them asunder,
 Just like he had done on the Tippecanoe.

Let Greece praise the deeds of her great Alexander,
 And Rome boast of Cæsar and Scipio too;
Just like Cincinnatus, that noble commander,
 Is our old hero of Tippecanoe.

For when the foes of his country no longer could harm
   her,
 To the shades of retirement he quickly withdrew;
And now at North Bend see the HONEST OLD FARMER,
 Who won the green laurel at Tippecanoe.

And when to the national council elected,
 The good of his country still see him pursue;
And every poor man by him thus protected,
 Should ever remember "Old Tippecanoe."

Let *knaves* call him "coward," and *fools* call him "*granny*"
 To answer their *purpose*—this never will do;
When rallied around him, we'll route *little Vanny*,
 And give him a Thames—or a full *Waterloo*.

The Republican banner of freedom is flying,
    The eagle of liberty soars in your view;
Then rally my hearties—all slanders defying,
    And thunder huzza! for "Old Tippecanoe;"

Among the supporters of brave General Jackson,
    There are many Republicans, honest and true;
To such we say "come out from among them,"
    And "go it for Tyler and Tippecanoe."

HARRISON AND LIBERTY.

TUNE, "*Jefferson and Liberty.*"

From Mississippi's utmost shore,
    To cold New Hampshire's piney hills;
From broad Atlantic's sullen roar,
    To where the western ocean swells,
How loud the notes of joy arise
    From every bosom warm and free!
How strains triumphant fill the skies.

Turn to the scroll, where patriot sires
    Your Independence did declare,
Whose words still glow like living fires—
    His father's name is written there.
That father taught that son to swear
    His country ne'er enslaved should be;
Then lend your voices to the air
    For Harrison and Liberty.

O'er savage foes, who scourged our land,
    When Wayne so wild and madly burst,
Among his brave and gallant band
    The youthful Harrison was first.
And when on Wabash's leafy banks,
    Tecumseh's warriors gathered free;
How swift they fled before the ranks
    Of Harrison and Liberty!

When Meigs' Heights, his army held,
    And haughty Britons circled round,
His conquering legion's cleared the field,
    While notes of triumph pealed around;
And though on Thames' tide again
    His progress Proctor sought to stay,
Dismayed he fled; and left the plain
    To Harrison and Liberty!

Now honored be his hoary age
   Who glory for his country won:
Shout for the hero, patriot, sage,
   For William Henry Harrison:
Of all our chiefs he oftenest fought,
   But never lost a victory,
And peace was gain'd and plenty brought
   By Harrison and Liberty!

A HYMN.

TUNE, "*New Durham.*"

Hark! through the land a doleful sound!
   Our ears attend the cry;
Ye living Whigs come view the ground
   Where your oppressors lie.

Great Van, with thousand twenty-five,
   Rides in his English coach,
While all the menials in his hive
   Still urge him to encroach.

Their numbers hungry legions are,
   A hundred thousand told,
Whose daily cries assail our ear,
   "Oh! give us, give us gold."

And yet amidst this golden shower,
   All trades do prostrate fall;
The gold and silver, paper power,
   Van keeps and uses all.

Our cotton sells for half its cost;
   Our wheat lies up in store;
Our tools are all laid by to rust,
   We cannot use them more.

The great ones, too, who rule our State,
   (Obedient to Van's frown),
Have hurried on the pressing weight,
   And crush'd us fairly down!

And is there for these blighting ills,
   No healing balm or cure?
No remedy but quackery's pills?
   No physic which is pure?

There is. Send men to legislate
  Who are not demagogues,
Who work, and think, not those who prate,
  Or howl, or croak like frogs.

Tom Corwin place in the first chair,
  To guard and to advise;
And banish all who have a share,
  In the foul frauds and lies.

Lo! see, near yon log-cabin pile,
  Just weary from his plow,
(While his good dame, with placid smile,
  Sits milking of her cow):

There sits the man, upright and pure
  Who will the laws rescue;
Will all our rights guard, and secure
  The Hero of Tippecanoe.

Give him your votes, ye freemen all,
  And stop Van Buren's games;
And run, ye spoilsmen, one and all,
  Like Proctor at the Thames.

Then, when the busy hum, once more,
  Shall make the welkin sound,
When Harrison and Tyler soar,
  We'll pass hard cider round.

LOG CABIN DEDICATION.

Our cabin now we dedicate,
            Hurrah, hurrah, hurrah!
To Harrison, the good and great,
            Hurrah, hurrah, hurrah!
We've rolled the logs up straight and true
And columns made of buckeye, too,
    Hurrah, hurrah, hurrah, hurrah, hurrah, hurrah.

For cabins erst our hero fought,
            Hurrah, hurrah, hurrah.
And to their firesides safely brought,
            Hurrah, hurrah, hurrah
Did freely every danger brave
Our own beloved West, to save,
            Hurrah, hurrah, hurrah.

He beat our foes upon the Thames,
               Hurrah, hurrah, hurrah.
Then settled on his farm again,
               Hurrah, hurrah, hurrah.
There by his plow content he lives,
And to the needy freely gives,
               Hurrah, hurrah, hurrah.

But hark! the cabins sound alarm,
               Hurrah, hurrah, hurrah.
They groan beneath the oppressor's arm,
               Hurrah, hurrah, hurrah,
They call on Harrison the brave,
From tyrant power their rights to save,
               Hurrah, hurrah, hurrah,
Cabin boys, then onward stand,
               Hurrah, hurrah, hurrah,
Rescue your misgoverned land,
               Hurrah, hurrah, hurrah.
Come to the work, press bravely on,
And "shoulder arms" for Harrison,
               Hurrah, hurrah.

THE WHIG BALL.

[Annapolis Tippecanoe Club, Aug. 18, 1840.]

Hail to the ball which in grandeur advances,
  Long life to the yeomen who urge it along;
The abuse of our hero his worth but enhances;
  Then welcome his triumphs with shout and with song.
      The Whig ball is moving!
      The Whig ball is moving!

See that light in the South and the West that's dispelling,
  The dark cloud that hangs o'er our once favored land,
Let us hail it with joy, while our ball we're propelling,
And firm in our purpose as honest Whigs stand.
      The Whig ball is moving!
      The Whig ball is moving!
Then let ev'ry true Whig with shoulder to shoulder,
  Give speed to the ball and that light wider spread,
'Tis a duty we owe to our father's who molder
  'Neath the sod where they fought—the sod
    Where they bled.
      The Whig ball is moving!
      The Whig ball is moving!

They were feeble in number, were weak in resources,
　Yet they won and they left us the boon, liberty.
Let us vow to maintain it, in spite of Van's forces,
　And teach panders and place-men that Whigs will be
　　free!
　　　　The Whig ball is moving!
　　　　The Whig ball is moving!

Yes, Whigs will be free, and the liberty dear,
　Which their fathers bequeathed them they'll jealously
　　tend.
And the charm in the wand of the Kinderhook seer,
　They'll dissolve by their shouts for the sage of North
　　Bend.
　　　　The Whig ball is moving!
　　　　The Whig ball is moving!

A SONG.

Tune, "*The Bonnets of Blue.*"

Here's a health to Tippecanoe!
　Here's a shout for Tippecanoe!
And he that won't drink to the pride of North Bend,
　Is neither a wise one nor true;
It's good for the people to rule;
　It's base to be fed by the few;
It's good to stand for the popular choice;
　Then shout for Old Tippecanoe!

Hurrah for old Tippecanoe!
　Hurrah for old Tippecanoe!
It's good to cheer him who has often cheer'd us;
　Then shout for old Tippecanoe!
Here's a health to Tippecanoe!
　Here's a shout for Tippecanoe!
Here's a health to the Chief who was never yet beat;
　Three rounds for the honest and true!

Here's luck to the hand that will toil !
　Here's luck to the seed that is sown !
Who's a poor man himself is a friend of the poor,
　And values their rights as his own.
Then shout for old Tippecanoe !
　Hurrah for old Tippecanoe !
It's time to turn out all the profligate herd,
　And put in *Old Tippecanoe!*

THE GATHERING SONG.

They're rousing, they're rousing in valley and glen,
  The noble in soul, and the fearless in heart;
At freedom's stern call, to the combat again
  They rush with a zeal she alone can impart.

From wild Madawaska's dark forest of pine,
  To the far fertile glades where the calm Wabash flows,
True sons of their fathers! The people combine
  To shake off the chains of their tyrants and foes.

They're gath'ring, they're gath'ring, on hill side and plain,
  They warm every vale and o'ershadow each river,
Each hamlet and dale is made vocal again,
  With the soul-thrilling cry of "Our Country Forever !"

The flag of the free to the breeze is unfurl'd,
  Around it they rally to guard its fair fame;
And well may the foes of corruption be bold,
  In the glory and strength of their Harrison's name.

Where the noble Ohio in wild beauty sweeps;
  Where the swift Susquehanna bears onward its waves,
And e'en where the Hudson in calm grandeur sleeps,
  There are thousands of freemen who scorn to be slaves.

Arouse then, true hearts! to the battle once more!
  And the spoilers shall quail at your gallant array!
Despair fades behind us—Hope's morn dawns before!
  It will brighten full soon to a shadowless day.

A LOG CABIN LYRIC.

Sons of freedom, awake! your wild slogan is pealing,
And hark to the voice of prophetic revealing,
If ye sleep on in peace—if ye rouse not the nation,
And fight as of yore for your country's salvation;
Then the lightnings of freedom forever are clouded,
And her war-shiver'd fanes shall in darkness be shrouded.

Lo! the Genius of Union from her airy flight stooping;
Flings the mists of the clouds from her swift pinion swoop-
    ing ;
And the roll of her war cry our foes is appalling,
As her oft shielded sons to her rescue she's calling.
Rouse! lovers of law—of your rights—and of nation,
E'er ye mourn in the dust of your own desolation.

Look! see ye not on your mountains now gleaming,
The watch-fires of liberty brightly there beaming?
Stay not to hail the first beams of to-morrow,
Ye may read by its light naught but trouble and sorrow,
For the fire-cross has sped over valley and plain,
And the clans of Columbia are summoned again.

And the king bird glares fierce through the dim, misty
        morning,
As the flash of his keen arrowy glance is discovering,
Where creeps those vile vipers who his eyrie entwining,
Dared to blot with their slime a fair star-gem there shining.
And his crest glows more bright, as he proudly deriding,
The hiss of these reptiles on the tempest is riding.

See! the stars in our flag shed no longer a ray,
For they mourn their bright sister torn ruthless away,
In honor no more shall they float o'er the main,
'Till New Jersey's lost Pleiade shall be hailed there again.
Oh! why did they snatch her fair gem from its station,
And alone leave the stripe of her own degradation?
        Then freemen, awake,
        And your fetters now break!
Down, down with the tyrant, and dare to be free.

NEW HARRISON SONG.

AIR, "*A Life on the Ocean Wave.*"

Awake to the stirring sound!
    Hark, hark, to the loud alarms!
A shout on the breeze is heard—
    'Tis the people up in arms!
Then rouse to the rescue, rouse!
    In a body, all as one—
Let your watchword be, " Our Rights! "
    And your war-cry " Harrison! "
                Awake, etc.

In vain did our father's toil
    And fight for the rights of man,
If tyrants may scorn us now,
    And to take our freedom plan,
We'll let them know we'll fight
    For the cause our sires have won,
And our shout shall go forth aloud,
    " The people and Harrison! "
                Awake, etc.

Let us teach those men in power
  What they seem not now to know,
That they cannot stay an hour,
  When the people utter, "Go!"
Then up and with the shout again,
  Press the cry of victory on—
" The rights which our fathers gave,
  The people and Harrison!"
                    Awake, etc.

———

LINES TO NEW JERSEY.

Baltimore, July 28, 1840.

General Green :

  Dear Sir: I am a Jerseyman. I have been absent from my native State
now for about two years, but had it been twenty instead of two, I could
not feel otherwise than anxious for her welfare. In looking over one of the
morning papers of to-day, I saw an account of the reception of the rejected
members of Congress at New Brunswick, some day last week. The writer,
speaking of the banners displayed upon that occasion, says, " There was
one of remarkable beauty and exquisite workmanship, worked by the ladies
of New Jersey, and presented by them to the Tippecanoe club of New
Brunswick." We had not time to inspect the banner, nor to copy the inscriptions, but as it spread its folds to the breeze, we could discover that the
battle of Princeton, and an *obliterated star*, formed a part of the emblems.
I cannot describe to you the feelings that rose in my breast at the time, nor
do I wish to trouble you with a recital of all that I felt ; suffice it to say that
I determined to make an effort in the cause of the soil on which I first drew
my breath, and the following lines were the result:

And is it so? has that bright star then faded?
  Is Trenton, Monmouth, Princeton, all forgot?
The mangled victim of the field invaded;
  And must it be that they have bled for naught?

The gore that dyed thy shores—groans of the dying,
  The widow's tears—the orphan's helpless wail,
The anguished mother for her children crying—
  Thy wrongs were then revenged, though now ye fail.

Where now the spirit that thy son's once boasted?
  Where now the sons of those who for thee bled?
Has all the valor of their sires departed?
  And is thy glory buried with the dead?

Oh shame upon the recreant who would waver,
  Or dare to falter in so just a cause;

The State disowns the sons who will not save her,
From foes alike to freedom and its laws.

E'en now the gallant sons of sister States,
Are gazing on thee, anxious for thy good,
'Gainst common enemies they'll join their fates,
But would not help thee now, e'en if they could.

No! when thy sons have dastard like, allowed
Their chosen servants, by their laws elected,
Bearing thy seal (of which they once were proud),
To be 'gainst right and reason disrespected;

When this they've done—when freedom's fire has faded—
When cowards tread the soil where heroes trod—
When that is lost which now is but invaded—
And they have recreant proved to man and God—

Who then would aid thee? or thy sons in need?
Who'd heal thy wrongs? or strive to hide thy shame?
None! none! would own thee after such a deed;
And foul reproach would fasten on thy name.

But no! it cannot be—land of my birth!
And thou—my brothers—say, shall this foul stain,
This incubus that bows thee to the earth,
Say? shall this damning blot of shame remain!

No! by thy blood-bought freedom I adjure thee,
By honor, fame, by hope of Heaven's rest;
By those who bled and died but to secure thee,
The sacred rights that from thee now they'd wrest;

Arouse thee! to the strife! that banner waving,
Point to the space where once thy star shone bright,
Blanch not! but to the breach! all danger braving,
Show to the world ye dare maintain your right.

———

THE BOSTON TIPPECANOE CLUB SONG.

AIR, "*O! 'Tis My Delight.*"

Did you ever see the paintings
Just front of Concert Hall?
There's something there of every kind
For Locos, Whigs and all—
There's Harrison, the farmer brave,
Who beat his country's foe;

O! we'll win beneath his banner
  Who conquered long ago.
O! we'll win beneath his banner
  Who conquered long ago.

There's all the story Johnson tells
  About the brave old chief,
Who ever at his country's call
  Came first to her relief—
Who never left the battle-field,
  But he might victory know.
O! we'll win beneath his banner
  Who conquered long ago.
              O! we'll win, etc.

Who says that Gen'ral Harrison
  Was ever found behind,
"When rifle balls were whizzing past,"*
  And death rode on the wind?
He always bravely led the van,
  To deal the victor's blow;
O! we'll win beneath his banner
  Who conquered long ago.
              O! we'll win, etc.

But soon another victory
  The gallant chief will gain,
Though 'tis not o'er the savage foe,
  Or on the battle plain—
For dread misrule, with fearful band,
  He soon will overthrow;
O! we'll win beneath his banner
  Who conquered long ago.
              O! we'll win, etc.

THE IRISHMAN'S SONG.

AIR, "*Sprig o' Shillelah and Shamrock so Green.*"

Success to the man at that place called North Bend,
Bad luck to the spalpeen who would not defend
The fame and the name of Old Tippecanoe.
His heart for his country has ever beat true,
Her interest and honor were ever his view,
Whether fighting her battles or guarding her pelt,

---

* See Col. R. M. Johnson's speech.

Sure its little he cared for his own noble self—
And such is the hero of Tippecanoe.

Sure you've heard of that little *pond* called St. Clair,
And that nate little river that empties in there;
To the banks of that river marched Tippecanoe,
Och! there he found Proctor with all his big troops,
With bastes of wild Indians, with screaming and whoops;
For the scalps of our boys, Och! they sharpened their
        knives,
In hopes to make widows of all their swate wives,
And take off the scalp of Old Tippecanoe.

But you should have been there, at that nate little place,
To have seen the red coats turn the "right-about face!"
From the brave Yankee boys, under Tippecanoe,
And very soon after they got on the trail,
(A devil a bit could you see but the tail!)
Those red looking blackguards, without any clothes,
Show'd a set of clean heels, as you may suppose,
And got but few scalps from Old Tippecanoe.

Success to the hero! Och! sure would we sing,
Who trimm'd the red coats of that foolish old king
Who sent Proctor to fight that same Tippecanoe.
Long life, too, to Johnson, who fought on that day,
And killed that big savage called Tecumseh;
May each true hearted boy, in this land of the free,
Whether Yankee or Irish, just sing out with me,
Hurrah! for the Hero of Tippecanoe.

SONG.

[Written for the Celebration of the 5th of May, 1840, at St. Louis.]

AIR, "*Rosin the Bow.*"

Come all ye young men of Missouri,
    And all ye gray headed ones too,
Turn out on this bright day of glory,
    And shout for Old Tippecanoe,
            And shout for Old Tippecanoe, etc.

When red foes our country invaded,
    He boldly stepped forward for you,
And though red coats were boldly paraded,
    They ran from Old Tippecanoe,
            They ran from Old Tippecanoe, etc.

And if ever again they attack us,
　Which just now there's a chance they may do,
Let's have the right spirit to back us,
　The spirit of Tippecanoe,
　　　　　　　The spirit of Tippecanoe, etc.

Van Buren may do to spend money,
　Price or Swartwout would just as well do,
For like drones they eat up all the honey,
　But there's work in Old Tippecanoe,
　　　　　　　But there's work, etc.

Dark clouds are now gathering o'er us,
　There's nought but disaster in view,
But they'll fly at the loud echoed chorus,
　Of—hurrah for Old Tippecanoe!
　　　　　　　Of—hurrah, etc.

Then let all with new vigor inspired,
　Stand firm to their posts and be true,
And the vessels by gold mint drops hired
　Can ne'er keep out Old Tippecanoe,
　　　　　　　Can ne'er keep out, etc.

Come along to this log-cabin raising,
　The ladies will all be there too,
And bright eyes will sparkle in praising
　Our choice of Old Tippecanoe,
　　　　　　　Our choice, etc.

Van Buren may quaff his Madeira,
　Hock, Sherry, and Burgundy too,
But hard cider to us is far dearer,
　It reminds us of Tippecanoe,
　　　　　　　It reminds us, etc.

And his health shall be pledged in full glasses,
　Toasts will spring from each heart that is true,
Like nectar 'twill seem as it passes,
　'Tis the drink of Old Tippecanoe,
　　　　　　　'Tis the drink, etc.

When you come to this log-cabin raising,
　Bring along honest Democrats too;
Tom Benton can't keep them from praising
　The deeds of Old Tippecanoe,
　　　　　　　The deeds, etc.

For those deeds are remembered in story,
　Yet still there is much he will do,
And our country will add to her glory,
　By electing Old Tippecanoe,
　　　　　　　By electing, etc.

And when at our helm he is seated,
　Sunshine will again be in view,
And Columbia with honor be greeted,
　Commanded by Tippecanoe,
　　　　　　　Commanded, etc.

BY THE SAME AUTHOR.

HISTORY OF KNOX COUNTY, OHIO.

ANNALS OF KENYON.

LIFE OF SAM HOUSTON.

HENRY CLAY AND HIS FRIENDS.

RHUS.

THE WHIG PARTY,
Its Leaders and Principles.

NEMESIS OF THE REBELLION.

THE UNIONISTS OF THE SOUTH.